WHISTLER INDEPENDENT
WINNER
BOOK AWARDS

I0720064

"*Charlee LeBeau & The Gambler's Promise* is a rollicking adventure of the wild west, packed with tall tales of treasure and romance, tragedy, and the dark deeds of villains. But it is also a deeper story about a young woman struggling with loss and finding, in her grief, the ability to not only cope, but to forge her own identity and independence, even in the face of cruel societal norms that force her to hide who she really is. Charlee is an engaging and spirited character that many young women will relate to as she refuses to allow circumstance or prejudice hold her back."

— GAIL ANDERSON-DARGATZ, AUTHOR

"…I suggest this be read, and then discussed, by whole families, not only for its evocation of time, place and character, but for the themes it fleshes out so well: the strength of girls, the nonsensical cruelty of racism, the human costs of greed, the redemptive power of friendship."

— DARCIE FRIESEN HOSSACK, AUTHOR

"This is one of the best books I have read in a long time. I was captivated from the first word to the cliff-hanger ending."

— CANADIAN AUTHORS WIBA JUDGE

CHARLEE LEBEAU HISTORICAL ADVENTURE SERIES

Charlee LeBeau & The Gambler's Promise

(Book 1)

1st edition 2019

2nd edition 2024

Charlee LeBeau & The Salish Wind

(Book 2)

1st edition 2021

2nd edition 2024

Charlee LeBeau & The Golden Deception

(Book 3)

2024

Charlee LeBeau

&

The Golden Deception

c. v. gauthier

TUANN ANDREWS PUBLISHING

Steveston, British Columbia, Canada

www.cvgauthier.com/tapublishing@shaw.ca

Art Direction & Cover Design: Marty Dolan & Raman Dhoot

Deception Island Map: Josephine Steeves

ISBN

978-1-7388902-0-0 (Paperback)

978-1-7388902-1-7 (E-Book)

1. YOUNG ADULT FICTION/Action and Adventure/Survival Stories

2. YOUNG ADULT FICTION/Coming of Age

3. YOUNG ADULT FICTION/Métis

Legal Deposit, Library and Archives Canada, 2024. Distributed to the trade by The Ingram Book Company

ɫax̣áyam–tə́mtəm

A great oppression in spirit, of both heart and mind. Deep sadness and longing for something that was lost or never known.

*(from Chinuk Wawa, a trade language
spoken in the Pacific Northwest)*

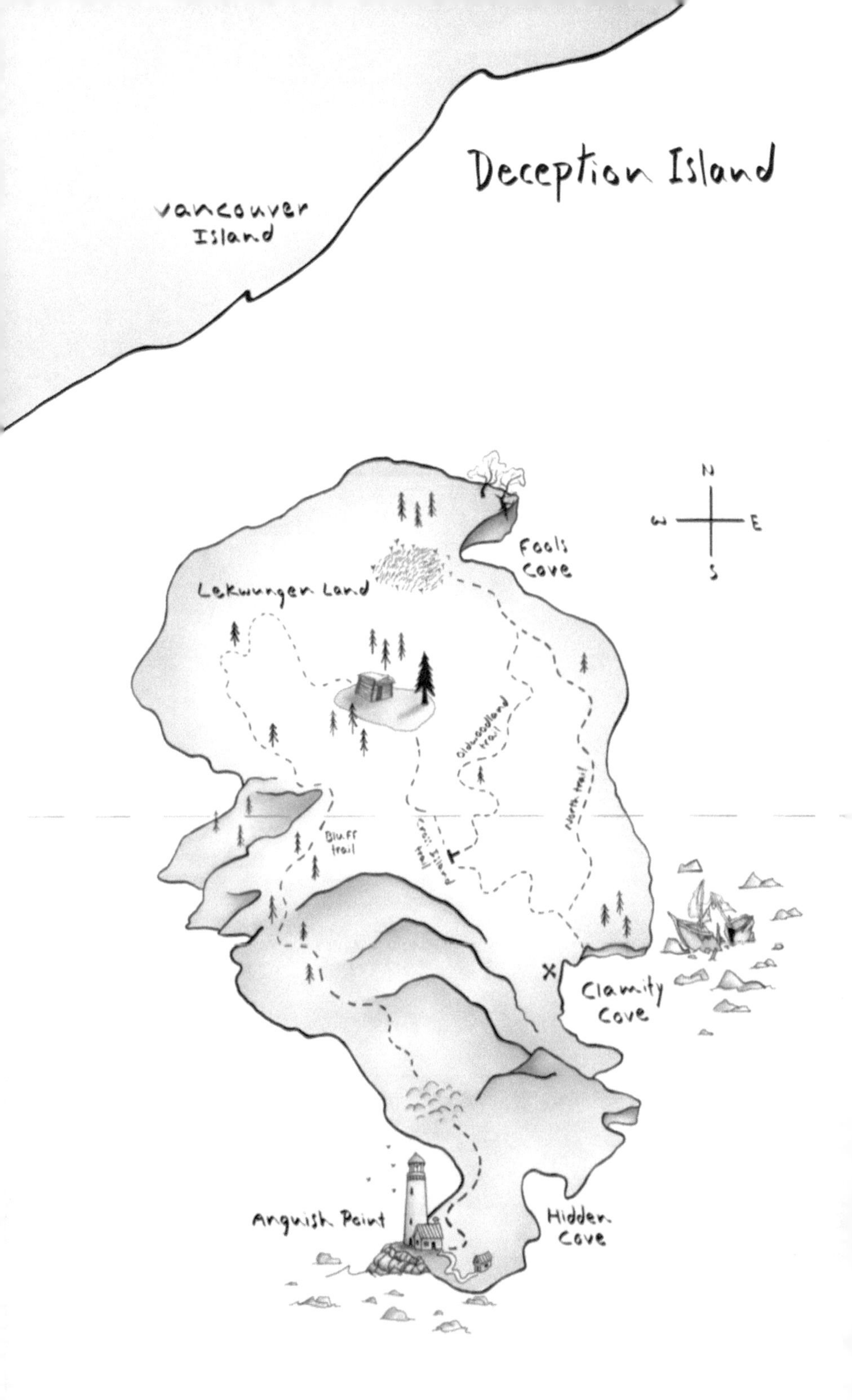

Deception Island
Vancouver Island
Fools Cove
Lekwungen Land
N
W E
S
Oldwoodland Trail
north trail
Bluff trail
trail Island trail
Clamity Cove
Anguish Point
Hidden Cove

CHAPTER ONE

"Maybe those greasy pirates were right. Maybe this island is cursed."

I'd just skimmed a chapter on magnification and lens formula in one of Edgar Dalworth's science books, but when I looked away, I couldn't picture any of it. It was something I'd always been able to do. Until Deception Island.

"Nonsense. You're not superstitious," Mrs. Dalworth said without looking up from her needlework.

I threw down my pencil and shoved myself away from her kitchen table, chair legs screeching across the wood floor. A piece of dry cedar in the fireplace snapped. The clock on the mantle clanged as I rubbed my forehead and paced around the table. Mrs. Dalworth's rocking chair squeaked in slow, predictable intervals.

"I'm going to oil that thing. Doesn't it bother you?"

Mrs. Dalworth halted in the middle of a forward rock.

"I've always found it quite soothing."

She set her needlework on the table beside her chair and picked stray bits of colored thread from her lap. She didn't look over at me as I circled the room like a trapped animal.

"You don't want to hear this, Charlee, but I'm going to say it, anyway. You're pushing yourself too hard with those books. You aren't doing yourself any favors by it."

"There's nothing wrong with me. Not a scratch or a bump or a cut left anywhere."

I stopped in front of her, held out my hands for inspection, but yanked back my left arm when the nasty horseshoe scar on my wrist appeared from under my sleeve.

"That's the outside. The inside heals different. It can take longer."

I glared at her, even though I knew she was right. I had buried myself in books because they helped me escape the long, dark months of winter. It hadn't taken long for the novelty of living at the Deception Island lighthouse to wear off. The boredom that followed was enough to drive a sane person mad. I'd also hoped losing myself in books would help me get my memory working again. But like a tough knot that gets worse with every wrong pull, my head was more tangled up than ever. Reading and studying had thrown new things into the mix, and the result was a scrambled mess. I'd go over and over things I'd already read, and I wouldn't let up.

"I want my memory back. I want it to work like it used to."

That sounded pathetic. The only thing missing was stamping my feet and throwing a tantrum like a spoiled child, as if my scrambled brain and constant frustrations were her fault. I'd already blamed her that morning for moving my notebook when she hadn't touched it.

Mrs. Dalworth had her own share of problems. After losing her husband Edgar in the spring, she was alone with an uncertain future. A young navy recruit had been hastily assigned to help her run the lighthouse until a replacement for Edgar could be arranged. She had reason to be irritable, but I was the one who let my problems darken the household mood, and I often took my frustrations out on her. She had put up with six months of me, and never once complained.

Mrs. Dalworth pushed herself out of her chair and took a few stiff steps in the general direction of the kitchen. Mr. Jones, who had been curled up on the braided rug at her feet, felt the nudge of a wayward foot and skulked out of the way. He arranged himself closer to the warmth of the fire, a safe distance away from being stepped on or tripped over. To prepare for warmer weather, we'd shorn his wooly coat like a spring lamb. He was right mad about that, even if it wasn't his first haircut, but he seemed happier with the weight of his thick white fur gone. He had shivered the whole time we snipped, and I figured that was an act because we'd left a good inch of his coat behind. When I told him his haircut made him look young and handsome, he'd forgiven me. Dogs don't carry grudges like people do.

I stared out the front window at the morning drizzle, a blanket of gray shrouding the land and blending into the dull morning light.

"I never used to get headaches at all. At least I remember that. I get them almost every day now, don't I?"

"Yes, lately, almost every day. But notice you don't wake up with them." Mrs. Dalworth clanged a heavy lid onto a pot and my hands shot up to cover my ears. "Sorry," she said.

I didn't wake up with the headaches. They came when I forced myself to study and remember.

"Look, I know where you're going with this. You think I read too much."

Books from Edgar's collection were scattered across the kitchen table and I'd plowed through all of them. While only two dozen volumes, they were more advanced than any I'd ever laid my hands on. Ordinarily, I'd have figured through them without too much trouble, but so far, what was in them felt like spectacular fragments of refracting glass.

"Those books won't vanish. You need to give them a rest, lass."

"I can't. Time is running out and I'm not finished because I keep forgetting."

"Is that why you are half frantic with them? Goodness! You can have the lot!"

"I can?"

"Edgar would want you to have them. His notebooks, too. Do you think I'll ever make heads or tails out of 'em? Not a chance. I don't need those dust collectors following me to Victoria."

Edgar had few belongings, and yet she was giving me the things he loved the most. The house lost its dreary gloom then. Its gray stones and dark woods became soft and enveloping, like a warm winter quilt.

"That's very...I promise I'll take good care of them."

I looked away as my eyes blurred and ached. A different headache loomed behind them.

"So, you'll ease up since there's no hurry?"

"I'll ease up."

I pressed my face to the window glass and peered through the drizzled pane into the muddy yard. A spring storm had settled over the island and the rain hadn't let up for more than a few hours in almost a week. A drab figure crossed the yard, slicker flapping in the wind. Squinting into the downpour, he pulled open the door of the lighthouse and disappeared inside.

"Perkins is checking the lantern again."

Mrs. Dalworth frowned. He was doing so in between the scheduled times she'd set out for him.

"I suppose the lad needs something to do. We don't need him underfoot in here with us, now do we?"

"No, we do not. But it's insubordination, if you ask me."

"You forget, I'm the temporary lighthouse keeper, not his naval officer. He doesn't report to me."

"Still, you're in charge here. He listens to what you say, and then goes and does whatever he wants."

"I'll admit that gets on my nerves. But some would say he's being responsible by doing more frequent checks in this weather. Going beyond the call of duty, even."

"That's probably what he wants you to say when the time comes. I bet that's why he does it."

Mrs. Dalworth studied the parchment calendar hanging on the wall behind the front door. A beautiful English garden scene had been hand-drawn and colored on it, with the months of 1860 laid out in neat, lettered boxes. It had been a gift Mr. Miller had sent to Mrs. Dalworth for "all of her kindness", he'd written. She adored the gift. I figured the garden pictures reminded her of where she was born because she always got a little dewy-eyed when she looked at it. She stood in front of it often, as if the passing time kept catching her by surprise.

"It's April already," she said, shoulders slumping.

"Finally, you mean."

"I suppose that's a better word, if one can't wait to get off this island."

"Can't wait, but must wait. I hope Brody..."

"That's Mr. Brody..."

"...Mr. Brody brings news from California with the supplies. My December letters have worn mighty thin these last three months."

"Even the one from your friend Jake?"

"That one in particular. He said nothing about anything. You'd think he was the one who smacked his head and knocked some screws loose."

"Well, I'd trade you that letter for the syrupy thing I got from the Colonial Ladies' Circle in Victoria. Did I mention they've invited me to join them again when I return to town this summer?"

"How do they know you're going back?"

"Word travels fast through the grapevine."

"The grapevine?"

"Gossip and talk. That ladies' circle can move news faster than one of those new-fangled telegraph machines."

Edgar had notes on the codes used with that invention. For a moment, I lost myself trying to figure out which of his notebooks I'd read it in. I couldn't recall, but realized I'd at least remembered reading about it. That was a good sign.

"Will you give the ladies' circle another try, then?"

"If Edgar was still with me, I wouldn't touch them with a barge pole. But once you're gone, I won't know what to do with myself and won't have anyone to talk to. So maybe. Oh, I don't know."

Her voice quivered. Was she saying she'd miss me when I was gone? I'd been so ornery all winter, I thought she'd be glad to be rid of me.

"I know! You should come to California!"

Mrs. Dalworth turned in surprise.

"California! And what in heaven's name would I do there?"

"Make a fresh start. You're good at lots of things. Besides, they want people to come. And it wouldn't rain all the time."

"I don't mind the rain. Rain reminds me of England."

We both stared out the window at the drizzle. It was a stretch to see it as an attractive quality.

"And Edgar is here," she said.

I could have sworn the clock skipped a tick at that moment. Edgar. Of course, she couldn't go away, particularly somewhere far away, and leave her late husband behind in an unmarked, make-shift wilderness grave.

Mr. Jones got up from the hearth. He strolled over to his empty breakfast dish, nails clicking across the wood floor. He sniffed it to be sure no new morsels had arrived, and then drank noisily from his water bowl.

"Do you think Mr. Jones is ready to go with you to California?"

When I was going to leave in the fall, Mr. Jones had run off to Clamity Cove, to the place where his friend Kuno had died aboard the sunken *Salish Wind*.

"I tried to set the record right, but I failed. He knows it's over now."

"You didn't fail, Charlee. The matter was out of your hands."

Mr. Jones looked at me with sad eyes, his disappointment heavy as my own. Still wearing Kuno's yellow bandana, he shuffled back to the warmth of the hearth and curled up in his favorite spot. He would leave with me for California this time. I knew he would. But I wondered if it was wrong of me to take him.

CHAPTER TWO

Seconds before three o'clock that same afternoon, two sharp raps came upon the cottage door. Mr. Jones growled.

"The man is like clockwork. I'll give him that," Mrs. Dalworth muttered as she hurried a tray of dishes to the table. I followed with a warm pan of apple crisp. "Come in!" she called out, while setting teacups on matching saucers.

At least Perkins had the manners to wait for an invitation. A chilly wind gusted in when he entered, and he pressed the door shut behind him. Mr. Jones, having recognized the intruder and given him an indifferent pass, returned to his warm spot by the fire.

"Good afternoon, ladies," Perkins said, as he did every day at teatime.

The clock on the mantle chimed as he placed his boots in the puddle catcher beneath the coat rack. He removed his dripping rain slicker, corralled it into neat folds lengthwise, and hung it on a hook by the door.

"Rain letting up yet?" Mrs. Dalworth enquired, even though the answer was obvious with a glance out any window. Adults like to warm up conversation with small talk about the weather when there isn't anything new or interesting to say.

"Not yet. Looks like a break over to the east, though. Figure it'll let up by suppertime."

"Let's hope it clears soon so the supply boat can make it out to us. I'm afraid it's baked beans again tonight."

If Perkins didn't like the idea of beans for dinner, he didn't show it. I was used to scarcity, so it didn't bother me a bit. But Mrs. Dalworth took pride in her cooking. She fed us as if we were both house guests and wasn't happy unless she could provide a well-rounded, satisfying meal with a wholesome dessert.

The British Navy had assigned Archibald Perkins to assist Mrs. Dalworth at the lighthouse in the fall of last year. I'd already decided to stay on the island to help her while I was waiting for the shipwreck investigation to get underway in Fort Victoria. But according to the government, womenfolk can't manage a lighthouse on their own. So, we got Able Seaman Perkins, an earnest young man with the habit of lining up dishes and utensils to form perfect geometric patterns in front of him on the table. To amuse myself, I'd set the table and place something crooked or in an unusual spot. Then I'd watch him go through his routine, correcting placements and spacings. I suppose there are worse habits a man could have. That's what Mrs. Dalworth said when she caught me loosening the cap on the salt shaker by half a turn. "Don't torture the poor fellow, Charlee," she'd said sternly. On the bright side, we didn't have to serve him hand and foot, or do anything for him other than feed him meals. The government had been generous with food stores because of him, so it wasn't all bad. He'd set up separate sleeping quarters in an outbuilding attached to the main house, and kept to himself. He only came into the main house to eat, and when the weather turned particularly cold and ugly.

Perkins washed his hands in the basin by the door, first

soaping his left hand up to the wrist, then the right one just the same. Four soapy revolutions of both, a quick brushing of each set of nails, and two rinses followed. Then he shook the water from both hands over the basin and reached for the hand towel. His routine was the same every single day. It occurred to me that island madness might happen in two ways. First, it might make a person a slave to mindless routines, in some effort to keep life meaningful. Second, it might make a person notice every little daily detail, as if it were an important event, when it wasn't. I was suffering from the second affliction more than I cared to admit. My eyes tracked his every move, waiting for some unfamiliar gesture to appear. Nothing was out of the ordinary. All of it got on my nerves.

"Have a seat, Mr. Perkins," Mrs. Dalworth said, lips pursed into what I now recognized as a polite smile.

She gathered up our playing cards, but rather than putting them away, she placed the deck smack in the middle of the table like some kind of grog house centerpiece. Perkins couldn't help but notice the display as he settled into his usual chair at the table.

"You ladies are playing cards now?" he said, a goofy grin scrunching up his freckled nose.

Now we had something to talk about. He rolled his sleeves down over thick forearms and fastened the buttons on his cuffs, first left and then right.

"Charlee's teaching me poker," Mrs. Dalworth replied.

He smirked. "Well, that'll be good for a few laughs."

My hands tightened around the back of the chair across from him.

"And why is that?" I said.

"Now, Charlee…"

"No, I'd like to know what he means. Explain what you mean, Mr. Perkins."

"It's a man's game. Requires sharp thinking and clever strategy."

I leaned on my palms and stretched across the table at him. "Ah! I gather you don't play then."

"On the contrary, I play rather well," he said, missing the three-pronged insult I'd thrown at him. "In fact, I'm one of the best in my crew."

"You don't say! You must be destined for success in naval service. Don't you agree, Mrs. Dalworth? A quick mind like that? The absolute grasp of complex maneuvers. Oh, my! What a fine candidate for a future officer!"

Mrs. Dalworth shot a warning look at me from behind Perkin's back as she brought the teapot to the table. She hadn't missed a drop of my sarcasm, even if all of it had missed Perkins by a country mile.

"I'm new to the navy, so I must complete my general service first. But I'll admit, they do fancy me as a future leader. Running the lighthouse for the winter will look exceptional on my record, I'm told."

Running the lighthouse? The arrogance and nerve!

Mrs. Dalworth caught my arm and squeezed it. "Yes, your timely help at the lighthouse will be quite a feather in your cap," she said sweetly. Perkins looked pleased. I fumed.

"We'd have managed fine without you," I said, refusing to let him swoon in his imaginary greatness. What I said wasn't true. He had been quite useful. Barrels of whale oil were back-breaking and when I first arrived at the lighthouse, I was in no shape to do much of anything. Still, there was no way I'd give Perkins more credit than he was due. Mrs. Dalworth changed the subject before I could take another run at him.

"Mr. Perkins, how was the lantern after lunch? The wick on the far side seemed weak this morning."

"Indeed, it was. I trimmed it and it's performing well again," he replied, oblivious to the daggers I stabbed into his head with my eyes. I dropped into my chair across from him. You can't fight with someone who doesn't notice the battle.

After tea, when Perkins had returned to his quarters and we'd finished our chores, we returned to our game at the table. I said to Mrs. Dalworth, "I'm going to play poker with him and make him swallow his words."

She glanced at me sideways. "I don't think that's a good idea. If he's as good as he says, you may not win. But then, it's only luck anyway, isn't it?"

"If I had to rely on luck over the past year, I wouldn't be alive. It's hard work that makes luck happen. He's blind with overconfidence."

"Nonetheless. If his weakness is overconfidence, yours is impulsiveness. You'll have to manage that. Otherwise, you'll forever face unnecessary hardship."

"I didn't bring any of this on myself."

"Didn't you? What were you doing on the *Salish Wind* then? Taking a sailing vacation?"

"I sailed north to claim gold shares," I replied, proving her point. The gold mine didn't exist, the shares were worthless, and it had been a near-fatal trip.

Mrs. Dalworth smiled as she shuffled the cards for another game. The rounds weren't much fun, as she had no concept of the bluff and was slow as molasses when it was her turn. But she was doing her best, and it gave us both something to do while the rain continued.

"Edgar said that for one to be good at poker, one has to weigh all consequences, make concessions and tolerate deception."

"Really."

It impressed me that Edgar even knew the game. Having spent so much time with his notebooks, I felt like I'd gotten to know him. I hadn't taken him for a card player, but since he must have been, of course he'd see the mental side of the game.

"My Uncle Jack believed you have to listen to your gut. He said you gotta go with the feeling and sometimes stick your neck out on hunches to make the greatest gains."

"From what you've told me, his way didn't work out."

"You mean how he nearly got me killed?"

"I was thinking more about his get rich quick scheme…"

"Oh yeah. The one I fell for, like all the other fools."

I tossed a penny into the pot. "I call."

Mrs. Dalworth peeked over her cards, forehead wrinkled. I knew she had something in her hand. When she'd drawn her last card, her face lit up. But the odds that one card had turned into something big were slim.

"What's your opinion, then? Who's right? Edgar or your uncle?" She laid her cards on the table with pride. "A pair o' Queens."

"I think both are right. Head and hunch go hand in hand. But the best advice? Know your opponent." I laid my cards down. "Three of a kind beats a pair."

CHAPTER THREE

The report of a rifle rang out across the rocks of Anguish Point. A flock of at least a hundred geese honked and flapped as they took to the air. They swung low under the overcast sky, circled around, and coasted down to the northwest end of the field, away from the source of the disturbance.

Mrs. Dalworth and I were hanging out the wash in the stiff morning breeze. Although the rain had stopped, the supply boat could not come until the wind let up and the ocean settled. I blew on my icy hands, shoved them into my pockets, and looked out across the field at Perkins.

"Did he get one?" Mrs. Dalworth asked, pegging a shirt to the line and squinting into the distance.

"No. He'd have done better with his eyes closed. If you had your heart set on roasting an Easter goose, you should have sent me."

"Now Charlee…"

"It's true. He said it himself. He grew up with shotguns. You don't learn good aim when you're spraying lead in the general direction of a target."

"He'll figure it out."

A second shot rang out. The flock rose and descended farther away.

"By the time he does, they'll be gone and you'll be out of ammo."

I dropped a wet shirt in the basket and stomped off through the muddy yard. Mr. Jones, bored with my domestic duties, jumped up and followed, eager for whatever adventure I'd decided upon.

Perkins stood in the middle of the empty field, fumbling with a box of cartridges, the breech-loading chamber of Mrs. Dalworth's rifle gaping open.

"My turn," I said to him, hands outstretched. He held the gun away from me in protest, but I wasn't in the mood to hear him tell me why girls couldn't shoot. "If you'd like something other than beans for supper, hand it over."

He shoved the rifle at me with disdain. I took a bullet from his open box.

"Only one?" he snickered. "You figure you're that good?"

I walked away from him before the urge to clock him with the barrel got the better of me. Part way down the field, I kneeled by a large boulder. Mr. Jones leaned into me and we studied the resting flock, nibbling away on the early grasses.

"Circle down to the other end, Mr. Jones. I'll let you know when to stir 'em up."

Mr. Jones trotted off with an air of importance. I loaded the chamber of the rifle and braced myself against the rock. At the end of the field, Mr. Jones assumed a proud stance away from the birds and waited for his signal. I whistled, and he sped around the far edge of the flock, scattering them into the sky in my direction. Fifty or more would pass right above me. Breathe, Charlee, I could hear Papa whisper. Mind the wind, the direction of flight.

A warmth flowed through my body into my hands. As the geese flew over, I set my sights on one in the middle, flying steady and smooth, adjusted my aim for its speed and direction, and squeezed the trigger. The gun kicked back into my shoulder as the shot fired. The goose lurched and tumbled to the ground, oblivious to its mortal injury. I lowered my head and said a few words Papa had taught me, to honor its life and the food it would provide for the three of us. Hunting was part of life when I was a child on our homestead. Learn to shoot or go hungry and become the hunted.

Perkins joined me as I made certain the bird was dead.

"Right through the neck. That was lucky."

"It's not luck."

"I mean, most girls…"

I cut him off. "You should know by now, Mr. Perkins, that I'm not most girls. Also, if you hadn't noticed, girls can do hard things."

"I'll give you that. First you whip me at poker, and now this."

I'd played him at poker, as I pledged I would. He was a good player and took a couple of games, but then I started tracking cards and estimating odds. The memory of how to do that had appeared out of nowhere. He was no match for my system.

"Card-sharking crack shooter, that's what you are," he added, paying me an unheard-of compliment.

My knees felt weak and black bubbles danced in front of my eyes. I stuck the rifle into the ground like a crutch and bent over it.

"Miss. Are you okay?" His faint voice reached through the ringing in my ears and I felt his alarm.

"I'm fine," I said, straightening up too fast and tipping sideways. He caught me and I stared at his hand on my arm like it had scorched my sleeve.

"No, you're not."

"Yes, I am. I'm fine." I pulled my arm away, ready to argue with him.

"Then let me take care of the bird and the gun." He pried the rifle from my hands. As I walked away, he added, "That was a helluva shot."

Mr. Jones and I picked our way back to the yard, where the wash line was almost full.

"You got one," said Mrs. Dalworth. "You don't seem very happy."

"I guess I'm not."

"There was a girl I met in the fall who might have crowed for the rest of the day, having shown that young navy whipper-snapper how it's done."

"I know. That's not it. I knew how to shoot that goose and didn't have to think about it."

"Maybe that's the secret."

"There's more. Right after, unanswered questions about the shipwreck filled my head and I felt sick. Like, all I can think of right now is why those pirates didn't use guns when they raided the *Salish Wind?* No one fired a shot. They used knives. Why? And how come the *Salish Wind* didn't fire on them when they came alongside and attacked? We had guns on board. Not good ones, but we had guns."

"Oh, Charlee. We've talked about this. You said the Captain wouldn't take up arms, and you figured they used a stealth approach so navy ships in the area wouldn't hear gunfire and come looking."

"I said that? See, this is what I mean. I go over and over things around that shipwreck and nothing sticks in my memory or gets sorted out. I go around and around."

"You've sorted out most of it, even if we're the only two who know the complete story. But lately, you've been trying to remember things you never knew."

"What?"

"There's a difference. Between what you know, and what you never knew."

I mulled that over for quite a spell. If true, this was much worse than I'd imagined. Messing up the things I remembered was bad enough. But had I made up things that didn't happen?

"You don't believe me! Is that what you're saying?"

"That's not what I'm saying at all. Of course, I believe you! I remember everything you've told me and one thing I know for sure is the details are the same every single time you bring them up, even when you forget them."

"They are?"

"Exactly the same." Mrs. Dalworth went on. "Give it some room. What's there is hiding from you but not lost. Your sharp-shooting just proved it so."

We watched Perkins take the dead goose into the shed. For all of his dumb ideas about girls and women, he wasn't a moody, grudge-carrying sort of fellow. His disposition was the same, day in and day out. But today, he'd shown something new. He had been almost friendly, appreciative even. For the first time in six months, if only for a few minutes, he'd seen me as an equal.

After a dinner of roast goose and potatoes, Perkins stuck around longer than usual and helped clear away the dishes.

"I can do that, miss," he said to me as I lifted the roasting tray and prepared to empty goose fat into a tin can.

This was also new, him calling me "Miss". I liked it better when he didn't call me anything and didn't acknowledge me.

I frowned. "You can call me Charlee. 'Miss' sounds weird."

"All right. Then you must call me Archie." He stretched out his hand to me, like we'd just met. I took his hand, rough and calloused, and shook it.

"Pleased to make your acquaintance."

Perkins laughed. "The pleasure is mine."

Mrs. Dalworth gawked at us with amusement, and I rolled my eyes at her.

With supper cleaned up and Perkins retired to his quarters, Mrs. Dalworth and I settled into our usual chairs by the fire.

"You know, Archie is only twenty."

"Don't start with that."

"Well, he's loosening up around you. You ought to give him a chance."

"A chance at what?"

"To be friendly."

"We're friendly enough. Civil, I'd even say."

"I think maybe he fancies you a little."

"Eeew." But the thought had crossed my mind when he was nice to me after so many months of treating me like I was invisible. "Thankfully, I'm leaving soon and will never see him again."

"Well, there is that. Besides, you have your clever fellow waiting back in San Francisco."

"You mean Jake? He's not my fellow. He's my best friend. We grew up together."

"Seems to me you are mighty fond of each other."

"Of course. But it's not like that."

"Like what?"

"Like, you know, all mooshy and goo-goo-eyed and stuff."

"That's quite a description. I don't think I'm familiar with those words."

"You know what I mean. All lovey dovey."

"Ah! Where did you get it in your head that being in love is something bad?"

"I don't think it's bad."

"Mooshy and goo-goo-eyed aren't exactly flattering. Who've you seen in love like that?"

I thought for a moment. "Mr. Miller, Jake's father."

"And?"

"He'd practically lose his mind around The Missus. That's what we hired help called his second wife, Jake's stepmother.

She's gorgeous, absolutely stunning in fact, but she's also a mean and horrible person. He couldn't see it."

"What about me?"

"You?"

"Am I mooshy and goo-goo-eyed over Edgar?"

"No."

"Yet I loved him with all my heart and still do."

Their love was different. More like the kind between Papa and Mizzy, even though they had to hide their love from everyone because of stupid prejudice. Mrs. Dalworth got up and added a couple of logs to the dying fire.

"I get why you loved him. I can tell from his books he was thoughtful and kind, a very interesting man."

She settled back into her rocking chair, wiped a tear from her cheek, and managed a sad smile.

"I hope you find love like ours one day. Promise me you won't settle for anything less."

"I promise. But how will I know?"

"Oh, you'll know."

CHAPTER FOUR

"Charlee! The boat's coming!"

Mrs. Dalworth stood on the front porch overlooking the waters of Fuca Strait. Moments earlier, she'd stepped outside into the overcast April morning to empty a pan of gray dishwater from breakfast. I dropped my pencil on my books and ran outside.

Perkins had seen the boat coming, too. He was across the yard before Mrs. Dalworth could pull her boots on. Without looking to her for direction, he picked his way down the steep path, oblivious to the treachery of the slope, still muddy from two weeks of rain.

"Hmph," she said. She'd told him over breakfast that she'd greet the supply boat.

"Perkins is half billy goat," I said. "He's just missing a set of horns."

I poked Mrs. Dalworth in the shoulder. Her scowl relaxed, and she chuckled.

"Oh, we've both seen his horns come out. He doesn't enjoy being told what to do, but I'm still boss around here until they drag me off."

Mr. Brody and the supply boat had made it out to Deception Island, ten days later than expected. The supply boat came every three months, give or take a week, weather permitting. They brought the barrels of oil needed for the lighthouse lamp and basic goods needed for the lightkeeper assigned to the post. In the fall and winter, bad weather or storms often delayed deliveries. We'd last seen them on the second day of January, when a stretch of clear, crisp weather had provided a window for their year-end run out to Deception Island.

The supply boat chugged its way into the tiny protected cove on the eastern shore. It was the last friendly spot for a boat to approach the rugged island. In pleasant weather, and with the light of day to navigate the gamut of hazards below the waterline, it was a pretty little cove and an easy venture. But when the weather was poor, nobody dared approach. Underwater rocks fiercely protected every part of the island, reaching well out into the strait. It was as if the beauty of the place lured sailors to her and then she made them pay for their desires. Or an experienced mariner, like the foolish captain of the *Salish Wind*, would think he could handle the island domain with his elegant maps and shiny instruments. Deception Island had taught him a terrible lesson. I'd seen that with my own eyes.

"Still a bit of a gamble coming out today," Mrs. Dalworth said as we made our way down the path to the top of the cliff, "but I'm happy to see them."

None of us expected the boat to come, since afternoon gusts had churned the waters of the strait into a frothy green. But in the morning, the sky was a tedious, flat gray in every direction and the sea was calm. That was how fast conditions changed on this difficult coastline.

"I hope they've brought mail. I'm dying for news from home."

"Yes, from home," she repeated, and I realized I'd never called California my home before.

Brody brought much-needed supplies and a handful of correspondence for all of us. Mrs. Dalworth showed her usual hospitality, inviting Brody up to the house for fresh coffee and biscuits, but after a concerned glance at the weather vane in the yard, he declined. Mrs. Dalworth seemed relieved. She didn't linger to watch him board the supply boat and leave, and returned to the house without saying a word. Settling at the kitchen table, she reviewed the papers delivered to her concerning her upcoming replacement.

I plunked myself down across from her. I'd finished reading my three letters minutes after Brody had handed them to me—a warm and cheery greeting from Mizzy, a formal note from Mr. Miller regarding my return to San Francisco, and a short, uninspired letter from Jake, which I'd saved for last.

Jake Miller was the oldest Miller boy and my best friend. Before Mr. Miller remarried and had more children, we were the only two on the ranch. We did everything together in those days. So, I looked forward to his letter the most, and it left me slumped in a chair with disappointment. I read it through a few more times, hoping to find something I'd missed, but it wasn't more than a few lame paragraphs. He didn't even take the time to write in the usual double-meaning style we always used in our notes and correspondence.

"What's the matter with you, Jake?" I muttered.

"What's that, lass?"

"Nothing. This letter from Jake is odd."

She laid her smudged glasses on her papers and got up from the table. "What's it say then?"

"Well, it doesn't say anything. That's the problem. It's simple and boring. Not even a full page. It's not like Jake at all."

"Read me an example and I'll give you my opinion."

I looked over the letter and chose a section. "He says some

stuff about going home to the ranch and how it's not like it was before, and that his boarding house isn't any better because all the fellows are younger than him now."

"Why's that?"

"The boys his age moved on and a younger bunch arrived last fall."

"Maybe he's restless. Boys get restless when they're becoming men."

"Maybe." I wasn't convinced.

Jake had become moodier in recent years. He was almost seventeen and very different from the boy I'd left behind on the ranch almost two years earlier. But it seemed there was more going on that he wasn't saying. There was a strange comment about missing his one best friend, but I didn't mention that to Mrs. Dalworth because I wasn't sure if he meant me or one of his former classmates. I picked a safer section to share with her.

"Here's another. He says, 'much has happened since the fall, far too much to write about here…I'll tell you more when you get back. I expect you'll have the details of your journey soon. Father doesn't tell me much these days.'"

"Oooh. He definitely sounds out of sorts there," Mrs. Dalworth said.

"Out of sorts? I've been here all winter, stuck on this miserable island, and he's out of sorts?"

"Now, lass. You don't know what's gone on with him since you've been away. Why isn't his father talking to him, though? He doesn't know what his father wrote to you? That's a clue if I ever heard one."

I considered her point for a moment and then dismissed it. "He's got everything going for him. I can't imagine anything bad has happened."

"Have you forgotten he thought you were dead? He may have felt responsible."

"Responsible?" I snorted. "I doubt it."

When I'd lived in San Francisco, starving in the custody of my Uncle Jack, the Millers didn't check up on me. They assumed I was making out fine.

Mrs. Dalworth didn't acknowledge my complaints. She'd returned to her own letter. With her glasses back on, she tipped her head back and moved the page away to focus. I watched her lips move over the words. From her pinched brow, I could tell she didn't like what she was reading. She let the paper fall from her hand and left the table.

"Bad news?" I said, after she'd donned her apron and banged a couple of drawers and cupboard doors in the kitchen.

"Depends on whose news it is, I suppose. Not good news for me."

I had noticed an official wax seal on the envelope. "It's from the government?"

"Yes. They're booting me off the island. They've hired a new lightkeeper. A man with a wife and two sons to help."

"Well, that's not a surprise. They told you that's what they aimed to do."

"He takes over end of June."

"Oh. That's real soon. So where will you go?"

"Victoria. Says in the letter, the government is providing me with a modest accommodation, in appreciation of Edgar's service."

"That doesn't sound so bad."

"What am I going to do in Victoria??"

Wiping her hands on a kitchen towel, she stared at the floor as though Edgar had been laid to rest beneath it.

"They want to give him a proper burial. In the city."

A black pit opened in the bottom of my belly and I clutched the edge of the table. I'd buried him in the clearing and they would need me to show them where.

"Is that what you want?"

"I don't know," she snapped, and I sat back, a little startled.

Mr. Jones jumped into my lap. He'd never heard Mrs. Dalworth raise her voice.

She shook her head and sighed. "I'm sorry. It's a lot."

"It's all right."

I was all too familiar with having others decide things for me. It was something I'd complained about to Mrs. Dalworth many times over. To see it happen to her, though, a grown woman who could handle tough situations with one arm tied behind her back, that took all the wind from my sails.

"They didn't ask me. They've made plans for me and for Edgar and they didn't even talk to me about what I want. How do they know I want to stay in Victoria? I don't even know that. And I don't know if I want them to dig him up."

Mrs. Dalworth could take her forced retirement in stride. She knew she was going to be replaced after Edgar's death. But this business was personal. They were arranging her life. She hung her kitchen towel to dry and returned to the table.

"What are you going to do?"

Her hands trembled as she straightened the edge of the tablecloth.

"I need you to take me to him. Before they come with their shovels."

I shot to my feet.

"No. It's too hard, too much climbing, even with two good legs."

"My hip isn't that bad. You've seen. I go up and down the steep lighthouse stairs several times a day."

"But you can't leave the lighthouse."

"Mr. Perkins can handle it for a day."

Mrs. Dalworth was prepared to risk everything to see him. Trekking all the way to the clearing? Scrabbling over slippery rocks and steep bluffs? What if something happened?

"It's too risky." I meant too risky for her.

As if she read my thoughts, she said, "If something happens, you can fetch Mr. Perkins for help. But I assure you, I can make it and I will."

"We may not have the chance before I have to leave. We'll have to wait for a good spring day, for dry ground and clear skies."

"Now you are sounding like me," she smiled. "Sensible."

"What if we have to spend the night? You must be ready for anything."

"I'll manage with your help, but I have to visit Edgar's grave."

CHAPTER FIVE

I did my best to discourage Mrs. Dalworth from attempting the hike to the clearing, but she wouldn't listen to reason, and there was no talking her out of it. Before I left the island for good, she had to know where Edgar was buried. I found it hard to argue with her decision because if I were in her shoes, I would have wanted the same thing. I agreed to take her, but only if the weather was favorable.

The next morning, the weather vane in the yard was still, and the sky was bright blue. Mr. Jones took his morning nap on the porch, where the sun had dried and warmed the boards. Mrs. Dalworth pointed out that a trek the next day looked promising. Instant dread crawled up my spine. After lunch, when I could slip away, Mr. Jones and I wandered around the rocky point by the lighthouse so we could discuss the matter in private.

I did all the talking, which was a lot of complaining about the risks and responsibilities of taking Mrs. Dalworth to the clearing. After I finished venting, Mr. Jones suggested I might be making excuses because I was afraid of facing some things. I told him that was ridiculous, but then stewed on that for a good while. He was right, of course. I'd said nothing about the horror of having found and buried the unknown dead man, who turned out to be her missing husband. I had to get past my own feelings and apprehensions.

Papa told me about the city men who'd come to the northern territories long before I was born. Unfamiliar with riding horses, they were ill-prepared for the wilderness, yet determined to pursue their explorations and suffer through whatever happened. Papa was a Hudson's Bay Company guide in those days, and it was his job to keep the men safe and take them where they wanted to go. I thought about what Papa would do in my situation. He wouldn't avoid something because it was hard. He also wouldn't let his worries get in the way. I figured since Mrs. Dalworth had asked me to be her guide, I should honor her request and prepare as best as I could.

Later that evening, under clear skies and twinkling stars, we decided to go the next morning. I packed the gear while Mrs. Dalworth spoke to Perkins of our intentions, so we could turn in and get enough rest for an early start. Although I'd considered every circumstance we might encounter, the prospect of the trek kept me awake.

This wasn't my first sleepless night. I had a lot of them since arriving at the lighthouse. Sometimes I'd sink my empty, aching head into my pillow and puzzle over what my life had become. Other times, I'd toss around, wide-eyed and nervous, as if I were doomed to relive every single awful day over and over again. This night was different.

The ceiling flickered orange and yellow from the glow of the dying fire. As I stared at the grains in the wood, a map of the island appeared. Then the trails emerged, showing every twist and turn of our upcoming hike. I blinked at the vivid image, but it didn't go away. I caught my breath as the little map expanded into an epic topography of America, with my entire life journey marked upon it.

Born in the Red River Valley, I moved west to the Willamette Valley in Oregon when I was too young to remember, and then to a bush homestead with Papa somewhere out in the sticks after Mama died. I couldn't remember much from those days except we were alone, and it was hard living. When I was six, Papa rode us to Sonoma, California, where we started a new life working for a wealthy landowner by the name of John Miller. Pictures and places from the passing years scrolled by on the ceiling above me.

Jake Miller lost his mother on the wagon train coming west, but his father had struck it rich with gold and bought up a big ranch. He was Mr. Miller's only son, and only a year and a bit older than me, with hair that changed color with his moods and eyes like green pond water. Since we were the only two kids for miles, we became best friends. I taught him all kinds of things I'd learned while living on the homestead. I had a knack for anything to do with numbers. He taught me to read, shared his school lessons and brought me fascinating books from his father's library. One day, Mr. Miller decided I should learn from the teacher that came to the ranch for Jake.

A black leather cover of an old book appeared in front of my eyes, one that Jake had brought me just before I'd left. It was about a fellow named Odysseus who couldn't get home for ten whole years because he'd gone off to fight in an awful war. When the war ended, he was far from home, and bad things kept happening to him. My journey since leaving the ranch felt like that, even though I had only been gone about two years. What if it took me eight more to get back? I could run into more trouble, just like Odysseus did. I couldn't take anything for granted, that's what I knew. And I wasn't even sure Sonoma was my home anymore.

A remaining piece of wood on the fire ignited, and the ceiling brightened. There I was in a buggy with Uncle Jack, leaving the Miller ranch in August 1859, only days after my papa had died. Bernadette Miller, Jake's sister from his father's second marriage, had fallen into the corral of a wild stallion, and Papa had gone in after her to save her from being trampled. He'd saved her life, but a freak accident had happened. The terrified stallion knocked him sideways. Papa struck his head on a fence post, and he never woke up again.

I'd just turned fourteen, and all I had left was Mizzy Jefferson. She was cook on the Miller ranch, and she loved me and my papa. Mizzy raised me like her own from the time I arrived. She and her brother, Amos, had run from slavery in the south and Mr. Miller somehow got them free and working for him in California. On the ranch, everybody called her "Miss Molly". But before I left San Francisco last summer, she told me Mizzy was her real name, and she was claiming it back. I don't know the whole story, but Jake said they were among very few that ran and got out alive. Mizzy and Amos won't talk about any of it anymore.

My one known blood relative—Papa's older brother Jack— appeared out of nowhere to claim me when he found out his brother had passed. He led everyone to believe he was well-to-do and living in a luxurious mansion in the city. Turns out he'd gambled his fortune away, and took to the drink when he became destitute. Since Papa didn't leave him money, he put me to work, but I refused to gamble. I lived for a year with him in rough tenement houses, posing as a boy so I could work at a city livery. It all ended when Uncle backed a high-stakes card game and snookered some nasty fellas out of their mining shares. Uncle swore he'd won them fair and square, but those men came after him. He took off and left me behind with only my wits to escape, and the mining shares certificate he couldn't find.

Amos was working as a cook in San Francisco. Mizzy had told me to find him if I had trouble. Desperate to track him down, I stumbled upon the San Francisco Underground Railroad and ended up smuggled aboard the merchant schooner *Salish Wind*, in the middle of an important freedom mission. Amos, who went by Cook, ran the galley of the *Salish Wind*. Still posing as a boy to avoid drawing attention, I crewed on that schooner, bound for the British territories with a load of mining equipment and a group of Black passengers fleeing bounty hunters in pursuit of former slaves.

I thought my luck had turned. I had a mining share certificate and was heading to the place where the gold rush was in full swing. Turned out there was no gold to claim, I wasn't anywhere near the goldfields, and the company on the certificate didn't even exist in the territories. Jake Miller had pleaded with me to check with his father, to ask him for help. But I wouldn't listen, and it was a hard lesson.

Once we reached Victoria, Cook had to stay behind to help the Black settlers get set up on their island homesteads. That duty saved his life. Aboard the merchant ship *Salish Wind*, only hours out of port, on the return trip to San Fran, the *Salish Wind* was pursued. While attempting to outrun the attackers, the ship ran aground in a fog bank, and the pirates came on board. Drak, who had replaced Cook in the galley for the trip, shoved me in a hidden cupboard. It was as if he knew what was about to happen. Mr. Jones has never said how he survived the battle and carnage on deck. Before the ship sank, I slapped together a raft for us and we floated it to a nearby island.

The story of Odysseus took shape in my mind. I remembered he had had to deal with Poseidon, who, in a fit of rage, wrecked his ship when he was trying to get home. It was just like that on the *Salish Wind*, except our wreck was the work of greedy pirates, and not a ferocious sea god. Still, as stories go, Odysseus and I had a lot in common, and that made me more nervous as I thought about the hike the next morning.

Mr. Jones and I had survived, and the pirates didn't know. They hung around the cove where our raft landed, and we watched them from our hiding place. On the beach in front of us, they buried gold they'd stolen from the ship. When they left a few days later, a fresh terror descended. Nobody knew where we were. I finally got the courage to explore the island, hoping rescue wasn't impossible. All was going well until I stumbled upon a dead body in a clearing. My nerves were so frazzled by then, I panicked. Running down a steep and narrow path like a deranged fool, I tripped and crashed, knocking myself unconscious.

The only reason I didn't die where I fell was that a young woman found me. Her name was Shenoa, and she wore the traditional clothing of the local people. In the space above my head, I pictured her sitting beside me in the cave, weaving a basket and nursing me with strange tea. All of that still left me uneasy, like maybe I'd dreamed it all. She came out of nowhere and knew everything about me, everything about the island, and everyone on it. I was on the lighthouse island, she'd said, and the good lightkeeper would help me. She also said I should ask Mizzy about what happened to my mama. Then one day she vanished.

Weeks passed with me living in a cave overlooking that cove, struggling to get my strength back and make sense of things. While my body healed, my memory did not. Everything that happened after the shipwreck was a jumbled puzzle, with many pieces missing. Odysseus never had a whack on the head. Lucky for him. But he had way more backstabbers and enemies lining up to kill him than I did, so we both had our fair share of challenges.

I built up my strength day by day after Shenoa left, aware that each night was getting colder, daylight hours shorter, and my cave dwelling would soon be intolerable. Finally, I set out for the other side of the island, following a faint cross-island trail. I buried the unknown man in the clearing as best I could and then pressed on to the lighthouse.

The glowing embers from the fireplace cast a hint of red into the room. The ceiling disappeared, and I was in darkness. Another story memory popped into my head. I remembered a mythical nymph put a spell on Odysseus and held him captive on an island. Calypso. That was her name. I turned onto my side and fluffed my pillow. Mr. Jones grunted at having to accommodate my new position.

At least I wasn't held against my will on this island, even though I'd felt like a prisoner many times in recent months. Mrs. Dalworth wasn't a bit like Calypso. Even though she was alone at the lighthouse, she wasn't the type to lure sailors in from the sea. She would have no use for Calypso's pretentious golden loom, preferring her simple yarn and needles. She'd patched up Edgar's wool socks so many times, the toes and heels were the colors of the rainbow. She'd given me a favorite pair of them to wear in the morning.

Calypso was trouble, but she was just somebody that fellow Homer made up in his story so he could mess with Odysseus. Papa always teased me for doing the same thing, but that's what we storytellers do. But one thing settled me down and made me feel ready for the next day. I'd remembered the entire story and all the things that had landed me where I was. Mrs. Dalworth would laugh when I told her she had the role of island nymph in my version of Homer's Odyssey, particularly since I'd decided that Calypso was a superb name for a horse.

CHAPTER SIX

I awoke in the dark to the aroma of brewing coffee, having dozed off sometime after Mrs. Dalworth came in from her four-in-the-morning lighthouse check. I rubbed my sticky eyes, stretched my legs out from under my blanket. Mr. Jones jumped down and Mrs. Dalworth whispered a greeting to him as he clicked across the kitchen floor.

I rolled onto my side and peered out of my alcove behind the stove. She was already dressed for the day in the rugged trousers and shirt she wore when there was hard physical work to be done. I watched her move about her kitchen, preparing breakfast. She banged a wooden spoon twice on the side of a metal pot. Oatmeal. Something to stick to the ribs, I could imagine her saying, to keep us strong on our trek.

I dressed and checked my knapsack one more time. It was only a day trip, but I had prepared for anything—blankets, flint and steel, extra socks and gloves, a canvas tarp. At the kitchen table, Mrs. Dalworth was loading sandwiches into an already bulging pack.

"You're not bringing all that," I said.

She looked up. "Good morning to you as well."

"Good morning." I had come at her with a sharp edge. Not the way to start the day. "We agreed I'd carry supplies. You need to travel light."

"This isn't heavy. See for yourself."

She picked up the satchel by the strap and dangled it from a finger.

"It's too bulky. You could get hung up on something. What have you got in there, anyway?"

Mrs. Dalworth stared down at the bag, crestfallen. "A few things for Edgar."

Her cheeks tightened as pain passed through her expression. She wanted to take something to leave on his grave. She hadn't seen him since the day he'd set out for Clamity Cove in the lighthouse rowboat. She unpacked the bag, looking for something she could leave behind.

I slung my arm over her shoulders to cheer her up.

"How about we leave that extra blanket?"

"It was his. I was going to cover him."

That was about the saddest thing I'd ever heard anybody say. Tears sprung to my eyes, and I gulped them back. I remembered the blanket I clung to after Papa died. She had some other smaller items for him—a figurine of an angel, some dried flowers, a favorite pencil.

"I'll carry the blanket then. You can take the rest."

"No. I'm being silly. The blanket stays."

There was a knock on the door then, the usual two knocks announcing Perkins. He was earlier than usual because Mrs. Dalworth had told him we were leaving with first light. She moved her pack to the floor and called for him to enter.

"Now remember, Mr. Perkins," she said, as he dug into his oatmeal. "You're to stay here no matter what. You cannot leave that lighthouse unattended."

"Yes, ma'am. But I must protest one last time. This trip is unwise."

His friendliness of a week earlier had worn off, and he'd returned to treating me like I was an ornament.

"It's none of your business. I'll see to her safety. Do your job as she asks," I said.

Perkins clenched his coffee mug and glared at me.

"Stop it, you two," Mrs. Dalworth ordered. "I'll not start this fine day with your nonsense. We'll be fine, Mr. Perkins. I am not helpless, as you well know, and Charlee has planned everything. We'll be back before dark. If we run into trouble, we are prepared to overnight. You mind the lighthouse. Stay the course. You are in charge."

Perkins had been grumbling something under his breath, but straightened up when she handed over the temporary command of the lighthouse.

"We'll leave you with the dishes. Do you think you can manage those?"

"Yes, ma'am." His ears looked ready to burst into flame, and I turned away to hide a smile. He despised taking orders from this fierce woman and, much as he'd wanted to be the man in charge of this place, he never was and never would be.

The air was crisp and cool as we set out, Mr. Jones leading the way across the rocky, uneven field. The recent rains had left the ground soggy in low spots and the mud sucked at our boots. I was pretty sure the bluff trail would have drained and dried, but it was a treacherous path to hike at the best of times.

Mrs. Dalworth chatted away as we began our gradual climb up the winding hill at the end of the field. As we moved into single file, I listened to her tell of walking the moors as a girl, reassuring me she was still capable of what we'd set out to do. The whole time, I kept telling myself that she'd be fine and taking her wasn't a huge mistake.

It wasn't long before the steepening climb made her fall silent. We stopped every few minutes so she could catch her breath. The hike that took me a good hour and a half was going to take double the time. I did a few calculations. Once we reached the clearing, Mrs. Dalworth would have only an hour to spend at Edgar's grave.

Mrs. Dalworth was slow and chatted about everything she came across. When we reached a craggy bluff, I tied off a rope for her to hang onto so she could use her arms to pull herself up. Luckily, the rocks weren't loose and she heeded my instructions about where to place her feet. She was not used to climbing, but she didn't complain or make excuses. Mr. Jones would show her the route, wait for her to catch up, then go ahead a little way, and wait again.

On the last steep section, I was so busy worrying about Mrs. Dalworth that I shifted my weight onto a loose stone. A small slide of rocks tumbled down the embankment, and I slid a few feet with it before catching the heel of my boot on a large root. A twinge of pain reminded me of the bad sprain I'd had in that ankle the previous year.

"Charlee!"

"I'm good," I said, clambering back to solid ground and dusting off my trousers. "That there is an example of how fast things can turn out here. Can't get sloppy for a second."

Mrs. Dalworth solemnly nodded. She muttered to herself the rest of the way, analyzing and coaching every step, vigilant for dangers.

We reached the clearing by late morning, later than I'd hoped, but still within a safe window of time. The sky was a perfect blue, no sign of weather in any direction. Birds of spring created an enthusiastic chorus of song to celebrate our arrival.

Mrs. Dalworth was weary from the climb and tried to disguise the limp that always set in when she did too much. I led her to the spot where I'd found and buried Edgar, marked by the mounded dirt and a simple stack of rocks I'd fashioned into a respectable headstone. The sun was out and had taken the dew off the ground. I laid out a blanket beside his grave, but she fell to her knees, placed her forehead on the ground and wept. My own grief bubbled up like a fiery volcano, choking me, making my breath burn in shallow puffs. For a moment, I was standing beside the dirt hole in Sonoma where Papa's wooden coffin had been placed. My hands went to my waist where Mizzy's arms had encircled me, but her warmth wasn't there to hold me up. I turned away, wandered out to the middle of the clearing and dropped onto a patch of grass. I couldn't bear to look at Mrs. Dalworth, so broken up with pain and loss. Mr. Jones stayed behind, leaning against her as she sobbed, comforting her when I didn't know how.

Something about this clearing always made me feel unsettled, like someone was watching me. I looked up at the top of the tree, the one I'd buried Edgar beneath. High on a broken branch jutting out from the thick green foliage was a solitary bald eagle. His feathers ruffled as the morning breeze swayed the treetops. He turned his white-capped head to one side and peered down at me. "Eagle Looking". I remembered. The wife of the Lekwungen chief had given me that name when we'd met at the lighthouse. It was as if she'd seen me before, here in this clearing, watching and searching, just as I was again now.

When I agreed to take Mrs. Dalworth to the clearing, she proposed I carry on down to Clamity Cove, the site of my original camp and where I believed Mr. Miller's gold still waited for me to find it. I'm sure she thought adding a gold-hunting side trip would be irresistible to me. It was. It gave me a chance to search the cove one last time before leaving the island forever.

I stopped some distance from Mrs. Dalworth and waited for her to acknowledge me. She blew her nose in a handkerchief and turned, face blotchy and red, eyes puffy and swollen.

"Will you be all right here?"

"Of course, lass. Seeing his grave made it final. I'd hoped for so long…"

"I don't have to go down to the cove. I doubt there's anything new to see."

"Don't be silly. Go check for that gold one more time. Maybe it'll come to you, where you put it. I'll be right here when you're done." She blew her nose in her handkerchief again, a loud honk that sent little birds fleeing from the nearby bushes.

"If you're certain…"

"Go! While you have time. I'd like to talk to Edgar for a while."

"All right then. Mr. Jones, you stay."

Mr. Jones had been inspecting the tree, sniffing around the base as if he knew the eagle was hiding up in the branches and he aimed to flush him out. He stopped his investigation when I spoke his name.

"I'll see you both in one hour. We'll start back right away."

"Take a sandwich," Mrs. Dalworth replied, digging a cloth package out of her knapsack. I wasn't hungry, but took it since she'd gone to the trouble.

As I set out for the path at the south end of the clearing, Mr. Jones followed me.

"You need to stay."

"Let him go if he wants. I'm all right. Just going to sit right here."

I pointed at Mrs. Dalworth and Mr. Jones took up watch duty at her side. Then I waved and disappeared alone into the trees.

CHAPTER SEVEN

The path hadn't changed much from the last time I'd walked it. The smell of the forest was rich, and the air felt fresh and invigorating in my nose. Ferns covered the forest floor beneath the cedars, but the overgrown path was easy to follow. This was Lekwungen land. Mrs. Dalworth said the local people had a fishing camp on the north end, but nobody had been here since last summer. I was probably the last person to have walked the path in the fall.

Returning to Clamity Cove cinched my stomach into an unexpected knot. With my head a lot clearer than before, I had one last opportunity to figure out if the gold was still there, or if the pirates had found it and taken off with it.

The day Brody took me to the cove, when he was beginning his investigation into the sinking of the *Salish Wind* last fall, my memory had failed me. The place where the pirates had buried the gold was dug up. Three ugly mounds above the tide lined remained, a scar left behind by their greed and haste. But what they dug up and made off with that day was three barrels of stones. Before they returned, I'd replaced the gold with beach rock and moved the actual gold to another spot up the beach. That's where my memories got messy. I'd left a marker, a small piece of a broken hatch, pointing to the new spot so I'd know where to find it. But when I returned with Brody, there was no such marker. Brody and some of his crew combed the area looking for anything that belonged to the *Salish Wind*. One man wondered out loud about the mysterious three mounds, and he leveled them out with his boot when nothing interesting was found around the holes. Clam diggers, he figured, of all things. 'Giant clams, those,' Brody had said, and he studied me as if I knew all about them and wasn't telling, which was true. I hadn't told him about the stolen gold.

I paused at a twisting section of the path. When Mr. Jones and I began exploring the island, we'd climbed this path from Clamity Cove and gone all the way to the clearing. This was the place I'd stumbled and knocked myself out, this sharp bend in the narrow path where my knapsack had caught on a branch, yanked me off balance and I'd lost my footing.

I put my boot up on the big, menacing rock where I'd hit my head as I plunged to the ground. For a moment, I saw myself sitting in the dirt talking to an Indian woman who had appeared out of nowhere and found me knocked senseless on the path. She helped me back to my cave and stayed with me for several days until I was well enough to manage on my own.

But this is where my memories were tangled or lost. I remembered she'd told me I had to bury the man I'd stumbled upon. She said I needed to help him, and one day I would understand why. It was months later when I realized the body I'd buried in the clearing was Mrs. Dalworth's husband, who she believed had drowned when his canoe capsized off Deception Island.

Something touched the back of my leg. I caught my breath and jumped aside.

"Mr. Jones! For heaven's sake! You frightened me, sneaking

up like that! What are you doing here? You're supposed to be watching Mrs. Dalworth."

He ignored my comments, strolled over to the ugly rock, and lifted his leg.

I laughed. "That's what I think of it, too. All right, then. If you insist on coming, let's go."

We emerged from the grove on the eastern shore of the rugged island a short time later. The hike seemed so easy now. It had taken less than fifteen minutes to get down from the clearing, and I wasn't pushing myself.

As we passed through the grove, Mr. Jones went straight to a sheltered spot and sat down. I joined him there, remembering it as the place I'd first slept after reaching the island by raft, that protected place under the canopy of trees, where I'd shivered under a wet canvas tarp, while Mr. Jones sat nearby watching the black water for the pirates and their ship.

"I remember this spot."

Mr. Jones lowered himself to the ground, paws placed in front of him, awaiting instructions.

"You're feeling awful sentimental. I guess I am, too. But c'mon now. We've got to comb the high tide line."

I had half an hour to figure out if the gold was still there, and if it was, where I'd put it. I remembered moving the gold and marking the new spot. But since my marker was gone, had the pirates come back and found it? I'd been over this hundreds of times and, as I pushed myself to recall, I felt a headache creep up the back of my neck. I could hear Mrs. Dalworth telling me to ease up on forcing myself to remember. I rolled my neck and shoulders around.

"Nope. Not going to have a spell. Not doing that now." I took a few deep breaths. "Let's check our cave."

Mr. Jones led the way from the bottom of the path, up along a narrow rock ledge. Tucked into a hidden crevice, the cave we'd lived in at the end of last summer was the same as before, but strewn with bits of debris blown inside from winter storms. One thing was certain—the gold bundles were never in the cave. I was sure of that. I'd kept a few nuggets aside and stashed them here for emergency use, but the rest was buried somewhere outside.

Mr. Jones nudged the knapsack with his nose.

"Good idea. We could both use that sandwich."

I unwrapped the cloth bundle Mrs. Dalworth had insisted I bring along. The air filled with the aroma of smoked fish, and Mr. Jones moved closer to ensure he got a fair share. I tore off a portion off the double slices of plump bread filled with yummy fish spread. Mr. Jones took the chunk from my hand and devoured it in three large gulps before I had chewed my first bite.

"That's all you get," I said, and then gave him another piece, unable to turn down his expression of sad hope.

With our sandwich devoured, and chased down with a little water from my canteen, we set to work on the beach. Hand shovel at the ready, I eyed the location where the pirates had first buried the gold. I let my thoughts drift to where I would move something important if a storm was bearing down and there was little time to act. I closed my eyes and let the lapping waves create a quiet rhythm. When I opened my eyes, Mr. Jones was sitting in the spot I imagined, waiting for me to join him.

"Are you telling me that's where I moved it?"

I kneeled down and examined the area, about half way between the original burial spot and the cave, and also above the high tide line. It was an excellent spot. A logical spot. I was about to plunge my shovel into the ground when my arm froze in mid-air. Papa was telling me to study the ground before destroying all the clues in front of me. I bent over for a closer look. The rocks in one spot formed a different pattern than those around them, as they would do if someone had dug in this spot and then taken great care to return the ground to its natural appearance. Seeing the changed pattern in front of me, the actual size and location of what had been dug up was obvious. This spot was significant and the digging was my work!

At the time, I'd been in a hurry and had only this small shovel. I would have buried the canvas bundles just deep enough for them to be fully covered. If the gold bundles were here, I'd be able to run my shovel into them. I pictured a grid in my head and inserted my shovel at an edge, then into the ground at about six-inch intervals, cutting through what I guessed was the center of the burial site.

"It's not here," I said to Mr. Jones, who was trying to get a piece of bramble unstuck from his back paw. "It has to be here."

But something was wrong. I'd dug up this spot, I was sure of it, but if I'd hidden the gold there, the pirates must have come back and found it, which would explain why I couldn't find the broken hatch. Maybe they'd figured it out after realizing I'd tricked them. But no way they'd leave the ground like this. It would have been another pile of rock and rubble, like the original burial spot down the beach that they'd torn up. It didn't make sense. I dug a hole about a foot deep in the middle. I found beach rocks mixed into the deeper sand, more evidence that it was the right spot. But the canvas bundles with Mr. Miller's gold were not there.

Time was running out. I examined other possible burial spots, but found nothing out of place. At the trailhead, by the grove where we'd spent our first night, Mr. Jones and I sat down and looked out over the bay one last time. I put my head in my hands. Once again, I'd tried and failed.

Scenes of the shipwreck gushed into my sinking mind. The dispute over directions between the Captain and Kuno, our First Mate. The thick, disorienting fog that swallowed us. The deafening crash when the ship slammed into the hidden reef. Drak forcing me into a cupboard in the galley to hide from invaders and emerging hours later with the ship in peril and everyone missing or dead.

Images of the shipwreck made me sick all over, and that usually brought on fierce headaches followed by a dark, paralyzing mood. I had learned not to go there with my memories, to stop the flashbacks and bad dreams, always of the same awful pirate opening the cupboard and throwing the head of one of my friends inside with me.

Mr. Jones licked my hand and I pulled him close.

"I know you remember. I wish you could tell me what happened. I've got nothing to prove that a black sloop robbed us and killed our friends. They don't believe me. They think I imagined it."

Back in the fall, I'd overheard Brody say to Mrs. Dalworth that I'd suffered a terrible trauma and my account was confused. I got up and dusted the dirt and leaves from my trousers. Mr. Jones sniffed with disgust and pawed at the ground.

"I don't want to give up either, but there's no point searching anymore."

I started up the trail back to the clearing. Mr. Jones didn't want to leave, but I told him Mrs. Dalworth was waiting and we had to get her home safe. He looked down the trail one last time and followed me, tail down over his haunches.

It was a long shot trying to find the gold, but the trip wasn't a total waste. I was clear about one thing: There was no way those pirates came back, found the gold in my new spot and tidied up after themselves. I had recognized my work. That meant I'd moved it again, and the gold was still out there somewhere.

CHAPTER EIGHT

On the last long hill winding up to the clearing, Mr. Jones bolted ahead. Five minutes later, I found him sitting beside Mrs. Dalworth at Edgar's grave.

"You're back already? Oh dear, the time went so fast!"

I checked the angle of the sun. "Keeping an eye on the light."

I helped her to her feet and she shuffled the kinks out of her legs.

"I told Mr. Jones he'd have to fetch you if you lost track of time. Did you eat your sandwich? We enjoyed ours, didn't we, Mr. Jones?"

What was she on about? Mr. Jones had been with me the whole time. He avoided my bewildered stare.

"I ate, yes. You made Mr. Jones' favorite."

Mr. Jones licked his lips, remembering lunch with one or both of us, and stole a guilty look at me sideways.

"I take it you didn't find the gold."

"No, I didn't. Checked every logical place."

"Help me fold the blanket, lass. I can barely bend over. I'm going to be slow going back, so we'd better not dilly-dally."

"If you're ready." She had weeded and groomed Edgar's

humble grave, and placed an angel figurine on the rock head-stone I'd made for him.

"As ready as I'll ever be."

I glanced up at the sky, still clear, with a faded slice of crescent moon showing against the pale blue. The low angle of the sun made long black shadows across the clearing. We had a few hours of daylight left and we'd need every minute. As Mrs. Dalworth said her last goodbyes to Edgar, I stuffed her remaining things into my pack so she wouldn't have to carry anything. Mr. Jones led the way, Mrs. Dalworth followed, and I took up the rear.

As we left the clearing, I thought I heard someone call out behind me. It was the young woman who had saved me after my fall. But when I spun around to see her, she wasn't there. An eerie silence hung over the clearing, and my skin prickled. I looked up into the gigantic tree. No sign of the eagle. A light breeze rustled the treetops. Probably what I'd mistaken for a voice.

As Mr. Jones set a steady pace along the trail, I wondered if Mrs. Dalworth had decided what to do about Edgar's ultimate resting place. She seemed at peace when I returned from the cove, but I didn't want to ask to satisfy my curiosity, so I hummed a little tune to break the silence.

"I recognize that song," Mrs. Dalworth said, turning her head to look at me, which caused her to trip and tumble head-first into the thick salal clogging both sides of the narrow path.

"Oh, no! Are you okay?"

"I think so. Help me out of here, will you?"

I untangled her arms from the dense foliage, grabbed the collar of her coat, and hauled her back onto her feet. She steadied herself and brushed bits of dead leaves and debris from her trousers.

"Appears I've only wounded my pride."

"The shadows make the uneven ground tricky in this light. Watch your step. There's no need to hurry."

"Good point. You know, ever since I came to this outpost, I've disliked those infernal bushes. They grow everywhere, you can't get rid of them and the berries they produce are more work than they're worth. Well, they just cushioned my fall. Didn't even hit the ground. So maybe they aren't so bad after all."

Mrs. Dalworth had disheveled hair. She'd also wiped her nose and smeared dirt on the end. The sight of her made me smile, and I was relieved she wasn't hurt and had returned to her old self. Then I had the sobering thought that we were still on the simple part of the route back.

I spotted a sturdy branch lying beside the path, and after trimming off the scraggly branches, gave it to her to use as a walking stick. It gave her fresh confidence and energy.

"I was thinking," she said, when we stopped for a brief rest and water at the highest bluff. "Maybe you'd like to come back and visit me in Victoria. You're always welcome, and you can stay as little or as long as you like."

"I'd like to, but it's a long way to come. I've got so many things to sort out in California."

"What about the unfinished business with the *Salish Wind?*"

"That's over. I have no proof pirates attacked the ship. I'm the only witness and my word isn't good enough. I don't even have the gold that I promised to deliver to Mr. Miller."

"But those men had a piece of it. They stole your island map and traded off that silverware from the *Salish Wind*. Doesn't that prove they were aboard the ship, that they knew about it or had the gold?"

"I wish it did. But for all we know, that gold was from someplace else. And the Captain's silverware? Who is going to vouch for that? S.W. could be anyone. With no evidence, I can't prove a crime took place. I hoped there would be justice, but the story of one girl doesn't bear any weight. It's best I forget about it and move on."

"You could ask the Lekwungen chief to provide an account. He was there."

"Never. All he could do, like you, is prove the men exist and were in Clamity Cove one day. Nobody saw their crimes but me. The chief and his people don't need any more trouble from the White man."

Mrs. Dalworth agreed. I took her arm and we continued on our way. By the time we reached the last bluff, the light was almost gone from the trees. The lighthouse blinked from the point, beckoning us home, the house beside it nothing but a diminished silhouette on the point.

"Looks like Mr. Perkins didn't think to light the house lanterns." Mrs. Dalworth said, already back in command of her light station. "Let's hope he's at least set a fire on the hearth. Whoever marries him will have some work cut out for her."

I tied a rope around her waist so that if she slipped while descending the steep rocks, she wouldn't slide all the way down the cliff.

"Last difficult stretch. Once we get down this piece, we'll have it beat."

Mr. Jones had already picked his way down a narrow section of the cliff and watched us from the bottom.

"That dog is a showoff," Mrs. Dalworth grumbled as she clutched the rocks with stiff hands and began a slow and shaky descent.

"Careful, now. Concentrate."

I cringed as her trembling hands clutched at rocks and her feet searched for purchase on the smooth rock face. It was taking every bit of her remaining courage, but she was determined. Half way down, she looked up, face flushed by the effort, and grinned. "I feel like a girl again!"

I cheered her on, hoping she had enough strength to reach

the bottom in one piece. If she slipped and was dangling on the cliff by the rope, I wasn't sure I'd be able to swing her back to regain grip and footing. My rope harness could leave her flailing in mid-air. I didn't want to imagine that.

I exhaled and wiped nervous sweat off my brow when Mrs. Dalworth planted both feet on solid ground at the bottom. Mr. Jones congratulated her by jumping on her leg, and she beamed up at me with pride. I started down, wary of a risky misstep in the dim light, with nobody on a rope to catch me if I fell. Descending the bluff wasn't hard for me, but this was no time to take it for granted.

"You're mighty nimble," she said, slapping me on the shoulder when I reached the bottom. "How you manage in those cowboy boots is beyond me."

"Where the devil is he?"

Mrs. Dalworth paused on the porch while I groped my way into the dark cottage. Perkins was nowhere to be seen. I lit the lantern hanging by the door and the room flooded with amber light. Lunch dishes sat on the kitchen counter. The fireplace was cold. He hadn't been in the house for hours.

"He's got to be around somewhere. I'll check his quarters. Maybe he fell asleep or something."

I'd thrown out an explanation, but didn't believe it for a second. Perkins wasn't the sort to slide off for a nap when the boss wasn't looking. He had annoying qualities, but laziness wasn't one of them. He may have busied himself in a project somewhere, but even then, it wasn't like him to neglect his duties.

"I'll get the fire going. He's even let the stove go cold. He'll have to wait for supper, I mean to tell him. I'll give him a piece of my mind for this. He had very few instructions."

Mrs. Dalworth was still complaining as I left the house with a smaller lantern in hand. I crossed the yard and knocked on the door of his sleeping quarters. No answer. I checked the root cellar, the woodshed and the winery. No sign of him. Dusk made it impossible to examine the ground for his tracks.

I said to Mr. Jones, "He wouldn't have been foolish enough to come meet us. Besides, I would have spotted him from the bluff and you would have announced him with a bark. And Mrs. Dalworth told him not to come after us unless we hadn't returned by tomorrow."

Mr. Jones agreed, then stretched his neck to sniff the air.

"Can you find him?"

Mr. Jones trotted across the yard and waited by the lighthouse door. I yanked the door open and hollered up the staircase, voice echoing off the cavernous walls. A muffled reply came from up top.

"Go tell Mrs. Dalworth we found him."

As Mr. Jones hurried off to the house, I realized he couldn't tell her anything, but she'd figure I'd sent him because the mystery was solved.

"Perkins, what's going on up there?"

Another muffled reply. He was going to make me go up there to find out. Annoyed, I stomped up the stairs, my tired legs heavy as slabs of stone. They'd done enough walking and climbing for one day, and the spiral staircase seemed twice as steep and more precarious than ever. I debated whether to warn him that Mrs. Dalworth was going to have his hide for letting the house go cold.

I stopped half way up. The tower smelled like a wet campfire. The lighthouse lantern hadn't gone out—we could see it as we made our way back—and it still blinked in perfect intervals from above. But this strong odor wasn't right. My legs forgot their pain and I sprinted up the rest of the stairs.

CHAPTER NINE

"Perkins?" I scanned the stone platform that circled the massive oil lantern.

His reply came from the shadows opposite the staircase. He was slumped against the wall with blackened shirt sleeves and a barrel of spilled oil beside him.

I hurried to his side. "What happened? You've burned yourself! How long have you been like this?"

"What time is it?" His voice was quiet, weak.

The lighthouse reflector rotated beside us, its rhythmic clanking like a slow train leaving a station, moving on its tracks as if it had nothing to do with what had gone wrong. A small, unlit lantern sat in the puddle of spilled oil beside Perkins.

"Just past four. You're lucky you didn't set the place on fire."

He glared at me. "It's made of stone."

My sympathy for him vanished. He was well enough to be condescending.

"Well, I'm surprised you caught fire at all, since you're made of the same thing."

"My clothing…" he said, as if I didn't know what fire liked for fuel. It had charred his sleeves to the elbow.

"Get up, then," I snapped. "You'll live."

"I don't need your help," he said, getting to his feet without using his hands. "With the oil spilled, I couldn't risk lighting the lantern to see my way down." He clenched his teeth through the painful, jagged sentence.

"Whatever."

I grabbed his lantern from the puddle of oil and put it with mine at the top of the stairs. Perkins followed and examined his hands in the light. They were oily red and black. He couldn't grasp the staircase railing.

"I'll go first with the lantern. Lean on me for balance."

He ignored my suggestion and took the first two steps behind me without help. I moved to one side as he teetered on the stair behind me. I pictured him plunging head first down the spiral staircase and landing in a bloody heap at the bottom. That would be a fine mess to deal with. It crossed my mind he was in shock, wasn't thinking clearly, and didn't realize the risk in front of him.

I spoke in earnest. "If you fall, Archie, you might die..." This gave him pause, so I added in the most delicate tone I could muster, "...and if you fall, you'll take me down with you."

His eyes widened and I furrowed my brows for extra persuasion. I'd already decided I'd step out of the way if he tumbled. But appealing to his chivalry made him do the right thing. He lifted his elbows and I turned so he could rest his forearms on my shoulders. I knew he hated having to do it, but it was the only safe way down the steep iron stairs.

An odor of sweat and whale oil filled my nose as he moved into position close behind me. In a flash, I was back in the cave at Clamity Cove, sweat soaking my shirt out of panic and terror, cloaked in Drak's greasy rain slicker that reeked of the same fishy oil. It was after the big storm and an unusual king tide. In my cave, I'd realized I had to move the gold off the beach. The sudden image stopped me in my tracks, heart quivering like a captive bird.

"I moved it again," I said in disbelief.

"Moved what?" Perkins mumbled, and the bubble burst. I was back in the lighthouse, snapped back to the present.

"Nothing," I said. The flashback evaporated. "Slow steps now. Let's go."

I could feel Perkins' breath on my neck as we started down. I had never been that close to him. Once, our bodies collided while reaching for firewood, and last week, he'd steadied me when I had a dizzy spell out in the field.

He wasn't badly burned, I told myself. I thought of the gunpowder burn left on my wrist when the doctor in China-town had saved me from bleeding to death. I'd had very few burns from fire, thankfully, and none as bad as his, but even a minor burn hurt worse than almost every other kind of pain. He was suffering and doing his best not to show it, which made me feel a little sorry for him. But as soon as we reached the last stair, he moved away from me without a word of thanks. Nothing but a grunt as I opened the lighthouse door and let him pass. I shook my head and cut in front of him to lead the way.

"Found him. Tried to set himself on fire," I announced, as he followed me through the front door of the cottage.

"Oh, my goodness! Archie!" Mrs. Dalworth's kitchen knife clattered onto her chopping block. He tried to pry his boots off with his feet, but she waved him off the task and led him to a chair by the kitchen table.

"I've got water on, but it'll take a while to heat. Oil causes painful burns."

I stood in the door with my boots still on, hands squarely on my hips. I wanted nothing more than to plunk down by the fire, put my tired feet up on a stool, and think some things through. What had I almost remembered minutes earlier on the light-house staircase? With a little peace and quiet, I felt certain I could bring it back. But this ungrateful know-it-all had ruined the moment.

"I'm going to go clean up what he spilled." Perkins frowned in embarrassed silence.

"It can wait till tomorrow," Mrs. Dalworth said. "Fetch me that clean linen towel beside the wash basin, will you?"

I tossed her the cloth. "It won't take long. It's a hazard. Besides, he won't be in any shape to do it anytime soon."

Mrs. Dalworth nodded and Perkins looked at the floor. I couldn't resist one more dig, one more deserving kick at him while he was down.

By evening, a blazing fire had made the small living room toasty. Mr. Jones moved himself to a cooler spot on the floor under the kitchen table. I threw off the blanket I'd pulled over my shoulders when the house was still chilly. Earlier, I'd returned to the lighthouse to clean up the spilled oil. But before I set to work, I'd stood on the staircase as before, and conjured up the sudden memory I'd had. I recorded it in my notebook so I wouldn't lose it again.

'I'm in the cave. It's after the big storm. I've noticed that an extreme high tide combined with bad weather covers the entire beach. I realize I have to move the gold again. Again. What do I mean by again? I moved it once for sure, replacing the gold in the barrels with rocks and reburied those. That was before the storm. This is after the storm. Before or after I hit my head? Not sure. Did I move the gold to a third location? That would explain so many things, like why I couldn't find it in the second location and why the marker was gone, and why the second location was empty but concealed. I'd been careful not to leave evidence of my presence because the pirates didn't know I'd survived. So, I moved the gold to a third spot, but where did I move it to?'

Perkins caused me to lose the most important part of that sudden memory just before it was revealed. A few seconds more and I might have had it, might have had all the answers to the mystery of the missing gold. On the other hand, I might not have stumbled on the memory at all if Perkins hadn't nearly roasted himself like campfire quail over the lighthouse flame. I slapped my book shut. No way I was giving him credit for prompting my discovery.

Hunched in her rocking chair, Mrs. Dalworth poured over the final government report on the shipwreck that Brody had left for us to review.

"Good thing we got back without a hitch," I said. "Archie would have had a mighty grim night otherwise."

"What's that?" She marked a spot midway down the first page with her forefinger and looked up.

"Nothing. Are you finished your tea?"

She nodded and resumed reading. I carried our cups to the kitchen and washed them in the basin of water left from supper.

"Why did they give us a new copy of that report, anyway? Did Brody make a mistake on the first one? I don't remember seeing any errors in it, other than it was vague, and they got most of it wrong."

"That's 'Mr. Brody' to you, and I don't know. So far, it's almost identical. Maybe a word or two improved."

Mrs. Dalworth licked a finger, rustled the paper and flipped over to the second page. It had taken me months to get over my anger about the report. When Brody first brought it to us, I was furious for days. A ship had been seen floundering off Cape Flattery after a terrible storm in September, and initially, they presumed it was the lost *Salish Wind*. Since the schooner had left Victoria for San Francisco only one day before, and failed to arrive at her destination two weeks later, they assumed she'd been the vessel in distress.

When they discovered me at the lighthouse two months

later, it was a battle to convince them I was the only survivor of the shipwreck. They checked the ship's manifest, filed when the *Salish Wind* had been in Victoria. It identified me as "C. Harlee, Ship's Boy," and they were doubtful it was me, even when I pointed out the obvious play on my name. There was a lot of "How could I be that boy?" and "What was a girl doing on the crew of a sailing ship?" and "Why would the vessel have used a false name for me?" It was noise that had nothing to do with the accident and crimes, and they drove me out of my mind with it all. They didn't believe I'd built a raft and paddled it to the island until I led Brody to my cave at Clamity Cove. A piece of sail I'd tucked into the rocks was all that was left of the *Salish Wind*, and after I showed him how I'd cut it and used it for a door, there was no question that we'd both come from the ship. The report at least confirmed that the vessel in distress off Cape Flattery could not have been the *Salish Wind* and that the schooner had struck a reef and sunk off the waters of Deception Island.

I had no issue with that part of the account. My physical presence on the island was evidence to support the correct location of the shipwreck. But that's where it ended. In my statement, I'd described a ship following us, the Captain's bizarre reaction, and his fatal decision to evade it by entering the dangerous waters around Deception Island. His actions, and his navigational error in thick fog, led us to run aground on a reef. But my account was too fantastical to be believed.

Mrs. Dalworth stiffened in her chair.

"What's this now? It says your First Mate made a critical navigational error, placing the *Salish Wind* off course and too far north in the strait."

"What? Lemme see that!" I dried my hands as she handed me the second page, pointing near the bottom. My eyes flew over the words. A paragraph at the bottom was new. "This is a total lie! They're blaming Kuno! He told the Captain we were off course. Even argued with him about it. It was the Captain's mistake! I was there. I heard it all."

"There's more," Mrs. Dalworth said. "You'd better sit down for this."

I couldn't sit. I hovered by her chair, hands beckoning for the last page as I waited for her to finish reading it. Finally, she gave it to me, eyes wide with disbelief.

"As I live and breathe. There is another survivor of your shipwreck!"

CHAPTER TEN

"What! Who? There were only two of us left, me and Mr. Jones. I watched the ship go under. Watched the beach for days. There couldn't possibly be…unless those pirates took someone alive…"

"There's a thought."

"But they killed the crew. I saw…the bodies."

"Maybe they only killed the ones who resisted."

My eyes flew over the new evidence.

"'Based on the account of the other survivor…' Why don't they name him? '…the shipwreck was deemed an accident. The other survivor denies being followed or attacked by an unknown vessel. The other survivor was found unconscious in a small skiff and picked up by a passing vessel.' This is unbelievable!"

"But is it possible? You said yourself your raft got pulled by the current. What if that happened to him and he was lucky enough to be spotted floating around out there?"

"I saw the skiff. There was only one on the *Salish Wind* and the reef crushed it to smithereens."

But my memories were confused, unreliable. That's what the

"""

report concluded, without coming right out and saying it. The other survivor discredited me. Even worse, it dredged up my worst fear—that my memory had played a terrible trick on me.

My head pounded. I rubbed my temples.

"This news has done you in. You're pale as a winter moon." Mrs. Dalworth fought her way out of her rocking chair as I stood like a statue, staring at the wall behind her. "Charlee," she said, taking my limp arm. "Come now, lass. It's been a big day. We'll sort it out tomorrow."

My stomach churned. How could I have been so wrong? Another survivor, another witness, denied the *Salish Wind* had been raided and robbed. If true, it meant that nobody was murdered, Mr. Miller's gold was never stolen or buried at Clamity Cove, and I'd imagined it all.

During the drizzly days that followed, I fell into a terrible slump. I got up late, forced myself through daily chores, and then draped myself over the kitchen table, poring over the same few words written in the new report, as if they might correct themselves or reveal something new.

"I was wrong," I'd say, venturing into conversation.

"You were not wrong," Mrs. Dalworth would answer more firmly each time, but she left me to wallow in my brooding conclusion.

On the third day, Mrs. Dalworth had seen enough.

"This is no way for us to spend our last days together. Get your coat on." We strolled the fields surrounding to the lighthouse for much of the morning.

Mrs. Dalworth asked me to go over the shipwreck one more time, including my days as a castaway on the other side of the island. Nothing new shook loose, but it made me feel better, more anchored in my thinking. After lunch, we sat out on the porch and Mrs. Dalworth asked me to read from my notebook. I protested because it was private, and the things I'd written before the shipwreck were embarrassing. I'd blathered on about the stupid gold mine that didn't exist and how I was going to be rich one day. Mostly I grumbled about the hard work I'd landed myself in crewing on the *Salish Wind*.

"Why do you want to hear this childish stuff?" I said.

"It's quite delightful, actually. I think it'll help you see yourself as you once were. You're not the same girl, I'm sure you feel it. Still, you have the same determination and wit, and you don't suffer fools. Keep reading," she said. So I did.

With the turn of a page, I saw how everything changed after the shipwreck. Huddled in a cave on Deception Island, I was petrified and on the lookout for the pirates who'd raided the ship. I was obsessed with them, but also wrote in anger about what they'd done, and how I'd make sure they paid.

And then a drastic change in the pages after I had fallen and hit my head. The first entry was streaked brown with dried blood. Then nothing for days. Wrinkled and damaged pages followed, crammed full of strange symbols, nonsensical lines, and tiny handwriting, all of it smudged and uneven, as if I'd descended into madness. It went on for several pages until I reached a blank page, a gap over a month later, marking my arrival at the lighthouse. The codes were gone. My writing improved over the pages until it became legible again. The topics I'd written about after arriving at the lighthouse were a battleground of questions without answers.

"That middle section, when you were in the cave, shows how badly injured you were."

"Yeah, none of it makes sense."

"I think it shows you were of sound mind."

"What do you mean?"

"There's not much to go on, but if you go back to the pages before you fell and hit your head, you were scared to death that the pirates were going to find you. You knew you were a witness, and they'd come after you and kill you, too, if they knew you'd survived."

"Yeah, but what if I imagined it? What if it's part of the trauma of the shipwreck?"

"That doesn't fit. Everything you do is rational, sharp. You've got recipes. Foraging information. Instructions on wilderness survival. Descriptions of your surroundings. Weather, tides, times. All in incredible detail."

"True."

"And you wrote Drak saved your life because he made you hide in a secret cupboard. Why would he force you into a cupboard on a sinking ship?"

"Because he feared the human invaders worse than drowning."

"Exactly."

"I appreciate what you're trying to do, but it's no use. I can't prove any of it."

"There are two things going on here, Charlee. One is the truth. The other is the official account. It would be nice if they matched, but they often don't. What's more is two things can be true at once: that you are not wrong, and that the other survivor is not wrong."

That struck me like a lightning bolt. "What do you mean?"

"Perhaps this other survivor didn't see what happened. Is that possible?"

"I guess, but..."

"Tell me then. You're the writer, the storyteller. Tell me how one survivor might not experience the same thing as another."

I rattled off a story where a crew member got knocked unconscious, stuck into a boat by the pirates and shoved off into the strait. Then I made up another version, where the raiders sent one of their own out in a skiff, to be discovered as a witness and who'd provide a false account.

"That bit you wrote about the Captain bringing on new crew right before you left. Awfully coincidental."

"You think it's a set-up? I mean, what are the chances of being picked up in a skiff out on the open water?"

"Mighty slim, if you ask me."

The next morning was dull, almost overcast, a sign that the weather was turning but had not yet decided which way to go. Just before ten o'clock, the supply boat chugged into the black waters of Hidden Cove. Bobbing in a light ripple of waves, it anchored, and the crew launched a rowboat.

"They're coming ashore," I called into the kitchen.

This was the last time I'd look out over Fuca Strait from the lighthouse island. I hoped it wouldn't be the last I'd see of Mrs. Dalworth. Even though we tangled over some things, mostly because of my frustrations, we'd otherwise got on very well.

While my canvas bag was easy to carry, the small trunk Mrs. Dalworth gave me for Edgar's books was heavy and the handles dug into my hands. As I dragged it off the porch, thumping it down each step, Perkins appeared and volunteered to cart it down to the water's edge.

"What ya got in here? Rocks?" he teased as he shouldered the trunk with ease.

"Gold," I replied, and then I stood there, gaping behind him, images dancing in front of my eyes again. Clamity Cove. I'd emptied three small barrels of gold, made three canvas bundles, and buried them up the beach. I saw myself load the empty barrels with rocks and return them to the pirate's original burial site; I saw the pirates come back weeks later, dig up the barrels, take what they thought was their treasure out to their ship and sail away. It was early fall, the last time they'd been here. I saw the entire beach, the shovel in my hand, the dirt and blood on the knees of my trousers.

"Is something wrong, Charlee?" Mrs. Dalworth asked. I hadn't heard her come out of the house.

"I'm remembering."

"Do you want a pencil and paper?"

I caught her before she could dash back inside. "No, this is different. It's crystal clear."

"I knew it. It's all gonna come back. Which reminds me, wait till you've got Mr. Brody alone before interrogating him about the new report."

"I will."

"Don't know who might have ears out. Keep your cards close to the vest."

I smiled at her choice of metaphor.

"I'll be careful."

We walked down the path together, arm in arm. She wasn't about to say goodbye at the bluff and picked her way down the steep, rugged path behind me, right to the water's edge.

"I'll see you when I visit Victoria again." It was an odd, almost formal thing to say, but the farewell minutes needed some filling.

She shrugged. She knew I was unlikely to return.

Then there were a lot of repeated goodbyes, a lot of reminders about this and that, and when words became empty, nothing but deep sighs.

"Well, that's it then," Mrs. Dalworth said after Brody announced it was time to go.

"I'll write. Soon as I get there."

She smiled through trembling lips. Perkins saved the sad moment by stepping forward to shake my hand.

"Been a pleasure knowing you," he said, extending his bandaged hand and then pulling it back in awkward embarrassment. He clasped his hands behind his back to regain control of his arms. "I owe you one, if I ever see you again, Charlee."

He actually used my name. Mrs. Dalworth nodded with approval behind his back, and I knew then she'd put him up to a friendly farewell.

With my luggage loaded in the boat and Brody itching to leave, Mrs. Dalworth crushed me in her arms and whispered a little prayer in my ear, something about a road rising to meet me and the wind at my back, which ended with "until we meet again."

"Until we meet again," I said, inhaling the scent of sand and sea from her collar.

Then we broke apart and looked anywhere but at each other. I crawled into the rowboat with Mr. Jones tucked under my arm. Saying goodbye was hard and much too final.

Brody helped us to a bench at the stern and we shoved off. Mrs. Dalworth lingered on the shore for several minutes before starting the trek back up to the house.

"Mr. Perkins, get a shovel and fill that hole in the path before somebody breaks their neck!" she hollered.

"Poor Archie. Bet he wishes he was the one leaving," I said to Mr. Jones.

Not long after, from the deck of the departing supply boat, we watched the island cove fade away. Mrs. Dalworth stood at the top of the bluff, waving one last time.

"I'm going to miss her."

Words came to me, clear as if Mr. Jones had whispered back. "We will see her again".

I ruffled the fur on his forehead and said, "I hope you're right."

CHAPTER ELEVEN

With my small trunk stored in Brody's office at the government wharf, we set off on foot for the rooming house he'd arranged for me. During the ten-minute walk, where he insisted on carrying my duffle bag, he did all the talking, mostly outlining the rules of my stay.

While in Victoria, I was under his supervision. Until the *Sonoma Wind* reached port in the coming days, I was to be at the rooming house or at his office. I could walk the short distance between the two places, but only during daylight hours, and sightseeing of any kind required his permission and company. His rules seemed silly because everything in the town was within spitting distance. But getting lost wasn't his concern. The town was running amok with unruly miners who stopped in Victoria on their way to and from the gold mines on the mainland. Brody also informed me Mr. Miller was paying for everything until I was safely aboard the *Sonoma Wind*. But it was Mrs. Dalworth who had made him promise not to let me wander about the town alone.

The *Sonoma Wind* was expected to arrive in a day or so, but as with all sailing vessels, that could stretch for several more if the weather turned against them somewhere on their journey. One short week ago, a weather delay would have made me itch with impatience. But learning about another survivor had changed that. If the schooner was delayed, I could hang around Brody, get him talking about the shipwreck investigation and the new, unknown survivor.

"Mrs. Johnson, this is Miss Charlotte LeBeau. I trust you have a room ready?"

A rotund woman in a lavender floral dress greeted us at the front door of a pleasant white house. She eyed me with measured disgust.

"I do. But what's this getup now? And we don't allow animals." She looked down at Mr. Jones, who chose that moment to lick himself in a rude fashion. "It can't come into the house."

"It" is a "he", and he stays with me," I said.

"He can go in the tool shed out back," the woman snapped.

"If he stays in the shed, then I stay in the shed."

Our tense exchange flustered Brody, who blocked me with his arm as I leaned forward to argue in the woman's face.

"The dog stays with her, madam. Surely you can accommodate us this one time."

He took her pink hand and pressed money into it. She tucked it into her bodice and reconsidered the matter, while fiddling with a string of pearls around her sagging neck.

"Well. I have small quarters for hired help. There's an extra room right next to the back door. It's decent, if a little plain. She can stay in there with him, but that dog can't roam the house. I won't have it. She'll have to use the back door for coming and going. And if I hear so much as a whimper or a bark, they're both out."

She talked about us as if we weren't there. Brody looked to me, hopeful I'd accept her terms. I looked at Mr. Jones, who said he preferred a room to the tool shed, and so it was settled.

"Fine," I said, under respectable protest on behalf of us both.

The woman escorted us around the back and showed us to our room. After pointing out where the dining room was, the woman said I could get table scraps from the kitchen for Mr. Jones. Brody must have slipped her a nice sum to have gained that concession.

The room was tiny and lacked the decorative touches of throw cushions, fancy curtains and such to make it attractive. There was a bed with a plain wool blanket, a wash basin on a stand with two drawers, and a chamber pot tucked underneath. There was one wall picture with a king on it, one rag rug on the wood floor, and a small looking glass. I smiled as I realized I'd done inventory, the tallying of objects that surrounded me in unknown places. It had been a long time since I'd done that.

Since I had nothing to unpack and nothing to do, Mr. Jones and I returned with Brody to the wharf for the rest of the afternoon. There, I counted more things to pass the time—ships in the harbor, the number of crates on a wagon across the street, and how many boards unloaded into a pile from a merchant vessel nearby. I wondered if this sudden mental counting was another sign of my brain fixing itself. When Brody came back from the wharf to his office and nobody was around, I followed him inside.

"Excuse the disarray, Miss LeBeau. My clerk left and I haven't had time to hire a replacement."

His inner office was a sea of papers, filling every available surface and flooding over his desk on every side. It looked like he was handling the paperwork of the entire harbor.

"Mr. Brody?"

He didn't look up from his desk. "Yes?"

"Do you know...um...could I get a book out of my trunk?"

"Of course." He rifled through a pile of papers in search of something.

"Say, I was wondering." I watched his face to gauge his reaction. "I was wondering why the other survivor from the *Salish Wind* wasn't named in the report."

His hands paused in mid-air and he frowned.

"That is a very good question and I don't know the answer."

He left his office with me on his heels. "But it was your report. Wasn't it?"

"It was, at first. The government office took it over when new information came in about another survivor. I had no part in it after that. Excuse me now, I must get back to the dock."

He hurried off before I could form another delicate question. So, the government had cut Brody out of the investigation. Why? He had done all the work, drafted the first report, and even if he got it wrong, I couldn't blame him. He'd done what he could with almost no evidence.

Outside his office, sitting in the spring sunshine, I thumbed through Edgar's book. As soon as I flipped open the cover, I remembered having read it before. Not all of it, but many sections of it. So many times over the past winter, I'd pick up a book I'd been reading and look at it like I'd never seen it before.

A short time later, Brody returned.

"Mr. Brody, why did the government take over your investigation?"

"Are you still pondering that?"

"I mean, do government offices typically handle investigations around here?"

"No, they don't, but it is their prerogative," he said over his shoulder and was gone again. I watched him until he vanished into stacks of lumber waiting to be loaded onto a ship.

"Something's off about this," I said to Mr. Jones, who had been eavesdropping while monitoring the inner harbor for the *Sonoma Wind*.

Brody returned within the hour, and I followed him inside once again.

"Sorry to be a nuisance, but the report said they recovered the other survivor in a skiff. Where's that skiff now?"

"I don't know. You sure have a lot of questions."

I remembered Uncle complaining about my persistent questions, but I pressed on.

"Do you at least know who picked up the other survivor?"

"Sorry, no. Listen. It's getting late. I'll escort you back to the house."

"You don't have to. I can almost see it from here. Impossible to get lost."

"All right. Directly there, then. I'll see you in the morning."

As I walked back to the rooming house with Mr. Jones, we mulled over what we knew. Brody had completed his investigation, prepared a report, and the case had been closed. Then, sometime over the winter, another survivor had turned up. The case was reopened and, for some reason, the government office took it over, cutting Brody out altogether.

I couldn't think of one good reason why a government office would take on that kind of task, unless they had something to add that the original writer might not agree with. What was the matter with Brody? Why did he let them take over his work?

The next morning, after sharing breakfast in my room with Mr. Jones, I packed my things and walked the short distance back to Brody's office. The sky was clear and the breeze stiff, so if the schooner had come up on the entrance to the strait the night before, she'd make the inner harbor by noon. Sheltered in a beam of sunlight on his office porch, away from the bustle of workers, I leaned my head against the wall and closed my eyes to think. A curious image suddenly popped into my head and I straightened up. A few minutes later, Brody appeared, heading into his office.

"Excuse me, Mr. Brody? The final report on the *Salish Wind*. You didn't sign it."

I'd pictured the last page of the report. It bore his name, and the signature of an official on his behalf. Brody stopped on the porch, looking perturbed. His usual pleasant expression had vanished.

"And good morning to you as well, Miss LeBeau. No, I did not sign it."

"But you wrote it."

"Not the final."

"But you agree with it." His eyebrows tightened into a dark line. "You agree with it, don't you, Mr. Brody?"

He rested his clipboard on his hip.

"Is there something specific you'd like to know, Miss LeBeau?"

"I can't figure it. You investigated the shipwreck and did all the legwork. Then, a government man, who'd never set foot on Deception Island and never talked to me once, took over your report."

"Let's just say, I could not reconcile the facts as reported."

"You mean my facts."

"And those contrary to yours."

"Which means one of us two survivors lied." He stared at the wall over my shoulder, nostrils flaring. "One of us lied...and you didn't think it was me."

He disappeared inside without answering.

CHAPTER TWELVE

By afternoon, I'd had enough of sitting on the porch, so I asked Brody if I could watch for the *Sonoma Wind* from the beach. No doubt happy to be rid of me and my questions, he agreed at once. Mr. Jones and I set up in a spot where we'd see the ship as soon as she rounded the point at the harbor entrance.

I'd just finished laying out our blanket when a commotion on the next wharf over caught my attention. A group of dock-workers were unloading a huge draft horse from a barge. They hauled on it by the neck to get it to step over the low gunwale onto a floating dock. Frightened out of his wits, it thrashed and resisted. I imagined it toppling into the water, tangled in ropes and sailors.

"Stay here, Mr. Jones." I raced up the beach, ran along the dock, and hollered at the men. "Stop that! It's dangerous!"

The fools had hobbled the horse's back legs to keep him from kicking, which made it difficult for him to balance.

I leaped onto the barge deck and shoved past the surly men.

"All of you, get out of the way. I'm a wrangler."

"Hey!" said the man holding the ropes as I snatched them out of his hands without asking.

The horse sensed a new presence and stopped yanking his head around. He was like the carriage horses I groomed at the Livery in San Francisco—a powerful animal, the type that could drag a plow through heavy sod and make it look like a child's winter sled.

A familiar buzz shot through the rope, up my fingers and into my arm. In a flash, I was back on the Sonoma ranch with Papa, working with the horses in the Miller stables. I reached up and circled my arms around the horse's broad neck and leaned into him. I was close enough for him to hurt me if he wished, but I knew he wouldn't. He was gentle by nature, only driven to violence out of fear. I saw myself reflected in his dark brown eye.

The men behind me murmured. I shushed them as the horse made a nervous scuff on the wooden deck in response.

"Who hobbled him?" I whispered and a man behind me confessed like I was some kind of preacher who'd caught him in a cardinal sin. "You'll undo him when I say."

"Now wait a sec…" he protested.

"Do what she says," another man growled, and no one else spoke.

I took my end of the rope and tied it to the horse's halter. Then I untied the other end that had turned into a noose and had already left marks on his broad neck. I held him steady and whispered reassuring words. He bent his head down and touched my cheek with his nose while the sailor freed his feet.

With the men standing aside, the horse stepped off the barge on his own like he'd done it every single day of his life. As I led the horse from the rocking dock to the beach, the men grumbled and made rude comments about me. The sailor who'd let me help them caught up and walked beside me. He was familiar.

I hoped he wasn't one of Brody's crew on the main wharf and wouldn't tattle on what I'd done.

"Don't mind them boys. They're just sore 'cause you made 'em look bad. To be honest, I never seen no one handle a horse like that, let alone a pretty gal like yerself."

His words struck like a bolt of lightning. I knew then where I'd seen him before. He had replaced one of our regular crew members on the *Salish Wind* on the morning of the shipwreck!

My heart pounded. I turned my back and fiddled with the horse's halter to calm a rogue wave of panic crashing over me.

"Yeah, I'm no sailor, but I know horses."

As I handed him the rope, he eyed me from head to toe. I was different now, taller and more filled out, with longer hair framing my face. Despite wearing men's trousers and a work shirt, I wasn't trying to look like a boy anymore. He'd seen me only once, in the dark, aboard the *Salish Wind*, as the ship's boy. I was pale and scrawny then, with short hair hidden under a wool cap. He didn't recognize me.

"You are something," he said, straightening his cap with a sheepish smile and tucking bits of stray hair behind his protruding ears. My stomach flipped as I realized he was flirting.

"None of us are what we seem," I replied with a sugary smile, and handed him the horse's lead.

"Hope to see ya again, miss," he said after me. "Wait, I didn't catch yer name."

I didn't answer. "Miss" was now the identity that saved me.

Mr. Jones had waited at the blanket as instructed, straining forward, fur on his back raised, ready to come to my aid if necessary. He growled at the sailor up the beach as he led the horse away.

"You recognize him, too! One of the Captain's last-minute hires."

Mr. Jones whimpered. Realizing I would not give him permission to go rip the fellow limb from limb, he dropped his haunches to the ground. We watched until the man and the horse disappeared from the beach.

"The *Sonoma Wind* is not coming today. Let's go."

I waved to Brody like nothing had happened, and let him know we were returning to the rooming house. He waved back, none the wiser. As we started along the main street above the harbor, the shock of my discovery sunk in. I'd stumbled upon the other unnamed survivor!

"That's the man who denied that pirates chased the *Salish Wind*. The one who claimed Kuno made the navigation mistake. That man survived, and here he is, working the docks like nothing happened. And right under Brody's nose? It doesn't make sense."

Mr. Jones stopped and barked. He was still as mad as I was about it all and wanted to go back. I hushed him up and he fell into step.

"Here's what we're going to do, Mr. Jones. I'm going to follow that sailor when he gets off work. You have to stay away. He didn't recognize me, but he'll figure it out if he sees the two of us together."

Mr. Jones hated being cut out of the investigation, but agreed it was the only thing to be done. Just that morning, I'd noticed a modest clothing shop on the way to the harbor. The allowance that Mrs. Dalworth had given me for helping her at the lighthouse all winter was about to come in handy.

I'd no sooner crossed the threshold when a well-dressed man about my size cut me off and steered me out the door, like I was some kind of vagrant. Mr. Jones had been standing guard outside, and when he saw me escorted out under protest, he barked at the man, who then used his foot to shove Mr. Jones off the boardwalk into the deep muck.

"You shouldn't a done that," I said, grabbing the man by his tailored lapels and walking him backwards into the store. Volcanic rage bubbled in my chest and burned through my limbs. First, the poor horse on the barge. Now, Mr. Jones. The man grabbed the front of my shirt, and it locked us in a tense standoff.

"Goodness me! Ralph, unhand her!" A stern woman with penciled eyebrows, probably the man's wife, marched out from behind the shop counter. The man let go of me, straightened his cockeyed eyeglasses, and brushed off his vest. I released my grasp as well, surprised at not being blamed for the altercation.

"I came in to shop. He threw me out and kicked my dog into the gutter."

"I did not!" The veins in the man's forehead looked ready to pop.

Mr. Jones, no worse for wear, had come right back out of the mud and followed us into the store. He barked at the man then, and we all gawked at his filthy evidence.

"You stay out of this," I said, wagging a finger at him. He sat down, clearly indignant, mud covering one side of his body and right ear. His ridiculous appearance brought a hint of a smile to the woman's face.

"I'm sorry for the disturbance, ma'am. Please. I need to buy a dress."

I thumbed a wad of bills to prove my intentions. The woman's eyes softened as she sized me up.

"Apology accepted. If you could have your muddy companion wait by the door, I'm sure we can find something. Nobody will bother him there."

"But..." the man began.

"I'll handle this, Ralph," she said, waving him off, and he disappeared behind a curtained door in a smoldering huff.

Back at the rooming house, I unpacked my purchases—a new dress with undergarments, and a knitted shawl. The woman in the store had given me a good deal, and didn't even stick her nose into my business by asking questions.

"I can't abide cruelty," I said to Mr. Jones, who stood with his two hind feet in my washbasin, nose in the air, while I washed the stinky crud from his coat. "Of course you can handle yourself. But nobody mistreats an animal in front of me and gets away with it. Which reminds me. Do you like horses? I sure hope you do, because I adore them and you will have to be friends with Magic. He's the best horse ever. Pure black, and carries his tail high, just like you."

Mr. Jones said he didn't mind horses at all, donkeys and mules were also among his trusted friends, and that he only hated pirates. He thought the name of my horse was charming.

"His real name was Majestic. You know Jake? Well, he has this sister, Bernadette, same age as me, and Magic belongs to her, even though she is too sickly to ride him and he tossed her off into the shrubs one time, because she was so annoying."

Mr. Jones listened, as if trying to picture this girl he'd never met. I dried him off as best I could and he finished the job by rubbing his back on the thick rug.

"Getting Magic back is a long way off yet. I can't even set foot on the ranch, thanks to The Missus. Besides, Mizzy is in San Francisco right now. There's this smart lady, Mrs. Plea, who is a good friend of Mr. Miller's. I think you'll like her. Anyhow, she'll get us set up. But just between you and me, I'm going to expose these lies about the *Salish Wind*. And that other survivor? He knows what happened out there."

Mr. Jones positioned himself in front of the door as I changed out of my work clothes and did my hair.

"I know you want to come along, but we can't risk being recognized." I twirled in my new dress. "Now. How do I look? Will I pass the test?"

CHAPTER THIRTEEN

Just before four o'clock, decked out in my new dress, I returned to the wharf where I'd last seen the sailor. Ominous clouds had rolled in from the west, which meant worse weather at sea. The *Sonoma Wind* would not sail into Victoria until it cleared.

At shift change, groups of men trailed off the main dock and others arrived to take their place. I counted thirteen men arrive and eleven leave. The sailor I was watching for wasn't among them, and may have been assigned to some other location.

As I stewed over what to do next, he emerged from the hold of a fishing boat, jacket slung over his shoulder and lunch pail in hand. I draped my shawl over my head to fend off the damp chill coming off the water, and to conceal my face if he looked my way. I followed him at a safe distance, defying Brody's strict orders to stay on the main road, and attracting long looks from the dockworkers I passed.

He stopped at a nearby hotel, a two-story slapped-together wooden shanty on a narrow side street, no place for an unescorted lady to be any time of day. I hung back, strolling and looking in shop windows. He passed a group of workers loitering at the hotel entrance. They exchanged familiar greetings as he went inside.

"C'mon fellas. Scram," I said. I knew better than to get near them, so I pretended to read a menu posted in a cafe window.

The threat they presented almost made me lose my nerve. Mrs. Dalworth, Mr. Miller, and Brody talked in my head all at once about the dangers of being a young woman out alone. *It's still daylight and there are others around. Even in a dress, those men'll have their hands full with me if they try to pull anything,* I told the voices back. My debate was short-lived as the sailor came back out of the hotel, joined his pals, and they swaggered off up the street.

"That turned out well, Mr. Jones," I said, and then remembered I hadn't allowed him to come.

The hotel lobby was dark and tiny, and reeked of stale tobacco and fish. A scuffed path on the wooden floor led to a ruddy-faced man of small stature tucked behind a desk. His pen paused in mid-air as he squinted at me in the lantern light.

"Good afternoon, sir." I said, summoning the delicate tone The Missus had always used around men when she needed something from them.

He grunted and rose from his chair, smoothing down a long strand of hair doing the impossible work of attempting to cover a balding head. "A gracious good afternoon, miss."

"Oh, please. Don't get up. I don't wish to take you from your work."

He paused halfway to his feet, smiled proudly, and plopped back into his chair.

"I'm looking for a gentleman. He came to my aid the other day, and I didn't catch his name. I understand he stays here."

"No gentlemen here," he said, shoving the chewed end of a cigar into his mouth.

"Surely a good working man can also be a gentleman?" I said, with a puzzled expression of innocence and dismay.

"What's he look like then?" He squinted at me through the smoke that rose from his cigar into his right eye.

"He's a sailor."

"Most of 'em are."

"Dark hair and a beard, about as tall as me."

"Still describes half my tenants."

"He's American..."

"Still..."

"...and he wears a distinctive kerchief—blue and red with white stars."

"Ah! That's Lenny Falette. You just missed him." He pointed up the street. "Went thataway less than five minutes ago."

Of course, I knew that.

"Oh, what a shame! Well, thank you anyway." I turned to leave.

"He'll be at the tavern up the way. Goes there every night for supper and drinks."

I let a hand flutter to my throat in shock, as if the idea of a young woman entering a drinking establishment was beyond the pale. He realized his suggestion was scandalous.

"No. Of course you can't look for him in there. Who can I tell him came by? And where can he find you?"

I opened my mouth to speak, but nothing came out. I scrambled to think of a reply.

"Unfortunately, I'm leaving town. Right now. I mean, shortly. By boat. With my family. Just tell him the young lady he helped the other day was very grateful...for his kindness."

I swallowed and hoped he didn't notice the lump going down my throat. The man tipped his head with curiosity. If I'd made him suspicious by fumbling over words, he didn't show it.

"Kindness, eh? Doesn't sound like Lenny, but who knows? He has a way with the ladies." His eyes roamed over my body and settled on the cowboy boots poking out from under my hem.

"It's a shame I've missed him. I'd be grateful if you'd thank him for me," I said, dragging his eyeballs back up to my face. With my face burning and pulse racing, I wished him a good evening and hurried from the lobby.

I felt breathless from my risky venture, like I'd dodged a falling tree but got hit by its heavy branches. What if Lenny had returned and caught me asking the clerk about him? I hadn't considered that. What if he hadn't had any recent contact with a young woman other than the girl on the dock? The clerk would tell him about me. Describe me, no doubt, in awful detail. Would he be leery of a young lady asking about him? Not likely. If he spent his evenings in a saloon, he'd have met several young ladies serving up pints of ale. He'd think he'd missed an opportunity and nothing more.

Back on the main road and away from the hotel, my shoulders loosened and the stiff chop went out of my stride. I stopped looking over my shoulder for trouble. As I passed the dress shop, now closed for the evening, I congratulated myself on a successful mission.

"Not bad, Charlee. You're a mite rusty, but that was pretty good," I said to myself. Jake would be impressed. Of course, when I told him about it, I'd make the account much more dramatic and dangerous. I smiled, a familiar sense of clarity having returned to my thinking.

A fat raindrop splattered on my cheek and ran down my face like a teardrop. The streets emptied as I hurried to get back to the rooming house before the skies opened.

Lenny Falette. I had the name of the sailor who had been on board the *Salish Wind* before she sank. I had the name of the other survivor, the other witness. Why was his identity kept a secret?

~

By late morning the next day, the rain had stopped, but the wind was up and the sky hung low with heavy, grey clouds. At Brody's office, I dried off a wooden chair and dragged it under the cover of the eaves. Mr. Jones took up a half-hearted watch for the *Sonoma Wind*, but we both knew she wasn't coming given the turn of weather.

The delay didn't bother me. It gave me time to figure out how to tell Brody what I'd discovered on my unauthorized side-street investigation. When he appeared at the office steps, he beckoned me to leave my chair and follow him inside.

"You don't need to sit out in the rain. You can see the harbor from that table by the window." He cleared the surface of a few strewn papers, tossing them onto another pile near his desk.

"I'm fine waiting outside."

The chaos in his small office made me feel anxious, but I couldn't tell him that.

"As you wish, but you're welcome in here if you get cold or change your mind."

"Thanks all the same."

I couldn't avoid the hard questions any longer.

"Mr. Brody, do you still have a copy of the manifest from the *Salish Wind*?"

He looked up from his desk, brows pinched together.

"I do."

"Could I see it?"

His expression changed from interest to concern.

"May I ask why?"

"The first mate who died. He's got a wife in San Francisco. I thought I should look her up when I get back—pay my respects —but I never knew his last name."

I stopped talking and let my string of lies settle and anchor. Mr. Jones coughed and I glared at him.

Brody reached behind him for a file and laid it open on his desk. The top paper was the ship's manifest. He dragged his finger down a list and stopped beside a name. I looked where he pointed, but before he took the file away, I took in everything on the page.

A pendulum clanged against the inside of my skull. If I let my head ache with the sound, I'd lose the detailed picture in my mind. I closed my eyes to make it stop.

"A wife in San Francisco, you say?"

"Pardon?" The ringing in my head subsided.

"I said, 'A wife in San Francisco'. Seems odd for a Hawaiian sailor."

"I know. Maybe he was pulling my leg. He told stories all the time. But I think he was serious, and maybe nobody's even told her, you know, what happened."

Brody accepted my explanation, as well as my sudden decision to return to the rooming house. Mr. Jones was not happy with me. He wanted to stay and watch for the ship, and I'd made up things about his lost friend. On the way back, he trailed several feet behind. I had to wait for him to catch up several times.

"Don't be mad, Mr. Jones. I made up that stuff about Kuno to get information. It's how to conduct a proper investigation. Now hurry up, before I forget what I saw."

As soon as I was through the door to my room, I flipped open my journal and scribbled. It was a race against time before the picture of the document I held in my head faded.

Muster roll. September 10, 1859. Two-masted schooner, *"Salish Wind"*, Reg. Bear Drilling Inc. Owner J. Miller. San Francisco, USA.

Sebastian Hart, 34, Captain, Philadelphia, USA.

Kuno Kai, 28, First Mate, Sandwich Islands.

Cookie J, 23, Cook, San Francisco, USA.

C. Harlee, 13, Ship's Boy, San Francisco, USA.

~~C. Chou, 20, Seaman, San Francisco, USA.~~ Leonard F, 21, Seaman, Boston, USA.

My pencil stopped. There it was. One of the sailors the Captain had brought aboard at the last minute. Someone had added the name of the replacement sailor next to the name of the original sailor, who was detained over paperwork in Fort Victoria. Leonard F. That had to be Lenny Falette.

I placed my pencil back over the blank lines on my page, but my memory had gone blank. The rest of the image had vanished like smoke in the wind.

CHAPTER FOURTEEN

On the third morning in Victoria, I awoke to Mr. Jones nudging my hand. A chorus of birds sang in a hedge outside my window. The dawn sky was clear and a light breeze rippled the new leaves on courtyard trees. Conditions were perfect for a ship to sail into port from the Pacific. I untangled myself from warm blankets, dressed and washed, and tidied the room so some poor worker wouldn't have to do it later. Before leaving out the back, I snagged three pieces of buttered toast off a covered stack in the empty dining room.

Mr. Jones could feel the ship coming, too. He led the way to Brody's office and immediately set up a watch of the harbor from the office porch. I paced the uneven planks of boardwalk and mulled over what to say to Brody. If I told him I'd found the other survivor, I'd have to tell him tell him about the incident with the horse and sneaking back to the wharf to follow the sailor from work. My unauthorized visits to the dress shop and hotel would cause him even more alarm. And what if I was mistaken about Leonard F? He might think I was delusional. I needed more proof before I started talking.

When Brody appeared, the favorable weather, or maybe the

thought of being rid of me, had put a spring in his step. We both knew the *Sonoma Wind* would arrive, but it would also take several hours to sail Fuca Strait. I couldn't stand to watch the water like a kettle that takes too long to boil, and I was too nervous to read, so I offered to tidy up his office files. Brody was reluctant to have me work, but when I told him I could get his sea of papers in order by lunch, he agreed there was no harm in giving me something to do.

The first thing I did was look for the file he'd shown me the day before. It was gone! Mr. Jones didn't see it because he wasn't inside at the time, but I was absolutely certain I hadn't imagined it. I decided Brody had tucked it away somewhere safe. It's what I would have done with an important file when a key witness was present and oddly curious. At the same time, I hoped I'd come across it, and get one more thorough look.

Throughout the morning, Brody would come in for some-thing, and I'd say, "Any sign?" and he'd reply, "Not yet". By mid-morning, I'd trained him to answer without being asked. By late morning, he complimented me on my efficient work, even saying he wished he could hire me to stay on. Just before lunch, as I was finishing up, he said, "Thank you kindly. You can stop now."

Sliding the bottom drawer of a cabinet closed, I straightened up and stretched, eyeing my organization with a fair amount of pride.

"I'm done, anyway." And then, because he hadn't provided the expected ship-watching report, I added the tired question. "Any sign?"

A deeper voice answered. "I won't take it personal you're too busy to notice me."

"Cook!"

The familiar frame of Amos "Cook" Jefferson towered in Brody's doorway. I leaped at him, threw my arms around his neck, and he swung me around in a ragged half-circle.

"Whoa, you've grown! I'm gonna throw my back out!"

Grinning, he set me down. I danced up and down, almost stepping on Mr. Jones, who barked a reminder of his location. Brody stood back, surprised at our display of warm affection.

"And if it isn't our loyal Second Officer of the *Salish Wind*! Come say hello, Mr. Jones!" Cook crouched down and ruffled his ears. "It's very good to see you, mate."

Mr. Jone's tail ticktocked three times in an uncharacteristic burst of enthusiasm. When Kuno was still alive, nobody dared to pet him for fear of losing a hand. But Cook was one of the few people he tolerated from the start.

Cook whispered, "You're a brave dog. Kuno would be so proud of you."

My eyes filled with tears and I pretended I hadn't heard to make them go away. I gazed out the window and spotted the tall masts of the beautiful schooner, *Sonoma Wind*, identical to her sunken sister ship. Unbridled joy and overwhelming grief spilled out of my chest. I gripped the sill to keep the flood from washing the floor away from under me.

As we walked down to the wharf, Brody and Cook exchanged information regarding port schedules and our departure from Victoria. Cook thanked him for taking care of me on behalf of Mr. Miller, handed him an envelope, and they shook hands. It was strange, not knowing what Mr. Miller had arranged—or what it may have cost him—to see me returned to San Francisco. He didn't have to do any of it, and I wondered why he'd gone out of his way for me, even though he'd always been generous with me and my papa.

Cook and I watched as Brody took charge of the men securing the schooner to the wharf.

"He's a decent fellow," Cook said.

"Yeah, he's all right. He did most of the shipwreck investigation."

Cook noticed the dark cloud that came over me.

"Now, why do I think you have a tale to tell about that?"

"Because I do."

"Save it for later. Right now, I've got a surprise for you aboard. You good to climb Jacob's ladder?"

I eyed the thick web of rope draped down the side of the ship.

"Of course."

He slung my duffle bag over his back as I tucked Mr. Jones under my arm and climbed. I didn't get far. It was much harder than I remembered and my feet swung around under me. Dizzy, I stepped back down.

"You'll have to take Mr. Jones, too. I'm rusty. Gonna need both hands."

"Better yet, let's wait for the boys to drop the loading ramp."

"I'm not waiting one minute more." Stuffing Mr. Jones into his arms, I clambered up the ropes, swung a leg over the gunwale and peered back down. "There. How's that?"

"Haven't lost your stubborn streak, I see," he replied, as he scaled the rope ladder in record time.

Mr. Jones grunted as Cook handed him back. He'd have to get used to being carted around like a sack of potatoes again. While the ship was under sail, he wasn't allowed to roam around underfoot. I'd have to get used to the motion of the boat all over again. My legs felt like noodles, and I hung on to keep my balance as the boat swayed next to the dock.

Cook glanced past my shoulder and smiled. "Ah. Here comes your surprise now."

A head popped up from the steps leading into the galley, strawberry blond hair sticking out of the bottom of his wool beanie.

"Jake!"

"Charlee!" We ran to each other, reached out to embrace, but stopped short by gripping each other's forearms instead and doing a weird shuffle dance. Then I pushed him away.

"What are you doing here?! Why aren't you in school? You didn't run away again, did you?"

"Ooo-ee! Lots of questions from our Charlee, hey Jake?"

Jake cracked a weak smile. Dark purple circles underlined his sunken and tired eyes. His face was pale but for two smudges of red in his cheeks. There was trouble around him being on the *Sonoma Wind*. I could tell by the look of him.

"The nine lives of Charlotte Lee LeBeau," he said.

"Don't change the subject. Besides, I've only used up two."

"Two's plenty," Cook replied. "Your family can't take no more of your disappearances. Mizzy's going grey, thanks to you. And Mr. Miller's hair is half torn out over the pair of you." He thumbed at Jake, who looked away in glum silence. I was still stuck on the part where Cook had called me family.

"You're assigned to the galley, same as before. I'll take your gear below. Jake's on opposite watches, so you'd better catch up while you have the chance."

"Wait. I've got a small trunk in Brody's office."

"Mr. Brody told me. They'll bring it over later."

Jake and I watched until he disappeared below deck.

"So. You wanna tell me what's going on, Jake?"

"Not really. I mean, where to start?"

"Then answer this. Did you quit school?"

He shook his head. "I took a leave."

"Isn't that the same thing?"

"No. I withdrew, temporarily, with the headmaster's permission. I can return, pick up where I left off."

"So you're going back then."

"Eventually, I guess."

"Eventually. Why didn't you tell me this in your letter?"

"It was too hard to explain then."

He rubbed his temples with both hands. My questions had triggered some kind of awful pain. I knew what that felt like.

"It's okay. I'm shocked to see you here, is all. I'm not mad at you. Truly."

He looked up, letting his arms drop to his sides.

"Yeah, well, you may be the only one who isn't. Father was furious and, you know him, he never gets angry. The disappointment from everyone, well, it's a lot…"

I leaned against the gunwale and shifted Mr. Jones to my opposite hip. Jake reached out and patted Mr. Jones' curly head, a greeting which went well once again. I realized Mr. Jones was a changed dog since last aboard the *Salish Wind*.

I listened as Jake spoke of the past winter. He told me how they had waited, hopeful that the *Salish Wind* would show up, until news came of her shipwreck and lost crew. My apparent death was a terrible blow. He tried to concentrate on school, but couldn't do it. By the time he learned I'd survived, it was too late to salvage his year.

A huge pang of guilt came over me. But before I could tell him how sorry I was for all the grief and worry I'd caused, he said that wasn't even half of it. The rest of his family had gone east and wouldn't be returning to San Francisco. Jake had refused to go, and his father was caught with a family divided by the continent.

"Oh," was all that came out of my mouth.

I knew Mr. Miller had been away during the winter, but I didn't know it was because his second wife and children had moved back to where The Missus had come from. The battle that must have happened when Jake wouldn't go must have been intense, since he couldn't use being in school as an excuse.

"So you stayed behind."

Jake pinched his lips into a flat smile. "It's complicated. I did it for me and for Father."

"I don't understand."

"He was miserable and didn't want to move back. But he said

if I insisted on staying, he'd stay, too, and the two of us would carry on like before, like when we first came to California."

"Ooo, I see. That's very complicated."

"So that's what I did. I dug in my heels. I decided because he couldn't."

"What about Bernadette? Will she get proper medical help there? I don't think the ranch did her a bit of good."

I listened to myself say the words, like I'd forgiven her for causing the accident that killed my papa. Had I forgiven her? I didn't feel any anger towards her anymore.

"You'd better sit down. There's more to that."

A wave of dread came over me. I wasn't sure I was ready to hear what he had to say, but sat on a nearby crate, arms wrapped around Mr. Jones. Jake sat down across from me, his shoulders rounded from the weight of heavy thoughts.

"Bernadette is ill."

"Worse than before?"

"Much. She's in a hospital. She can barely walk."

"What!"

He nodded, blinked through misty eyes. "I don't expect you to be sad. I know you hated her."

"I never hated her. She tormented me and I lashed out sometimes."

Or had I hated her? She'd come to the corral to give me flowers for my birthday, and to apologize for causing me trouble with her mother, The Missus. Then the accident happened. My stomach clenched as I remembered wishing her dead. Blaming her for my papa's death had probably made her illness worse.

"I'm sorry to hear it, Jake." I pressed my fingers to my lips and sighed.

Jake tipped his head. "You mean that?"

"I do. She was lonely, I think, didn't mean any harm."

Suddenly, a deafening boom rang out and the deck boards

quivered under my feet. I jumped up from the crate, away from the noise, clutching Mr. Jones to my chest in a panic, panting and scanning above us for a falling mast. The similarity of the schooner carried me back to the deck of her sister ship, the *Salish Wind*. In a flash, I was shipwrecked again, and was hearing the horrific sound of a dying ship.

But Jake was there, gripping my arm, talking to me, comforting me. I could hardly hear him. I latched onto his words and he reeled me back to the present.

"Hey, hey! It's all right. They just dropped the loading ramp a little hard."

"Right. Just the loading ramp. It scared the wits outta me. I was back…"

"Is everything all right here?"

The voice behind me sent a shudder up my spine. I spun around, eyes wide in disbelief. It was the former captain of the *Salish Wind*, in full blue uniform, and very much alive!

"Welcome aboard, Miss LeBeau. It's very good to see you again."

My eyes roll back in my head and darkness slammed down upon me like a coffin lid.

CHAPTER FIFTEEN

Sometime later, I felt Mr. Jones lick my wrist. Then I heard a voice call my name over the steady creak of the ship's riggings. When I opened my eyes, I was propped against a deck box with Jake kneeling beside me.

"You fainted," Jake said, steadying me as I sat up. "Never seen you do that before."

As I remembered where I was, an old familiar headache crept up the back of my neck. Jake chattered a mile a minute, but his words grated on me like a dull blade screeching over a sharpening stone. I put my hands over my ears and told him to hush up. Wounded, he leaned back, filled a ladle of water from a nearby pail and held it to my lips.

"I've got it, Jake. Please don't be a mother hen," I said, spilling some of the water into my lap as I wrenched it from his grip.

"You're welcome."

"Sorry. What I meant is fussing only makes it worse." I swallowed the cool water, washing away a sour taste that lingered in the back of my throat. "C'mon, help me up."

"Too soon. You're white as fog." He took my hand in his own, which was sweaty and cold.

Mr. Jones put a paw on my leg, taking sides with Jake.

"I know how this goes. If I can move around a bit, I can stop a headache from coming on."

"Then wait a little longer. You were out cold. If I hadn't caught you, you'd have slammed onto the deck like a whale and flattened Mr. Jones."

"That's a flattering image."

"I mean, you're taller now…bigger than last September."

Jake jabbered on about my growth spurt and ungraceful collapse. I couldn't get past how he'd described my face. White as fog. White. As fog.

Memories swirled around in my head. I was on the deck of the *Salish Wind*, right before she struck the reef that sank her. The captain had deliberately taken us into thick fog along the northern side of the strait, to evade a black sloop that had followed us from Victoria. Kuno, unable to reason with the captain, yelled at him about our ship's position and how we were running straight for the treacherous coastline on the northern side of the strait. The captain disagreed, and behaving like a man possessed, ignored him and ordered us to stay our course. The crew looked at the captain, jaws hanging open. We had a disoriented leader at the helm, and it was a side of our captain we'd never seen. In the short time I'd known him, he had always trusted Kuno's experience at sea.

Drak, the sailor who had replaced Cook in the galley for that fateful last voyage, swore under his breath in Russian and clutched the cross around his neck. We all knew right then that something bad would happen, and there was no stopping it. I remembered squinting into the blinding fog, feeling cold, confused, and alarmed.

The memories fell away. I was sitting in warm afternoon sunshine, on the deck of the Sonoma next to Jake, who was poking my arm.

"Hello, am I talking to myself here?"

"Where'd he go?"

"Who?"

"The captain."

"He went to get Cook, to send him for a doctor."

"Oh, great. Only half a year too late. Give me a hand up."

Jake extended his palm, and I pulled myself to my feet.

"By the way, you're the one who should see a doctor. What's with those clammy hands?"

"Nothing's wrong with me," he said, but shoved his hands into his pockets.

"Aren't we both just barkin' at a knot?" I replied, nudging him to break up his sullen mood. Mr. Jones looked around for the knot I'd mentioned, as if he'd been called upon to bark at it, too, and that made both of us smile. Jake and I both had our problems and frustrations. We could see it in each other. We also knew they weren't things that doctors fixed.

"This is so messed up, Jake. The Captain...he's supposed to be dead."

I glanced around, half-expecting to spot him lurking in the shadows, watching.

"What do you mean, dead? Sure, we thought everyone was dead at first. But he survived, just like you."

"No, he did not. Not like me."

"A ship heading offshore picked him up. They said he was in rough shape. He turned up months later, like you, memories muddled up, thinking he was the only survivor."

"I don't know about any of that story. I'm talking about what happened in the shipwreck. Those facts. His aren't the same as mine."

Just then, the Captain came out of his quarters.

"Here comes the dead captain now," I whispered and steeled myself as he approached us with an expression of grave concern.

"Miss LeBeau. Good to see you've recovered from your spell. I thought I might have smelling salts in my cabin, but alas."

"I'm better, thank you, sir. These happy reunions were a bit too much all at once."

"I'm sure. It's quite a lot of excitement being reunited with old friends again, particularly since your terrible ordeal."

"And seeing you reminded me of the *Salish Wind*."

His eye twitched for a moment, like something had flown into it, but his jaw remained set in a hard line. Jake cleared his throat and shuffled his feet. He knew me well enough to know I was poking a bear.

"I imagine it would. It's quite a miracle that both of us survived when everyone else drowned. I must hear your story when you feel up to it, and I will share mine if you wish to hear."

They did not drown, I screamed inside my head. Pirates killed them. There is a third survivor. You must know that. And your name was purposefully left out of the final report. My heart pounded with rage, but I hung a stony expression on my face to hide my turmoil.

"I would very much like to hear your account, sir. I'm afraid mine will disappoint though, because I recall little."

No doubt he'd read the report, which concluded I was an unreliable witness because of memory loss. He was setting me up to fit into his official story, the one he'd told to whoever took over Brody's investigation, the final account that was full of lies. Had he wanted to catch me off guard, to confirm that my memory had indeed failed me? Or was he saying these things for Jake's benefit, to make sure my friends remained his allies? He was clever. A worthy opponent. I hadn't forgotten that. We eyed each other in an unblinking standoff.

"It's remarkable how we both survived without seeing each other," I said.

The Captain bristled. If he insisted on playing the game, I'd take him on. He still didn't know that I remembered every awful moment of the shipwreck. He also wasn't aware I'd stumbled upon one sailor he'd hired at the last minute. That was an ace up my sleeve, if I could get the rest of my cards in order.

"I was knocked out when the ship struck the reef," he began.

So that's his angle, I thought. Conveniently unconscious during the pirate raid.

"When I came to, I was in the skiff. To this day, I don't remember how I got there, but the ship was gone and I had been drifting out to sea for days. But let's not talk about this now. It's distressing to revisit, and it makes you unwell. I've sent Cook for a doctor. Before we sail tomorrow, I need to know it is safe for you to travel."

"I'm fine, now that I'm over the shock of seeing everyone."

"We'll have you checked over all the same. Mr. Miller would expect nothing less of me."

And with that remark, he excused himself. Jake elbowed me as I glared after him. We didn't speak until the Captain had crossed the deck and descended into the main hold.

"He wants the doctor to check my head for loose parts," I muttered to Jake.

"Why?"

"I'm not sure. Maybe he's worried something incriminating might tumble out of my skull. Did you see how he was studying me?"

"Something incriminating? What are you talking about? He wants to make sure you're okay."

"There's a lot you don't know, Jake. He's worried I'll contradict him and people like you might believe me instead of him."

Jake paused for a moment, considering what I'd said. "Tell me everything you know." He glanced over his shoulder and lowered his voice. "One thing Cook can't get past. He blamed Kuno for the shipwreck. Cook said Kuno wouldn't make a mistake like that."

"And he didn't."

Mr. Jones shoved his nose into Jake's arm. "Mr. Jones agrees with you. C'mon. Let's wait for the doctor in the galley."

With Mr. Jones tucked under my arm, Jake led me down the steep stairs. Seeing a doctor wasn't the worst outcome. Worrisome fainting spell aside, I hoped he might tell me how to fix my memory.

"You'd better get back to work," I said to Jake once he'd helped me settle at the galley table.

Jake didn't want to leave me alone, but I assured him I wouldn't budge. I told him I wasn't the slightest bit dizzy anymore, which was true, but decided not to mention a lingering headache. I wanted time alone to make it go away and prepare for my examination. If I appeared a rattled mess with the doctor, he might tell the Captain I couldn't sail and I'd be stuck in Victoria for another month.

Mrs. Dalworth had warned me not to talk about the shipwreck when things were still jumbled inside my head. I trusted Jake and decided to tell him everything—how I doubted many muddled memories but was convinced his father's gold was still buried on Deception Island. But there was no hurry. We had the journey back to San Francisco, and I felt I was on the brink of truth and clarity.

CHAPTER SIXTEEN

"I understand you've had some hallucinations," said the young man who claimed to be a doctor. He plopped his brand-new black leather case with a shiny clasp down on the galley table.

"Hallucinations?" I laughed. Cook must have told him I'd smacked my head and imagined things. "No. I've lost some recent memories since hitting my head last fall. I still get headaches."

"Hmmm," he said, tipping his head back so he could get a better look at me through the small, round spectacles that sat on the end of his wide nose.

"I'm Doctor Calvin Bough, by the way. That's bough like the tree, not the boat."

"Doctor Bough. You're too young to be a real doctor," I examined the shadow of his mustache as he leaned closer. It seemed fake, like he'd penciled it in, which is what I'd done when posing as a boy for much of the last year.

"I assure you, young lady, I'm qualified for surgery and the apothecary. I graduated in December with honors."

"Good to know. But that's only three months ago."

"I'll note that you are aware of basic mathematics and the passage of time." He exaggerated his words for sarcastic effect. I smiled. A doctor with a sense of humor. I liked that.

"How about we start with your name?"

"LeBeau."

"Full legal name, *s'il vous plaît*." Professional with second language ability, I thought. He didn't look up as he flipped to a fresh page in a little black notebook.

"Charlotte Lee LeBeau. I'm only part French."

He paused, as if deciding whether to ask about the other part. He let it go and pulled a few instruments out of his bag.

"So you get headaches. And today you fainted."

"Oh that. I never faint. But there was an awful lot of excitement today." I leaned forward to whisper, "And I'm in my, you know, flow time."

A complete lie, but I figured it would get him to dismiss concerns about fainting. Men, even good doctor men, blamed a lot of things on women's monthly problems.

"Ah. That explains a lot."

"I didn't want to mention it in front of the fellas. You know…"

"I see. You appear well enough now. Excellent color. But this head injury from some months ago, that's worrisome. Let's check you over, starting with your vision."

He looked into each of my eyes with a huge magnifying glass, which turned his own eye into a monstrous, swirling grey blob. He stretched each eyelid open with stained brown fingers. These weren't tobacco stains. I imagined he'd tanned fur or polished boots on the side to put himself through school. His suit jacket was proper but faded on the cuffs and lapels. He definitely didn't come from money.

I'd only seen one other doctor in my life. That was the Sonoma county doc who took care of folks around Santa Rosa. That doctor only showed up if someone was shot or dying.

Most of the time he arrived too late to fix much, like when he came to the ranch after my papa's accident.

"What's the difference between a doctor and an undertaker? I asked.

He gave me a blank look.

"The number of miles between her and her patient," I said.

His cheeks lifted into a toothy grin. He caught himself and smoothed it into a curious smile. Then he said, "Her?"

"Why not, her?"

"Of course. Are you in the habit of telling jokes to strangers?"

"It's not a joke. It's commentary on the state of medical access."

The doctor sat back and ran a hand through his receding brown hair.

"Quick witted and clever. Duly noted," he said, pursing his lips with amusement. "Now, if you could follow my exercises, we'll get through this faster."

I shrugged, pinched my lips closed, and sat obediently awaiting instructions.

He held up his fingers, asked me to follow them with my eyes, and then to count them, which I did with childlike exaggeration. He sighed. I was wearing on his patience. I decided not to make an intentional counting mistake, even though the exercise was ridiculous.

But then he asked if I could read.

"Of course I can read," I replied tersely, careful not to raise my voice. I figured he'd put violent mood swings on my medical record, and then he'd refer me to an asylum, and that would be the end of me.

"Look, I have to ask the question. I don't want to conclude you have a problem with your vision when you couldn't read in the first place. You'd be surprised how many people can't, and are too embarrassed to say."

I thought about Tubby, my old boss at the San Francisco Livery. And Papa and Mizzy, whose reading wasn't very good even though they could get by.

"You're right. Sorry about that. I'm kinda giddy, but it's because I've been reunited with friends after being stuck on a dreary lighthouse island all winter."

"Isolation aside, injuries to the head can take a very long time to heal. I'm attempting to rule out obvious physical issues." He dug a paper out of his bag. "It would appear your command of spoken language hasn't suffered. An excellent sign. Read this then, since you know how."

I unfolded a square of soiled paper, flattened it out on my thigh. It took my left eye a few moments to focus, but I read the paragraph with ease after that.

"No law shall be passed restraining the free expression of opinion, or restricting the right to speak, write, or print freely on any subject whatever; but every person shall be responsible for the abuse of this right."

I handed the paper back to him. It sounded like something Jake might have quoted from his government studies.

"What's that from?"

"The new Oregon Constitution," he said with obvious pride.

"You're American then."

"I am. From Oregon City."

"I like the person part."

"The which?"

"...Where it says, every person shall be responsible, and not every man..."

Dr. Bough leaned on the bulkhead. "Yes, of course. Deliberate choice of words there."

"We the People of the United States, in Order to form a more perfect Union, establish Justice, insure domestic Tranquility, provide for the common defence, promote the general Welfare, and secure the

Blessings of Liberty to ourselves and our Posterity, do ordain and establish this Constitution for the United States of America.'"

It was as if the words, all jumbled somewhere in a dark corner, stood up and marched out in an orderly line.

He folded his arms. "Impressive."

Now he was looking at me the way the Captain did the first time we'd met. I no longer felt bold. I felt heat burn up the front of my neck into my cheeks.

"How long ago did you memorize that?"

"A couple of years ago. I can recite more."

"I'm sure," he said, making notes in his little book. His handwriting was large, slanted right and had lots of swooping tails. Very educated.

We talked about whether I'd had dizziness, or vomiting, or ringing in my ears. I'm not sure what made me tell him the truth, but I did. I emphasized that the worst of it was when my head was first cracked open.

"Do you remember what you hit your head on?" he asked.

"A big rock," I said. "This side, on the back." I didn't tell him I had my head whipped a second time by a nasty pirate who'd flung me hard onto the beach at Clamity Cove.

"Much blood?" He dug through my hair to check my scalp. I told him it had not bled at all, but I'd had an ugly lump. Some other clear liquid ran out of my ear. Ear tears, I called them.

"And what do you recall in the minutes, hours, days after? What you were doing and so forth."

"I know where I was, but only remember bits and pieces of things that happened. I lost track of time for a few weeks."

"Hmmm," he said again. The information meant something to him, but he wouldn't say what.

He banged a little hammer on my left knee, and I almost kicked him. Then he got me to stand on one leg, close one eye then the other, switch legs, touch my nose with the little finger of my left hand. I did all of those things, even though the boat rocked back and forth as we floated at anchor. I didn't mention that too much more of this would make my head woozy and I might throw up on his shoes.

He put his notebook and instruments away.

"You've had a serious injury. I suspect you broke your skull. A fracture, we call it. That causes swelling, which is why you're having trouble with recall around the time, and with your memory and vision since. You are suffering some effects, much like one might expect after a hard night of drinking."

I remembered how Uncle Jack staggered about, fell down, sometimes passed out, and then forgot all of it. "It's very much like that."

"You are capable of travel, but you'll have a bad time of it if the voyage is rough. It would be best to wait until all symptoms are gone."

"I can't. I have to get back to California. I'll handle it."

"Very well. You're of sound mind, so it's up to you. I'll tell the Captain I've cleared you to go."

"I have a question, Doc. How long does it take for a broken head to heal? I mean, will I remember things like I did before, eventually?"

"I would say so, but memory is a strange thing. You might never recall some things around the time of your injury. Or they may all come back."

"So you don't know."

He laughed. "No. Not for certain. I can tell you what you need to do to have the best outcome. Number one. Be very careful not to hit your head again. That's the most important thing."

"Number two," I said. "Avoid exertion. Pumping blood increases the volume of circulation and that will cause more swelling. Number three, avoid consumption of spirits, which will aggravate the symptoms and increase risk of re-injury." He raised his eyebrows in surprise and I shrugged. "I read some medical books on the island."

"You seem to have retained that material."

"What about reading? Does reading make it worse?"

"It may be harder and you may feel ill if you do too much. You've got a worrisome problem with focus in that left eye. It's like you are trying to read without glasses. In fact, if it doesn't improve, you may require lenses."

"It's not as bad as it was."

"Good. Then your vision may return with time. Don't push yourself. If you feel unwell—"

"—rest," I said. The old medical standby, which was not bad advice.

He snapped his bag shut and adjusted his spectacles. I followed him to the stairs that led up to the deck.

He paused with his foot on the bottom step. "How old are you?"

"Sixteen...almost."

"You'd make an excellent doctor. You're intelligent and knowledgeable far beyond your years."

"Did your school allow girls?"

He looked past me as if his classmates had lined up behind me and he'd just realized none of them were female.

He sighed. "As a matter of fact, no."

CHAPTER SEVENTEEN

octor Bough didn't offer unnecessary tonics or medicines, and he didn't blame any of my lingering symptoms on female problems. Before he left, I had to know if I could trust my memory of the shipwreck, because it happened only days before hitting my head. I told him the basic story of the sinking schooner and how I'd made my way to land, leaving out all the parts about the raid and murdering pirates. He listened with wide-eyed dismay, nodding and then shaking his head and when I was done, he said, "My word," and sat down on a nearby barrel to take it all in.

He told me to imagine the shipwreck was like an injury that nobody could see, and it was as troublesome as a crack to the skull. As he explained, I felt like my spine might crumble into dust, so I sat down across from him, staring at the deck boards by my feet. He was telling me why nobody believed me. All they saw was a girl with a broken head. But when he said, in answer to my question, that the mind was more likely to hide painful memories than alter them, I lifted my head and asked him to repeat what he'd said. "Trust the things you remember", he said, "because your mind will reveal things when it's ready".

Back in the galley, I dug out my notebook and began scribbling down what he'd told me from his tests and observations. On a separate page, I made a chart and labeled the sections. In one column, old memories. These were untouched. In another column, memories of the shipwreck. Despite trauma, not likely wrong. A third column, memories immediately before and after hitting my head. I may have lost those forever. The last column was for memories from the days and weeks following my accident. Tangled up at first, but as my head healed and time passed, the knots were coming undone and settling into a kind of order. Everything the doctor said made sense. As I jotted notes about the shipwreck on my chart, I remembered Mrs. Dalworth had said the facts I told her about the shipwreck had never changed, even though I had struggled to remember them from one day to the next.

Cook appeared, and we set to work on supper for the crew. I kept my notebook handy during the meal shift and added to my chart as things came to mind. After stopping half a dozen times during cleanup, Cook told me he'd scrub the last of the pots so I could finish what I was working on.

I sat at the table and studied the latest entries on my chart. I'd already forgotten a few items I'd written that same afternoon.

"Hmmm," I said, just like the doctor.

"Didn't the doc say your eyes need rest? That don't look like rest to me."

"You eavesdropped!" I said, not surprised he'd stuck close by while the doctor was checking me over.

"Not on purpose. Have to be stone deaf not to hear a conversation through these wood panels."

"Say, what's the name of the street where the Hudson's Bay Company store is?"

"Government. Why?"

I put a checkmark in a little box on my chart. "Testing my recall."

"I'm going topside for a puff. You should come along for some air."

I opened and closed my left eye as I looked up at him. It was slow to focus, just like the doctor had said. It needed rest. I shut my notebook.

"Why, Miss LeBeau! I do believe you're winking at me!" Cook said. He bowed and stuck out his hand.

I let one hand drift to my throat in flirtatious surprise and delicately placed my other hand on his palm.

"Well, seeing as how you're still an available bachelor, sir, I'm inclined to enquire about your intentions. I have other prospective suitors, one with a naval position at a lighthouse, don't you know, and the other, a rather charming man of medicine whose acquaintance I have made only today. It is only fair to warn you, sir, I'll choose the one who will offer me the best station in life."

Cook laughed. "That counts me out. Are you playing one of them ladies in a book you read? 'Cause except for the bit about all your suitors, you lost me. And when did you start sizing up the gentlemen?"

"I'm not sizing them up. I'm managing them."

"Managing them? Nah, I think you like the attention. And what about our young Mr. Miller? You forget about him on your list of suitors? Ain't he more your age and style?"

He clamped his lips shut to keep from grinning and carried Mr. Jones up the stairs to the main deck for me.

Boats tied up and at anchor in the inner harbor were vibrant in the cool night air. Music, laughter, clanks, thumps and hollers came from all around us. On shore, the lights of Fort Victoria formed a bright clump while the scattered, flickering fires from the Indian camp across the bay fanned out into the darkness like stars in a black sky. The cool air smelled of burned wood and campfires. With the sun gone, a dampness came off the water. I pulled on my jacket as we picked a place on deck to sit and look up at the sky.

"How was your meeting with the Captain?" Cook asked, plopping Mr. Jones into my lap when I'd settled into a comfy spot. I'd been called to his cabin right after the doctor left.

"He was all right. Cleared me to sail, but I already knew that. He usually likes to talk, but he was preoccupied today."

"You survived the same shipwreck. You understand."

But I didn't understand. I could explain my survival, but the Captain's made little sense.

Cook dropped the conversation, rolled himself a smoke, and gazed up at the stars. I didn't want to tell him that the Captain had been peculiar, like he'd become a different person. The quiet, soft-spoken man with a love of poetry had turned into an obnoxious fellow, clenching a wine glass and stumbling around his cabin with simmering contempt. It took me back to the *Salish Wind*, the day of the shipwreck. The thoughtful captain, who always consulted and deferred to Kuno's expertise, had been ill-tempered and irrational.

The Captain's survival was a mystery. There was only one skiff on the *Salish Wind* and the reef had smashed it to bits. I saw it. I'd hoped to use it to save myself and I wrote that coherent memory into my notebook earlier in the day. So what skiff was he found in and who put him in it?

"Cook, what do you know about the Captain's rescue?"

"Same as you, I expect." He blew smoke into the sky and leaned back. I said nothing for another minute.

"I saw the final report, and it didn't give any details. It didn't even name him as the survivor."

"He told Mr. Miller a passing vessel rescued him near the mouth of Fuca Strait. It was a stroke of luck someone spotted his little boat before it sank."

"Very. When did you find out he was alive?"

"January, I think it was. The rescuing ship was off to the

Sandwich Islands and it wasn't until they made port in Honolulu that he could report the shipwreck and send word to Mr. Miller."

So that fit. That would be why the report wasn't revised until spring. The Captain confirmed my account of where the ship sunk. But that was the only thing we had agreed on.

"He blamed Kuno for the accident," I said.

"I know."

"Kuno didn't make a mistake. Drak and I were there. Mr. Jones, too. We witnessed it all."

Cook sat up. "Now don't go dredging up the past, Charlee."

"But he lied! It was his fault we crashed."

Cook's eyes widened as he put up his hand to stop me from saying anything more. He didn't want to hear it.

"What's done is done. It's bad enough that everybody else died. No good will come of going against his account."

He butted out his smoke and stood. I followed him.

"Kuno was your friend. Don't you want people to know the truth?"

His limbs stiffened. Pain distorted his face. He'd known Kuno and Drak for years, and their loss had been a terrible blow.

He grasped my shoulders and squeezed. "Not if getting the truth will harm you, too."

"It won't."

"You don't know that."

True, I didn't, but he imagined the worst.

Back in the galley, I let it rest and changed the subject. We chatted over menus, the watch schedules, my duties and routines. Once I saw he'd returned to his old self, I brought the subject up again.

"You ain't gonna let go of it, are you?" he said, shaking his head.

I shrugged. "I can't. How do you figure he ended up in a skiff?" I asked.

"Someone must have put him in it. Probably Kuno. He'd be strong enough. He'd have thought to save him."

"Say it was Kuno. If he was alive, don't you think he would have turned over every board on that ship to find me and put me in the skiff, too?"

"Yeah, but…"

"He didn't look for me because he was dead, Cook."

"Look, Charlee. You can't blame the Captain. He was unconscious."

"So he says."

"And what, you don't believe that?"

"I don't know. I keep thinking how Kuno didn't like the replacements the Captain brought on when the others got stuck ashore."

"Those last-minute hires."

"Right. Drak didn't like the sudden crew change, either. He and Kuno had never seen those sailors around. Real bad luck, they took a job on a doomed ship."

"And good for me and the other two boys who got stranded in Vic. What are you getting at?"

"I ran into one of those sailors on the dock yesterday."

"What?!"

"I helped some fellas who were having trouble unloading a horse. He didn't recognize me. So I followed him to find out his name and then checked the manifest from the *Salish Wind* at Brody's office. How is it he also survived the shipwreck and nobody knows? Back from the dead and nobody, including Brody, is the wiser?"

Cook furrowed his brows. "What's he look like?"

I described him as best I could and added that he wore a red, white, and blue bandana.

"With stars and stripes on it," Cook added.

I grabbed his arm. "You've seen him!" I whispered.

"Now don't get all worked up. Yeah, I think I did. The Captain was talking to him when I came back with the doc. It was a little odd because they were away from the wharf and it wasn't anybody I knew."

One thing was obvious. The Captain knew the sailor was also alive, and he hadn't told anyone.

CHAPTER EIGHTEEN

By morning, the crew had loaded the schooner with goods for San Francisco. With the black waters of the inner harbor dark and still, the sun yet to appear on the eastern horizon, sailors bustled around the deck preparing for departure. Jake said a quick good morning as he hurried by with coils of rope. He'd worked most of the night, loading the hold, and wouldn't see his hammock for a few more hours yet, when we'd go into full sail past the outer harbor. I tucked my hands in my pockets to keep my fingers warm, feeling guilty about being assigned to an easier shift and light galley duties.

"You're looking well this morning," the Captain said, appearing beside me as I watched the crew scurry about. I didn't like him coming out of nowhere like that. He'd never done it before. When we'd sailed on the *Salish Wind*, he'd kept a polite distance.

"I feel good. Thank you, sir," I replied. I was tired, jumpy, and not good at all. I'd tossed all night in my galley hammock, thinking about what the doctor had told me about my memories, and about what the Captain had to do with the wreck of the *Salish Wind*.

"The doctor expects you'll see a full recovery."

"Yes. In the physical sense, he said, I'll be fine." I replied, hoping the good doctor hadn't been loose-lipped with everything I'd told him.

"The physical sense?"

"The dizziness, fainting, and such. They'll go away with time. Like what happened yesterday."

"Ah. But are there other things?" He tossed the question out like a fishing line on a lazy summer afternoon. Despite feeling tired, I took the bait, ready to see his reaction to my answer.

"Um, like, my memory isn't good. I haven't forgotten things from a long time ago. My schooling, growing up on the ranch, things like that. I remember all the old stuff."

"But not more recent things."

"It depends. I remember some things clearly and other things not at all. Like I remember everything about living at the lighthouse and I'm glad to be out of there, I tell you. That foggy outpost can make a person go crazy."

I widened my eyes and swatted at an imaginary fly. He stepped back with a tight smile on his face.

"You remember the woman lightkeeper, then?"

"Mrs. Dalworth? Who could ever forget her? Such an amazing person. And her cooking! Was it last year I landed there? Somehow, I swam to that island, what's it called…"

"Deception Island," he said, his blue eyes so cold they could splinter a diamond.

I gazed back with the emptiest look I could muster.

"That's it. And I wandered around and found her lighthouse. Don't tell Cook, but her biscuits are as good as his. Different though. Fluffier. I think it's the soda. She gave me the recipe."

I flashed a honey smile and brushed a strand of hair from my eyes.

"You built a raft. When the ship sank. You built a raft."

"Oh! That's right. Apparently, that's what I did. I only remember if somebody reminds me. It's the silliest thing."

"You don't remember the shipwreck, then."

"We ran aground in a terrible fog. But I guess I hit my head when we crashed because when I woke up everyone had abandoned ship. So I swam for shore."

"You built a raft."

"I mean, yes, I built a raft somehow."

Uncle Jack would have been proud of me. Such a gambler. It was a dangerous game, and one I took way too much pleasure in. If I slipped up, he'd know I was bluffing.

"Your memory hasn't recovered."

"The doctor says that part might never. Unless…"

"Unless?"

"Unless something similar triggers it. Like, for example, if I was on a sinking ship, I might remember what happened the last time. But the *Sonoma Wind* won't run aground, will it, Captain?"

"I would be cursed if such a disaster should strike me twice."

"Yes. Two shipwrecks would be horrible luck. What are the chances?"

"Slim to none. Now if you'll excuse me, Miss LeBeau, I'm needed."

He tipped his hat and hurried off to where his crew beckoned. I glared after him, scowling at his First Mate, even though he'd been nothing but friendly since I stepped aboard. He'd replaced Kuno, my murdered friend, and I couldn't bring myself to like him.

My earlier courage faded into uncertainty as I thought about the conversation I'd just had. What kind of fool was I, trying to pull one over on the captain? Not a fool, said my confident self. I knew what had happened, and I'd get to the truth if it killed me. It might kill you, said my doubtful self. I put my head back and pinched my eyes shut, seeking to find peace between the two parts of me tugging in opposite directions. The Captain wouldn't sink another ship. Not over me. He'd find a simple way to deal with me if he had to. I imagined him strangling me unconscious and throwing my weighted body overboard, watching me slide away from the stern into the deep, black waters of the vast Pacific Ocean. Or maybe he'd make it an accident he witnessed, and shout "man overboard", and they'd bring the ship around and circle the dark waters despite it being hopeless. They'd search because Mr. Miller would expect them to, but they wouldn't find me. Nobody lost overboard at night from a moving ship was ever found. If he thought I'd lied to him, or knew the truth of what had happened on the *Salish Wind*, could he be so ruthless as to get rid of me?

Since the Captain had cleared me for light duties, he told Cook I could serve him dinner in his quarters. Cook had raised an eyebrow at the unusual request. Not like the Captain to request personal galley service, he'd said. Jake was plain annoyed about it, and whispered under his breath that the Captain was taking advantage and I must be very careful. I convinced them both I could handle it and told them I would call on them to rescue me, like a fragile damsel in distress, if I ran into trouble, which made Jake frown because he knew I was taunting his chivalry. None of us could argue with a request from the ship's commanding officer, even if the request seemed odd. But I also knew what the Captain had in mind. He wanted to get me alone so he could root around in my memories and see what he might uncover. It was unnerving, knowing his purpose, and I didn't know if I could keep my thinking clear under the stress of it all.

Gloom descended upon me as soon as we left Victoria harbor. I didn't want to think of my last voyage on the ill-fated *Salish*

Wind and have that dread spin out of control into a paralyzing fear. While the trip would be much the same, this time we didn't have bad weather looming, and only a small window of time to make open water. Still, the similarities were unsettling.

Working in the galley kept me from thinking the worst. Since I'd lost my sea legs since last aboard, balance demanded my full attention. The angled floor of the ship under sail made me totter around like a newborn colt. When I toppled into Cook for the fourth time, he sent me topside to get my bearings. Swaying about below deck was also making me queasy. I hoped a few minutes of fresh air and looking out at a steady horizon would sort me out. It did, but I couldn't settle my nerves.

The sun climbed into a cloudless sky off our stern, carrying with it the promise of a warm spring day, while the salt air filling our sails from our port side still carried the cold, sharp bite of winter. I pulled my beanie down over my ears, buttoned my coat and flipped the collar up around my neck. Jake was working the mainsail with two other sailors. He touched his brow in a playful salute when he saw me, and I waved back.

Jake's face had lost the last cherub traces of childhood. His jaw had become angular, and he was attempting sideburns like the older men. He'd trimmed back his strawberry blond hair that had always flopped in his eyes, so only a few light-colored ends stuck out of his cap. As I watched him haul on the sail, I realized he was stronger than his pale, lanky appearance suggested. Lucky for me, he'd caught me when I fainted, and laid me down on the deck without so much as a jolt or a scratch. He'd caught Mr. Jones before he tumbled from my limp arms as well. I'd been ungrateful and still hadn't thanked him for saving me from another disastrous crash landing.

"Enjoying the scenery?"

The Captain's voice whispered in my right ear. He'd come up on me again and caught me watching Jake. If anyone else had done that, I would have blasted them out of their boots. Instead, I side-stepped away and pressed my lips into a stiff smile.

"I am. It's a lovely morning with no fog. Isn't that a relief?"

He bristled. "Indeed, it is. And look. There's your island."

"My island?" I scanned the horizon with a puzzled look.

"Where you landed after the shipwreck. Where you stayed at the lighthouse."

He pointed to a dark mound off in the distance on our starboard side. This time, he'd set a course well away from the perils on the north side of the strait.

"Oh, right. The lighthouse. On Desertion Island."

"Deception Island."

"I mean, Deception," I said, tapping my temple with my fist. His tense expression told me not to overplay my memory loss.

"Do you remember the lad who worked for the lighthouse lady?"

"I wouldn't call him a lad," I said, and then turned away, realizing he wasn't referring to Perkins. I changed the subject. "What time do you take your dinner again, sir?"

"An orphan lad like yourself, wasn't he?"

I pasted a blank look on my face and stared at him. "I don't recall."

"Never mind. Seven as usual. Cook will remind you. If you forget."

He wandered off then, our conversation not revealing any new secrets. What lad had he been talking about?

A sailor called out that a ship approached ahead of our port side. It was quite a distance off, tacking on a southeast course.

Cook appeared on deck, and I waved him over.

"How's the ship's boy? Thought maybe you'd toppled overboard."

"Much better. And that's not funny for a bunch of reasons."

As the ship sailed past us in the distance, its details became visible. It was the single-masted sloop that had pursued the *Salish Wind,* the sloop that belonged to the raiding pirates!

I glanced over at the Captain who was watching me. Had he seen me recognize the ship?

In an instant, his curious question about Mrs. Dalworth's lad made sense. When the pirates had captured me in Clamity Cove, they'd called me Mrs. Dalworth's helper and I'd gone along with it. They hadn't realized I'd survived the sinking of the *Salish Wind.*

The Captain couldn't have known about that unless he'd heard it from the pirates. And that meant he knew those men and was in on all of it!

CHAPTER NINETEEN

At seven hundred hours on our first night out, I stood in front of the Captain's quarters, bracing myself for tricky conversation. Balancing a plate of cheese and fruit on a clammy palm, I rapped on his cabin door with my free hand.

"Please enter, Miss LeBeau," the Captain said, sweeping me and the fresh sea air through the open door with one hand, and swirling whiskey in a crystal glass with the other. "You've found your sea legs, I see. Splendid."

"Thank you, sir. I expected to be unsteady for a few days, but conditions so far have been so favorable."

My measured reply did not betray a crazed heart, which hammered inside my chest and urged me to flee for my life. He took the plate from me as he considered my words and studied my calm expression. I let my trembling hand drop to my side.

"You know, the doctor was quite impressed with you the other day. He was delighted with your clever repartee. You seem to have a knack for engaging educated gentlemen."

I wondered how much the doctor had told him. Probably about reading the Oregon constitution or our discussion about medicine. Since the Captain was making small talk, I didn't feel obliged to join in. I smiled at his comments and awaited instructions.

"If you would be so good as to set my table, you can stack those maps and papers on my desk. Let Cook know I'll take dinner in half an hour," he said.

"Aye, sir."

"Leave my cabin door open. You may come and go as required," he added, turning back to his desk.

Back in the galley, I rummaged through a cupboard for the Captain's china, linen napkins and tablecloth. I piled the items onto a tray along with his fine utensils.

"Huh. I see he hasn't got around to engraving the new silverware yet," I muttered.

"What's at?" Cook asked as he came out of the pantry.

"Nothing. Captain wants to eat at half past seven."

"Good. You doing all right? You're a mite flushed."

"I'm fine. If he keeps guzzling whiskey though, I might need you to call me back to the galley. Make something up, you know?"

Cook scowled. I told him I was joking and not to worry.

When I returned to the Captain's quarters, he was behind his desk, head bent, immersed in reading. I steeled myself and entered. He glanced up but immediately continued his work. I set my tray on the table, careful not to disturb him with clinking dishes or rattling utensils. His disinterest was a relief and helped to smooth out my jittery nerves.

The Captain's cabin was full of interesting objects. It reminded me of being locked in the pantry of the Sunshine Cafe, where I'd counted items into math problems to keep myself calm and sharp. This wasn't the same thing. I wasn't a prisoner. But feeling a bit trapped must have brought the pantry to mind. It was like the doctor said—similar situations might trigger memories. I would add that to my notes later. In the meantime, I could put my serving time to use by doing an inventory of his cabin, and test my memory of it later. It would pass the time and distract me from worry.

He had thirty-two books filling two small shelves, all arranged in alphabetical order as before. The Captain had been quick to assemble a new collection on the *Sonoma Wind*, but I noticed the titles were not the same. How did I know that? I couldn't remember all the titles of his last collection, but somehow, I knew these were different. I thought of his precious books on the bottom of the ocean, fluttering in deep ocean currents on the watery shelves of the sunken *Salish Wind*, the Whitman book of poetry he'd loaned me tucked in beside Yeats, sea life clinging to the blurry pages. My eyes moved on from the books, and from the sadness that came with the loss of the ones before.

In the corner, a fiddle lay in an open case lined with crushed blue velvet. Blue velvet, like the kind that lined Papa's coffin. A pain shot up behind my eye. That memory was still difficult. The fiddle was new. I was certain he didn't have one aboard the *Salish Wind*. I'd never heard him play a note.

A similar side table was next, with the usual navigation instruments and charts. Three rolled maps and one laid out. Five instruments, including a compass and a sextant, rested on top of it. One wine-colored rug with brown and green patterns covered the bare wood floor between the Captain's desk and his sleeping quarters. His wide hammock was made up with white feather cover and a thin muslin drape hung in front of the alcove. A book, a liquor bottle and a clock were tucked into a wall shelf on the end where his head would rest. Everything was so similar to his cabin on the *Salish Wind*. The same items except for the fiddle. I looked over to make sure I hadn't imagined it.

"What are your plans for San Francisco, Miss LeBeau?" the Captain asked, barging into my observations. Immersed in his work, I'd decided he wouldn't question me, so it startled me when he spoke. I slid items around on the table, smoothed the creases from the cloth, and didn't look over at him.

"I don't have any yet."

"School in the fall?"

"I don't know..."

"Could I trouble you to refill my glass?"

"Right away, sir."

I carried the heavy decanter to his desk and poured half a glass of red wine. He motioned for me to keep pouring, to fill it to the top. All the while, I sensed his eyes on the side of my face, watching my reactions.

"I haven't forgotten you are a reader. You are welcome to borrow a book from my new collection. I'd be delighted to make another recommendation, if you wish. Do you recall the book I loaned you last time?"

"Walt Whitman. 'Failing to fetch me at first, keep encouraged. Missing me one place, search another—I stop somewhere waiting for you...'"

The words spilled out of my mouth before I could stop them.

He straightened in his chair. "You remember."

Too late, I realized what I'd done. I'd remembered something from right before the wreck of the *Salish Wind*. My sudden recall was right under his nose.

I rubbed my head and did my best to look confused. I could feel his stare.

"Isn't that just the oddest thing? How can I recall a random passage like that? I guess I must have liked that bit of verse."

All of that was the truth, and those lines had comforted me. I'd spoken them over and over on my first nights on the island. I recited them while lying awake in the dark hours, all alone in the rock cave, with the fire flickering bits of light into the black, the night wind moaning outside like a wounded animal, when I didn't know where I was or if anyone would ever find me. Those lines of Walt Whitman's poetry had given me hope.

"Quite extraordinary... since you didn't have that book with you...in your island cave."

My body tensed, and I clenched the edges of the serving tray. How did he know about my island cave? It was not mentioned in the report. Who had told him?

"Excuse me, sir. I must get your dinner or it will be cold."

Thankfully, I was crew with a job to do. He squinted and pursed his lips into a thin smile.

"Of course. Please tell Cook it is not your fault. I detained you." He put his glass down and repeated to himself, "It's not your fault."

I didn't dare ask what he meant, but I knew he wasn't talking about cold fish for dinner.

He glanced up with a blank expression and waved me off.

"Carry on, then."

The wind was steady in our sails and the weather remained fair as we left Fuca Strait. We sailed west, away from the coastline, to avoid the long fog banks clinging to Cape Flattery on the northwestern tip of Washington. Cook said the journey south was easier and faster than coming north because of wind directions. And so it was. Where we had battled winds on our nose sailing north, the winds now favored us from behind.

But every good sailor knows that weather can change fast at sea. A passing storm could whip the ocean into a wild beast. It could last for hours or days. I'd been through that on my first voyage north on the *Salish Wind*. Where I'd been tossed around like a turnip in a hog trough, Jake followed only days later on the sister schooner, his ship skimming along over even, friendly waters. That was his kind of luck and it looked like it was already with us for the trip back to San Francisco.

Pleasant weather made crewing so much easier—up early in the morning, cooking and cleaning in the galley most of the day, and doing the evening watch with Cook until midnight. The work wasn't hard when the ship sailed in pleasant conditions. But the watch hours were deadly boring and long, staring into the black in the unlikely event a light should appear in front of us. To make matters worse, when I finally got a few hours in my hammock, I was wide awake. As each day passed, my lack of sleep took a toll. My body felt weighed down, as if tangled in a heavy chain.

I had two small breaks in my work day—one in the middle of the afternoon and the other right after dinner, before the evening watch. That's when memories bolted from my head like escaping prisoners. I'd catch them, write them down, and then doze off for a few minutes with my hand resting on a page.

On the fourth afternoon at sea, Cook poked me awake at the galley table.

"Hey, hate to ruin your nap, but the Captain wants tea."

I groaned and wiped drool off the side of my mouth. Mr. Jones dug his nails into my legs as he walked across my lap.

"Let's go, sailor," Cook said, plunking a silver tea service tray on the galley table. I dragged myself to my feet in a nauseous daze.

CHAPTER TWENTY

On the fifth night at sea, I was alone in the galley, heavy head resting in my palm, reviewing memories I'd add to my notebook. With less than an hour to spare before my night watch, Jake popped his head in the door.

"Feel like company?"

"Yes! Come in." I tossed my pencil on the table and rubbed the lead stain off my middle finger.

"Cook's covering me. Said you're sick of him."

"More like he's sick of me. Can't say I blame him. I'm sick of me, too."

Neither explanation was it. Cook knew Jake and I had spent no time together since leaving Victoria. I'd been grumbling over that earlier in the day, convinced the Captain had put us on opposite schedules to keep us apart. But Cook said it was the luck of the draw and I shouldn't imagine the worst of him every time something didn't go my way. It was a fair point. The First Mate had drawn up the watch schedule.

"Move over, Mr. Jones," Jake said, shoving him sideways on the bench as he took a seat. Mr. Jones wasn't about to budge from his after-dinner spot, not even for Jake, so I picked him up and dumped him into my hammock so he could finish his nap before we had to report on deck.

"Hey, that's the notebook I gave you! Looks like it's seen better days, though."

The leather journal Jake had given me for my fourteenth birthday lay open on the galley table, its edges scuffed and worn from two years of travel, its pages rippled from dampness, dirt and seawater. It was one of the few things I still had from the Miller ranch. I flipped it shut and tossed it into my hammock. Mr. Jones grunted as it landed on him.

"It's been through it all with me. Funny thing. When the ship was under attack, Drak told me to pack a bag. You know what I did? I packed like I was going on a holiday—books, snacks, this journal, ranch souvenirs, Papa's saddlebags of all things. Drak packed one small waterproof bag, and the stuff he put in it saved my life. I think about that a lot. My stuff was useless. But I'm glad I kept some things."

"Did you write in your book when you were alone?"

"Not much. I remember sitting in my cave by the fire, staring at blank pages, when I had no idea where I was or if anyone would ever find me. I wasn't even sure I was alive, to be honest. What do you write when you've just witnessed the horrific murders of your friends?"

"I don't know. I can't imagine. Look, we don't have to talk about this. I didn't come down here to do that. I came to cheer you up."

"Not talking about it is worse. Nobody believes me, Jake. They think I scrambled my brain when I fell and then made up all the stuff about raiding pirates. Sure, I knocked myself sense-less and I'm confused about a lot of things because of it. But I've never forgotten the shipwreck. That I remember."

"The lighthouse lady believed you, didn't she?"

"Mrs. Dalworth? Yeah, but even she doubted me at first because she knew those privateers. They'd come to the island to trade with her, so she thought they were harmless. But after they stole my island map off her kitchen table and cornered me over at Clamity Cove, then she believed me."

"And the authorities wouldn't accept her account?

"Account of what? She wasn't there. I could barely convince them I made it to the island on a raft. I had no proof those men had anything to do with the shipwreck, no proof they'd ever set foot on the island. Of course, there is your father's gold, but I haven't been able to remember what happened to it, other than I know it's still buried at Clamity Cove. Mrs. Dalworth knows about that, but we didn't tell anyone, because if rumors of buried treasure got out, gold diggers would have swarmed the island."

"Right."

"I wrote some stuff in my notebook after my accident, but it's absolute gibberish. I've been over and over it, and all it tells me is I was a mess after hitting my head. None of what I wrote makes sense. My handwriting is tiny, strange, almost illegible. Random letters and symbols. It's a lot of nonsense."

"Can I see it?"

I froze at the question. I'd shown the writing to Mrs. Dalworth, and it was so bad she'd advised me to keep it to myself. Since there was nothing in it to help my case, she thought it would hurt what little credibility I had. I didn't want to show it to Jake and have him doubt me, too. I'd also ruined the beautiful pages in his book with dirt and ash and mad scribbling.

"It's useless. I've been through it a hundred times, looking for clues."

"Show it to me. Pretty please? You've always said it's good to put fresh eyes on a problem."

I had said that to him, many times over, when I tutored him in mathematics and he'd get frustrated, stomp around the porch and threaten to give up. I'd show him a different way to figure a problem that he couldn't see. Maybe he could help me spot something new. I reached into my hammock for the book. Mr. Jones had roosted upon it like a hen. He didn't appreciate being disturbed in his nest and growled.

"Oh, for heaven's sake. It's me," I said, and he relaxed his curled lip in shame. I laid the book on the table and flipped it open towards the back.

"This is the last ordinary entry from aboard the *Salish Wind*. It's a bunch of childish complaining about what a lousy cook Drak was."

"To be fair, that was a fact."

"May he rest in peace," I added, frowning at my use of one of Uncle's favorite expressions. Jake squeezed my hand.

The next pages were smudged, dirty, and warped from dampness. There was even a streak of brown, where blood from cuts and torn blisters on my hands had stained the pages. "Pretty obvious where my time on the island starts."

"Whoa. I'll say. That right there shows how bad it must have been. It's like someone else wrote this."

"Yeah, a madwoman, as it turns out."

"What's the time gap? Between the last galley entry and the next one in the cave?"

"I dunno. It could be three days or three weeks. No idea."

Jake turned the pages, as if handling the manuscript of an ancient scribe. He shifted position so his body wouldn't cast a shadow from the overhead lantern.

"This can't be a bunch of meaningless scratches. I know you. Your brain had to be working at something. Look at this! I mean, messiness aside, it's written in deliberate lines and symbols, like some kind of foreign language or a secret code."

"I've applied every strategy I can think of to it and it makes no sense. It's like I thought I was writing in code. Like I pretended I was. Some weird way of coping with the disaster and the fear of being lost and all alone in some far-flung corner of the world. But it's garbage, trust me."

"Let me borrow it for a while. Maybe I can crack it."

"I can't give you my book." I snapped it tight and clutched it to my chest.

"I don't want to take it. I'll copy that one section out and work on decoding it. There's something to it, I swear."

"You don't have time to copy it. You've only got half an hour."

"We can get it copied, if we each do half."

"I don't have any paper."

One last half-hearted attempt to discourage him.

"I'll get some. C'mon, Charlee. Let me try."

"Oh, all right! But you can't let anyone see you with it."

"I'll keep it hidden. Promise. Pour us coffee. I'll be right back."

As he ducked out of the galley, he called back, "I drink mine black like you now."

I puzzled over that as I filled two mugs with fresh coffee brewed for the night watch. Jake didn't drink coffee back on the ranch. The Missus had got him on tea with milk, and I'd teased him half to death when I saw him cradling a delicate saucer in the palm of his hand and drinking out of a fancy cup, little finger sticking up in the air like the society ladies. It's a wonder he didn't knock me flat for making fun of him. He thought I was teasing him for acting like a girl and I said I would never do that because that would be like living in a glass house and throwing stones, particularly since I railed at being told I couldn't do things like boys. I teased him because he looked like a spoiled little rich kid and he never wanted to come off like that. Occasionally, I had to undo some of The Missus' training in manners before she ruined him like she'd done with Bernadette. As for me, I'd been drinking black coffee for as long as I could remember. Mizzy always had fantastic morning coffee brewed for the ranch hands. Tubby, the manager of the San Francisco Livery, boiled a pot of black sludge over the blacksmith's fire. We all griped about it every morning and drank it, anyway. Cook was like his sister Mizzy. He knew how to make a good batch, and he'd taught me on the *Salish Wind*. A sailor working the tedious, chilly night watch on a ship would drink a mug of hot, black dishwater if it kept him warm and awake. But Cook said all the more reason to make sure crew got a decent cup.

Jake was back with paper and pencils before I had the mugs on the table. When he handed me a sharpened pencil, I admired the smooth, undamaged length of it, and the fine point of the lead. Jake always had these simple pleasures around him. I could count on one finger the number of times I'd held a whole pencil.

We set to work copying the pages after my accident. Jake showed so much interest in the symbols, I lost my embarrassment at the deranged scribbles laid out before us. I wondered if he was right. Maybe something hid in the frightful mess. Maybe he could help me unlock the mystery of what I'd written.

Even if he was wrong, and what I'd written remained garbled nonsense, it didn't matter. Jake believed everything I told him, even when I knew it sounded wild and impossible. He believed in me, in all of it, and I knew he would be the one to help me find my way to the truth.

CHAPTER TWENTY-ONE

"Good news. We're less than a day out of San Fran, making good time," said Cook, nudging my leg.

I'd struggled through the dinner shift, then curled up in my hammock, feeling head-heavy and woozy in the rolling waves of a following sea. The trip home had taken its toll. Everyone had noticed, even though I'd tried to hide it.

"The Captain wants to know how you are feeling."

"Like he cares," I said.

"He's concerned, Charlee."

"About himself. Not about me."

Cook helped me out of my hammock. I clung to him, locking my knees to brace my stance. Loose pieces of hair fell in my face, but I felt too wrung out to fix them.

"He mentioned Mrs. Plea will take charge of you."

"I know that. Mr. Miller told me in his letter, because he knew he'd be away. Jake will stay on with you, right?"

"That's the deal. But only till summer, before school goes back in. I hope that's where you'll end up, too."

"Maybe. But if school is too boring, you'll have to take me back in the galley next spring."

"Not a chance. Your sailing days are over. Besides, Mr. Miller's going with steamships starting in August. Schooners are too slow on these merchant runs. And less reliable. Losing the *Salish Wind* shook him up."

"But what are you gonna do then?"

"Run a new diner Mrs. Plea bought. Time all of us got our feet on solid ground."

Someone descended the stairs from the main deck. These were light, careful steps, unlike the hurried thumps typical of crew. Mr. Jones, still in my hammock, lifted his head and growled.

"Am I interrupting?" the Captain said, lifting a polished boot over the bulkhead into the galley. Cook said he wasn't, and they exchanged a few respectful pleasantries as I wobbled my way to the galley table. I sensed the Captain wanted to speak to me alone, but Cook ignored the awkward pauses that signaled he should leave. Instead, he moved to the far end of the galley and made himself busy. Cook had his doubts about the Captain, despite always saying otherwise and encouraging me to cooperate.

The Captain approached the table with an odd stagger in his stride, like he'd stepped in a bit of manure somewhere and didn't want to track it across the floor, but it probably had more to do with the wine he'd quaffed with dinner. He stopped some distance away and grasped a cupboard handle for balance. It flung open, and he almost toppled into our water barrels.

"So. Miss LeBeau," he said, catching himself before he fell. "You must be happy to be going home."

"I don't have a home."

I could not curb a grumpy retort. Cook shot me a warning glance.

The Captain took no offense, as if the melancholy chord it struck with him had drowned out the bitter tone of my reply. He seemed saddened by my situation.

"Home. Yes, well. Literally speaking. I see that. Happy is hardly the sentiment."

There was a lengthy silence as his thoughts carried him somewhere far away.

"I'm thinking about going to school, if they'll take me."

I hadn't thought about school at all until Cook brought it up moments earlier, but somebody had to say something to move the conversation along.

He clasped his hands behind his back. "Splendid idea. I'm certain you'll do well." He took a quick breath through his teeth and added, "Once you've recuperated, of course."

Cook caught my eyes, stopping me from blurting out another snide reply. "Yessir, once I'm better."

"Mr. Miller made arrangements with Mrs. Plea for you to stay at the house where Cook's sister works. I'm sure you'll make a speedy recovery in her care."

Cook dropped what he was fiddling with. "You get to stay with Mizzy. Charlee, that's wonderful! She's going to be over the moon to have you back!"

I'd assumed Mrs. Plea would put me up somewhere with strangers. Hearing I was going to be staying with Mizzy lifted my spirits, but I felt so rotten, I couldn't enjoy the happy news for long.

We sailed into San Francisco Bay under a clear blue sky the next morning. Blue waves frothed off the hull of the schooner and swirled away behind us as we cut across the water, pushed by a damp April wind. Even the stubbled line of city buildings was mesmerizing from a distance. The sight of the city brought many feelings up inside me. There is a kind of sad happiness one feels, returning to something that's no longer there, to a place remembered but no longer the same. I swallowed a lump that had formed in my throat.

I stood on the starboard side, gripping the gunwale for balance with white hands, teeth chattering despite heavy wool clothes and cap. Cook took off his coat and swaddled me in it, while blocking the wind with his body. The warmth clinging to the inside of the wool enveloped me, and I stopped shivering. The fresh sea air on the main deck soothed my heavy head. I couldn't spend one more minute staggering around the galley below.

Our arrival took the whole morning, first holding at the bay entrance waiting on a pilot boat, then maneuvering into the busy harbor, and finally docking where the ship would unload. I couldn't wait to get my feet on solid ground. Doctor Bough had been right. The trip had been tough, even with light duties and a pretty smooth sail the whole way.

I didn't like the idea of Jake staying on without me, but that's what he'd signed up for. Jake and Cook would stay aboard, working most of the few days in port, before heading out again to Victoria on the May expedition.

Cook was both thrilled and relieved I'd be with Mizzy, and he couldn't stop talking about it. That news had kept me going through the last hours aboard ship. If all Mrs. Plea could spare was a couple of planks for a bunk in a closet, I'd welcome it. I couldn't wait to leave my rope hammock behind, swinging with every rise and fall of the ocean waves, the water rushing past the hull next to my head reminding me of my time trapped in the cupboard of the sinking *Salish Wind*.

The San Francisco docks were many times bigger and busier than the little port of Victoria. I spotted Mrs. Plea, in a black dress, next to a black carriage with two shiny black horses. At first glance, undertaker came to mind, but it didn't fit. She had a distinguished look, an air of prestige.

She spoke to the Captain at length while Cook and Jake loaded my trunk and bag from the *Sonoma Wind*. As I watched their serious faces, I was convinced they were talking about me. But when I disembarked, she welcomed me with warmth and delight.

She greeted Cook, and then Jake, with little personal conversations that left them smiling at her like royalty. When I introduced her to Mr. Jones, she said she was pleased to make his acquaintance and offered him a seat for the buggy ride. Unfortunately, Mrs. Plea's lovely black dress accentuated the white fur he left on her hip as he wedged himself between us. Mr. Jones was inclined to be a snob when meeting someone new, but I'd told him about her being an underground operative for freedom and he'd liked her immediately.

The noisy crowds and the stench of the city streets rose to greet us as we pulled away from the docks. The sights and smells had shocked me when I first arrived in the city, the day Uncle brought me to the city after Papa died. But now, as we drove through the muck and bustle, the place was wildly familiar. I knew these streets, the businesses that gave fair deals, which back alleys to avoid, the bakery that handed off stale bread to the hungry kid who waited in the shadows by the back door at closing. These streets had been my home for almost a year.

The brick buildings and wooden shanties disappeared as we left the heart of the city. A fresh salt air breeze carried the scent of fresh flowers and cut grasses. We passed through streets of neat little cottages, lined up side-by-side on wide, tree-lined avenues. I'd come this far once before in a hack, when we were short a driver at the Livery. Tubby had sent me out here to deliver a German couple who'd arrived by steamer. "It's a lot o' money," he'd said. "Don't mess it up." I promised him I wouldn't. The horse he'd given me was the sweetest in the stables.

Mrs. Plea was taking the same route. We turned a corner, and I recognized the house where I'd taken the couple along with their enormous trunks of luggage. I spotted the wife tending rose bushes by the gate.

"*Wie geht's*, Mrs. Kern! *Es ist schön, dich wiederzusehen!*" I hollered as we passed by. A tall woman, light brown hair coiled high in a bun on the top of her head, turned and squinted at the passing buggy. The familiar wave of her arm didn't match her puzzled smile. Of course, she wouldn't remember me all this time later, no longer the scrawny cabbie sitting up front, and looking so very different now with my longer, braided hair.

"You know German," Mrs. Plea remarked.

"A little, I guess. I think I said how's it going, nice to see you again. At least, I hope that's what I said."

"How did you come by that language?"

"I don't know. Maybe the lady taught me," I said, equally perplexed by the words I'd spoken.

No, that wasn't it. I had a vague memory of a book some-where and someone speaking words to me and eating some kind of warm, delicious apple thing. Strudel! The recipe was somewhere in my notebook. But where was I? Did Drak teach me? That didn't seem right. He was Russian and a terrible cook. It had to be Mrs. Dalworth. Did she know German? I didn't think so. I stopped trying to sort it out, as I was already tired and could feel a headache coming on. We rode along without talking for some distance. The motion of the buggy had made my head wobble and my neck feel like it could snap from the weight of it. I closed my eyes and let the familiar clopping of horse's hooves carry me away.

"Are you feeling ill?" Mrs. Plea asked. I sat up and looked out. She was taking in the late afternoon scenery while Mr. Jones rested his head on her lap.

"I'll be all right. Still got the sea in my head." I swallowed hard, thinking conversation might take my mind off my upset stomach. "Did Mr. Miller make all these arrangements for me?"

"I did. On his behalf. I'm sure Jake has told you why he had to go east."

"Yeah. The Missus wanted to go home. Jake said she wanted the whole family to move to Philadelphia."

Mrs. Plea frowned. "The Missus?"

"Mrs. Miller, I mean. The Missus is what the help called her back on the ranch. Nobody liked her."

"Nobody?"

"Well, Mr. Miller did. But only because she cast some kind of love spell over him. And her kids 'cause they're a chip off the old block. But that's it. In the long run, I think Mr. Miller will be glad to be rid of her."

She muttered something that sounded like, "Won't we all," but my ears were ringing and I may have imagined it.

CHAPTER TWENTY-TWO

The house was like all the others on the road—a pleasant, two-story affair, with a wide veranda wrapping around the front and sides. The groomed yard was large, with some acreage out behind. Mizzy had been waiting for us and waved from the front porch as we pulled up. She looked exactly as I remembered.

I leaped from the buggy, but my legs buckled as I landed and I fell hard to the ground. Mr. Jones jumped down and circled around me, barking with alarm. Mizzy flew down the stairs and Mrs. Plea was at my side before I could figure out what had happened.

"My feet fell asleep," I said as they helped me up and checked me over.

Seeing I wasn't injured, Mizzy wrapped her arms around me and squeezed me tight. I inhaled her familiar scent of wild roses and baked bread. Tears backed up behind my eyes and my head pounded. I hung on to her and willed myself not to collapse into a sobbing heap. After a long minute, she held me at arm's length, cheeks wet with tears.

"Look how tall you got! I'm lookin' up at you now. Gonna have to buy a set o' heels to keep my eye on you!"

"I'm so sorry. Your hair…"

A few grey curls poked out from under her head kerchief. I'd put her through so much worry and grief.

"Never you mind. You're back, thank the good Lord."

Mrs. Plea sent us inside as a man dressed in farm clothes came for the buggy. Mizzy wouldn't let go of my hand, even when she showed me around her kitchen, and to the small room in the back she'd made up for me, right next to hers. Mr. Jones stuck to my leg like a burr, and I explained how I'd survived thanks to him, and how he seemed to think it was more like I'd saved him. And anyway, we were inseparable. Mizzy crouched down, rubbed his cheeks, and thanked him for taking care of me. Mr. Jones sat solemn and straight. He looked sideways at me, embarrassed at all the fuss, but I could tell her friendly words meant a lot to him.

Mizzy promised a full tour of the house the next day. She set me up at her kitchen table with a blanket around my shoulders and fed me a fluffy, warm scone with butter and jam, and hot tea with honey. Mr. Jones got his own blanket beside the stove, which he appreciated, but he kept a steady watch on the new situation.

Mizzy wanted to hear my story from beginning to end, but not all at once and maybe starting with the nicer bits, she said, if I could recollect some. So I skipped the shipwreck, the murderous pirates, the buried gold, and the traitorous schooner captain. I started with Mrs. Dalworth and the lighthouse island, which she had a hard time picturing because she'd never been off land in her life. During a pause in our conversation, I put my head down on the kitchen table, and Mizzy massaged my shoulders until I felt the knots loosen. I fell asleep.

When I woke up, it was dark. I thought I was in Mrs. Dalworth's kitchen at the lighthouse until Mizzy put her arm over my shoulder and told me she'd let me sleep because I needed it so badly. I rubbed my left cheek, imprinted with the texture of a linen towel, and wiped sticky drool from the corner of my mouth. My head felt like a massive anchor, my neck a thick, rusty chain.

"Mr. Jones has had his supper already. I saved yours. It's keepin' warm on the stove."

"Thanks, but I'm not hungry." My mouth was dry and sour.

"I made one of your favorites." She placed a galette in front of me and my eyes popped at the sight of the rolled-up pancake stuffed with what looked like ham and gooey cheese. Papa and I loved these. Mizzy always made them for us back on the ranch.

"Well, I think I'll give that a little try," I said, pulling the plate toward me, and she brushed a wayward strand of hair from my eyes with a hopeful smile.

"Don't have to eat it all. Just as much as you want."

Although we'd talked about what had happened to me, I hadn't brought up the one big subject that had haunted me since my time in the island cave. I ate half of the galette, the whole time mulling over how I could bring up my mama. There was no easy way. I had to get it out.

"Mizzy,"

"Mmm," she said, without looking up from her dishes. She wiped droplets off a glass and placed it beside the others in an overhead cupboard.

"There's something I have to ask you."

Her hands paused in mid-air. She turned, leaned a hip against the kitchen counter, and braced herself for a difficult question.

"About what? she said.

"About…my mama." She looked down at the floor, then out into the dark hall, as if looking for approval from somebody standing out there in the shadows. "You know what really happened to her, don't you?"

She sighed and shook her head, not to say she didn't know, but that she didn't want to say, or didn't want to have this conversation.

"You have to tell me."

"I will. I'll tell you all I know. But not tonight."

"I can take it."

"It's…no, look at you." She took my face in her hands and examined me. "That left eye o' yours is swollen half shut."

If I was overtired or slept on that side, that would sometimes happen. My weak eye would puff up, like a bee had stung me. Mizzy's eyes widened as she did a closer inspection.

"How long has that been goin' on?"

"Since I fell."

"I got some medicine…" She rummaged in a drawer across from me.

"Tell me about Mama."

I thought I'd try one more time while she had her back turned.

"I promise I will, but not right this minute. You're barely in the door."

She rubbed some sharp-smelling salve around my eye. "Besides, that story ain't goin' nowhere. It's waited this long, it can wait a few days more. You need to rest."

Mizzy helped me to my feet, took my arm and led me down the hall to the back of the house. Mr. Jones' nails clicked on the hardwood floor as he followed close behind.

"You get some sleep and some of Mizzy's home cooking in your belly, and you'll be right as rain in no time. Cook didn't feed you proper. He shouldn't have made you work. I'm gonna give him a piece o' my mind when I see him."

"Oh no, he tried to make me eat, and I asked to work. It was the motion of the boat that got me. I couldn't eat or sleep much the whole way back because I was too dizzy."

I didn't mention gigantic waves still rolled around inside of me, like I was aboard the ship.

Mizzy lingered, tended to little things in the room, helped me change into a nightshirt and wash for bed. Someone had brought in my trunk and she asked what was in it. So we talked a little more about my time at the lighthouse with Mrs. Dalworth, and about her husband Edgar, whose books she'd given to me and which filled much of the small but heavy trunk. She asked me to help her write to Mrs. Dalworth, to thank her for how much she'd done for me, and I realized they would like each other very much if they ever had a chance to meet.

I let Mizzy tuck me in like she'd done when I was young, soaking up the happy memories of earlier years with her and Papa on the ranch. Mr. Jones dug a nest for himself in his blanket beside me and when we were both settled in, she told me to rap on the wall right beside my head if I needed anything and she'd be there in a flash. She kissed my forehead, turned out the lantern, and clicked the door shut.

The bone-chilling shivers I'd had on the schooner set in as soon as she left and my body couldn't warm the cold seeping out of the mattress. Mr. Jones wedged himself against me, but even he wasn't enough to keep my teeth from chattering. To make matters worse, the room was pitch black and the motion in my head felt worse, with nothing to fix my eyes on. I tried to sleep but couldn't. Whenever I drifted off, my legs would jerk, like I was falling, first from the top of a towering mast, then down the steep iron staircase at the Deception Island lighthouse, finally on the winding island path where headless pirates chased me with long swords. I sat up in a shivering sweat. I couldn't stay in this cold, dark place, with my thoughts circling a drain of imagined horrors. I opened the door to my room and peered into the hall. A thin beam of moonlight shone through a window in the back door. Its dim light helped me get my bearings. I tiptoed toward the kitchen, careful not to make a sound.

Mizzy found me in the morning on the floor behind her stove, tangled up in blankets I'd dragged from my room, curled up around Mr. Jones. I woke up to her shaking me, eyes wide with alarm. I assured her I was fine, that I'd slept like a log behind the toasty stove and didn't have a single bad dream. She seemed relieved to hear it, although she sighed a lot through a quivering smile and tears flooded her eyes as she helped me out from the tiny nook I'd found between the stove and the wall.

CHAPTER TWENTY-THREE

During the buggy ride from the wharf, I had asked Mrs. Plea if she knew of a job I could do for decent pay, because I didn't want to be a burden on anyone, to which she replied that there was no hurry, and I'd been through a lot and I could think of myself as her house guest to start and enjoy a bit of rest. I thanked her for her kindness, but I told her I meant to find a job so I could pay my way. I had already worked my passage home aboard the *Sonoma Wind*.

"I don't have any positions at the house, but I can find something for you, if that's your wish. Tell me your skills then, what you think you might be suited to."

I'd landed myself in an unexpected interview for some unknown position.

"Well, I can do simple accounting and inventory. I can tutor a little, although I'm not good with spoiled brats. I scare them with my threats...so maybe skip tutoring. I'm good with animals of all kinds. I can tend and train horses. Manage livestock. Drive a buggy. I'm an excellent shot, but a little rusty coming from an island that had one sorry old rifle with sights that weren't true. Oh yeah, I can almost run a lighthouse, but there aren't a lot of those around."

Mrs. Plea grinned. "That's a fascinating list of qualifications. And how about domestic work?"

I rolled my eyes. "Yeah, I can do that. Cleaning, mending and such, if it's all that's available. I can cook a little. Not like Mizzy, though. Nothing fancy."

Mrs. Plea said she'd see what she could do. To start, I could give Mizzy a hand in the kitchen and tidy the parlor each day. She warned me to expect a job that was much the same. I already knew it. When I first came to San Francisco, I discovered orphaned girls like me had two options: work as a housekeeper, or work in the seedy saloons and opium dens.

Mizzy didn't need help, so she made me rest with my head on the table because I refused to go lie down in my room. The parlor didn't need cleaning either. I tidied it in minutes and spent the rest of the time yawning and browsing the bookshelves.

There were many books I hadn't seen before, not in Mr. Miller's parlor or on the shelves in the Captain's quarters. Most houses didn't have books at all because folks either couldn't afford them, or they couldn't read, and I figured the house guests here mustn't have either problem. I picked up a beautiful leather-bound book by a fellow named Emerson and took it over to the polished mahogany desk. My eyelids drooped before I made the bottom of the first page. I had to lie down.

"Charlee." Someone nudged me. "You can't sleep under here, dear."

I opened my sticky eyes and tried to focus. Mrs. Plea was crouched down, peering under the desk where I'd tucked myself away when sleep overtook me. Mr. Jones was also looking at me with similar concern, the traitor, as he'd been having a secret nap along with me, but probably heard her coming and pretended he had nothing to do with sleeping on the job. I unfolded my bent limbs, stiff from being cramped into the small area, and crawled out with the book and feather duster I'd taken with me.

"It won't happen again," I said, not convinced I could keep myself awake for a whole day with nothing to do but loiter about looking for traces of dust in a spotless room.

"You're not ready to work," she said, eyebrows furrowed with concern.

"Ready? Oh no! I need more to do, not less, now that the floor isn't moving under my feet. Mizzy doesn't need me and this room doesn't either. I'll wear the covers off the books, dusting them all day long."

Mrs. Plea smiled. "Some people think reading is a frivolous pursuit. I gave you this task so you'd have an excuse to be in here. Same with Mizzy's kitchen. I wanted you to rest more than work for a few days. But you can't sleep on the floor. You must sleep in your room, in your bed."

"I can't sleep there."

"Why not?"

"Because it's haunted."

"Haunted! Oh, my!"

"I swear, Mrs. Plea, I shiver like I've got the icy breath of a dead man on my neck. Like somebody's climbed out of a fresh grave and is sinking down and smothering me like a thick fog."

I played the air like a piano. Mrs. Plea listened with wide-eyed concern and I continued.

"When I close my eyes, I see picture after picture of horrible things. I hear muffled yells and agonizing screams and...and death is everywhere."

After blurting it out, I realized I'd gone too far with the part about hearing voices. She might have decided then and there that I was out of my gourd. But instead of appearing shocked, she raised a skeptical eyebrow and motioned for me to join her on the settee. Mr. Jones jumped into my lap and I hung on to him, worried about what would come next.

"I know a lot about haunted places, Charlee. Matter of fact, some people in this town think I'm a witch. A voodoo queen, if you please." She seemed amused by her reputation. "You'll read all about it in the newspapers, so I might just as well tell you myself."

"Are you really?" The possibility enthralled me. I had a million questions for her, but caught myself. "I mean, that's terrible gossip."

"Let's just say, if there were ghosts in this house, I would have met them by now."

She smiled as Mr. Jones jumped from my lap, chose a spot in the middle of the floor and stared at an empty chair in front of the bookshelves. Her eyes swept the room and came to rest on the same chair, as if acknowledging an invisible guest. It's nothing, I told myself. She's playing with the idea, adding to her mystique. Just then, I picked up the scent of tobacco and magnolias, like some cigar-smoking gentleman had entered the room with a bouquet of fresh flowers. My skin prickled. I remembered having a similar feeling in the clearing on Deception Island, like I wasn't alone.

"I read somewhere spirits can hang on to a person and cause all kinds of mischief for them. What if I brought one back with me? I've been around a lot of dead people lately."

"I hadn't thought of that," she said, placing a forefinger on her lips, and I couldn't tell if she was serious. "In which case, you must let them know this is my house and they are welcome, but they had better behave."

"W-I-T-C-H. In witch case." I slapped my thigh. "Oh, I'm going to write a story and call it that! What a superb title!"

"Write that story and you will end up scandalized along with me."

And then she was back to the real problem at hand. Her

smile fell away as she adjusted a silver brooch with a blood-red stone pinned at the collar of her dress.

"You know, this sleeping in odd places is likely the result of the terrible things that have happened to you."

"Yeah, I know. That's why I blame the ghosts. Because if it isn't ghosts keeping me up at night, then the problem is in my head, and people will think I'm crazy."

"For the record, I don't think you're crazy. Not for a minute. You have a busy, rather delightful imagination, and you've been through much hardship. It's also obvious the journey home has exhausted you."

"Until last night, I hadn't slept more than a few hours since leaving Victoria."

"Goodness gracious! That explains a great deal. Mizzy mentioned she found you behind the stove this morning."

So she knew the ugly truth about my sleep problem.

"She said you slept in an alcove in the lighthouse kitchen. A cozy little nook behind the stove?"

"I loved it. Never drafty, tucked away in the heart of the house.

"Makes sense, don't you think?"

It did make sense. I hadn't thought of that. I didn't want to ruin Mizzy's sleep, so I'd gone to a familiar place of comfort.

"But I wonder. What made you go under the desk in here?"

"It's kinda hidden, like the cave I first stayed in on the light-house island."

I stopped short of saying I needed to feel safe to sleep. The hammock aboard the *Sonoma Wind*, with its swaying and rushing water, brought back terrors of the shipwreck. The chilly room down the hall reminded me of staying awake with Mr. Jones to keep our fire going, terrified that I'd die in the dark and cold.

"Ah, I see."

"How did you know I was under there, anyway?"

She glanced at Mr. Jones, who was engaged in some important scratching.

"You've got good people around you, and one very special dog." Mr. Jones sniffed the surrounding air, as if he was too busy to listen in on our conversation, but I knew he'd heard her compliment. "Mizzy has suggested you stay with her for a while. We can fix up a cot. Would that help you sleep in a bed at night?"

"Oh, it would, if it isn't too much trouble." Mizzy's room made me feel calm and strong, like Papa was there with us, too.

"I had a wonderful job to tell you about—they were prepared to train you right away—but it's too soon."

"No, please. I want the job. I'm already better today. One more day and I'll be caught up on my shut-eye. I know I will be."

"Shut-eye."

I was about to explain what I meant, but she said, "I know what it means, cowboy. Now. You'll go straight to Mizzy if you're sleepy?"

"I will. I feel wide awake and pretty good right now."

"Let's see how you get on today. If all goes well, and you sleep through the night, I'll take you to see about that job in the morning. It's housekeeping, but in a medical setting, which I think you'll find interesting. And it's walking distance from here."

"I'll be ready. What should I wear?"

"An ordinary dress. I assume you have one?"

"Yes. I bought one in Victoria, just before I left."

"Very well. Now, forget the dusting and enjoy some reading in here this afternoon. But in a proper chair, yes? We don't want to scare the other guests."

She gestured to the empty room, and I wasn't sure if she meant real house guests or house ghosts. I shrugged in agreement anyhow. Then she rose and crossed the floor with the same floating stride I'd noticed when I first met her in the pantry of the Sunshine Cafe. It was as if her feet weren't in need of a solid floor. She was captivating and mysterious and I wanted to be just like her, except for maybe the voodoo part, which scared me just a little even though I was pretty sure folks had just made that up about her because she was Black and female and fiercely in charge of everything around her.

Like a proper gentleman, Mr. Jones escorted her into the hall.

"*Et tu, Brute*," I hissed at him when he returned.

He gave me a dismissive look that said he was only doing his job and quoting popular bits of Shakespeare didn't impress him in the slightest.

Shakespeare. Mr. Miller's library. Suddenly, I could picture all of his books, which Jake had borrowed for me one by one, all tucked into their proper places upon the walnut shelves in the parlor at the Sonoma ranch. The image was so clear, I could see each spine and title in front of me. I reached out to touch them, but my hand passed through the ghostly image of the library wall.

CHAPTER TWENTY-FOUR

Grace House was less than a mile from Mrs. Plea's residence, mostly uphill. At least the walk home would be easy. On this first day, to show me the way and to make proper introductions, Mrs. Plea had taken me over in her buggy.

Houses close together with small yards turned into bigger houses laid back from the road on broad pieces of land, where animals grazed in fenced fields and crops formed neat rows of lush green. Farther up the bluff, the houses turned into mansions, perched on vast estates with rolling fields that reminded me of the open land around Sonoma.

We followed a winding road up to a point that overlooked San Francisco Bay.

"Not too shabby a spot for a hospice," I said to Mrs. Plea, as I peered out at the rolling lawns and manicured gardens. "It must be expensive to stay here."

"It is. Grace House is a private hospice and I'm well-acquainted with Dr. Benjamin, the owner. He's an associate."

What kind of associate, I wondered. This is how men did business. They called in favors with each other. It dawned on me that Mrs. Plea had a lot of favors she could call upon from the gentlemen, a measure of her personal influence around the town.

"The work won't be hard, and Dr. Benjamin is an excellent doctor."

I clutched the side of the buggy.

"I'm not coming here as a patient."

"No, no. You aren't," she said. "But while you're here, I've asked him to meet with you. You said yourself, you're suffering terrible flashbacks and memory loss. If anyone can help you through those things, it will be him. It's his area."

We rode in silence for several minutes. Trust Mrs. Plea, I heard Mizzy saying to me last summer, right before her people drugged me, loaded me into a bin of vegetables, and smuggled me aboard the *Salish Wind*. She'd been forced to do that, to keep me from blowing her midnight mission for runaway slaves, but that didn't mean I had to agree with her methods. Trust her, Mizzy had whispered to me again, as I got in the buggy half an hour earlier to ride to the hospice. Mr. Jones didn't like me leaving without him and I'd shut him in Mizzy's kitchen so he wouldn't follow. I had to do this alone.

Mrs. Plea knew my head wasn't right the moment she'd laid eyes on me. The Captain must have informed her I'd suffered the journey back. Mizzy told her about my troubled first night, and then she herself had found me under the desk in the parlor. I sat back and rubbed my aching neck. She meant to help. She was smart and well-connected. Trust her, I heard Mizzy say again.

"Did you go to school, Mrs. Plea?"

"Not formally. But a few good men have schooled me."

"Oh. Like the way Mr. Miller let me join his children for tutoring?"

She laughed. "Kind of like that. One must choose carefully among the gentlemen."

"I've got Jake. He's going to go far once he gets himself sorted out."

"No doubt he will. But don't you stand in his shadow. You're clever and resourceful. Times are changing for your generation. You could do many things if you have the courage."

I could do many things? Like what? I was good at math and science and writing and wrangling horses. But nobody wanted a girl to do those things. Jake was going to be a politician or a lawyer or something important one day. I once dreamed of going to school like him to study. But serious subjects weren't an option for girls, let alone a girl like me. My future hung around my neck like a heavy yoke on a mule.

The buggy swung into a shaded drive lined on each side by tall oaks. A sprawling, two-story residence of red brick stood on the highest part of the hill. As we pulled up to the front entrance, a man and a woman came out to greet us. The man was short and had a trimmed, black beard. He wore a crisp white cloak over a herringbone suit. Mrs. Plea introduced him as Dr. Benjamin, and he welcomed her like they'd known each other for a very long time. The woman, white-bib apron over a grey dress, and clean white shoes, stood back from him, awaiting instructions. She'd pulled her black hair back so tight, her eyes looked stretched on each side. Smiling was out of the question. She looked at Mrs. Plea with a sour expression, her unpainted lips pursed in disapproval.

Half an hour later, the woman who had been introduced as Nurse Killey showed me into the second-floor staff room. It was a plain affair, with a row of wooden benches next to cupboards, some washing basins and a looking glass in a wooden frame at one end, and a few small lunch tables and chairs at the other. But it had sheer curtains and a tall window that looked northeast across the bay.

Nurse Killey would never smile, no matter what I said. When she asked if I knew what my job was, I said if I'd been told, I'd already forgotten, and she might have to remind of a lot of things in the coming days. I told her to picture that my head was a watermelon that had dropped off a wagon and rolled down the steep hill towards Mission Road, maybe splitting itself open half way down on a large boulder. Her blank look told me I wasn't funny, she'd heard every hospital joke before, and I should just put on my uniform and stop wasting her time.

"Before your shift each morning, you will wash and change from your personal clothing." She snatched my satchel from me and rummaged through the contents, pulling out anything her hands couldn't identify. She even inspected my extra under-clothes, which was uncalled for given she didn't even know me, but I supposed it was her job and she'd seen it all before. The only thing that gave her pause was my worn copy of Uncle Tom's Cabin. She frowned, told me I wasn't at the hospice to read, and chucked it back in my bag.

"This is your cupboard, although it appears you have nothing of value. We aren't responsible for lost or missing items. We'll feed you lunch. Tie your hair back neatly. There are ribbons in the drawer underneath the basins. I'll return with your first assignment in ten minutes."

"Aye aye, Captain," I said with a salute.

She shot me a mean glare. "You are not aboard a mangy seagoing vessel here, Miss LeBeau. I will not tolerate rude and uncouth behavior. That is the first thing you will do well to remember."

I'd become accustomed to the language of cowboys and sailors. But that kind of familiar banter had set me off on a bad foot with Nurse Killey. She shoved some folded clothing at me that felt scratchy and stiff to the touch, and marched out of the room.

The uniform wasn't as bad as I thought it'd be. Although the cotton apron was starched and stiff, the undergarments were soft and smelled fresh like the ocean. I donned matching white leggings. The water in the basin was clean, unlike at the light-house, where Perkins always greased it up whenever he came in for a meal, leaving it for me or Mrs. Dalworth to empty and change. I washed with strong soap that made me sneeze when I sniffed it, and put my hair in a tight braid. The shoes felt a little stiff and snug, so I left them undone.

While I waited for Nurse Killey to return, I scuffled around the room and touched everything. The brick walls, rough and cool and strong. The slippery curtains that were sashed at the window. The smooth ledge and clean glass of the open window. I gazed at a pretty garden below, where some residents were enjoying the afternoon air. They were all dressed the same. As I watched, I realized if I didn't get my head right, I might end up like them. No doubt I'd sent Mizzy and Mrs. Plea into quiet alarm with my odd behavior. My actual job here was to sort myself out and show them I wasn't damaged beyond repair.

I vowed I would not have any more spells in front of people. I knew what set me off—the horrors of the shipwreck and fear of the unknown. It would start with a buzz behind my eye, then turn into shooting pain through the side of my head, followed by blurred vision, ringing in my ear, and panic. Panic was the point of no return. If I reached panic, I'd lose control and would say or do things I couldn't remember. I would not go to that place again, at least, not here with the doctor watching for signs of mental problems. Oh, I knew he would be. Mrs. Plea didn't say it. She made it sound like I was only here to do gentle work in a tolerable situation and get checked out for future placement in school. But I knew it was more than that. She had to be sure I could be in public without having dangerous fits. When someone is out of control, people get frightened. What better job to test the waters than light domestic work in a hospice owned by a trusted friend?

Dr. Benjamin rapped on the door and waited for me to

acknowledge him before entering. Nurse Killey barged past him, eying my appearance, hands on her hips.

"All's well, I see," said Dr. Benjamin, halting half way across the room. "So. I'd like to meet with you for thirty minutes each day at the start of your shift."

"Half an hour!" Nurse Killey exclaimed and then caught herself when Dr. Benjamin admonished her with a stern glance.

"After that, she's yours for the rest of the day."

"Of course, Doctor. Your office, I assume?"

"No. We'll meet here." He turned to me. "How does that sound, Miss LeBeau?"

"What about the other nurses? I don't want to hog their room." I said to Nurse Killey, whose expression melted ever so slightly at my consideration of her other staff.

"They won't be in here at nine, am I right, Nurse?"

"That is correct." She snipped her words like surgical stitches.

"Now. I've brought some schoolwork for you to tackle, so we can get a sense of your general competencies." He placed a folder on the table. "Do as much as you can, or feel up to, and then Nurse Killey will show you around. Now don't overwhelm her on her first day, Nurse."

"I'll be fine," I said, once again siding with the woman I didn't even like, and knowing full well that if she set me off, I might not handle things at all. A pang of anxiety filled my chest as I realized I was at the mercy of these two strangers. I hoped Mrs. Plea knew what she was doing.

CHAPTER TWENTY-FIVE

After they'd gone, I made myself comfortable at the table and flipped open the folder of work he'd left with me. A set of basic math worksheets. Some pages of lettering to copy onto neat lines. A piece to read and summarize with questions to answer on simple content. It was work for a child, but simple work meant I didn't have to strain my head. I'd slept nine solid hours in Mizzy's room and woke up feeling strong and prepared. But I figured Mrs. Plea had been right. I didn't need to push myself to prove anything.

The writing exercise had potential, even though it was basic. The assignment was to write a paragraph describing someone you'd met. I ignored the small space given. On the backs of the other worksheets, I wrote a story about a man I'd notice in the courtyard from the staff room window. In my story, he was a wonderful stonemason, an immigrant fellow who'd come over from Germany as a young man. One day, when he was finishing a gigantic two-story fireplace, there was an earthquake, and he got buried under a load of heavy river rocks and when they pulled him out, he couldn't talk or walk again and everyone thought he was dumb as a brick. But he knew what was going

160

on and just couldn't say, and a kind woman doctor saw it in his eyes. I was about to add a mystery woman to the story—a German lady, maybe his wife, who was forced to work in the brothels to provide for them, and she'd come to sit with him every Sunday, sadly hoping for his impossible recovery—when the shuffle of soft shoes on the hall tiles told me company was coming. I slapped the file shut and gazed out the window in calm repose.

"You are not working," Nurse Killey said.

"I'm done. It's way too easy."

She marched a lunch tray over to my table. Earlier, Mizzy had declared I wasn't going anywhere until I could finish a meal she put in front of me. Even though I'd cleaned my plate for her only hours ago, I found myself hungry all over again.

Nurse Killey clunked the tray onto the table in front of me. There was a cucumber sandwich, made with thick white bread. Chocolate pudding that some cook had swirled into a crooked peak to make it look elegant. Orange slices fanned out on a saucer. Tea in a plain cup, allowing a person to hold it in a good grip. Not bad at all.

I reminded myself to eat at a speed befitting a young lady. I overcame the urge to dip my finger into the pudding and made sure I didn't slurp or smack like some unmannered sailor. Nurse Killey would watch for things like this. I could see her checking a box under the heading "manners," adding a harsh note that said, "barely acquired, eats like a raccoon."

She picked up the folder and thumbed through the papers, her surprise soon replaced by annoyed suspicion.

"What about the reading book? Surely…"

"That book? I read it when I was nine. Twice. Ask me anything." I shoved it into her hands on top of the papers. She nearly dropped the works.

"You are quite the know-it-all young lady, aren't you?" she said, her black eyes flashing and her thin upper lip curling back on one side. She hadn't liked me from the start and I hadn't improved the situation.

"Look, I'm supposed to be going to high school. College soon. That work is for children. Simple writing? Basic arithmetic? Please. Do you know algebra, Nurse Killey? I know algebra and calculus. And the periodic table. Laws of physics."

"I see," she said, crossing her arms. "Listen to me, Miss High and Mighty. There is a patient in here who composes classical music for full orchestra. Hailed as the most brilliant musician this country might have seen, everyone thought he was going to be another Mozart. Well, they found him dancing around his parlor with the body of his dead wife, weeks after he'd lopped off her head with a kitchen knife. He'd propped her up in a chair by his piano, head in her lap, and played to her for days."

Now that was a great story. It crossed my mind that Nurse Killey might be a better writer than nurse. I put my hands to my mouth, feigning horror, as she expected that reaction. Then I took another bite out of my sandwich.

"That happened?" I mumbled as I chewed.

"It did. That one insane act canceled out all of his brilliance. You are very much at risk of crossing that delicate line yourself."

The mouthful of sandwich I'd swallowed lodged in my throat. I washed it down with a gulp of tea.

"Ladies take smaller bites. Enough chatter. There is work to be done. Bring that tray. And do up those shoes!"

I tied my laces and followed her out of the room without another word.

I arrived early for my shift the next morning. Changed and ready with fifteen minutes to spare, I paced around in nervous anticipation, tidying a few things, and moving some things to better, more logical places. Nurse Killey had increased my dread by criticizing me as she passed the staff room. I'd accidentally creased my apron by putting it away incorrectly the day before.

After another lap of the room, I turned at the far wall to see Dr. Benjamin standing in the doorway. He was wearing the same white coat from yesterday over another expensive suit. He was right on time, and I was expecting him. But like the Captain, I felt like he'd snuck up on me.

"Nurse Killey swiped my boots," I said, placing my hands on my hips in protest. I almost called her Nurse Killjoy, the name I'd given her when I was telling Mizzy and Mr. Jones about my first taxing day at the hospice.

"Good morning to you as well, Miss LeBeau," he said, ignoring my hostility. "That was my doing. You'll get them back at the end of your shift."

"I can't be separated from my boots. Cowboy policy. I'd appreciate it if you'd return them. You got plenty of empty drawers in this room. I can keep them with my other things."

"Your boots are unique and we do not need them stolen. Surely your cowboy policy has something to say about that." He strolled across the room. His own black shoes were scuffed, like it was the one part of his otherwise dapper wardrobe that he failed to notice.

"You've rearranged some things," he said, motioning for me to sit with him at the table I'd moved under the window.

He opened his folder and scribbled something down. I realized everything I did and said would end up in that folder. Later, he'd sit down at his big fat desk somewhere and he'd start today's entry with, "found patient agitated, pacing room, in a disagreeable mood, furniture rearranged."

I smoothed out the furrow in my brow and smiled as I took the chair opposite him.

"I should have asked before moving the table. It's such a pretty view from here. And how lovely for the nurses to sit by an open window during breaks, don't you think, Doctor Benjamin? Fresh air is so very good for the health."

I'd poured it on too thick and he could tell I wasn't sincere. His smile formed a flat line of patience and amusement, and he made more notes in his folder.

First, I'd greeted him with guns blazing and then I'd dumped half a sack of sugar in his tea. I had to find a balance between brutal honesty and sweet manipulation. He was taking notes on everything.

"So we get off on, shall we say, a good foot," he said, with emphasis, "Your boots are safe in my office, just down the hall."

I grinned at the intended pun, and it pleased him to see I'd caught it.

"This table is nice by the window. I can see why you'd like to sit here, and why you think the other ladies might enjoy the view as well."

Sly bit of empathy to get me to go along with him, but I already realized I had no choice but to do whatever he saw fit.

"What is it about those boots that are so important?" he asked. "Beyond cowboy policy, as you call it?"

My stomach clenched. He was digging.

"They were a gift from my papa on my thirteenth birthday."

"They are special then."

"Very, yes."

"I thought as much. The left one appears to have been cut and repaired. Is there a story about that?"

I pictured myself in the island cave with Shenoa, the young Indian woman. She'd had to cut my boot to get it off my foot. Days later, I'd sewn it back together. I remembered it like a vague, patchwork dream.

"The time I fell, I also twisted my ankle. You know what it's like to get a boot off a swollen foot?"

"I do indeed. Was it broken then?"

"No. But very swollen and painful for...for days. Weeks, actually. Wasn't sure I'd ever get my fat foot back in a shoe."

He'd been writing notes. Talking about my ankle injury was good. It was part of my accident, and it steered the conversation away from Papa. I didn't want to talk about his death since it had nothing to do with my head problems. I didn't need some doctor poking too deep into other dark corners of my life. He was still writing. Watching how he formed letters on the paper, I decided he was cautious, fussy with details, but warm and kind. But like his shoes, he didn't catch everything. He didn't notice me watching and making mental notes about him.

When he'd finished, he laid out a plan for me, and I was relieved it matched what Mrs. Plea had said. He would give me some tests to start, and assignments to take home, if I was willing, to assess my readiness for school. As an aside, he mentioned he'd help me deal with trauma and memory loss. He said he knew that Nurse Killey was severe and demanding, but she was also the best nurse he'd ever come across and hoped I'd get along with her in the coming weeks. He didn't see me doing the hospice job for long, but if it worked out, I'd be welcome to stay on. Everything he said brought immense relief, because he wasn't deciding anything for me. And even though I didn't know what I'd study if I went to school, I saw no harm in finding out if I had the brains for it, or whatever else a girl like me might do.

CHAPTER TWENTY-SIX

Besides a mental assessment, I had to pass a physical test before Dr. Benjamin would allow me to work at the hospice. Like the young doctor on the *Sonoma Wind*, he conducted a standard examination by looking in each eye with a magnifying glass, then asking me to count fingers he held up and moved from side to side.

He followed this by asking me to read from a card, while covering one eye and the other. Dr. Benjamin's card had a passage printed in huge block letters. I recited the four lines of "Mary Had A Little Lamb" with considerable drama, and then giggled.

"Straightforward, I see. But what do you find so funny?"

"The doctor I saw in Victoria gave me the same test, but he had me read the Oregon Constitution."

"My word! For an eye examination? I didn't think Oregon had one of those yet."

"It's in the works. I think he used what he had handy."

I rattled off a few more lines of what I'd seen a few weeks earlier, surprising us both with my accurate recall. He studied me for a long moment, then slapped his notebook shut.

"C'mon.. Let's go outside. You'll have to manage in the nurse's shoes, though. Nurse Killey says they're easy on the feet, so perhaps that makes up for what they lack in style."

His eyebrows lifted with a playful smile. I could see why Mrs. Plea liked him. His warmth and wit could soften tough new leather. The uniform shoes didn't even pinch when I laced them up.

A set of stairs outside the staff room led down to a court-yard, where we settled at a sunny table with two wooden chairs and talked about my accident and what I remembered from the time. We had a view of the entire courtyard and the rolling fields surrounding the hospice. The beauty was impossible to ignore.

As we talked, the nurses brought patients out into the fresh air and sunshine. There was an older man with disheveled grey hair and a drooping face. With help from his nurse and a wooden cane, he shuffled to a chair. Once seated, he looked at the ground by his feet, mumbled to himself, and fell asleep with his head on his chest. There was a frail, bird-like woman in a rolling chair. The nurse who wheeled her out tucked a colorful knitted blanket around her legs, but as soon as she left, it slipped off and the woman did not try to catch it. I left Dr. Benjamin in mid-sentence, crossed the courtyard and tucked it back around her legs. She looked up with cloudy eyes and a puzzled expression. I didn't know what to say to her. All I could come up with was, "There you go, ma'am."

"That was kind of you," Dr. Benjamin said as I returned to my chair. Then he made a note of it.

"What's wrong with the people in here?"

"Many things. This isn't a place where people get better, typically."

"Palliative, then."

"Yes."

His eyes met mine, a twinkle of surprise quickly concealed behind his calm doctor expression.

"But I'll get better, right?"

"Mrs. Plea believes so."

"What about you? You're the expert. What do you think?"

"I'm just getting to know you. What do you think I believe?"

"I think, as a doctor, they trained you in science. Science seeks to find evidence for things, which is why you take so many notes. For example, back in the old days, they thought the world was flat. And why do we now know the world is round? Because when a boat sails away, it doesn't fall off an edge or sink into the ocean as it disappears on the horizon. It comes back. Unless it's robbed and sunk, of course. Or some other misfortune happens that has nothing to do with the shape of the earth. Anyhow, its journey away and back provides scientific evidence. So I think you are looking for evidence that my mind hasn't sailed off for good, like that poor lady over there, one map short of ever finding her way home."

The doctor leaned forward with his elbows on his knees. "That's accurate, albeit rather colorfully explained."

"But how does evidence work with people and their minds? How do you know what's in there other than by what people tell you? Like me, for example."

Dr. Benjamin scratched his beard.

"Well, I noted you moved the table in the staff room by yourself, without marking the floor. Evidence that you have considerable physical strength for a girl of your age. Also, evidence of an attitude of non-conformity." He paused. "Do you know what that is?"

"High-spirited, they called it when I was young."

"You still are young, but yes. A high-spirited nature. It can be a mark of intelligence."

"Or madness."

Dr. Benjamin didn't respond to that, which confirmed he still wasn't sure which one applied to me. On the way back inside, he asked me what it was like to sail on a schooner and when I described the incredible beauty and the terrifying power of the ocean, he said "how magnificent" and other such remarks, and didn't stop to take any notes.

Nurse Killjoy was in the staff room, struggling to drag the table back to its original spot.

"Leave it by the window, would you please?" Dr. Benjamin said as we walked in.

"Yes, Doctor." She shoved it back against the wall, its legs screeching over the tile. "If you're sure she won't stand on it and jump out."

Dr. Benjamin's face drained of color, as if he'd imagined me climbing on the table and flinging myself out the open window. In an instant, he'd seen me crashing in a broken heap beside the hydrangeas, blood oozing from my smashed skull, arms and legs bent in all wrong directions, hospital dress pulled up, a puddle of red snaking out from under my torso. It had crossed his mind and left him shaken, thanks to Nurse Killjoy.

And what kind of place was this, if tables had to be kept from windows so even the staff wouldn't leap to a messy death?

"Don't worry," I said, in a sing-song voice. "If I wanted to die, I'd have thrown myself overboard sailing back to San Fran."

I plopped down at the table and ran my hands over its smooth wood, enjoying their shock and horror at my matter-of-fact comment.

"This is a perfect place to sit and think. Do you allow staff to read or write in here on lunch breaks?"

My question snapped Dr. Benjamin out of imagined horrors.

"Of course! We'll provide you with materials. Like me, Nurse Killey, I suspect the only thing that will drive her completely mad is to be without a book or pen."

His joke smacked a bent nail a little too hard on the head, but it was still mighty funny. He chuckled along with me, no doubt relieved that his awkward remark had landed without breaking anything.

Nurse Killjoy didn't smile. The woman had no sense of humor.

"I'll see to it," she said, bowing her head, annoyance lurking behind narrow eyes.

After my shift, as I was collecting my boots in Dr. Benjamin's office, he asked how my day had gone, to which I replied it had been pretty good. Nurse Killjoy had already gotten to him, and told him I had coped with my assigned tasks, but was prone to distraction.

Of course, I was distracted. I was bored to death. I had to think about other things to make time move faster. Plus, knowing I was under close watch, I was careful to behave like an ordinary girl, even though I hadn't fully caught up on sleep and wobbled now and then from lingering sea legs. Overall, I'd had a good day and Dr. Benjamin said Mrs. Plea would be pleased. On hearing that news, I exhaled like I'd been holding my breath. Managing myself all day was hard work.

Dr. Benjamin sent me off with homework. He noticed I was tired and said I didn't have to do it all in one night. When I told him I looked forward to it, he seemed encouraged, but repeated his caution. Yet another adult telling me not to push myself. It seemed to be the common message, and I realized I'd heard it so often I'd started telling myself the same thing.

The work turned out to be arithmetic problems, and some written passages with questions. A dozen pages in all. I cut through it in fifteen minutes while sipping tea and reading a daily newspaper at the mahogany desk in Mrs. Plea's parlor. Some of the last pages required a little more attention—introductory algebra and written analysis—but they were still a breeze. I finished that work at the kitchen table while Mizzy put away dishes and we chatted about what we'd all done that day. The biggest news was Mr. Jones had escaped the kitchen and met me on the road by the hospice. On the walk back, he vowed he'd wait at the foot of the drive and never wander off, so I told Mizzy he didn't have to be kept inside anymore. That made all of three of us happy.

Doctor Benjamin reviewed my homework the next morning as I swapped out my boots for my nurse's shoes in his office. His eyebrows danced as he flipped through my papers, only stopping on the last page and placing his finger on a comment I'd written in the margin, criticizing the vague wording of a particular question. Aside from that, I was sure there were no mistakes.

"Good," was all he said.

That night, he gave me harder homework. No more grade school worksheets to fill out. This work required concentration. I had to read, think, analyze, write, and remember. The last skill was the hardest. I knew I could recall things I'd learned before, but it often took me a while to find where old information was hiding, to dig it up and bring it to the front of my mind.

The chart I'd made on the way back to San Francisco had helped me untangle and make sense of my memories. I'd also used it to test myself on random things, like objects seen when passing by an open door, because I could picture things like that with ease before my accident. Since leaving Victoria, a lot of memories had fallen back into place.

At first, memories came to me daily, and they didn't fade away. If I closed my one weak eye, I could even glance at a page, picture it in my head and remember it the next day. I was excited to feel the fog lift from around my head, but also nervous about what I'd see lurking around me. But then memory fragments came at me fast. I scribbled them all over my chart, turning it into a chaotic list of circled words, bad guesses, crossed out thoughts and demanding questions. My notes piled up in a menacing heap and I used them against myself like an angry juror who'd conspired to find me guilty. I was losing sight of my evidence.

CHAPTER TWENTY-SEVEN

On the third day of work, Dr. Benjamin cut our meeting short because of an emergency. I was immersed in a Latin phrase book he'd left with me when there was a light knock at the open door.

"*Introvenio*," I said, expecting Nurse Killjoy with my first tedious chore of the day. I snapped the book shut and turned to see Jake Miller standing in the doorway.

"Jake! What are you doing here?"

He shuffled from one foot to the other, his thumbs tucked into his trouser pockets as he'd always done when he'd hung around the stables with me growing up. His cheeks were flushed, like he'd run all the way up the steep hospice drive.

"We sail today and I had to talk to you." He looked around the room. "What do they have you doing in this place? Is it all right?"

He gazed at my hospital dress and apron, down at my sock feet, and the ugly shoes I'd cast off under the table.

"I start with a morning meeting to help me get my head sorted out. Then I do simple nursing jobs for the rest of the day that nearly make me mental all over again."

"Sounds all right. Did I hear you speak Latin when I came in?"

"You did."

He could never get me to learn a word of it when we lived on the ranch. He smacked his forehead with a palm.

"*Veni, vidi, vici.* I have conquered."

I ignored his claim to victory and offered him a chair, which he carried over to the door.

"Where are you taking that?"

"Over here, so I can keep an eye out." He eased into the chair, his long legs folding up like a spider. "I gotta say, you already look a million times better. I knew Mizzy would bring you around. Your hair is nice like that, by the way. Kinda pretty, like old times."

I had braided my shoulder-length hair and tied it with a small red ribbon, according to orders. On the ranch, my hair was long and always in a single braid. I didn't think he'd ever noticed, or even liked it.

He leaned back and squinted down the hall. "That Nurse. She's a tough bag of hammers, that one."

"Her name's Killey, but I call her Nurse Killjoy."

Jake snickered. "Well, Killjoy gave me strict orders. She wasn't going to let me in at all, and not without a chaperone, but some doctor passing by told her to allow it. She said she'd be watching and if she heard so much as a chuckle from this end of the hall, she'd throw me out. I don't think she likes me."

"Don't take it personal. She doesn't like anybody."

He leaned back again, tipping the chair precariously back on two legs, and checked the hall. I looked him over from head to toe. He'd lost most of his boyish awkwardness. His broadening shoulders balanced out his long limbs, but his feet still seemed a few sizes too big for his height.

"I've only got a few minutes," he said, leaning forward, speaking in a whisper now.

"You came all the way for a few minutes?"

"I shouldn't have come at all. But I saw something you should know about."

Jake told me that while talking with the Captain in his quarters the night before, he saw an unusual hand-drawn map sticking out of a book on his desk.

"It was the map you told me you drew of Deception Island."

I shot out of my chair. "What? Are you sure?"

"Positive. I know how you draw, from the maps we made when we were kids."

My mind raced as Jake described the mapping symbols we'd used and how he'd seen them on this drawing. How did the Captain get his manicured mitts on my island map? The pirates had stolen it from Mrs. Dalworth. If it was now in his possession, he had to be in cahoots with them.

"Does he know you saw it?"

"I don't think so. But he stashed it as soon as I wasn't looking."

The news made my eye twitch. I rubbed it before it became worse.

"This is a big deal. It means he's in on it."

"It means something, that's for sure. Do you want me to steal it back when I get a chance?"

"Absolutely not! He can't know we're on to him. Just watch him."

A rhythmic clicking on the hall tiles caught Jake's attention, and he stretched his neck outside the room. "Oh no!" He almost tipped his chair over as he got up, flapping his hand at someone to hurry.

Mr. Jones appeared at the door, looking at both of us like a dog wandering a hospital corridor was nothing out of the ordinary. Jake snatched him up from the hall. "He followed me! That nurse will have our heads if she sees him. I'll smuggle him out."

"I mean, he has a white coat. He kinda fits in," I said, amused by Jake's fear of Nurse Killjoy's wrath.

Just then, the rattle of a trolley echoed in the hall. Jake said, "She's coming! What'll we do?"

"I'll distract her." I said, lacing up my ugly shoes. "When I've got her busy, take the stairs on the left. They exit into the garden. Cut through the tall hedge to the drive."

"What do I do with him?"

"Drop him down by the road. He'll wait there till I finish work. Won't you, Mr. Jones?" I added. He stole a look at me sideways, knowing he'd put all of us in a sticky situation.

Jake slung Mr. Jones under his arm and I peeked around the door jamb. Nurse Killjoy had paused at the end of the hall, outside the supply closet.

"Wait till I get her back turned."

"Aye. See you in a few weeks."

"Keep your wits about you, sailor."

"You as well." He squeezed my arm and I hurried up the hall.

It didn't take me long to get Nurse Killjoy boxed into the supply closet with her cart blocking the way out. It was worth the reprimand I got for my clumsiness to make sure Jake and Mr. Jones made a clean getaway.

When Mr. Jones spotted the trolley in the hall, he mistook it for some large, dangerous animal. He was about to launch into a loud round of barking, but Jake clapped a hand over his snout and only one muffled woof escaped. Fortunately, Nurse Killjoy had her head behind the stacked towels and was none the wiser.

Nurse Killjoy was a problem I had to learn to manage. That morning, she'd showed up when I was fixing my hair and had taken exception to how quickly I brushed it. One hundred strokes was required daily, she said, and I told her there was no science to prove brushing that much made hair stronger or improved health. When I added too much brushing might even make a person bald, she yanked my braid and called me ill-mannered and disobedient.

Jake's inappropriate visit, plus the incident in the supply closet, all happened before ten o'clock. It was a deep hole to dig myself out of, with still a whole day left for mistakes to be noted. To make matters worse, they served tripe stew for lunch. Never mind that I didn't like it on a good day, or that it looked as appealing as something down an outhouse hole. Maybe I would have eaten it last year when I was starving. But this wasn't last year.

"Blech!" I exclaimed after she demanded I try it. "It's horrible. If you make me eat it, it'll end up all over your clean white shoes."

"It's not that bad. You exaggerate everything."

"Not this. My stomach will not keep it down."

"Very well. I will note on your record that you refused to eat and were hostile."

"No, please don't do that! See, I'm thinking about maybe... becoming a nurse."

Nurse Killjoy straightened, pleased by this unexpected news.

"A nurse. Like me," she said. Her nostrils widened. The corners of her mouth were dying to smile. If she'd had tail feathers, she would have spread them out across the room.

"Maybe you have some simple nursing tasks I could help you with? Like what duties does a nurse have, anyway?" I rested my chin on my hands to make myself look interested.

She launched into a very enthusiastic description of every little thing she had to do in a day, as well as things she had to be prepared for, and the horrific situations that she'd seen in her nursing days. I knew five minutes into her lengthy presentation that nursing wasn't for me. Most of it sounded like a calling, and it wasn't calling to me. It was yelling at me to run the other way.

The most interesting part of her work was dealing with patients much more difficult than me, and I wasn't sure I'd be any good at that, as I wasn't inclined to patience with people. But I made a mental note of the tedious things that made her tone sour, things she said were not the glamorous part of the work. None of it sounded glamorous to me, but I saw a way to get her on my side.

"How about I clean the staffroom for you? I'll come early to scrub the floors before I see Dr. Ben," I offered. "Besides my usual duties."

She considered the offer. The idea of me taking on more work had to be irresistible.

"This isn't a ship. You'd have to scrub them with disinfectant and as I instruct."

"Of course. And I saw you fill out a chart as you put things away in the supply closet. Why don't I do that for you as well, after folding the morning laundry? I have a knack for inventory."

She brightened a little. "You have the penmanship. Still, you must write plain and be precise."

One more suggestion for the win.

"If it isn't too much to ask, do you have a nursing book you could loan me? So I can study the basics?"

She was beaming now. She leaned in to share a confidence.

"The first book on domestic management in hospitals is excellent. I'll lend you my copy."

Domestic management. The tripe stew of books. I imagined it would cover making up sick beds, cleaning bedpans, and, yes, folding laundry. There would be nothing about how to overlook a banned book concealed in a pillowcase, or how to turn a blind eye to the apple pie stashed in a bedside drawer, or how to catch a thief stealing from the infirm. Still, I'd read anything to get her on my side. I needed favorable reports going to Dr. Benjamin and Mrs. Plea.

Nurse Killey pushed aside the cold bowl of stew on my lunch tray.

"You know, I couldn't eat that myself today. Some days, they get it quite wrong in the kitchen."

She put her hand up to her mouth and burped. Her face contorted as she tried not to laugh, which resulted in a gulp of air and an unladylike snort. That set both of us off into suppressed giggles. She knew how to laugh, after all. She just wasn't in the habit of it.

CHAPTER TWENTY-EIGHT

"You know, this nurse I'm assigned to is a real strange bird," I said to Mizzy later that week as we got ready for bed.

"Maybe so, but she's head nurse and you gotta mind what she says."

"Oh, I do. I'm figuring her out. Do you ever wonder how some folks turn out the way they do?"

"I look at you and think it all the time. I see Luke in you, but I know you also got your mama. The spitting image of her, Luke said, plus headstrong and fierce like she was."

She'd sat on the end of her bed facing the door, and I sensed she was getting ready to tell me more. I kept my mouth shut and didn't move so as not to ruin the chance.

"Luke told me everything the day before he passed. He'd had another bad spell that day and he started on about dying."

"I don't understand." I sat down beside her and Mr. Jones hopped into my lap.

"It's like he knew his time was up. They say some folks know when their time is close. But I told him to hush that foolish talk, thought he was worryin' over nothin'."

The conversation had not gone in the direction I expected.

"What do you mean, 'he'd had another bad spell'?"

"He had a condition."

I stared at her in disbelief. "What? What kind of condition? He had a bad shoulder, if that's what you mean."

"Weren't his shoulder. His heart gave out, just like he feared it would. He told me it was gonna happen, and I didn't wanna hear it."

"I didn't know."

"Me neither, till that day, right 'fore he died, I never knew his heart was bad. Mr. Miller and Doc knew, but he kept it a secret from us. I was mad at him, then upset, and he said, 'See there, that's why I didn't tell y'all.' He didn't want a cloud hangin' over us, and both of us watching him like a hawk, thinkin' every time he had a slight pain, the end was near. I woulda worried and pretty sure you woulda, too. He was going to have a talk with you the next day, but he never got the chance. Maybe he was right—it don't make no difference one way or the other how it happened in the end."

Knowing wouldn't bring him back. That much was true. But I'd blamed Bernadette Miller for causing his death. He'd sprinted to the corral and leaped over the gate to save her from getting trampled. She shouldn't have climbed up on that stallion's fence, but she did, and Papa ran to save her. It wasn't just his job, it was his nature, and it cost him.

"He should have told me, and you."

My words had hard edges. I'd never criticized Papa about anything.

Mizzy handed me a fresh nightshirt. I buried my face in it, the soapy scent a comfort and a reminder of the good years we had together on the Sonoma ranch.

"Don't be mad at him, Charolat. He was lookin' out for you, for both of us, best he knew how."

"I know. And I was still a kid then."

"You still are," she said, hugging my shoulders. She got up and turned down my bed.

"Now, let's get back to Nurse Killjoy…or whatever her name is. Your Papa's situation is a good lesson. We don't always know a person's whole story, what they been through, or what burdens they carry. If she seems mad all the time, she's probably hurtin'. Most folks ain't ornery for no reason. That don't mean it's right for her to take it out on you, though."

I'd never even thought of Nurse Killey as a real person, with another life away from the hospice. I didn't know if she had family anywhere, where she came from, or what she had to put up with to become a nurse. I knew nothing about her and had been acting like a know-it-all, just as she'd said.

"I guess I'm a poor judge of character."

"You ain't quick to trust folks, is all, and you got some mighty good reasons. People gotta earn your trust. But judging a book by its cover don't always work."

I smiled at her choice of metaphor, using my love of books to make her point. I pulled off my socks and crawled under my quilt.

"And look at this fella." Mizzy lifted Mr. Jones onto the bed beside me. "How many people were scared o' him before they knew him?"

"I wasn't."

"Just like your Papa that way. You and animals got some kinda secret language."

Mr. Jones waited for me to make room for him in his usual spot. He circled three times, and then curled up beside me.

I tucked myself around him. Mizzy patted his shoulder, kissed my forehead, and turned out the lantern.

At the table in the staff room, by the window that looked into the courtyard at Grace House, I watched the last grains of sand funnel through a gigantic hourglass on the table. I reached out to flip it over, but my fingers felt clumsy and odd and wouldn't grasp it. The hourglass wobbled and tipped, then fell end over end towards the tile floor, as if time had halted. I gasped, the shattering of glass and flying shards inevitable. "Catch it, Charlee," Papa whispered. "Catch it before time runs out." My hand flew out and caught the hourglass inches above the floor. I set it back on the table, steadied it with two hands, and the sand began to run again.

My body lurched and my eyes sprung open. Bright moonlight shone through a gap in the sheer curtains on the window, lighting up the entire room and casting Mizzy's bed against the opposite wall in a pale glow. Her breathing was deep and even, her thick bedcovers an unmoving mound. She'd turned onto her side, facing away from me. Mr. Jones wasn't beside me anymore, but the spot where he'd been sleeping was still warm.

I sat up and let my bare feet touch the cold floor. The hourglass from my dream lingered in the space in front of me, transparent and bobbing like a jellyfish in tidal waters. As it faded away, everything that had happened to me in the past year appeared in my mind, in particular, the time I'd lost following the shipwreck and my accident on the island trail. All the missing days became clear. The memories were as fresh as if they'd just happened.

I flung my covers aside, dug my notebook and pencil out from under my mattress and pulled on the socks I'd thrown on the floor by my bed. I swung a foot around, feeling for Mr. Jones, but he wasn't there. As I eased myself to my feet, a spring on the cot squeaked out a loud complaint. Mizzy always slept with one eye open, but this time, she didn't stir. I groped my way over to the small table by the window, lit up in a perfect beam of eerie white moonlight.

I stared at the remaining blank pages in my notebook, remembering my time on the island, calculating the number of pages I had left and how many days I might have until I ran out. My small handwriting from that time wasn't the work of a troubled mind. Not knowing where I was, or how long I'd be there, I'd written small to conserve space! Now, with only a dozen pages left in my notebook, I shrunk my handwriting down to the same tiny script I'd used on the island, just as I'd done before. Every single memory of my island survival poured out of me onto the paper. I tried to keep up with the gush of details, letting my pencil fly across the page, keeping pace with the sand running through the imaginary hourglass in my head.

I wrote for what seemed like hours, my hand cramping from writing small enough to get everything onto the empty pages. My pencil grew dull and annoying, but I couldn't stop to get my pocket knife and sharpen it. I drifted around the room, chasing the light of the moonbeam as it traveled. I'd finished writing all I could when the moon moved past the back of Mrs. Plea's house. In the disappearing light, I rubbed my aching hand and stared at the shadowy pages of memories. They were all there, except for one, and it was the most important thing of all that was still missing. Mr. Miller's gold. Where had I moved it a second time? I wracked my tired brain, pencil in hand in case it came to me, but my brain would not reveal it. I sat back down at the table and laid my head on my arms. It will come to me in due time. I know it will.

"That's enough for tonight, Charlee. You nearly wore that pencil down to a nub."

Papa had said those same words to me in our cabin on the Sonoma ranch the day before he died. I turned and saw him sitting on the end of my bed, looking alive and well, repairing tack, as he'd often do in evenings on the ranch. It was like nothing had happened to him.

"Papa?" I closed my eyes, pressing the heels of my hands into each socket. He was still there when I took my hands away.

"That's a fine howdy do. Haven't seen you for a blue moon and that's the sad welcome I get?"

"You're not real. I'm making you up."

"How 'bout I'm the real one and I'm making you up?" A wayward lock of black hair fell down over his forehead, just like I always remembered. His clear grey eyes twinkled with amusement.

"That's not funny. I've had a hard time telling the difference."

"I know. Put them papers away now. I rode a long way to come tell you a story." He patted the blankets beside him.

I shoved my notebook under the mattress and crawled back into bed.

"Hush now, we don't want to wake up our Mizzy."

I was dreaming. If I wasn't, Mizzy would have woken up at the sound of our voices. He stood beside her now, tucking the patchwork quilt up over her shoulder. Our Mizzy, he'd said. What she wouldn't do to see Papa again! Even though it was my dream, I couldn't arrange it for her. I blinked, and he was sitting on the bed beside me.

"Now then. You were too little to remember, not even three years. One night out on the trail, you heard the wolves howling and wouldn't sleep. Your mama was making a basket by the campfire. She held you in her lap as she worked. It was a beautiful summer night, warm and full of life."

I became that small child again. I looked up into the face of my mama, glowing in the firelight. For the first time, her face was clear in my mind. Hundreds of stars, twinkled like pretty beads, sewn into the black sky above her head.

"I remember," I said.

"You asked her, plain as can be, 'Mama', you says, 'where did we come from?' Smart little one right from the start. Your mama says, 'Chalala,' that's what she called you, 'Chalala,' she says, 'we come from the stars. Every star you see is an ancestor, so if you are ever alone or frightened, ask and they will help you.'"

"Chalala. I remember her now."

CHAPTER TWENTY-NINE

S oft morning light filled the room. Mizzy bent over me, poking my shoulder with one long finger, like I was some kind of possum playing dead.

"Ahhh!" I hollered, bolting upright. She shrunk back in surprise, steadying the coffee cup she held in her other hand.

"Lordy! You scared me, Charolat, comin' to life all of a sudden."

I rubbed sleep from my eyes. "What time is it?"

"Seven. You were sleepin' so peaceful. I let you be."

I looked around. Nothing was out of the ordinary in the room except my bed, which was torn apart like I'd pitched the entire night with a mad fever. The sheets on my cot were wrapped around my legs like thick vines. I'd jammed my pillow between the cot and the wall.

Mr. Jones jumped up and pressed himself against my side.

"And where were you?"

He looked at my tangled sheets as if the answer was obvious.

"The moon woke me in the middle of the night. And then after, I had some pretty wild dreams."

"The moon?" Mizzy looked puzzled. She set the mug down

on the table. I'd left my pencil there, but it was gone now. "What moon?"

"It lit up the entire room. It was so bright. But guess what, Mizzy? My memories came back last night. Almost all of them."

"I knew it! You been doing so well, good color in your cheeks these days. C'mon, wash up and get dressed. You can tell me all about it at breakfast." She handed me a towel and added, "Weren't no moon last night, though. You musta dreamed that."

No moon? As soon as she was gone, I slid my hand under the mattress and felt for my notebook. Still there. Did I write in it or had I just dreamed I did that, too? I flipped to the back. The pages were full!

I let the book fall into my lap as a memory on the open page became a vivid picture in my mind, like wind filling a waiting sail. After my fall on Deception Island, the young Indian woman who found me had helped me return to my cave, and cared for me. I would have died without her. She told me the ancestors had sent her to help me, just like Papa told me in his story. She told me I should ask Mizzy about what happened to my mama.

Mizzy was half way through the breakfast dishes when I made it to the kitchen. I grabbed a drying towel, but she swatted me away.

"Your breakfast's keepin' warm on the stove. Never known you to be such a slowpoke gettin' up. You must be cartin' around a load of big thoughts this morning."

"Oh, I am. But things are making sense now. It's all becoming clear."

I rattled off all the things I remembered as I ate breakfast at Mizzy's cooking counter.

When I was done, Mizzy filled our mugs with coffee and said, "Somebody watchin' over you, Charolat. I swear you got a mission God wants you on."

"Sometimes I think so, too. But one thing is in the way. I have to know what happened to my mama."

She moved a stack of plates to the end of the table, a pointless relocation undertaken to put the conversation in a less painful place. She clenched her skirt.

"The very day before your papa died, he was fixin' to tell you. He told me, in case something happened to him. You recollected something about that time last night?"

"No. Just island stuff. Her face is clear, though, and something that dangled around her neck and made a clacking sound that I liked to play with. I always thought I'd imagine those things, just to have something of her to keep with me. Most of my memories start at the bush cabin in Oregon, but Mama wasn't ever there."

"No, she weren't. Luke took you there after the trouble at the homestead."

My heart dropped into my belly. "What trouble?"

She rubbed her forehead and began.

"When you were still a baby, your papa and mama left the Red River Valley with some folks and come west to the Willamette in Oregon."

"I know that. Papa told me."

"They made a new start on a tough piece of land given to them by the Hudson's Bay Company. That sorry deal broke a lot of promises—they got west and found there weren't enough livestock, seeds, or tools to go around. And some settlers didn't like the Red River Indian folk getting a fair share."

I already knew most of that, too, but if she had to take a run at the rest, I'd keep quiet and let her. She paused, pressed the back of her hand to her lips. I could tell what I was going to hear pained her to repeat. A terrible pressure enclosed me, crushing my chest with heavy dread. I took a breath and pulled a chair over for her.

"I'm ready. Go on."

She sat down across from me, clasped her hands in her lap, and stared at her fidgeting thumbs.

"It was late fall. Your papa had gone hunting. Usually, you'd all go, but this time, your mama stayed back 'cause she weren't feeling well. Your mama could handle herself, Luke said, so it weren't unusual. But when your papa come home three days later, he found you in a horse stall in a frightful state and she was gone."

"Gone? What do you mean, 'gone'? She left?"

Mizzy took my arm. "She left, but…"

"But what? She ran away and left me?"

"No, Charolat. Your papa said…" Mizzy took both of my hands in hers. "Your papa said she left against her will."

"Wha…why'd he say that?"

"Venison stew on the stove, picked vegetables in a basket on the porch, none of her things gone, not even her most special things, and you, hidden away in the stable. It was sudden, like she'd been in the middle of making supper. Her horse was gone. There were two sets of tracks with it. Your papa followed them until they disappeared at the river."

I gripped the edge of the table as my eyes blurred. The surrounding room flashed blood red. I didn't recognize the sound of my voice.

"Somebody took her? You're saying somebody came…and took her?"

"Your papa searched for weeks. Left you with a neighbor. Even went to the local sheriff, but that man laughed and told him your mama's kind were always takin' off and he wouldn't waste anyone's time lookin' for her. Your papa found her horse in a town some fifty miles away. A couple of traveling preachers claimed she'd sold it to them."

My entire body shook as I pushed myself away from the table. I wanted to clear every single dish onto the floor with my arms.

"Liars! They stole it from her and…"

My head pounded and I choked on the words. Mizzy

wrapped her arms around me as I collapsed back into my chair. My voice was torn, nothing more than a raspy whisper.

"They killed her, didn't they? Those men?"

She didn't answer right away, which added to my worst fear.

"We won't never know. But one thing I know for sure is your mama hid you in that barn to save you. When your papa told me, I knew it in an instant 'cause I woulda done the same if I saw trouble ridin' in."

My breath caught in my chest. I remembered a horse stall. I remembered playing a game with Mama and hiding in a pile of straw, waiting and waiting and waiting for her to come dig me out. She never did.

My anger burst into a flood of pain and unstoppable tears. Mizzy pulled me to her shoulder and rocked me back and forth, cradling my head with her hand. She held me like that for a very long time. Then I wiped my eyes with my hands and she handed me a dinner napkin for my slobbery nose.

"See why I didn't tell you? Why your papa kept it from you? Still don't know if tellin' you is the right thing. Some things are better left in the past."

I blew my nose, which made my head throb worse than it did from crying.

"I think I always knew there was more. Papa let it slip once, when I asked him why we didn't get sick and die with Mama. He said the sickness only picked on women. Why are some men so cruel, Mizzy?"

Mizzy brushed away her own tears and set her jaw into a hard line.

"Might as well tell the whole truth, Charolat. Get it all out, once and for all. She ain't the only one. They started coming for me when I was younger than you, and don't ask me to talk about it 'cause I can't. All I'll say is I survived 'cause when I was sure I'd die, Amos dragged me to my feet and made me run.

Your mama ran into the worst kind, though, the kind that don't go away, the kind that make us disappear."

"I'll never let them get me."

My voice was strange, like I was playing in a game of hide-and-seek where the consequences of getting caught weren't horrific. It was all too awful to imagine—what had happened to my mama in Oregon, and to Mizzy before she fled slavery.

"Never, never, never," I said, and reached for the safety of her arms.

"That's good. I'm gonna take that as a promise," Mizzy said, squeezing me close to her and not letting go. "I prayed every day you were away for the Lord to watch over you and keep you safe."

"Somebody's been watching over me the whole time, so your prayers helped. Maybe Mama and Papa have had an eye on me, too, from heaven or the stars or wherever they are. It doesn't matter who, where or what, does it? As long as we know we aren't alone?"

"You could put the preacher at my church right outta his Sunday employment, with such wise talk."

She wiped my cheeks with her thumbs and straightened up, as if to say it was enough serious talk for one day.

"Women aren't preachers, though. We only get to be witches."

Mizzy sat back in shock, but I poked her ribs and bit my lip so she'd know I was teasing.

"Mrs. Plea's been telling tall tales again. My, oh, my! That woman's got a streak. Can't resist stirring up a little mystery."

I told Mizzy a wild story I'd heard about Mrs. Plea and the Underground Railroad. It didn't match what Mizzy had heard, but that came as no surprise to either of us.

"I wonder which parts are true," I said.

Mizzy shrugged. "After a while, the past won't tell."

I understood then why Mizzy felt so helpless when I left for

San Francisco in the custody of Papa's no-good brother. When he told the Millers we were moving east, and that he'd send me to one of the finest schools, Mizzy didn't believed him. She knew better than to trust the likes of Uncle Jack. But the Millers took him at his word and I figured they were glad to hand me over. Thanks to Uncle's lies, my trail very nearly went cold, just like my mama's had done.

CHAPTER THIRTY

Mr. Jones insisted on escorting me to and from the hospice. Since he couldn't come to work with me, he'd wait all day under a shade tree down by the road. I told him it would be more interesting to stay with Mizzy, but he wouldn't hear of it. As days passed, the boredom got to him, and he took to sneaking up the hospice drive.

During my second week on the job, I spotted him watching me from the cover of the courtyard shrubs. So did a gentleman patient, who happened to be fond of dogs, and who promptly coaxed him out of hiding. Seeing a dog in her courtyard, Nurse Killjoy had a fit and swatted Mr. Jones with her broom. Before I could stop myself, I'd wrenched it from her hands and lectured her about the treatment of animals. There was a time I would have lost my temper and clobbered her with that broom. But I was calm and rational, and only a little uppity and indignant. She listened, straightened her nurse's cap, and, to my surprise, quietly apologized.

I worried she may have frightened Mr. Jones off for good, but he was adept at ducking trouble and persistent about what was right, even if it meant risking a bit of rough treatment. Sure enough, as soon as Nurse Killjoy was gone, he was back in that gentleman's lap, and the fellow was chattering to him about the cackling witch with a broomstick who'd shooed him away.

This gentleman, who had been in the hospice for months, hadn't uttered a single word to anyone until Mr. Jones showed up. I told Nurse Killjoy she had to come see the fellow talking. It was such a big deal, she brought Dr. Benjamin along, and didn't the old fellow say to him, clear as a bell, "Hello, Doctor. I'd like to introduce you to my new friend, Second Officer Mr. Jones, formerly of the *Salish Wind*." After that, Mr. Jones spent a good portion of his day visiting with patients. I told him he was still not permitted inside, which he accepted as a fair compromise.

By the third week at the hospice, Nurse Killjoy was my new best friend. Ever since mentioning nursing, she'd taken a keen interest in me. Where I thought the incident with Mr. Jones may have spoiled our friendly relationship, it made her appreciate me more, like almost with respect. She took to giving me hand-picked nursing tasks. Even though none of the jobs she gave me were hard, I'd ask her opinion on how the work should be done and then do it exactly as she wanted. That pleased her to no end.

Since we were getting on like a house on fire, she surprised me one morning by letting me keep my boots. I could only wear them outside, which I said was reasonable, having taken to cleaning the floors myself and seen up close the dirt that was tracked in. She gave me a hospital satchel, like all her other nurses had, to carry important personal and nursing items with me. It was a gesture of trust from Dr. Benjamin, she said. Trust was an issue for him, I said, which caused her to laugh and snort simultaneously. Her unusual laugh got me going along with her every single time.

Some days, Nurse Killjoy would hang around the staff room or sit beside me in the courtyard and I couldn't get rid of her. She'd say "don't let me interrupt your folding" or "don't mind me taking a wee rest here". At first, the sight of her coming was an irritation. But then I remembered Papa telling me how Mr. Miller used to come down to the stables to visit while he was busy. He'd hang over a stall door and chat about nothing. Papa would just wait and keep doing his work because he figured Mr. Miller just needed somebody to talk to, and if he had something on his mind, it would come out. So I'd be quiet and let her hang around as long as she pleased, and she'd talk if she felt like it.

Nurse Killjoy said nursing wasn't about all the cleaning I'd been doing. She said any good domestic worker worth their weight could do that part well. She said the harder work was understanding the patients, and I had a knack for that, so she gave me more time with them.

I liked that part of the job, talking to people and helping them feel better. Since I'd caught up on my sleep and my head wasn't fuzzy anymore, I offered to work weekends, which was almost entirely spent with patients, helping them with exercises for recovery. I had nothing else to do with Jake away at sea, and I found this work settled me, like a young seedling transplanted into a spring garden, its roots eager to expand and put down a strong and healthy base.

One sunny afternoon, Mrs. Plea appeared at the hospice.

"Charlee!" she called out from across the courtyard. I placed some selected plant cuttings into a pail and waved.

"What's this now? They've got you gardening?"

"Oh no. I'm minding patients. One of them is a botanist, and he's instructed me to collect samples for his research." I winked and tipped my head at a seated gentleman running a hand over the tall fronds of some decorative grasses.

"That's quite the outfit."

I'd taken to wearing one of Dr. Benjamin's white lab coats over my nursing uniform and had donned my boots for work outdoors.

"And Mr. Jones is allowed to mingle with patients?"

"Many residents find him a great comfort." Mr. Jones was in the courtyard swing with a frail man, whose back was so stooped he couldn't lift his head anymore. Mr. Jones heard his name, and I motioned for him to stay and carry on with his duties.

Just then, a woman nearby called out. "Doctor, is that my Evelyn?"

I crouched beside her rolling chair. "Evelyn's not here, Mrs. Gothman. She's tending the farm today. Remember your farm? She's coming this Sunday, right after church."

"Isn't today Sunday?"

"No. It's in two more days."

"Oh dear. Will you remind me?"

I picked up a rag doll she'd dropped on the ground. "Of course, I will." I tucked the doll into her arms and straightened the shawl hanging off her bony shoulders.

"She thinks you're her doctor," Mrs. Plea said when I returned.

"I know. How ironic. It takes the mind to be gone for it to lose its narrow thinking."

She regarded me thoughtfully, like she had a lot to say on the matter, but changed the subject instead.

"So Dr. Benjamin gave me a report on your progress, all of which he says he's shared with you."

"He's a straight shooter, for someone who likes to snipe around in a person's skull. I'll give him that."

We sat in a couple of vacant chairs beneath a shady oak.

"You know, then, I've looked into schools on your behalf." I nodded as she picked a piece of lint from her sleeve. After a long pause, she added, "I'm afraid I have some disappointing news there."

"But I aced all the entry tests, didn't I?"

"Yes. In fact, it's plain you don't belong in grade school."

"Well, that's good, isn't it?"

Mrs. Plea shook her head. "You belong in higher education."

"College, like Jake."

"Yes, but you aren't old enough yet…"

"…and I'm a girl."

"And you're a girl. And, well, you're…"

"You can say it. I know what people think. I'm a little crazy."

"Oh dear. That's not it. You're…like me…mixed blood," she said with an exasperated sigh. "You don't look like it much, but many schools will not take any mixed race, let alone girls."

"So there's no place for me to go unless I lie about who I am, and even then…"

"Even then."

Mrs. Plea set her lips in a thin line. I matched her flat expression, and we both sighed. Finding a school for me would be like trying to find a brown button in a barnyard.

"Nurse Killey says you show considerable promise for nursing, but I suspect your display of interest is how you manage her."

I shrugged and didn't deny it. She gathered her skirts and stood.

"For now, you have this job, a place to live for as long as you wish it, and you're recovering well."

Well enough, I thought. I'd gotten good at hiding scary problems.

"But even working weekends, I'm not making enough. I'll never be able to support myself."

I'd earned a few weeks of part-time wages working at the hospice, but it was nowhere near enough to live on, let alone pay for school. As an orphan girl, working oneself out of poverty was impossible.

"You are Mizzy's family, Charlee, and my guest. Dr. Benjamin intends to pay you full wages starting next month if you wish to stay on."

"He mentioned that, which helps, because I'm not sure I want to go to school, anyway."

"Well, school isn't the only path to a destination."

Just then, a nurse wheeled a patient past us. The patient glared at Mrs. Plea.

"What is that woman doing here?" the woman said, spitting her words. The nurse steered the patient away from us to the opposite side of the courtyard. Mrs. Plea glowered after her, eyes fixed and steady like a wildcat on the hunt. Then she broke her gaze and straightened her shawl.

"Mrs. Plea. I have a question. It's a little personal."

"Go ahead."

"How much does it cost to buy a house?"

"That is not the question I expected," she said with a laugh. "Anyway, not a lot, if one has money, that is. I own the house you're staying at, for example."

I spun sideways in my chair and gaped at her. She kept looking out over the courtyard, but smiled at my reaction. I knew money wasn't a problem for her, but she had way more of it than she let on.

"Is that the end of your questions? Don't you want to know how I could afford a house?"

"Yes! I mean, of course. I'm confused though, because you're a domestic worker. Mizzy said you run the staff at the house."

"And that's correct."

"But you own the house."

"Houses. I have more than one. But I'm sure you're aware that women can't go about purchasing properties. I have a wonderful husband and a few trusted associates, like Jake's father, who are willing business partners. They hold my assets for me since I cannot do so myself. I prefer not to draw attention to my finances, so it's an excellent arrangement."

"But you didn't go to school to learn business, did you?"

"Where might I have done that?"

"Right."

"No, I learned on my own, with excellent mentors."

"There! That's what I want to do! I want to be just like you!"

"Listen, Charlee. Being a woman in business is difficult. You must work twice as hard. You'll trust and you'll be betrayed. You'll get cut down, cheated, and you have to pick yourself up, lick your wounds and carry on because you have no recourse. If you're good, despicable things will be said about you, written about you. If you're great, you will be demonized. Every day you must wake up pledging to stay one step ahead of those who are determined to destroy you. Why choose such a hard path?"

"I don't know. I gotta pick something, and nursing isn't it."

"There's no hurry. You don't have to decide right now. Figuring out what you don't want to do is also important."

"I guess. I just want some choice."

"I know. Now. I'm hosting a cookout this Sunday, when the *Sonoma Wind* is due back. Will you help Mizzy prepare?"

"For pay?"

My brazen question caught her by surprise. I scrunched my nose so she would think I'd been kidding, and she laughed.

"Very enterprising of you to ask. No. Not for pay."

I thought about that for the rest of the day, even talked to Mizzy about it before we turned out the lamp at bedtime. I didn't expect to be paid for everything, I argued, embarrassed to admit I'd even suggested Mrs. Plea pay me, but I needed to make money if I was ever going to fend for myself. Mizzy asked why I didn't charge Jake for all the bookwork I'd helped him with over the years, to which I admitted that his trouble with math alone might have made me a small fortune and it had truly been a missed opportunity, but I got her point. Good will, when it comes from the heart, is worth more than money.

CHAPTER THIRTY-ONE

The *Sonoma Wind* arrived home late Saturday, and the Captain accepted the invitation to Mrs. Plea's cookout on behalf of the happy crew. They arrived all at once the next afternoon, a raucous bunch rolling about in the back of a hay wagon, and in the company of an oak keg of ale. Staff from the house, and other employees I hadn't seen before, trickled in with little plates of assorted desserts. Most of them declined offers of beer, so the fruit punch and ice tea I'd made under Mizzy's instructions were popular with everyone but the sailors.

Cook took charge of the grill, and the aroma of hickory wood and grilled meat soon filled the air. Jake worked by his side, squinting through the thick smoke, slathering Mizzy's special sauce on chicken and ribs. They laughed and joked around with the men who'd been drawn to the grill like moths to a lantern. Mr. Jones patrolled underfoot, in the event a morsel fell from the grill. Everyone else mingled about in the sunny yard, spirits lifted by the friendly gathering on a warm spring day.

Mrs. Plea had also invited her current house guests. The first gentleman to appear on the back porch had two bottles of wine tucked under his arm. He made his way straight for the naval officer in the sea of unfamiliar faces. The Captain, in his crisp blue uniform, stuck out like a lone palm tree on a deserted island. After Mrs. Plea introduced them, they uncorked the wine, sniffed it, sloshed it about in crystal glasses and sipped it in an elaborate tasting ritual. I heard the gentleman say the rare wine was from the Miller Estate, which was obviously a fancy name given to the new wine produced at the Sonoma Ranch. Glasses filled to the brim, they stood in the middle of everyone, debating some important matter with the enthusiasm and volume of stage actors.

A solitary woman came out of the house and hesitated at the top of the stairs. Mrs. Plea led her down into the group of strangers, where Mizzy handed her a tall glass of ice tea with a lemon slice dangling off the side. Mizzy always said that people can get through uncomfortable situations as long as they have something to do with their hands. The lady took the glass, saved the lemon slice from falling onto the grass, and was soon chatting with the women like she'd known them her whole life.

Then Mrs. Plea was back by the porch, having slipped away unnoticed, her profile striking and elegant, like it belonged on the side of a coin. She watched her gathering with mischievous satisfaction, like she was breaking somebody's rules and witnessing something good at the same time. As if she sensed eyes on her, she turned and caught me watching her. She winked, or at least I thought she did, before heading up the stairs to greet an overdressed couple who had appeared at the screen door.

After the cookout, people lingered in the yard, even as dusk brought in damp air from the ocean. Mrs. Plea handed out blankets to some ladies, a couple of guitars appeared and folks settled around a large fire pit tended by Cook and his mates.

As I put food away, Jake appeared with a stack of plates, insisting on helping me with the dishes. Mizzy told us the cleanup could wait, but I wanted to talk to Jake alone. It was a chance to catch up, and find out if he'd uncovered anything more about the Captain, and neither one of us felt much like sitting around with the adults.

Jake had nothing new to report on the Captain, but was pretty proud of his work on my notebook pages.

"I thought you'd be excited to hear I've almost cracked the code."

"I am."

But I was staring into the yard, thinking about my mama. She'd been on my mind since I'd found out what happened from Mizzy.

"That is not a look of excitement."

"I have something to tell you, and I don't know where to start."

He pulled a stool over for me and took the clean silverware out of my hands. After reassuring him nothing bad had happened, I told him what I'd learned from Mizzy about the death of my mama. Jake listened to the story with a solemn expression. He nodded from time to time, shoulders tense, arms wrapped around his chest in a protective embrace. When I was done, he leaned against the counter and gazed at the ceiling in stunned silence.

"I feel like I should go investigate myself, back in the Willamette Valley."

Jake straightened. "That's futile."

"No, it's not. Somebody might remember something."

"You'd actually run off again, go to Oregon, all by yourself?"

"Well, I haven't figured the details, but yeah, I guess I'd have to go alone.

"Charlee, you can't."

"What if she's still out there somewhere? Wouldn't you want to try, if it was your mama?" Jake ran a hand through his hair, and pressed his lips into a tight line. "Well, wouldn't you?" I demanded.

He mumbled something, and I snapped at him to speak up.

"I said, you should think of the living. You're not the only one who has ever lost someone."

He left the kitchen without looking at me. I hadn't meant to scorch him with the hot ashes of my smoldering anger. I caught up with him outside, before he could cross the yard to join the others.

"Wait. I never said I'm the only one..."

"Look. I get why you want answers. But your papa did his best, right when she vanished, and he couldn't find her."

"Maybe he missed something."

"You can't believe that. Your father was the best tracker around."

I didn't believe it, but I also wasn't ready to accept that I would never know the truth.

"So I should give up? Where's the justice in that?"

"Where's the justice in throwing your life away trying to fix the past? Nobody wants you to leave home to do that."

We'd been intensely whispering in each other's faces. Mizzy was suddenly there, taking each of us by the wrist.

"I think maybe my eyes are fooling me here. You haven't seen each other for almost a month and you looking mighty riled up over something. And on such a special day, with our family back together."

Family. That word again, like when Cook had said it. And Jake had just called this my home. I swallowed hard as my swirling past receded in the presence of Mizzy's calm resolve. Her words also settled Jake. He uncrossed his arms, said we were debating something, and it was nothing important. A borderline fib to avoid trouble, like old times.

"Then why were you looking mad as a couple o' hornets?"

"I had another hare-brained idea and Jake was setting me straight. You know how I can get carried away, how I don't like to be told what I can and can't do…"

Mizzy raised her eyebrows, suspicious. She looked at Jake for confirmation and he shrugged on cue.

"All right then. Nothing wrong with a difference of opinion, as long as you don't forget you got ears on the sides o' your heads for a reason."

We watched in silence as she walked away.

"She's right…I need to listen more."

"I just don't want you to, you know, disappear again."

Until that moment, I hadn't realized how much heartache I'd caused him.

A new song had begun around the fire, some old thing about a miner forty-niner that was popular with the adults. Jake winced and I scrunched up my nose.

"Let's go inside," I said, taking his elbow. "Show me what you decoded in my notes."

Sitting side-by-side at the parlor table, Jake explained the patterns he'd figured out in my scribbled pages. He was close, but something was still missing. I flipped to the end of the book and showed him the new entries I'd made the night I dreamed of Papa.

I shuffled playing cards someone had left on the table while he skimmed the pages.

"You remember it all," he said when he was done.

"All except where I moved the gold the last time." I dealt two hands on the table. "Do you ever play with Cook and the crew on the *Sonoma Wind*? Those boys are easy cash."

"I tried, but I was so bad they couldn't enjoy winning. Besides, I prefer my books."

"Better watch out. The Captain is fond of readers."

Jake scowled. "I'll have you know I used our mutual interest in government to learn more about him. Did you know his father is the top naval commander in Washington?"

He told me how the Captain's father wanted him to follow in his military footsteps, how he was forced into the naval academy despite his hatred for it, and how he disgraced his family by leaving a bride standing at the altar. Jake had extracted a lot of personal information from the Captain.

"Don't think I'm going to feel sorry for him. He's a liar, a coward and a crook."

"I can't see him as a crook. He doesn't care a whit about gold and riches and he thinks miners are fools."

"Why would he work with those murderous pirates then? Maybe he needs money since his family cut him off."

"I don't think so. He's too philosophical. He plays chess, not cards. Said to me that gambling and women are two vices to avoid."

"Really. He might want to cut back on wine while he's giving out advice. C'mon. I'll teach you a card game the fellas like, one you can win. It was the first game Uncle taught me. I'll even show you a couple of tricks."

Under protest, he agreed, but I had to remind him to pay attention more than once because his mind wandered. Finally, I threw down my cards and gave up. I was about to tell him to never play because he was hopeless when he put a finger to his lips. He pulled cards across the table with a forefinger and flipped them face up.

"What are you doing? You can't turn them over." He shushed me and organized the cards in lines.

"What's the name of this game?"

"*Vingt eh un.*"

"Charlee, that's it! That's the missing piece! I cracked your lettering patterns, but the numbers and symbols didn't make sense. You used this card game! The four suits are markers and your letter code resets at twenty-one! It's brilliant! And you worked your French in there, too."

In an instant, I could see it in my head and it jumped off the illegible pages. My memory of the shipwreck hadn't failed. The Captain made a terrible navigational mistake and ran the ship aground in the fog. I'd heard the pirates say the Captain had squealed and told them where to find the gold in the pantry. The skiff on the *Salish Wind* was crushed, so the Captain couldn't have drifted away in it. Dead bodies everywhere, Mr. Jones emerging from the shadows, and a desperate race to build a raft and paddle it to the nearby island. The pirates anchored in the bay, unaware of my survival. How they buried Mr. Miller's gold on the beach, and how I'd moved it as soon as they left. It confirmed what I always believed had happened.

And the last revelation sprung from the page. After a stormy day, with a king tide pushing water well past the high tide line on the beach, I'd gone back and moved the gold again, this time, up and away from the water. Up and away from the water.

"It's off the beach!"

"But you don't say where? You remember now, right?"

Before I could answer, something rustled behind us. We whipped our heads around so fast we nearly knocked them together. The Captain stood in the library's doorway, swirling wine in his glass, dangerously close to sending it out over the rim and onto Mrs. Plea's imported carpet.

"Sorry to barge in," he said, amused at catching us up to something. I closed my journal and slid it into my lap.

"Not at all, sir," Jake answered, rising from his chair, always the polite and respectful one. "Charlee and I were…getting caught up…" His cheeks turned pink as he spoke.

"I see that. We're leaving for the ship in fifteen. Better catch up fast," he said with a wink, and left us.

"Do you think he heard what we said?" Jake asked after he was gone.

"You bet he did. Watch what happens next. I need to return to Deception Island immediately, and he's gonna find a way to get me back on the *Sonoma Wind*."

CHAPTER THIRTY-TWO

By morning, I was no longer confident the Captain would come up with a compelling reason to take me. I meant to go, even if I had to sneak aboard the schooner later that night. But as Nurse Killjoy and I arranged patients in the courtyard for their afternoon air, Dr. Benjamin appeared with the conniving Captain on his heels.

"I'm afraid something has come up," Dr. Benjamin said to his nurse. "Miss LeBeau has to leave."

I feigned surprise, but was secretly relieved.

"What!" Nurse Killjoy couldn't conceal her anger. "When?"

"Unfortunately, right away. She has to return to Victoria regarding a pressing legal matter. The Captain has papers requesting her appearance."

The Captain nodded in solemn agreement, a pained expression hanging on his face. He hadn't mentioned anything about legal matters yesterday at the cookout. Yet now he'd appeared with official documents in hand.

"But I've just trained the girl to be useful! She has duties now. Responsibilities! She can't abandon her post without proper notice!"

"I'm so sorry, Nurse Killey, but I'm a key witness. I'll be back in three weeks' time, before you know it."

The Captain avoided my hard gaze, but added to my reassurance.

"I understand the terrible inconvenience it causes, but it is quite necessary. It's become something of an international matter. We must keep peace with the British, you know."

That was funny, but Nurse Killjoy wasn't having any of his humor.

"The British are more important than nurses for these people? If you'll excuse me, gentlemen, I have important work to do, doubled now, thank you very much."

She marched off in a huff.

"I'll see she has help," Dr. Benjamin said to the Captain. "Nurse Killey's become rather fond of her understudy." Then, turning to me, he added, "Go change and get your things. Let's not keep the good captain waiting."

"You seem to have made yourself indispensable," the Captain said ten minutes later, as the buggy pulled away from the hospice. "That was quite a scene."

He smirked and began humming some old sea shanty. We weren't even out of the yard and he was already tormenting me.

At the bottom of the drive, I told him to stop. I whistled and Mr. Jones sprinted from the long grass. He stuck his foot out to block him from jumping in with us.

"The dog can't come."

"I need him. I can't remember things unless he's with me."

He slid his boot back. "In that case, looks like the old sea dog is back on the crew."

I waved Mr. Jones up and he took a spot on the floor by my

feet, as far away from the Captain as he could manage without falling into the road.

Mizzy was in the vegetable garden when we pulled up at Mrs. Plea's house. Surprised to see me back in the middle of the day, and in the Captain's company, she dropped her basket and rushed over to find out what was wrong. The Captain told her my presence had been requested in Victoria because of new developments in the investigation into the wreck of the *Salish Wind*. With Mrs. Plea away on business for the day, Mizzy begged the Captain to wait for her return.

While the Captain explained why he could not wait, I ran upstairs to change into my sailing clothes and pack a small bag. I wrote a note to Mrs. Plea, telling her that the Captain was taking me to Victoria because I'd remembered Mr. Miller's missing gold was buried on Deception Island, stolen from the sinking ship by pirates and murderers known to the Captain, and likely in cahoots with him.

If I disappeared, I'd left a brief account in shrewd hands. Jamming the paper into an envelope, I scribbled a few lines to Mizzy on the front, telling her not to worry, and to see that Mrs. Plea got the envelope as soon as she was back. Then I left it on her pillow.

In the entrance hall of the house, Mizzy wrung her hands while the Captain attempted to reassure her of my safety. Mr. Jones was stationed on the porch to make sure he wouldn't be left behind during our hasty departure.

The Captain looked at me with exasperation and said, "Perhaps you can talk to her. She's not willing to let you out of her sight, even with Dr. Benjamin's approval and orders from a British court."

"I can't let you go, Charolat! I let you go last time, and you nearly died. I can't do it again."

"You must, Mizzy. The shipwreck is finally getting a proper

investigation. Besides, I'll be in the Captain's capable hands. He'll make sure I stay safe, won't you, sir?"

Our eyes locked for a long moment, both of us defiant.

"I assure you, Miss Jefferson, she will be back before you know it. Your brother will watch over her. Surely you trust him, if not me. And young Mr. Miller is also aboard. It's quite the happy little family. Come now."

"And Mr. Jones will be with me."

"It's that big ocean I don't trust. It could gobble up all of you in one go. And what about your job at the hospice?"

"I've explained everything to them and they understand the urgency," the Captain replied. "She'll resume her work the moment she gets back."

He was so convincing when he spoke, I almost believed that a shipwreck investigation was the reason he needed me to return to Victoria.

The afternoon was cooling as we left Mrs. Plea's house. A damp fog had rolled in from the water, hiding much of San Francisco Bay and the city below. It drifted in wisps and patches across the growing fields of wheat and barley as we passed by. I tucked my hands under my legs to keep my fingers warm. Mr. Jones found himself a warm spot between my shins. He knew riding on the seat beside me was out of the question and he didn't like the Captain, anyway.

I took in the familiar sights as we headed down toward Market Street and the harbor. The Captain knew the streets to avoid, the ones with steep hills or nasty wagon ruts, so I didn't offer route suggestions. When the harbor came into view, I felt like I'd returned to a difficult home.

As we drove through the downtown area, Mr. Jones had quite a few things to say about the numerous stray dogs. I said I couldn't remember so many running loose everywhere. The Captain remarked that San Francisco had to do better with them. Except for one pair that the city had turned into ridiculous celebrities, most strays were neglected and at risk of being shot in the street by angry shopkeepers. Mr. Jones had seen and heard enough. Curled up by my feet, he made himself tiny. He'd been a stray in Victoria, Kuno had told me, cast out because of injury or illness. When Kuno found him, scrawny, matted and quivering, under a dock near the *Salish Wind*, he'd been fending for himself.

I knew the back alleys, back doors and hiding places in San Francisco like a human stray. Like Mr. Jones, I still felt that old life nipping at my heels and worried I might land there again with one wrong turn.

He turned the buggy into a street that led through Chinatown and pulled up in front of a row of businesses.

"Why are we stopping?"

I gripped the edge of the seat. What if he had no intentions of taking me to the *Sonoma Wind* and back to Victoria?

"I need to pick something up. It'll only take a minute."

He handed me the reins, an immediate connection to the large draft horse in front of us, who turned his head to acknowledge me. No need to panic, I thought. If the Captain was going to throw me in a dungeon or something right here in San Francisco, he would not leave me unattended, tempted with a simple escape. Or maybe he was testing me, to see what I might do. Maybe he figured I wouldn't run because I wanted to go after the gold as much as he did. The Captain swung down to the street and disappeared into a shop that had jars of herbs and medicines displayed in the window.

I'd walked this street many times, on my way to and from the Livery. Over six blocks and up another four, and I'd be on the back steps of the awful tenement where I last lived with Uncle, where desperate miners had come after me, and where the old man across the hall had sent me to Mrs. Plea and the Underground Railroad when I couldn't find Cook.

"This is my old neighborhood, Mr. Jones."

He pressed himself against me and peered out of the buggy, growling at a mangy dog sniffing garbage on the other side of the street. He didn't like the dog or the place one bit.

The Captain returned in minutes with a small package and we were on our way.

"I used to work there," I said, as we passed the Good Fortune laundry just outside of Chinatown. I turned in my seat as we passed because it didn't look the same. There was a boardwalk in front of it now, and pallets of bright-colored bins were stacked on each side of the doorway.

"I thought you worked at the Livery?"

"That was my main job. I did occasional jobs here, too."

It was much more than that. Taitai, the proprietor of the tiny laundry, had noticed the skinny, haunted girl passing by her shop each night after work. She knew I wasn't the boy I pretended to be, hiding myself in baggy clothes and darkness. Her daughter, Jing Yi, was only a few years younger than me. She invited me in, gave me meals and safe company, in exchange for made-up chores.

Down at the harbor, we passed the old Livery, boarded up and ready to tear down. It had closed, and that meant Tubby was gone. While stewing over how many things had changed while I'd been away, the Captain spoke as if he'd read my mind.

"There's progress for you. Railcars are here and the liveries are getting pushed out to the country."

I wasn't surprised. Even Tubby knew it was coming last year. He'd dreamed of getting out of San Francisco anyway, maybe getting himself a small ranch somewhere. I pictured him sitting on the top rail of a fence, open fields behind him for as far as the eye could see, smoking a cigarette and waving at me with his gnarly, brown fingers.

The Captain interrupted my melancholy reflection.

"You seem to remember your days in San Francisco. The laundry, the Livery. That bodes well for recalling what happened to the *Salish Wind*, doesn't it?"

Strategic question. I couldn't let my guard down with him, even if he tried to put me at ease with casual banter.

"I remember old stuff. The doctors don't know about more recent things."

"Dr. Benjamin said you've recovered well and your abilities are…what was the word he used? 'Exceptional'."

"He said that?"

I wondered what else Dr. Benjamin had shared with the Captain. I hadn't counted on the Captain plying him for information about my condition.

"In any event, your laundry lady at the Good Fortune isn't there anymore."

"How do you know?"

"Because Mrs. Plea owns the place now."

"What?! What do you mean, she owns it?"

"It closed last fall and I gather Mrs. Plea bought it off the bank for a song. She's good at that sort of thing. And that shop we stopped at back there? She owns that, too. I thought a smart girl like you would have figured it out by now. She's the wealthiest woman in San Francisco."

CHAPTER THIRTY-THREE

A light breeze tinkled the riggings of the *Sonoma Wind*, tied up at the end of Clay Street wharf. The schooner sat heavy in the water, her hold loaded with goods, ready for departure. The sailor monitoring the ship exchanged a few words about wind and weather with the Captain, who thanked him for the report and dismissed him ashore.

"Where's everybody?" I clasped Mr. Jones a little tighter under my arm.

The ship was deserted. No sign of Cook, Jake, or any of the crew. Sails were down and tucked away, ropes coiled, deck spotless. Tarps and chains battened down what looked to be large pieces of mining equipment.

"They have shore leave until dusk."

That meant I was alone on the ship with him. At least I had Mr. Jones. I wanted to run down to the galley, but shuffled my feet and waited for instructions instead.

"Do you remember our cargo on the *Salish Wind*?" the Captain asked as he pulled out his pipe. Now he wanted to chat and socialize. I set my bag down on the deck and swung Mr. Jones around to my other hip.

"Building and mining equipment, mostly."

"That's right. And people." He raised his eyebrows and watched for my reaction.

Twenty Black passengers had gone north with us that first night I sailed out of San Francisco. I had never forgotten about that mission, even after smacking my head, but he didn't need to know that.

"Of course. I remember now." I made myself look perplexed.

He tipped his head to one side as I pretended to be flustered by the sudden memory.

We had taken a group of Black passengers out of San Francisco, leaving the harbor under the cover of night. These people had bounty hunters hot on their trail. Former slaves, people without papers, people running for their lives. We had slipped out of San Francisco harbor late at night, and ran into a nasty squall on the open ocean that made me seasick for days. I remembered it clearly, but thought it best he believed I'd forgotten much to do with the *Salish Wind*.

"Do we leave tonight?"

"Dawn tomorrow." He turned his back to the breeze and lit his tobacco. "I have to tell you, despite how it may appear, and what I said to Miss Jefferson, I have major reservations about allowing you to sail again, but this is the timeliest way to return you to Victoria. Several people shall have my head if any harm comes to you, not the least of whom is my benevolent and forgiving employer, Mr. John Miller."

I was still thinking about the passengers. Mrs. Plea was in charge of the mission, and had probably funded it. People had risked the journey north, seeking refuge in the British colonies, a place unknown to them but offering freedom.

"Don't you find? he said.

"Pardon, sir?"

"Ah. Lost in your thoughts. Never mind. It wasn't important."

The Captain puffed on his pipe. The smoke of the tobacco drifted past my face—a sweet smell like fresh hay—and then rode away on the evening air.

"Did anyone ever catch on? That you were smuggling people?"

My bold questions surprised him, and he stiffened.

"If they had, I wouldn't be standing here. But work on that campaign is over. The railroad took a severe blow in the east, before our last trip, and all of it has ended amid greater concerns of civil war."

I nodded. Jake had told me how the southern states refused to give up slavery. It was tense, with constant disputes between the north and south. Thanks to miles and miles of natural land, California was far away from it all.

"Mrs. Plea was there, in the east, wasn't she?"

"Yes. Cook, too. Up in Rupert's Land, for a time."

That was why Cook was nowhere to be found when I'd searched for him the previous winter. He'd gone east with Mrs. Plea, on railroad business.

"They won't come after her, will they?"

"No. There is no proof of her involvement. But they've tried to catch her at something ever since. I've never seen a woman so admired and so vilified in the public eye. Remarkable, really."

Her warning to me was fresh in my mind. She was relentless and brave. If I wished to be like her, it would be hard, and I didn't like the idea of being hated.

I scanned the nearby ships at anchor.

"Didn't you ever fear being caught?"

He shrugged. "Caught for what?"

A trick as old as time. If you never admit to something, it didn't happen. At least, that was the law as applied to the white man. He wasn't about to confess to anything without proof or evidence, which meant he'd never admit to what he'd done on the *Salish Wind* either. Panic tightened my stomach. A sharp pain under my ribs felt like the stab of a knife.

"For...helping. For participating in the...the smuggling."

He looked out at the horizon with a narrow smile.

"I have too much value as a...negotiator. Nothing to see for a price. They'll always turn a blind eye when distracted by the dollar. Bribery. Let's call it what it is, shall we? Money talks. Money can buy almost anything, except happiness."

Did he have money? If he had money, why did he want me to take him to Mr. Miller's gold? He did not sound happy at all. None of it made sense.

"I guess it can buy freedom," I said.

"I wish it were that simple. It's a ruthless business. One must always keep an eye over one's shoulder, in case someone betrays you for a better offer."

The Captain was like two different people and I never knew which one I was getting until he spoke. Since the shipwreck, I had been certain of one thing. He was devious and untrustworthy and he'd conspired to sink the *Salish Wind*. Sailing back to San Francisco, he'd taken far too great an interest in my memory of the shipwreck. There had to be a reason. And then there was Jake's discovery. The Captain had somehow ended up with my island map, the one that stinky pack of privateers had stolen off Mrs. Dalworth's kitchen table. He could only have come by that if he knew those men and was in on the raid.

Now here he was, speaking candidly about risking his life to help a group of people escape slavery, with significant disgust when acknowledging the money that changed hands to have others look the other way. Who was he? It was maddening. He could make me drop my guard, forget who I was talking to like nobody I'd ever met. I rubbed my temples, feeling the sudden sway of the ship on the water.

"What is it?"

He'd been watching me think again, which unnerved me even more.

"Ah. I was wondering. Can I work the galley for pay while I make this trip back to Victoria? I'm losing at least three weeks of wages, not to mention, I was about to get a substantial raise at the hospice."

"As you wish. Cook will be happy to have you once he gets over the shock of your sudden appearance."

"He doesn't know I'm coming?"

"I didn't know myself until this morning. Same pay as before. No raise. And you'll work the watches as before."

A natural negotiator, all right. He didn't need to know I made more crewing as a ship's boy than I ever would at the hospice as a nursing assistant.

"It's a deal then."

He laughed, and I wanted to punch him.

One minute he was a reckless cad, the next minute a skilled diplomat. Devious in one matter, principled in another. Then, when away from his work, he could be thoughtful and interesting. It was hardest to manage his deliberate cool and clever charm when he was acting as ship's captain. Still, the good in him confused me, made it hard for me to hate him, made me almost forget that part of him was dark and dangerous.

I had to figure him out before we reached Victoria, before I returned to the island where Mr. Miller's gold waited for me, just out of reach. Whenever I closed my eyes, I could see my hands on the canvas bundles, feel the rain on the back of my neck. Clamity Cove was in view over my left shoulder. The only thing missing was exactly where I was kneeling.

I shifted Mr. Jones back to my original side, both of us uncomfortable, my arms tired and aching from holding him. The Captain noticed, announced he had work to do, and dismissed me so I could settle in.

"Cook will be along soon," he said, checking his timepiece.

I watched him until he disappeared into his cabin.

Down in the galley, I stood by the stove and surveyed the small space, this little, low-ceiling kitchen that was so familiar to me. If Cook had expected me, my hammock would be in its usual spot. Jake hadn't warned him I'd be on the next trip, even when I told him I'd come aboard as a stowaway, if necessary. But the Captain had made it easy for me, as I'd hoped he would.

I picked up the coffee pot on the stove. Clean, full of water and packed with fresh coffee grounds. Ready to go at first light. I sat at the galley table, dug out my notebook, and reviewed all the pages I'd written in the garbled code that Jake had helped me figure out. Then I read the pages I'd written in the middle of the night, when all of my memories came tumbling back. The accounts matched. Even when I was suffering from a head injury, I didn't get any of it wrong. Yet I didn't record where I moved Mr. Miller's gold the second time. I could see myself at the spot, knew it was off the beach, and knew I'd recognize the place if I put myself there one more time. Soft dirt, fragrant cedar trees, Clamity Bay over my left shoulder…

Just before dark, I heard the rumble of feet, laughter, and loud voices overhead. I scrambled up the stairs and popped my head through the open hatch to greet the crew.

"Hey, Cook. You let the stove get cold!"

Cook and Jake had been peering over the gunwale at the dock below. They both spun around in perfect timing.

Jake pointed at me and slapped Cook's shoulder. "I told you so."

"No way!" Cook said. "You are not coming along. Not again. Uh uh."

"I knew she'd find her way back on board! That's our Charlee!"

CHAPTER THIRTY-FOUR

Cook threw down his bag, told me to go pack my own, and said he was taking me back to Mrs. Plea's house immediately. My sailing days were over, he argued. I insisted it was only for one more trip, but he didn't want to hear it. The Captain overheard his protests, quietly explained the situation, and Cook had no choice but to follow orders.

We left San Francisco the next morning under clear, breezy conditions, but the warmth of California vanished along with the shoreline. By mid-afternoon, the wind picked up and heavy clouds darkened the horizon. By late afternoon, an icy rain lashed our faces and streamed off our slickers. The wind, which had a cold bite to it for the end of May, blew steady but fell short of reaching stormy conditions. I found my sea legs almost right away and turned in that first night feeling chilled to the bone, but not at all seasick.

On the third day out, the rain turned to a misty drizzle and then stopped. The motion of the boat changed from jarring heaves over grey, choppy ridges of water into a smooth up-and-down roll over frothing greens. Not wanting to see me suffer like the last time aboard, Cook kept sending me up top for regular breaks in the fresh air. I told him I didn't need to go and was doing fine, but it helped me keep my head clear, and often gave me a couple of minutes to talk to Jake.

Cook and I didn't rotate through other watches that required staying awake much of the night or sleeping during the day because those would interfere with meal preparations. Supper was served during the Dog Watch, between four and eight, which Mr. Jones insisted was named after him, and he supervised the galley as if he had invented the system. Our watch was the same every night, beginning at eight o'clock and ending at midnight. It wasn't hard to stay awake, but it left us with only five hours of sleep. Every morning at five o'clock, Cook would thump on my hammock to get me up for breakfast work. Staying at Mrs. Plea's house and doing an easy job had spoiled me. I'd be asleep well before ten in a quiet, cozy bed and didn't wake until six each day. Mizzy slipped out earlier each morning to get a head start on the day, but she never asked me to get up and help, and I'd never offered.

About a week into our journey, a brisk wind provided a steady push in our sails. We were making easy progress under the stars, heading north, far off the coast. On our evening watch, I gazed up to the top of the mainmast where the indigo canopy above us sparkled. A pale white moon was close to full and formed an eerie tail of light behind the ship. The serenity of it all was deeply soothing, and my head bobbed as I struggled to stay awake. After Cook had prodded me awake several times, he sent me down to the galley to warm up and make fresh coffee.

I stoked the stove, measured the water and grounds according to Cook's instructions, and plunked the heavy pot onto the hot iron surface. When Drak had taken over the galley on the *Salish Wind*, the coffee he made was the worst I'd ever tasted, including brew made over a campfire using swampy-tasting creek water. I didn't want to think about Drak. He had died aboard the sister schooner in the same spot where I stood.

I clutched the railing on the stove, feeling a sudden wave of nausea come over me. They had killed him while I hid in a secret cupboard under the side counter.

The two schooners were identical, which meant this one also had to have a hidden cupboard. I dropped to my knees and slid some bags of beans and flour out of the way. The wood from the outside panel was smooth. No handles or knobs to give it away. I studied the seam closest to me and noticed a tiny gap. Grabbing a spoon from the table, I stuck the handle into the gap and pressed. The panel popped loose, revealing a long and narrow storage area. I had not imagined hiding in the same type of cupboard aboard the *Salish Wind*.

I leaned in for a closer look. The cupboard had a musty smell. Rolls of canvas were stacked inside, just like on the *Salish Wind*. I remembered water rushing in behind the bulkhead as the ship sunk and Drak's blood all over the galley floor. The memories were too vivid, too awful. I stuck my fists in my eyes and rocked back and forth. I felt like I'd been clobbered across my chest with a huge stick and had the air knocked out of me.

The coffee pot sputtered as it boiled. I lined up the panel and pushed it back into place, sending a handful of beans rolling across the floor as I returned the sack to where it had been. I swept them up with my hands.

"Do you need help with something?" said the Captain from behind me and I banged my head on the counter in surprise. I scrambled to my feet, rubbing a spot on my crown.

"No, sir. I...I'm making coffee." The pot on the stove was boiling over now, splattering everywhere, coffee droplets sizzling as they hit the grill. I used a fat cloth to grab the handle and yanked it off the heat.

"Looks more like you were spilling the beans," he replied with amusement.

I was too frazzled for his humor. How long had he been

standing there? Had he caught me peering into the hidden cupboard?

"You may pour me a mug then, if it hasn't all boiled over. Or evaporated."

Teasing me again, but I kept my mouth shut and followed his request.

"I've been wondering, how did you survive on the *Salish Wind*? The report said you were in the galley, where you stayed until it flooded, and finding no other survivors on deck but the ship's dog, you built a raft and paddled it to Deception Island."

"Yes." My head pounded, and not because of the minor bump I'd just added to my collection. He was fishing for information and I wasn't ready. I poured his coffee with a shaky hand.

"And you saw no other survivors…including me."

"No other survivors. I figured you were in your cabin, sir, that you…didn't make it…" I would not mention the intruders and the murders.

"You did not check?"

"The ship was under water on that side and everyone below but me had drowned." An enormous wave of guilt struck me and I balanced myself against the counter. "I called out. The schooner was listing to port and the cargo of logs on deck threatened to break loose. I couldn't get aft to check. Nobody answered when I called out."

"I'm sorry to cause you further grief. I am only attempting to piece together how I came to be in the skiff drifting out in the strait."

That was his official story, the one Mrs. Dalworth and I had read in the revised report. But I'd seen our ship's skiff crushed to smithereens.

"All that must have happened before I made it on deck, which would explain why I didn't see you."

"Yes. You must have stayed below deck for a long time. What were you doing down there?"

"I don't know. I remember water rushing in, drowned sailors and somehow ending up on deck…with everyone gone."

His icy blue eyes cut my cheeks like a cold north wind. I held his gaze to convince him I was telling the whole truth. It was the truth, but with a few key omissions.

"I suppose I could have launched the skiff by myself, but I have the vague sense that someone helped me with it. Seems I'll never know who."

He looked troubled, as if he was attempting to figure out what had gone on. For a moment, I wondered if I'd been mistaken about the crushed skiff. It didn't matter. The skiff could have belonged to the black sloop.

"Sorry I can't be of more help. I didn't see you."

"What's the hold-up?" Cook said, barging into the galley, almost colliding with the Captain as he stepped over the bulkhead to leave. "Oh! Excuse me, Captain. Didn't realize you were down here."

"Not at all. Carry on. I'll get out of your way," he said, and left for the stairs.

Cook stared after him while Mr. Jones sniffed the floor and the panel around the secret cupboard.

"That was strange, him coming down here at this hour," Cook said.

"He wanted to talk to me. About the shipwreck."

"Again? How did that go?"

"Not the way he hoped, I figure."

"What happened to the coffee?" I picked up a rag and wiped down the outside of the pot. Spattered coffee had dried on the hot stove, leaving a blackened mess.

"I'll clean that up. Sit for a spell. You look like you seen a ghost."

"I'm fine."

But I wasn't. I had seen ghosts. My head was full of horrible images of the sinking ship, and I couldn't block the ugly memories anymore. They'd come raging back along with the good ones. Forgetting had given me time to heal, time to become strong enough to handle the worst of them. I felt strong enough now, but that didn't make any of it easy.

"The Captain forgot his coffee. I guess I'll have to take it to him in his cabin."

Cook scrunched up his face.

"Don't bother. He doesn't drink the stuff."

We arrived in Victoria late one afternoon under cloudless skies and a gusty spring wind. Once sheltered by the inner harbor, the sunny warmth of May soon cooked the crew out of coats and sweaters. By early evening, the wind died off entirely—no clinking of riggings against masts, no whistle of wind through battened sails, no steady sloshing of water against the ship's hull. As the sun dropped low in the sky, a salty dampness rose off the water. I stood on the port side of the *Sonoma Wind*, taking in the last of a spectacular sunset.

Mr. Jones stood on a crate beside me, his paws resting on the gunwale. I'd asked Kuno one time if he ever worried that Mr. Jones might dive overboard after a seal or seabird, and he said as a trained naval officer, he would never stoop to such simple canine urges. I watched him scan the water. The only thing missing was a spyglass to get a closer look at items in the distance. He assumed we were still on watch duty even though we were at anchor, which was partly true, but not like how watches go when at sea.

Mr. Jones spotted something moving near us in the water. A long, narrow boat passed alongside, heading for the opposite shore across the small harbor. It was a Lekwungen canoe, like those I'd seen at Deception Island, with a beautiful carved bow reaching high in the front. Mr. Jones snuffled a bark of acknowledgement.

"*Papa-eh-ah-cane,*" someone in the boat said, pointing at Mr. Jones. All heads looked up at us as we watched them glide past the schooner. Wool dog, they'd said. Mrs. Dalworth told me the local people bred dogs like Mr. Jones. Their thick fur had once been used to weave blankets and garments.

Jake and Cook appeared from below. I waved them over so they wouldn't miss the sun dipping into the distant forest, leaving sparkles of orange and streaks of pink fanning out across the sky, with the silhouette of the retreating canoe passing through golden light on the water.

"Never gets tired, and never looks the same twice," Cook said. Jake and I both murmured in agreement, and we stood for a long minute taking it all in.

We were at anchor, some distance from the dock, surrounded by merchant ships of all sizes. As ships arrived, they would get in the queue to be emptied and re-loaded. If the harbor was busy, as it was when we arrived, we had to wait our turn at the dock. Once in, the work was fast and hard, to keep everything moving.

"Harbor is hopping this week," Cook said. "We unload in the morning, but it looks like it'll be a day or two before we get our repair. And the Captain's got shipwreck business with Charlee here, so who knows how long it's all gonna take. I'm tired, though, and happy to put my feet up for a couple o' days. And now it's time to call it a night, you two."

"Aw, what's the rush, Cook? Can't we stay a few minutes more?" I said.

"Both o' you need a proper night's sleep. Lots to be done in port once they clear us in. You got fifteen, then I'll see you below, Charlee."

"Sheesh. He's like a big brother," Jake said, as soon as Cook was out of earshot.

"I could do worse. Is it true the ship needs a repair? I didn't hear of anything breaking."

"Nothing major, but a pulley is sticking when it's got too much pressure on it. It has to be looked at."

"I think the Captain's using it as an excuse to delay us."

Jake stiffened. "To give you time to go to Deception Island?"

"Yep. He hasn't said a word about it, though. But how many times has the *Sonoma Wind* ended up in a long queue to unload? Like never. And now this mysterious repair when nothing seems broken? I think he wants to give me time to go after the gold."

"Which is what you want to do, right?"

"Right. But not before I line up a few protections."

I pulled my notebook out from under my sweater. "Before I go ashore to do anything, I'll give you this for safekeeping. That way, if something should happen to me, you'll have my full account of the truth. You helped me decode the important section, so you can interpret it and see it through to the end. I appoint you as my legal representation."

"You can't do that. I'm not qualified."

"Yes, you are. Plus, you can verify that everything in this book is what I told you when I was of sound mind. When my memory came back, I added to it in clear language. Well, except for where I moved your father's gold the second time at Clamity Cove. But I'm inches away from remembering that last detail. I can feel it."

"You don't have to get the gold. Father thinks it was lost. It can stay that way. He wouldn't want you to risk going after it."

"The gold is bait. It's justice I'm after. Those responsible will show their faces. I'll make proper arrangements to get out to Deception Island. Everything I do will be right out in the open, where all kinds of eyes can witness. Nothing's gonna happen. Promise."

"Famous last words."

CHAPTER THIRTY-FIVE

"Captain says we may be in Vic for a week," Cook said as he came into the galley the next morning, and I hung up the last of the breakfast pots on the ceiling rack.

"That's a long time, given the short season, isn't it?"

"It is. But he has to get that pulley on the main repaired. Ignore it and it'll be what jams when you try to reef in the sail during a storm."

"Logical. Sure."

I began packing a few things I needed for a day trip. Cook put a hand on my satchel.

"What's that for?"

"A quick trip out to Deception Island."

"No way the Captain will allow it. Too many risks and not enough time, even if we are stuck here for a week."

"Nonsense. He wants me to go, I'm sure of it. Besides, nothing will happen."

But that's not what had been going around and around in my head all night and all morning. So many things could go wrong, I'd stopped listing them. But I'd come up with the best plan for the circumstances.

Cook stood in the doorway, blocking it, like maybe he wouldn't let me out.

I shook my head. "He knows I know what happened out there, that I remember everything. Don't you see? He's giving me room to see what I'll do."

"You can't be sure."

I rolled my eyes. "That first night on the ship, before you came back aboard? I already told him I wanted to go to the island. But I made it sound like it was to see Mrs. Dalworth. He's pieced it all together. He knows I want to get the gold, so he's making time for me to arrange it."

"You think he expects you to sneak ashore and run off?"

"No. He expects me to ask for shore leave, and to ask for his help to arrange a trip to the island."

"Which one's your plan?"

"The second one, of course. I'm going to ask him tonight. Now, are we going ashore for food and supplies or not?"

"Yes, we are. As long as that satchel of yours stays on board."

"I'm not taking the satchel, and Mr. Jones stays. Would I leave him behind if I weren't coming back?"

The schooner had been piloted to the wharf at first light. On the main deck, I made sure that everyone within a country mile knew I was going ashore with Cook, in case anyone was interested in my moves. Jake had to unload supplies with the crew, so he couldn't come along. He grimaced and threw me a half-hearted wave.

"You need to fill me in on what you're up to," Cook said as we walked along the skinny boardwalk of Wharf Street. "It's not like you to seek attention. The only thing you missed in announcing our trip ashore is an ad in the local paper."

"I'm hoping to draw out the crooks. If the Captain told them

I survived the shipwreck and I'm the one that dug up and moved the gold, they'll be watching me. I want them to show themselves before I go out to the island.

"What if the Captain has no part in this?"

"The way he's been digging around in my head? He has to be involved."

Our first stop was at the Hudson's Bay Company store. We wander around a little, in and out of the shops and I tried on a large winter coat that I didn't need. We'd been well-stocked for the trip and needed little. Cook picked up a few things he couldn't get in San Francisco and I bought a small hand shovel.

"Look at this, Cook," I exclaimed as we left the store. I tossed it in the air and twirled it around like a pistol. "I could dig up an entire gold mine with this. It's got a tough, sturdy handle."

"You going to holler and toss that thing around until we get back to the boat?" he hissed.

"Yessiree."

I skipped a few times on the boardwalk for good measure. Uncle Jack would have cringed at that, drawing attention as I was. But nothing was out of the ordinary, other than a few stares from people passing by.

From there, we headed to the wharf market to buy fish and vegetables.

"What am I looking for again?" Cook whispered.

"Anyone taking an interest, tagging along?"

A few streets later, as we turned down to the wharf, Cook nudged me.

"You got your wish."

"Where?" I didn't look around.

"Across the street, ten paces back. Sailor in a red and black checkered shirt."

We made a couple of stops and starts, and a few deliberate turns. The man stayed with us, closing the gap.

"I don't like this. I'll bust his head if lays a hand on you."

"No, don't do that. Listen, Cook. We're in a crowd. He won't hurt me. We go about our business and see what he does, if he has company."

"Well, slow down a little, then. Your goon is having trouble keeping up."

It was now mid-morning, and people packed the market stalls on both sides of the busy street. I pointed to a group of women with baskets of camas, shellfish and salmon.

"Hey! That's the women we bought from last summer. The one on the left, with the grey shawl? She came to the island last fall with the Chief's group."

We wove our way through people, horses, carts, and dogs. The woman in the grey shawl studied me for a moment, as if she knew I was familiar, but couldn't figure out from where.

"*Kla-how-ya,*" she said.

"*Kloshe,*" I replied.

We'd exchanged a common greeting in local trade jargon. Chinuk Wawa was a blend of mostly Salish, French and English, and widely spoken in the area. I'd picked up some words and phrases from Mrs. Dalworth, who had used it to speak to her Lekwungen friends on Deception Island.

"One salmon," Cook said to her, holding up a finger and pointing at a basket of fish reflecting rainbow colors in the morning light. The woman chose a large one. Cook nodded his approval, and she wrapped it in broad green leaves, binding them with woven string.

"*Tawnshi ta famee?*" I said.

The words flew out of me from some unknown place, and the woman in the grey shawl looked puzzled. I shook my head, momentarily flustered. I'd asked about her family, but in the wrong language. I'd used French Michif, the dialect of my Red River ancestors.

"*Nika tilicum?*" she asked, trying to understand.

"*Wii!* How is your family?"

"*Ah-ha. Kloshe.*" Fine, she said, with a warm smile.

"Where'd you learn trader language?" Cook said. I ignored him.

"Mrs. Dalworth," I said, patting my chest. "*Tenas illihee.* Island."

Her face lit up. "*Un ne! Mika Chak Chak Nan Itsh!*"

You are 'Eagle Looking', she said. She'd recognized me from the island and called me by the name given to me by her people. The other women stared.

"Do you know Shenoa? *Kum-tuks...Shenoa?*"

I had to ask about the young Indian woman who'd helped me on Deception Island, to know if she was a real person or if I had imagined her. But this question threw a wet blanket over our friendly exchange. The woman's smile vanished and she shook her head. Either she didn't know anyone by that name, or she didn't want to talk about her. The others looked away and busied themselves with their wares.

Cook jabbed me in the side.

"That fella is right behind you, two back," he whispered.

I glanced over my shoulder.

"*Le pome,*" the woman said, tugging my sleeve to get my attention.

She dropped a deep red apple into my hand. In an instant, I was in my cave at Clamity Bay. The apple was a smooth, warm stone I'd picked from the edge of my fire to warm my hands. My body shook beneath clothing damp from sweat and chilling rain, my muddy hands trembled from digging in the cold ground. Mr. Jones was curled up beside me on my bed of boughs.

The apple tingled in my fingers, sending fire up my arms and into my chest and head. My thoughts cleared, like a brushfire burning away deadfall. I saw myself moving three canvas bags off the beach, away from the high tide, to a place only I would have chosen.

"What's the matter? Did you hear what I said?" Cook said, snapping me back to the present. "He's right behind you now."

"I'm...yes, I know. I just remembered something."

I felt the man's thick hand close around my arm. It burned like hot grease.

I dropped the apple and confronted the man, recognizing him by the jagged scar that cut across his right eye. I hadn't expected to be grabbed in broad daylight!

I lunged at him, swinging the shovel I'd bought. He didn't have time to react.

"Robber! No good murdering thief!"

The crowd parted and formed a circle around us. Before he could get his arms up to defend himself, I'd got in a pretty solid hit on his head. The metal shovel rang off his skull, cutting his forehead above his good eye.

The man begged me to stop. I got a couple more licks in before Cook grabbed me from behind and hauled me off.

The man's fists were coming for me, but before he could land a punch square on my face, a couple of burly men grabbed him and his swing missed my cheek. The gathered spectators stood back and gaped. I'd expected someone in the crowd to jump into the fight sooner, and didn't count on them wanting to see how a girl would fare beating on a man who outmatched her in size. I was inches from having my nose flattened.

"Robber! Thief!" I yelled again.

The pirate's eyes were red with blood from the shovel cuts and he snorted like an angry bull. He'd tear me to pieces if they let him loose.

Just then, a whistle blasted and two policemen burst through the crowd. One policeman snatched the shovel out of my hand and grabbed me by the scruff of the neck so hard my feet came off the ground. He held me with my arms twisted behind my back, while the other policeman talked to the man in the checkered shirt without laying a hand on him. He even offered him a kerchief for his bloody head!

The police carted me away. Cook followed, but one of the policemen yelled at him, told him to scram or they'd arrest him, too.

"Get the Captain, Cook!"

Eyes wide in puzzled horror, he acknowledged my plea and took off for the *Sonoma Wind*.

CHAPTER THIRTY-SIX

The jailhouse stunk of stale liquor. Men in uniforms milled about behind a long, wooden counter. Rows of chairs formed a tight row across from the counter, occupied by a sorry crop of hard-luck miners and sailors, waiting to be stuffed into some dingy cell until a judge could hear their case.

"You can cool your heels along with this mangy lot," one policeman said, tossing me sideways onto the last empty chair like I was some kind of feed bag. I was smack in the middle of the crowded row, and the men on each side of me glared and refused to make room. I elbowed them until I could squeeze into the narrow space between them.

The floor under our feet thumped and rumbled, from the raucous prisoners detained below. Muffled obscenities seeped through the floorboards. The simmering rage, the sweaty stench, and the sheer size of the muscular men on either side of me was unnerving. What if I ended up in jail with all of them?

I hadn't expected the police to take me away and let the pirate go free. To make matters worse, I nearly got Cook arrested. Had it not been for the pirate sticking around to gripe about a mad girl beating on him for nothing, they might have blamed Cook for the disturbance. All he was doing was trying to pull me out of a fight.

Cook's pained expression had said it all—he couldn't help with the police. He had to keep his mouth shut and run for the Captain, who I now relied on to persuade the officials to release me. I was his responsibility, after all.

They did not leave me in the waiting area for long. The same officer returned and escorted me through a swing door, down a short hall and into the office of some judge-looking man in a dingy black robe. He motioned to the chair in front of his large desk. A white wig with curls sat on a stack of papers on the polished desk. Without looking up, he asked me to state my full name, age, place of birth.

As soon as I spoke, he put his pen down and looked up. Charlotte Lee LeBeau, I'd said with my gentlest voice, making it clear I was a girl, just in case he hadn't noticed. His expression was plain, hard to interpret, but he listened.

I explained I'd hit my head recently, had some trouble keeping things straight in my mind, and wasn't sure what had come over me out in the street. I got carried away with explaining where I was born, how I sailed from California, crewed on the ill-fated *Salish Wind*, and then had lived the past winter at the lighthouse on Deception Island. Of course, I left out the part about raiding pirates and buried treasure, which would have made me look like a liar, or even worse, a delusional danger to society.

The Justice set his timepiece down on the desk in front of him. Despite leaving all the best bits out, he seemed somewhat interested in my story, yet determined not to engage in it while the clock ticked and he had work to do. The policeman who'd brought me in appeared at the open door and handed him a piece of paper. I wasn't a very interesting case, I figured, judging from the small amount of writing on the page and how quickly the Justice skimmed it. As the policeman left, he instructed him to close the door. In an instant, I felt trapped, that my plan to flush out the pirates had backfired, and I was about to face the awful consequences of another one of my half-baked ideas. My armpits prickled with panic. I sat on my hands to keep them from trembling, and to remind myself that the situation was serious. One rash comment might land me behind bars.

"You claim the man you assaulted was a robber and a thief," he said, after perusing the paper and ignoring me for several minutes more.

"Yessir."

"Yes, your worship, if you please."

"Yessir, your worship. And when he snuck up on me like he did, well, I thought he was going to kidnap me. I made a terrible mistake, though."

"The arresting officer says the man never laid a hand on you. Am I to understand you mistook him for someone else?"

I couldn't argue that the arresting officer was wrong or lying.

"Yessir. That's exactly what happened." Doe eyes. Some fluttering of the lashes for added innocence. "I can explain. You see, these merchant sailors came to Deception Island last fall…"

He cut me off, beady blue eyes blinking with impatience. "Enough. I don't need to hear any more of your life story. At a minimum, Miss, er, LeBeau, I should charge you with disturbing the peace."

"Yessir, however, as I mentioned, it was a grievous error in judgement on my part. I deeply regret it and the trouble I've caused you when you are so busy with important matters."

My exaggerated attempt at a heartfelt apology didn't impress him. He returned a blank stare over his spectacles.

"The other man didn't wish to make a case of it. Lucky for you, because you are in the wrong. At least you admit it. I appreciate you owning up to what you've done and I will take that into consideration. But tell me, what is a girl doing in the company of merchant sailors? And do you always dress like a boy?"

There was that same old chestnut again, what girls can and can't do, not to mention what I wore so I could do my work. But I dug up a polite smile and hung it out for him like an honest shingle.

"Oh, it's only temporary. I've been working hard, hoping to save up enough to go back to school in the fall, to become a nurse."

"Ah! Nursing! An honorable calling. Quite ambitious, though, having to assist men of medicine."

Those doctors are busy turning skilled nurses into house-keepers for sick people, I wanted to say, but kept my salty opinion to myself.

"I hope I'm worthy."

"You are well-spoken despite your violent outburst. Where were you educated?"

"Nowhere, Your Worship, but I studied this past year with Edgar Dalworth. Well, not him exactly, as he passed away last year, and he didn't come back from the dead to hover over me and my lessons. That's not what I meant. What I meant is I've studied his journals and read the books he had on Deception Island."

A case of the nerves always made me chatter. I couldn't stop words from tumbling from my mouth. But my blather didn't make him angry. Rather, his jaw relaxed and his mouth fell open in friendly acknowledgement.

"I knew Edgar! He was a brilliant fellow, and a beloved friend. His passing was a terrible blow."

"I am sorry for your loss. How lucky for you to have had his acquaintance! I wish I had known him. His widow often tells me we have so much in common."

This was all true, but I had also glimpsed a path to his sympathy and needed to use it.

"Yes, I can see how she might say so. You must be quite clever to follow his scientific work. But he was not a man who believed in violence. In that, you are not similar. In fact, he was quite outspoken on the matter of capital punishment."

"He wrote about that. He wanted the death sentence abolished, as he believed it was excessive and inconsistently applied by…by the law… to control."

His expression flattened. He knew I'd stopped short of saying "excessive and inconsistently applied by judges like you…" and it snapped him out of his pleasant reflection.

"Yes, well. Enough chatter now. Your Captain will be here soon."

He adjusted his spectacles and shuffled the papers on his desk, which was my cue to be quiet. I wanted to thumb through the books he had on the packed shelves that lined the walls, but knew better than to lean out of my chair. A fat book lay open on the side table and I twisted myself sideways to read what was on the open page. Boring government stuff that Jake would have adored.

The Justice cleared his throat. He looked at me with disapproval, so I straightened myself in the chair, folded my hands on my lap, and counted the law volumes he had on his shelves to pass the time.

About ten minutes later, there was a knock at the door.

"Come," the Justice said.

The Captain entered, glaring at me with so much annoyance that I almost wished a trapdoor would open under my chair and drop me into the hoard of criminals below.

"Sir, my sincere apologies for the behavior of the young lady," he began.

He strode across the room and extended his hand. The Justice extracted half of his hind end from the chair in time for the greeting.

"Thank you for your prompt response, Captain."

"Your worship. My ship's cook has told me what occurred in the square."

"Then, as you know, she took a round out of some innocent sailor. Accused him of robbery and theft, but now claims it was a case of mistaken identity."

"Did she now?" He gazed at me with steely eyes, but I kept my face blank as a slate.

"She mentioned to me she has had some mental problems…"

"Yes, I'm aware."

Mental problems! How did a bang on the head turn into mental problems?

"And, for your information, your Black boy had no part in the attack. In fact, it would appear he did his best to break it up, my officers said. Don't be too hard on him."

Was he suggesting Cook had done something wrong? And talking about him like the Captain owned him, calling him "boy"? My breath was fast and shallow. I bit my bottom lip and gripped the sides of my chair.

"He's a good man, a free man," the Captain said, and the sharp edge to his words saved me from an outburst I'd regret. The implication that Cook was his slave offended the Captain. He clenched his jaw and continued. "Your recommendation concerning this incident, sir? I guarantee she will not be a problem if you release her."

"Excellent. Happy to hand her over. I have no room for females in here, and if I throw her in with the rest of them, they'll maul her beyond recognition. If you would take her home to Deception Island, the matter will be closed. I expect she can't get in any trouble out there."

The Captain spun around to look at me. "Deception Island?"

"Is that not where she lives?"

"No. She's from San Francisco."

They both stared at me and I feigned confusion.

"But I suspect it's where she wants to go," the Captain said, his words slow and even, his eyes narrowing as he fixed them on me. "She lived with the lightkeeper this past winter, but she has confused her memories of the time."

"Ah, I see. The mental problems…"

The Captain turned back to the justice. "What do you require from me?"

"Nothing. It's a case of disorderly conduct, which I see every hour on the hour in this gold-thirsty town. I'll waive a fine and dismiss her into your custody if you see she's out of this port forthwith."

"Very good of you, sir. She'll be gone for good as soon as my ship is cleared for departure."

And with that, the Captain escorted me in tense silence out of the police barracks and onto the dirty boardwalk of Bastion Street.

CHAPTER THIRTY-SEVEN

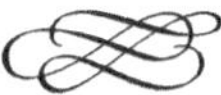

"D o you have any idea how much trouble you nearly got yourself in back there? It's a wonder he didn't lock you up, confiscate our goods, and throw the rest of us out of the colony. Wouldn't Mr. Miller be pleased with that, putting his business in jeopardy?"

The Captain hauled on my sleeve and marched us away from the police station at an angry clip. He made a sudden turn into an alley running parallel to the docks.

"Where are we going?"

"Keep up. Can you do that without causing a scene? Keep up and keep quiet. I've had enough of you today."

He spit the words at me in a raspy whisper, fists clenched in balls. I'd only seen him angry once before and that was when he gave the wrong command aboard the *Salish Wind*. He set a brisk pace, turned again into a side alley, a dark and narrow lane running parallel to the wharf with small doors embedded in the brick walls. He knew his way. I hoped it was a shortcut back to the *Sonoma Wind*, but we had passed all the familiar streets that led down to the harbor. My mind raced. I'd crossed a line with him, forced him to act. Now I didn't know where he was taking me or what he was going to do with me.

"Shouldn't we have turned down that last lane?"

"We're going to the shipyard. I should have been there an hour ago. No thanks to you."

"Oh." I felt bad for interfering with Mr. Miller's schooner business, but I hadn't finished setting up the Captain to go after the gold. "This place...I don't know. It's got me mixed up all over again."

Not the truth, not a total lie either, but my remark cracked his hardened surface. He stopped to wipe his flushed face, and his forehead changed from rows of hard-cut lines to soft, plowed furrows. He folded his white kerchief and placed it back in his tunic pocket as he eyed me with genuine concern.

"I can see how it would do, yes."

The thoughtful captain had returned, the one in control of himself and situations, the one who understood the world through poetry and literature. I almost expected him to quote something from one of his books. Instead, a flash of something troubling crossed his brow. Was it sadness? Regret? I couldn't tell. Whatever it was, it had brought a moment of empathy to him.

"C'mon," he said, steering me on with resignation. We walked on at a less frantic pace in the late morning sunshine and soon arrived at the back of an open building, where the broken hull of a whaler towered into the air, resting in a massive wooden cradle.

"Now, Miss LeBeau. I'd appreciate your cooperation while I see to the business of our schooner repair. Can I count on you to remain here, mind your business, and not pick a fight with any passersby?"

"Yessir."

My cheeks warmed. I shoved my hands into my pockets, as if keeping them put away would prevent me from embarrassing myself or him any further. So the *Sonoma Wind* needed a repair. The Captain hadn't made that up after all. But all the way back to Victoria, he hadn't shown interest in anything but my recall of details about the sinking of the *Salish Wind*. He had asked many questions about the shipwreck, but as I thought of it, I realized he'd gone no further. Then why did he have my map of Deception Island stashed in his quarters, the map the pirates had stolen from Mrs. Dalworth's kitchen table? What use was it to him, if not to help him find the missing gold?

As I sorted out my thoughts, the Captain returned, and we started back to the harbor. The Captain was in a buoyant mood, having learned his ship would be ready to sail in a few days. The needed repair also left me with enough time to get to the island and back.

"Sir?" I had to take advantage of his improved mood. "It's an awful time to ask, what with this police business today. And I'm real sorry about all that. I was wondering, since we must be here for at least two more days, could I have shore leave tomorrow? I need to visit Deception Island."

"That story you told the Justice about where you were from. You weren't mixed up at all about that, were you?" I didn't answer. I gazed at the harbor, in the direction of the elusive island to the west. "Tell me, why on earth do you want to go back to that godforsaken place?"

He had to know about the buried gold. Had to. "To see Mrs. Dalworth."

He was incredulous. "The woman lightkeeper? And how do you fancy getting yourself out there and back for a visit during our short time in port?"

"Well, I thought Mr. Brody might take me, or at least help me arrange it. After the meeting tomorrow, of course, which can't be too far from anywhere, as Victoria's not a big town. And since the ship needs a repair, it should be possible."

His shock wasn't an act.

"They almost ordered me to take you out there, thanks to that tall tale you told the Justice."

There was genuine horror in his expression, the look of someone haunted by terrible things.

"I must say, I don't share your appetite to return. I can't stand to look at that island and can't fathom how you'd want to set foot on that miserable piece of rock again, after all you've been through."

We walked on. I'd expected him to grill me about what I wanted to do there. Surely, he knew from his accomplices that Mr. Miller's gold was still out there. Maybe he was trying to throw me off, with all his chatter about hating the island. Time to put fresh bait on my hook.

"I left something important behind. Unfortunately, I'm the only one who can find where I put it."

He stopped and grabbed my sleeve.

"And what might that be? A sentimental collection of pretty beach shells? Or some cowboy memorabilia you kept from your dead father? Or maybe it's your mind? That's it. Maybe you left a piece of your clever but broken mind on that cursed island."

"No." I was stunned by his cruel remarks.

He scowled. "You're like a shark around blood."

"It's something real and valuable. I'm the only one who knows where it is. One last visit and I'll never go back again."

"While I'm grateful you've returned to Victoria at my request, I cannot allow such a flippant excursion."

What did he mean, "at his request"? He'd told Mizzy and Doctor Benjamin that the authorities had called me back to Victoria! And he wouldn't allow it?

"Please, sir. I need to go there. It will only be a day trip. We're idle here waiting for our repair, anyway. Besides, the Justice wants me out of here. He told you that himself."

"If I agree—and I haven't yet, as it is against my better judgement—but if I agree, there will be strict conditions. First, the expense comes out of your pocket. Second, you cannot go alone. Cook will accompany you. Third, it is weather permitting. Fourth, I will speak to Mr. Brody on your behalf, as I only trust him to arrange such a trip. Last, the trip is out if it cannot be arranged tomorrow following our meeting with him. We cannot pop by and pick you up on our way out of Fuca Strait if you get delayed out there due to weather. If that should happen, we won't wait for you. You'll remain here until we return next month. Understood?"

The list of precautions caught me by surprise. He wanted me to go, that was it, but he also wanted it to look like he'd done his best to keep me safe. It didn't add up. Why drag Cook into it if you weren't sincere? And why insist on Brody arranging the trip? He'd be the last person to ask if you were going after buried gold from a shipwreck he'd investigated.

"Can Jake go with me instead? You need Cook here."

"Absolutely not! Sending Miller is out of the question. I don't relish letting you out of my sight for the day either, given you are a magnet for trouble. Miller stays. He can cover the galley for Cook. By the way, Mr. Brody also has to agree to this, and we don't even know if he can pull it off, or if he is even willing to try."

We started back along the lane to the main street of the harbor, the Captain ahead, me trailing behind, the low-rank, reprimanded delinquent. I repeated the entire conversation to myself, confused all over again about the Captain and his unpredictable motives. The terms he laid out gave him no advantage. It was cautious and practical to a fault.

I had brought all my savings with me, and hoped they would cover the cost. Jake could loan me more if needed, I was pretty sure of that, but I was aware I was about to blow everything I'd saved on one hair-brained expedition to the lighthouse island. As we walked back to the *Sonoma Wind*, I tried not to get my hopes up, even though the morning sky was clear and calm, a sign that pleasant weather was likely in store for the coming days. I would beg Mr. Brody to take me if I had to, and felt certain he'd find a way. But the Captain's words didn't sit right with me. He hadn't behaved as expected.

"We have our appointment with Mr. Brody first thing tomorrow. I'll ask him about a trip to Deception then."

"Our appointment is with Mr. Brody?"

"Do I need to remind you that's why you are here again, and why I, regrettably at this moment, orchestrated your brief return?"

He clenched his jaw, his patience frazzled.

"Of course, sir. You told me. I didn't realize Mr. Brody was in charge of the matter again, is all."

"There is much you do not know. You would do well to consider that as you bash every shoreline you encounter with your stormy assumptions."

It wasn't the first time someone had accused me of brash and impulsive behavior, but his criticism was so poetic, his words swept me away. With no clever retort coming to the rescue, I shrunk into step behind him and mulled over what it was he thought I didn't know and what I'd assumed.

CHAPTER THIRTY-EIGHT

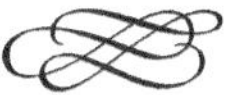

I scrambled up the steep wooden stairs to the main deck just before a quarter to seven the next morning. The Captain tucked his pocket watch back in his vest and straightened his cuffs and waistcoat. His eyes were tired, like he'd spent the entire night on the watch.

We were to meet with Mr. Brody at seven hundred hours regarding new information about the wreck of the *Salish Wind*. I was sure the Captain had invented a reason to get me back to Victoria. But here we were, going to that important meeting after all, and not a single mention of the gold buried out on Deception Island.

"Sir, do you know what new information Mr. Brody has?" I asked as we picked our way over slippery stones and crunching shells to the boardwalk. The tide was low, and the beach reeked of dead, fishy things.

"Yes, I'm familiar."

I waited for him to offer an explanation, but he didn't.

"It's because we're both witnesses and our stories don't match, isn't it?"

The Captain halted his steps and turned. I braced myself, thinking I'd angered him again, but in the faint morning light, he appeared shaken. "How so?"

"You left out the part about the black sloop that chased us, the one you tried to evade."

It was the most I'd ever revealed about what I knew. It was too late for him to disappear me overboard, too late to turn back. We were only minutes away from Brody's office. A few early workers were already milling about on the surrounding docks.

"You've remembered everything, haven't you? I told Mr. Brody I thought you had."

"Yes, almost everything."

At the corner, we joined the morning crowd of workers, pushing and shoving through an archway that merged single file into the narrow street. I was right behind the Captain, but everyone around me was so much bigger. We'd just cleared the passage when someone yanked me back. I reached for the Captain's coat tail, only inches out of my grasp, but the current of men carried him away. Someone yanked my wool beanie down, almost covering both my eyes, and stuffed a kerchief into my mouth. The last thing I saw was the Captain looking back, searching the crowd behind him in horror, realizing I'd vanished.

A man muttered orders to keep quiet and walk, as he shoved me into a side alley, past mounds of putrid garbage and simmering muck. I tried to spit out the kerchief, but he had jammed it in tight. It tasted like bitter oil and I gagged as it sucked the last drop of saliva from my dry mouth. My captor opened a heavy wooden door and shoved me into a dark hall that carried the aroma of cooking garlic. Someone pulled my cap up from my eyes.

In front of me was Sculder, the ringleader from the black

sloop, the man who had murdered Drak aboard the *Salish Wind*. The red-bearded sailor I'd seen him with at Clamity Cove was the one who'd snatched me in the crowd.

Sculder grabbed me by the collar and steered me through the back of a kitchen. Greasy smoke hung over a huge stove where two wiry Chinese men chopped and stirred food on the hissing grill.

The sailor I'd seen the day before came in through another door, still wearing his red and black checkered shirt. He had an angry gash on his forehead and a bruised left cheek.

"You look like hell, Quinn," Sculder said to him. "She did all that to you?"

The man clenched his teeth. "Aye. We was in public. I couldn't strike back, risk getting arrested." His fingers twitched as if he wanted to strangle me with his bare hands. "She had a shovel, boss."

Sculder burst out laughing and the sailor glared at me with a burning red face. I glared back.

"Well, she's more resourceful than all you lot. You have one job that isn't attached to a sail and you bungle it."

The two men looked at their shoes.

"Tie up her feet and hands. Think you can handle that? Hample, bring the loading cart to the back door so we can smuggle this feisty little piece aboard ship. We're going to the island right away." He pointed a dirty finger in my face. "And you, half-girl, half-boy, half-breed *siwash*, or whatever you are, you better keep quiet and do what I say, or you'll end up with the fishes, too."

Still winded by the exertion of my capture, the red-bearded sailor called Hample trundled from the kitchen. The cooks at the stove peeked in my direction, but wouldn't let me catch their eyes. Minding their business like I wasn't there, like they knew what was good for them.

I tried to speak with the kerchief in my mouth. My eyes pleaded with Sculder to remove it and he did with a dire warning that if I so much as raised my voice, he'd knock me unconscious. I nodded, knowing better than to argue. These men were dangerous. They'd pillaged the *Salish Wind* and murdered the crew. They were about to take me to Deception Island on their sloop.

"What do you want with me?" I croaked, almost matter-of-fact, as if underneath my calm expression, my heart didn't pound like a hunted animal. He shoved a cup of water in my tied hands. I managed a small gulp, enough to get my voice back, dribbling an equal amount down the front of my shirt.

"Well, turns out somebody—mentioning no names as I don't think we were properly introduced—turns out somebody saw where we buried some gold on that island. And that same somebody..." His face flushed red with anger. "That same somebody come along and swapped our treasure out for a bunch of beach rocks!"

"I don't know what you're talking about," I said, as he paced in front of me.

"Yeah, you do. You weren't just digging clams for Mrs. Dalworth that day we caught you in Clamity Cove, were you?"

I didn't answer.

"You were watching what we were up to, saw us bury our treasure."

"You stole that gold from the *Salish Wind!*"

Sculder stepped back as if slapped by the accusation.

"Took it, not stole. The Captain offered it in exchange for his life. That fool shoulda let us come alongside, kept everybody calm, instead of trying to outrun us. Sure, we woulda taken some goods, but everybody coulda sailed on happily ever after and been none the wiser. But we struck gold that day, thanks to him, and couldn't leave it to sink into the deep, now could we?"

His version of the wreck of the *Salish Wind* was a robbery gone bad. But this criminal had one fact right. He knew it was the Captain's fault that the *Salish Wind* ran aground.

"You could have rescued the crew. But you killed them!"

"In self-defense! That big Hawaiian started it all. A crazy warrior, that one, no reasoning with him. Took out two of my boys and then the battle was on. Meanwhile, the quivering captain hid under some tarps and begged for his life. So we spared him. We aren't monsters."

"You put him in a skiff, figuring he'd end up drowned or dead. Lucky for him, he got picked up floating out to sea and survived."

"How do you know that?"

Sculder pushed a stringy piece of hair out of his eyes and bent over to look me square in the face. His warm breath smelled of smokes and stale booze. My blank expression held, innocent and matter-of-fact as a critical fact came into focus in my head—he still didn't realize I'd been part of the crew, that I'd been aboard and witnessed the shipwreck and murders. I cleared my throat and took another sip of water to buy myself a little time.

"Oh. Well. The authorities gave Mrs. Dalworth a copy of the report...because the schooner sunk off the lighthouse island? And they did an investigation, the navy did. Got the Captain's testimony once he recovered. Declared it an accident. The result of a navigational error by the First Mate."

"He blamed the dead man? What a coward."

He turned away. Relieved that I'd spun a credible answer off the top of my head, the new information he'd given me sunk in. The Captain wasn't in on it with these scoundrels. He'd made a terrible mistake, and tried to conceal it to save his hide and his reputation.

"And then you, the lucky little clam digger, you come along and saw us bury something, didn't ya?"

"Yeah. That's what happened."

"Pretty slick, I'd say, although this bunch o' mine ain't hard to fool." He threw another disgusted side glance at the man in the checkered shirt. "But who knew Mrs. Dalworth's helper was a girl? That caught us all by surprise, although you were younger when we run into you over in that cove. You hadn't yet bloomed, or we woulda noticed fer sure."

Quinn snickered and wiped his mouth on the back of his checkered cuff. Posing as a boy had saved me many times in recent years, but as Mrs. Plea had pointed out, I couldn't get away with it anymore. The only way to stay safe was to use their friendship with Mrs. Dalworth. The only way to stay alive was to keep the gold just out of their reach. They couldn't kill me until I gave it to them because they'd never find it without me.

The door banged and Hample entered.

"Light breeze, we're ready. Wagon's out back."

Hample stuffed the oily kerchief back in my mouth so hard it made my eyes water. They were taking me to their sloop. This wasn't the way it was supposed to go. I'd been foolish to suspect the Captain had masterminded stealing Mr. Miller's gold.

As they rolled me up in thick canvas, I thought about the Captain. If I hadn't been so quick to judge him, I wouldn't have got myself into this deadly mess. He hadn't been part of the plan to rob the *Salish Wind*. I'd glimpsed his panic when I was snatched out on the street.

What would he do now, having lost me in the crowd? He'd go to Brody and tell him I'd vanished. Brody was the only one who could get me to Deception Island on my own, and I had no reason to run off since he'd agreed to ask him to make the trip. He'd know I hadn't been arrested because I vanished without commotion. But he also hadn't seen me kidnapped. Eventually, he'd return to the ship, tell Cook I'd gone missing, and they'd grill Jake. Cook would remind the Captain about the sailor I beat with the shovel the day before, a man I'd recognized from the shipwreck. Jake had my deciphered notes, describing how the black sloop robbed the *Salish Wind* and how they killed the crew before it sunk.

They would figure it out. I knew they would. But how much time would pass before they put together all the pieces and came after me to Deception Island?

CHAPTER THIRTY-NINE

A couple hours later, Hample unpacked me from the sail into the stale air of a cabin below deck on the sloop. My eyes bulged as he tore the sour kerchief out of my mouth. I tried to speak, but no words formed in my dry throat.

"Gahhh!" I croaked through burning lips.

"Holler all you want. Ain't nobody gonna hear ya out here."

I knew that. We'd already left Victoria harbor. At least an hour earlier, the ship's anchor grumbled, its heavy chain winding on a winch, and a couple sets of feet stomped overhead as sails were unfurled and raised.

The small quarters had just enough room to stand. A draft of sea air came through a small hatch in the ceiling, left open a crack to vent the place, which reeked of mold and rotting fish. I pointed at a half-full pail out of my reach.

"Water. I need water."

Hample shoved the pail with his foot and laughed.

"You ain't gonna want that. Here."

He tossed a canteen in my lap and loosened the rope around my hands just enough so I could hold it. I sniffed the contents and touched a little to my lips to make sure he wasn't tricking me. No smell and nothing sharp to the taste. I took a trial sip. A little on the salty side but otherwise cool and quenching. I guzzled a few mouthfuls.

"Lunch is served at high noon, Your Highness," he said, with a contrived accent. "Oh wait. You're just a meddler and a two-bit whore. No lunch for you." I swung my tied feet at his shins, but couldn't get a solid kick away. "Ow! That ain't very nice. I do like 'em scrappy, though."

He laughed so hard that he snorted. He was still laughing when he jammed the cabin door shut, rusty hinges squawking from lack of oil. A skeleton key clicked in a padlock and I was alone.

The cabin was bare but for a wooden bench, the bucket containing some combination of seawater and urine, and the drinking water canteen Hample had left behind. Although the door was flimsy, it was enough to keep me captive for the trip. The only real escape was overboard anyhow, and that would be a fast and frigid death by drowning. Escape would only be possible once we reached Deception Island.

I sat up on the bench to think. Once again, I'd gotten myself into trouble trying to fix things on my own. It was like the time I faked my death and didn't tell Jake, so he wouldn't get hurt or talk me out of another wild scheme. At least this time, I'd left a trail behind for him and others to follow. Cook knew the pirates were back. I told him the man I beat with a shovel had been at Deception Island. The Justice in Victoria knew where I wanted to go and so did the Captain. And Jake knew I meant to go after the buried gold.

But I didn't expect to be kidnapped on a busy street in broad daylight! That had been an unfortunate miscalculation on my part. Preoccupied with the Captain's deceit, I'd lost sight of my vulnerability. The thug in the market had been a warning—they were coming after me for the gold. I naively thought I'd be safe as long as I wasn't alone, and they'd snatched me before I'd finished arranging things. Jake and Cook would piece it together. I could count on them for that, but I had to buy enough time for them to figure it out and come after me.

There was one other problem to factor. Only the Captain knew someone had taken me. What would he tell Cook and Jake when he returned to the ship without me? He couldn't lie and say they had kept me in jail, and they'd never believe I'd run off. He would have to tell them I'd been kidnapped.

On the bright side, I reassured myself, my sudden trip to Deception Island was free. Of course, it wasn't a day's excursion to the lighthouse for tea and scones with Mrs. Dalworth. No, we'd be going straight to Clamity Cove, where the pirates would bash me around and demand I take them to where I'd hidden Mr. Miller's gold.

Although I knew I could find it now, it wouldn't seem real until I stuck a shovel into the earth and struck one of the lumpy canvas bags. And then what? As soon as I found the gold, they'd kill me. If I tried to fight, they'd torture me into giving it up. I shuddered at the mess I'd made for myself once again.

Rocking about in a small cabin below deck while the sloop was under sail was almost as terrifying as being trapped in the cupboard of the sinking *Salish Wind* while these same greedy men murdered and pillaged overhead. I stood on the bench and tried to look out of the small deck hatch. The crank to open it was missing. I wrapped my fingers around its iron hinges, but it wouldn't budge. It was much too small to crawl through, anyway. I stuck my nose up to it and inhaled the fresh, *saltchuck* air that rolled over the deck and slipped through the opening. My head cleared with every breath.

What did I do on the *Salish Wind*? I built a raft, that's what. I sighed. A raft wouldn't get me off the sloop and it wouldn't save me when I handed over the gold with the barrel of a gun sticking in my ear. I ran through options in my head, dismissing every scenario as hopeless. After a few minutes, I realized my survival was unlikely unless...unless I made them believe a story.

Rafts are like stories. You assemble the parts and make sure they hold together well enough to carry you. I returned to the bench, drank some more water, and pulled my knees into my chest. There had to be a way out of this, and I had less than two hours to think of it.

I had almost dozed off, rocked by the rhythm of small waves on the hull when the key jangled in the lock. Sculder ducked through the door, muttering to himself. The sailor in the checkered shirt squeezed in behind him and the two of them shoved and slugged each other as they took up most of the space. Suddenly, Mr. Jones shot by their feet, sprang onto my lap, and licked my face. I clutched him to me in surprise.

"Mr. Jones! Where did you come from?"

"That's what I'd like to know," Sculder said. "Musta snuck aboard when we weren't looking. Quinn, here, chased him around the deck, nearly lost a hand trying to shut up his fool barking. Got half the dock staring at us, so he had to come along."

I put a protective arm around Mr. Jones. Sculder was doing his best to sound mean and in charge, but his voice faltered. His eyes came to rest on the ropes they'd tied me up with, now piled in neat coils on the bench. He leaned back with a start as he realized I was loose.

"How'd you do that?"

"Magic." I whispered with a sly smile, wide eyes locking with his until he looked away.

It wasn't magic at all. Hample had loosened my hands and forgotten to tighten the ropes when he left. Still, Mrs. Plea would be proud of me for playing up the mystery. Sculder's eyes darted around the cabin, like he expected to find someone else in there with us. He swatted a fly off his neck and elbowed Quinn out of the way.

"Soon as we anchor in the cove, we're going ashore and you're going to show us where you hid our gold."

"I don't remember."

"We'll make you remember," Quinn snarled. "Besides, that dog'll show us if your memory fails. Ain't that right, Sculder?"

"Shut up. We wouldn't be here if you'd checked those barrels. Half way to Portland with three barrels o' beach rock. And you, Miss Smartypants, you'd better pray you remember when we get there, because if you don't take us to our gold, I'm gonna chop you and your mutt into tasty pieces for the crabs.

I'd been thinking they'd shoot me. Death by butchering was even more vicious. I held my breath as gruesome scenes from the *Salish Wind* filled my head.

"And nobody will ever know you were even here..."

"It's not your gold."

"Yes, it is. We salvaged it fair and square from an abandoned shipwreck. We have scavenger rights. You're the one that stole it."

I reminded myself they didn't know I'd witnessed their raid and murders.

"Say I'm lucky enough to remember where it is. You'll kill me if I find it and you'll kill me if I don't. So what's in it for me?"

Sculder shrugged and crossed his arms across his chest. "What's in it for you? Haha! The nerve of this one! What's in it for you? Well, how 'bout this, Missy? If you and your mutt don't find the gold, or try to pretend you don't know where it is, we'll get rid of your lightkeeper lady, too. You have a choice to make. Your life ain't worth a plug nickel, but maybe you think hers is worth saving."

"You wouldn't do that." I gripped my knees to keep them from banging together. "She had nothing to do with any of this."

"That so? As I recall, she handed out gold nuggets to them Injun friends of hers, the ones who bought you off me. So she knows, or you gave her a cut. Why else would you draw her a map of Clamity? You don't take us to it, she's next to try. I want my gold and you ladies are going to hand it over, one way or another."

Everything he said set me off, conjured up horrible memories. It should have triggered a terrible spell. But nothing happened. No sickness descended on me. Instead, I saw how he was playing his hand, and he'd started with a lame and predictable bluff. He wouldn't hurt Mrs. Dalworth. That empty threat might have worked in days past, but now I saw right through it.

"I'll take you to it."

"Wise choice. Cooperate and Mrs. Dalworth will never even know we were here. But you try to pull a fast one…that's something you don't wanna picture."

Quinn stepped out the door and Sculder followed.

"Is it really worth it? Killing for money?" I said.

"Money buys everything, kid. It bought you once. If those sorry locals show up, I'll tell 'em they don't get a refund. And this time, you ain't for sale."

He hooted with laughter and slammed the cabin door.

"How did you know I was in trouble, Mr. Jones? How did you find me?" I didn't give him a chance to explain. "Never mind that. Did Jake and Cook see where you went? You led them to me, didn't you? Good work. And I've come up with a way to stall the pirates until they can catch up to us."

Mr. Jones said what he liked about me was I always had a clever plan. But he hoped this one included some revenge this time, for Kuno's sake, and for the sake of the *Salish Wind*. A sudden chill surrounded me, as if the ghosts of the shipwreck had gathered, waiting for my answer. I rubbed my arms and shook it off. I'd wanted revenge at one time, but not anymore.

"Justice, Mr. Jones. Justice is far, far better than revenge."

Mr. Jones sighed, but I knew he understood. We both looked up at the small sliver of blue sky visible through the overhead hatch. A sliver of sky, a sliver of hope.

CHAPTER FORTY

Mr. Jones leaped out and ran up the beach as soon as the pirate skiff pulled onto the shore. He ran straight for a spot and dug furiously, sending scoops of sand flying into the air behind him.

"Ha. I knew it!" Quinn said, rubbing his hands together. "Yer mutt's showing us where you hid it."

I pressed my lips together, knowing Mr. Jones was too smart for that. The men shoved Mr. Jones aside and plunged their shovels into the rocky sand. It wasn't the spot, of course. They'd unearthed a two-foot section when Mr. Jones started on a new hole farther along.

"No, he's right. It's more that way," I said straight-faced, and the men hurried off with their shovels.

Soon, the beach behind us looked like a mad gopher had been at work, and the grumbling got louder as each new location yielded nothing. When Mr. Jones sniffed out yet another spot, Sculder lost his temper, whipped out his pistol, cocked the hammer and took aim.

"No!" I yelled, yanking the sleeve of his coat as he fired.

The shot fired wide and ricocheted off a log. Sculder pulled his arm away and fired a second time as Mr. Jones ran out of range. He curled his backend as if to duck the shot whistling past his hind end. But he didn't stop. He reached the bushes and vanished.

The three men encircled me then, flushed-faced, sweaty and furious. Sculder pointed his pistol at my chest and demanded I show him where I put the gold. I put my hands in the air and tearfully confessed that I'd hauled it off the beach to a mid-island clearing. It was a convincing performance from someone who should have been too terrified to lie.

"How much farther is this clearing?"

Sculder grumbled and jabbed me in the back with a walking stick he'd made from a tree branch. When I didn't answer, he jabbed me again, this time harder, and the end of the stick hit a bone in my spine. This horrible man had tried to shoot Mr. Jones. I wanted to rip the stick from his hands and beat him to a pulp with it, but I had to keep a cool head because he still had the loaded pistol.

"Answer me!"

"At this rate, say ten more minutes."

All uphill, I didn't need to add, as he'd noticed. He'd been puffing after only five minutes into the hike up from Clamity Cove. This trio was one sorry lot. I figured them all for ale house regulars, since they wore stale booze and tobacco like bad cologne. Their sweat reeked of garlic, onions, and unwashed armpits. They were terrible specimens compared to the trim and disciplined sailors I'd worked with on Mr. Miller's two schooners.

We walked in single file, which is all the narrow trail would allow. Since the path wasn't obvious, I led the way and Sculder followed close behind me. Hample and Quinn took up the rear, both of them dragging like an anchor that hadn't been set right, forcing us to stop every few minutes so they could lean over their knees and wheeze. Any time wasted helped my chances. And if the digging and hiking wore them down enough, I might get a crack at escape on this futile journey.

"Slow it up," Sculder barked from behind. We both looked back, hands on our hips, as the other two trudged to catch up.

"Man, you need a better crew."

Sculder nodded and sighed, as if the two of us were old pals sharing miseries over a pint, but then caught himself and snarled back.

"I don't need your snotty advice, thanks very much."

We set off as soon as they caught up to us. The other two were crestfallen when they realized they had to keep going.

A branch snapped in the bushes ahead and I peered into the forest shadows and thick salal. It could be Mr. Jones, if he'd doubled back and was following us. As we trudged along, I'd noticed his teardrop toe prints, like flower petals, dropped as clues in the fresh, damp dirt. He'd been moving at a trot and should be well ahead of us.

"Halt! said Sculder as he plunked himself down on a piece of fallen log. The other two groaned in relief and mopped their streaming brows with sleeves.

They'd made me haul their tools and gear like a pack mule, but we'd been so slow, I hadn't even broken into a sweat. I whistled a little cowboy tune as I screwed the cap off a water canteen.

"Gimme that!" Hample snatched it from my hands so fast, the leather strap burned my palm.

He drank half of it, then offered it to Sculder, who declined with a comment about slobber and backwash. Hample passed it to Quinn, who drained the last of it and threw it back at me empty. Whistling the same little tune, I waited in the middle of the path, scanning the surrounding bushes. I had a powerful sensation of being watched. Sculder's eyes darted around as if he sensed it, too. On this trail, I'd deliberately marched us onto Lekwungen land.

"Stop whistling. Move out," Sculder ordered, but his voice cracked.

I braced myself for what was to come. Once we reached the clearing, I'd run out of delaying tactics. They'd be in a rage when they realized I'd dragged them up there for nothing. But for now, I was still collecting advantages. I knew the path and the island. Mr. Jones had wasted a bunch of time for us down in the cove, and the hike was taking twice as long as it had ever taken me, even when I had a bad ankle.

The only gun I'd seen so far belonged to Sculder. It was a Colt five-shot revolver, and he had used up two rounds firing at Mr. Jones. The pistol was only deadly up close and was slow to reset between shots. If I could put five yards between us, the chances of Sculder shooting me were slim. I could tell by the way he handled his gun that he was no marksman. They'd never catch me past the clearing, if I timed it right. But then what? The only option was to run to the lighthouse.

The clearing had an eerie calm about it. Not a branch moved, not a leaf rustled. Even the birds were quiet, like they knew something bad had arrived. My legs felt heavy and didn't want to take another step, but Sculder forced me forward, out of the tree line and into the open space. I led them to the middle of the clearing, to the base of a massive cedar tree, to the place where I had buried Edgar Dalworth.

His gravesite wasn't the same. New grasses of spring torn away. Mounds of dirt left in two uneven heaps. The rocks I'd stacked for Edgar's headstone, knocked down and scattered. Edgar's remains were gone! This was the work of humans, and I hoped Mrs. Dalworth was behind it, that after I'd gone, she'd arranged to take Edgar with her when she left the island.

"Somebody's already been here!" I exclaimed.

"No. You are trying to trick us." Sculder pointed his pistol at my heart and looked around for more evidence. "You dug it up."

"How? I've been in San Francisco."

Sculder scowled. He knew it was impossible. He followed a trail of spilled dirt back to where we'd emerged from the forest.

His investigation gave me a precious minute to think. I hadn't expected Edgar's body to be gone. I'd hoped digging up a corpse would unnerve the men, since everything about the island already had them on edge. Now there was nothing to dig up. I was relieved I didn't have to do that to Edgar, even though I figured he'd understand, given the circumstances. But now I had to come up with something else fast.

I bent over to examine the grass and dirt over the shallow grave.

"This dig is fresh. Days old. I'd say the Captain beat you to it. After all, you gave him my island map."

Sculder's jaw dropped.

"We shoulda punched a hole in that boat and made him swim for it," said Hample. "That double-crossing yellow belly."

"I buried it in three separate canvas bags. Maybe he didn't get all of it."

I pointed to the first spot I'd tried to dig for Edgar. Hample stuck his shovel in the ground. It clanked against a rock. He slammed it down again and hit another rock. The island was like that. Rocks everywhere. Not like the friendly earth and fertile soil in Sonoma. I remembered spending weeks picking rocks out of Mrs. Dalworth's garden. They clustered in the ground like potatoes. I'd find one and then a whole family would appear in the surrounding dirt.

"Blast it all!" He kicked at a stubborn rock with his boot.

Quinn elbowed him aside and took over with his miner's pick.

Sculder paced nearby. He'd had a terrible experience on the

island the last time he'd come for the gold. But most of all, I'd got him thinking about the Captain and my island map.

"It'll be down about a foot," I said, helpful and timid as I could muster. "Just not sure of the exact spot."

The digging soon preoccupied the two men. If I could distract Sculder while they were busy, I could break away. Suddenly, Hample straightened and scanned the bushes.

"What was that?"

"Just the wind in the trees," Sculder said. "Onshore breeze is picking up. Dig faster."

The big old cedars stirred as if to prove his point.

"I hear the island is haunted," I said. "People say the ghost of a wild dog lives here and protects the island from all who do wrong."

"Nonsense," Sculder said, but he looked over his shoulder and back to where we'd entered the clearing.

"I heard him one night myself, howling, almost like a wolf, you know? The Indians say he's a spirit who'll take revenge on greed and evil."

Hample stared at me, aghast, and I shrugged. Just then, Quinn's pick struck something with a dull thud. The two men fell to their knees, moved the last of the dirt away with their hands, and pulled out a torn but empty piece of canvas. Salvaged from the *Salish Wind*, I'd used that canvas to gather the disintegrating limbs of Edgar's body, and slide him into a shallow grave.

"There you go. Somebody's taken it. You're too late."

"Listen!" Hample clambered to his feet. "That howl. You didn't hear it?" Panic filled his eyes, and his flushed face turned grey.

Sculder waved off his fear. "No animals here."

"No. I heard it, too," Quinn replied. He pointed his pick at the end of the clearing. "In the bushes behind that shed. It's there, right now. I can hear it move. It's coming for us." He took a step back.

A gust of wind came out of nowhere and the trees behind me moaned and then let out what sounded like a low growl. All three men turned to stare. I whistled a few eerie notes to add to the effect.

"Is something wrong?" I asked.

Hample backed away from the empty grave.

"That gold is cursed and…and she's a witch!"

Sculder ordered him to stop, but he didn't listen. Quinn, now wild-eyed, spun around, swatted and kicked as if he was under attack by a swarm of hornets.

"Ahhhhh! Shoot him! Get him off!"

He swung his pick, spinning around, chopping at the air. Then both men dropped their tools and ran for the trail.

It was at that moment Sculder made his error. Berating the men for their cowardice, he turned away from me and shot two rounds over the heads of the retreating sailors. I bolted for the end of the clearing.

CHAPTER FORTY-ONE

A crack rang out. The shot struck the wooden building a few feet behind me. I crashed through the brush onto the overgrown trail leading out of the clearing toward the windward side of the island. As a branch slapped my face, I didn't stop to think of whether I might fall or lose my way.

Sculder had fired his last round and missed. He would kill me when he caught up with me again, no doubt about that now, because I'd played him and escaped. But I knew he wouldn't follow me down this trail. He'd be lost in minutes if he tried.

It had been months since I'd brought Mrs. Dalworth to the clearing. I watched for the natural signposts I'd once followed—the fallen tree, branches I'd broken or stuck in the ground, small piles of rock. After a few minutes of running, I slowed up to catch my breath. Luckily, the route to the lighthouse was almost all downhill.

When I first tackled the trek to the lighthouse, I'd embedded clam shells in trees to mark the way. I searched the bark of tree trunks for them now, hoping I hadn't lost them behind the new spring foliage. I spotted the first one on the mossy side of a tall pine. The fear crushing my head like a tightening vice fell away and my thoughts had room to breathe. My mind set to work on what would happen next.

Sculder had an immense problem. He still didn't have the gold, his motley crew had mutinied, and in a flash of poor judgement, he'd given me an opportunity to get away. As I hurried down the path, I considered everything he might do next.

Of course, he'd round up his crew, threaten them back into line, and row back out to the anchored sloop. He'd reload that pistol and whatever other guns he had available on board. Then he'd sail around the corner of the island straight to the lighthouse, knowing that was the only place I could go.

The trail from the clearing to the lighthouse took about two hours in good conditions. I could trim fifteen minutes off if I kept to a good trot. How long would it take the pirates to get to the lighthouse? I did quick math as my feet found a steady rhythm.

The mutinous men were in lousy shape, but the return to Clamity Cove was also downhill. It wouldn't take them long to get back to the beach. Still, Sculder had to catch up with them and knock them back to their senses. I estimated it would take an hour before he rounded them up, sorted them out and got back aboard the sloop. Then it would take another half an hour to get under sail, make it around the island's southern point and anchor in Hidden Cove. It would take another fifteen to dispatch their skiff and row back ashore. An hour and forty-five.

I pushed myself as much as I dared, aware that I could not afford a single slip or tumble. Zigging and zagging through the forest undergrowth, it would also be easy to make a wrong turn. One mistake would cost me time. I had to beat them to the lighthouse.

I blew past the bluff without stopping to appreciate the incredible view, stretching west as far as the eye could see. But in passing, I noticed a telltale ribbon of grey along the horizon. A bank of sea fog was forming. A westerly breeze would bring it on land as the day cooled.

What would I do at the lighthouse? This pack of unscrupulous traders had befriended Mrs. Dalworth, so she wouldn't believe she was in danger, even if I could warn her. She'd invite them in as she'd always done. The long gun she kept for protection wouldn't be any help. She couldn't even load it without eyeglasses.

As for Perkins, he was a disaster with a rifle. He was a merchant sailor, recruited for his strong back and youthful spirit. Sailors in these modern times were solid working men, not snipers. They didn't have to worry about battles at sea as they did in the old days. While I'd left the island on good terms with him, I shuddered to think he might be my only ally. I hoped he'd trust me when I barged in out of nowhere and started giving orders.

Then there was Mr. Jones. I'd seen his fresh tracks, but nothing obvious since, and I couldn't stop for closer inspection. He had to have gone ahead of me. If he reached the lighthouse before me, Mrs. Dalworth would know I was on the island.

I wiped beads of sweat from my brow. The empty canteen reminded me of my thirst, but there would be no water until I reached the lighthouse. I'd been through much worse, I reminded myself, and made my legs pick up the pace.

The determined greens of spring spattered the rocky field by the lighthouse. A flock of geese gathered near the keeper's cottage, pulling at clumps of fresh shoots, undisturbed in the calm afternoon. I'd covered the trail in what I hoped was under an hour and a half, but I had no way of knowing for sure. The position of the sun as it dropped into the western sky supported my estimate, but I knew I could be off by fifteen minutes.

My first move was to head to the bluff above Hidden Cove to look for the sloop. I trotted through the field in a crouch, going from one hiding place to another, until I reached the lighthouse yard. I scanned the outbuildings and keeper's cottage. Nothing out of the ordinary. Two pairs of boots on the porch and smoke coming out of the chimney. Mrs. Dalworth and Perkins were in the house, which meant it was after three o'clock. I crawled through the windswept grasses to the bluff, got down on my belly, and popped my head over the edge of the cliff. No sign of a skiff on the beach below and no sign of the sloop anchored in the cove. Could I have beaten them by this much? That didn't feel right. They couldn't be that far behind me. I had to check the outer cove from the far side of the path.

The grass rustled behind me. I rolled sideways, fists up, legs ready to kick, expecting a pirate to throw himself on me. Mr. Jones jumped on my chest and licked my nose.

"I knew you were here!" I grabbed him and ruffled his ears, something he'd almost grown to tolerate. He pulled away, looked over the cliff and back at me. "You say they're here already?"

Mr. Jones started through the grass and I crawled along behind him until we reached the path that led down to the water. Just past the eastern point of the cove, the front end of the sloop came into view. She was dropping her sails, preparing to anchor.

"Good work, Mr. Jones! C'mon. We don't have much time!"

Knowing I'd beaten them to the lighthouse, I sprinted for the house.

I burst in the door with Mr. Jones on my heels. My explosive entry startled Perkins, who leaped to his feet, his teacup spilling as it clattered sideways onto its saucer. Mrs. Dalworth clutched her heart in shock, but then flew to me, wrapping her thick hands around mine in surprised delight. She scooped up Mr. Jones, who was not about to be left out of the reunion down on the floor.

Mrs. Dalworth launched a flurry of questions about when I'd come back, who'd brought me and why I didn't write to say I was coming. I cut her off to say we had maybe twenty minutes before her no-good pirate traders came ashore to hunt me down. Perkins hurried to the window to check the yard as I explained all that had happened. I told them the pirates had kidnapped me off the street in Victoria and marched me at gunpoint to the clearing on Deception Island. I told them Jake and the others would realize I was missing, but I didn't know how long it would take them to figure it out.

"They'll come here. I know they will. I've wasted a bunch of time already, but we have to hold the pirates off until help gets here. And if we can't, well, then I have to run again."

"Oh, Charlee, you're safe at the lighthouse. I know those boys. I'll talk to them."

"Of course you'd say that! Mrs. Dalworth, they are criminals! They want the gold and they'll kill me for it. Trust me, they will not listen to you because I've made them flaming mad."

"Gold? There's gold on this island?" Perkins asked, looking back and forth between the two of us.

"A small shipment stolen on its way to California. I buried it over at Clamity. I'm the only one who knows where it is."

Perkins yanked open a kitchen drawer where Mrs. Dalworth kept her ammunition. He took the rifle down from the rack above the sideboard and loaded it.

"There won't be any need for that," Mrs. Dalworth said, but he ignored her.

"We've only got the one gun, and you said there's three of them?"

Perkins was prepared to fight. As we threw together a plan, Mrs. Dalworth begged us to let her talk sense into them.

"No. Our way first. If it fails, you'll have lots of time to talk them out of killing all of us."

"Wait!" she said. "What do I do?"

"Stay in the house. If they get past Perkins and me, we'll pin 'em down in here. Be ready with your kitchen knife. They won't be coming for tea."

Perkins nodded in solemn agreement and followed me and Mr. Jones out the door.

In Mrs. Dalworth's wine cellar, I found what I needed to make exploding bottles and asked Perkins if he was up for a difficult feat. The job I had in mind required nimble navigation over slippery rocks in the damp fog while carrying one of my dangerous concoctions. The gravity of his assignment didn't concern him.

Perkins pointed out that since I was the better shot by far, it made sense for me to be the sniper. While he was scampering around the bluff, I'd be hidden away with Mrs. Dalworth's rifle, giving him cover and holding the invaders back. Hiding in the rocks on opposite sides of the path down to the cove, we wouldn't be able to see each other, so I went over a few whistles we could use as signals. Mr. Jones agreed to warn us if he saw anyone. Then we all took our positions.

We didn't have long to wait. Minutes later, Mr. Jones barked from his watch on the bluff. They were coming. I braced myself in my position and checked the rifle as I watched them pull their skiff up on the rocks in the long shadows of the afternoon. The butt of the rifle felt clammy, a combination of sweaty hands and humid air. With the fading daylight, patches of fog rolled over Anguish Point, past the lighthouse. The three pirates spoke to each other and then started up the path, single file, spaced several feet apart.

Mrs. Dalworth appeared on the bluff, completely exposed. The stubborn woman hadn't listened to me and was about to mess everything up, thinking she could negotiate. I couldn't stop her without revealing my hiding spot and the ambush we'd set up.

She called down from the top of the path. "William!"

I whistled low to Perkins. Stand by.

Sculder heard the whistle, stopped, and scanned the shadows along the path. Then he squinted up at Mrs. Dalworth.

"Ellen," he said with cool and measured annoyance.

William. Ellen. They spoke like old friends. I couldn't believe what I was hearing.

"I know why you're here, son."

"Then step aside, Ellie. We want the girl. We know she's here. Send her down and we'll be on our way."

"Not doing that, Will. You need to think about what you're doing. You harm her, they'll hang ya when they catch ya… and they will catch ya, I'll make sure of it. Leave now, while you're still a free man."

Sculder mumbled to the other two and started up the path again. His pistol dangled in one hand, no doubt reloaded. Horrified, I watched as Mrs. Dalworth started down the path to meet him.

"Tell you what. If that girl won't come out—and I bet she's watching from somewhere here—then you're coming with us until she turns herself over."

In an instant, Mrs. Dalworth realized the peril. She turned back, but it was too late. Sculder would overtake her before she could make it back to the top.

"You don't want anything bad to happen to the lightkeeper, do you, kid?" Sculder said to the rocks concealing me. Mr. Jones, hunched down beside me, growled in reply. Sculder heard and looked right at our hiding spot, then scrambled up the path after Mrs. Dalworth.

I whistled to Perkins and fired a shot that hit the ground, sending pebbles flying in front of Sculder's feet. My hands shook as I rushed to reload. Just then, a fireball flickered across from me and arced through the air like a comet. Glass splintered, and the flame set off an explosion on the path behind Mrs. Dalworth. Sculder cursed and retreated with his men. Moments later, another flaming comet came down from another spot on the bluff, exploding so close behind them it must have warmed their backsides. Perkins was a lousy shot, but he had an excellent arm.

The men ran for their rowboat as I shot another round from the rifle. It pinged off a metal oarlock, but Sculder forced them into the boat.

"We'll be back, kid. It's you or the old lady," he hollered as they shoved away from the shore.

CHAPTER FORTY-TWO

"That's it. I'm going with them," I said, as Mrs. Dalworth, Perkins, Mr. Jones and I watched the three men row back to the sloop, already invisible in the fog and fading daylight. "I'll take them to the gold. It's the only way."

"Out of the question," Mrs. Dalworth said.

"I thought you wanted to negotiate."

"I did. They weren't having it. They'll never let you go."

"Then what now, if I don't surrender?"

"We fight. We aren't out of ideas yet, are we?"

Perkins stepped forward, face streaked with sweat and dirt. "No, we're not, ma'am. In fact, I'm just warming up. Let them storm up the path when it's soaked in whale oil. I'm going to make some more of Charlee's bottles and next time, somebody's getting burned."

The looming threat had brought out a side of Perkins I'd never seen. He was sharp, fearless, and animated. "Be careful, Archie," I said. "If a bottle explodes before you throw it..."

"I know," he replied with a wink, and disappeared into the swirling mist.

"Smart idea, spilling oil," Mrs. Dalworth said. "All the guns and knives in the world won't help them if they can't get their footing."

"It'll force them to climb up the slippery rocks...where I can pick them off." The grim realization of what I said made both of us pause. "I mean, I don't want to kill anybody."

"Might only have to wound one to stop the others," she said. "They're big-talking cowards, those fellas. They weren't expecting a fight, and we've got them on their heels. But they'll be more prepared when they come back." She looked at the drifting fog with concern. "I must tend the lighthouse while I've got a chance."

We were in the middle of an invasion and Mrs. Dalworth was still mindful of her lightkeeper duties.

"Mr. Jones, you keep watch. One bark for every man who comes ashore, right?"

He'd already stationed himself at his post, standing at the edge of the bluff, eyes fixed on the water.

The fog descended on the cove along with the darkness. We wouldn't be able to see them coming until the last second, and that would give them a chance at a sneak attack. Defending the bluff wouldn't be easy. If they overpowered one of us, we'd be done. But they also had the disadvantage of having to find us in the fog as well. Worst of all, fog meant no chance of a rescue boat arriving anytime soon. We'd have to hold them off.

"We aren't out of ideas yet," I said, repeating Mrs. Dalworth's remark with even more determination.

I found Archie in Mrs. Dalworth's wine cellar. He had rounded up the last of the camphene oil and poured it into two empty wine bottles.

"That's it? That's all we have left?"

"Yes. But when I throw, I won't miss. Promise."

We stuffed the bottle necks with soaked rags and carried them out to the bluff like a precious tea service, careful not to stumble or shake the contents and blow ourselves to smithereens. We stashed them in strategic spots near the trail where Perkins would launch them on cue. Even if he hit nothing, I said to him, throwing them from different places would make them think there were way more of us up here.

I'd learned about camphene oil reading Edgar's chemistry notes. Camphene oil was highly volatile. With whale oil expensive and scarce, it had become a popular replacement for lighting fuel. But Edgar had cautioned it could explode for no reason, even when used with care. When Perkins threw our bottles, he had to light the soaked rag, wait for it to ignite inside the bottle's neck, and then toss the works in a hurry. The entire business was dangerous. If he timed it wrong, it could explode in his hands, covering him in splinters of glass and burning oil. Even though he had burned his hands in the lighthouse only months earlier, Perkins didn't hesitate. He knew the risk and volunteered anyway.

As we stashed the bottles, I spotted Mrs. Dalworth crossing the yard with a lantern from the house, which gave us some light, but also added an eerie orange glow to the top of the bluff. She'd also brought me one of Edgar's less bulky sweaters, which I welcomed because I'd been shivering in a damp sweat since the sun vanished. Mr. Jones appeared for the muster of our troops, reported no movement below, and with no new instructions, returned to his post.

Perkins shouldered a barrel of lighthouse oil and started down the path. It wouldn't take much to grease up the rocks and make the hike up from the cove next to impossible. While he was gone, I checked Mrs. Dalworth's box of ammo. Only half a dozen rounds left, but that was plenty. If I didn't stop my mark on the first try, I wouldn't have time to get a second shot off.

Mr. Jones barked three, no, four times. They'd landed on the beach and I couldn't see any of them! My heart sank. Even worse, they'd returned before Perkins could get back up to his position on the bluff. I hadn't heard a scuffle, and hoped it meant Perkins had escaped notice below.

Mrs. Dalworth stood at the top of the path with the lantern. She shouted down into the fog.

"I know you're down there, William."

No answer.

"I warn you. Set foot up here and you'll regret it for the rest of your life. Leave while you have the chance. No hard feelings."

That got a loud laugh in response. I pointed the rifle at the place where his voice had been and placed my finger on the trigger, but the sound drifted along with the fog.

"I told you. I want the girl, Ellie."

"You're not getting her," Mrs. Dalworth snapped back. She wasn't one to lose her temper, but she meant business.

"We'll see about that."

Mrs. Dalworth turned up the wick on the lantern to cast a brighter light. For a moment, the fog shifted and she was visible, but Sculder didn't shoot. She swung the lantern three times, set it down at the top of the path, turned and disappeared into the darkness behind her.

The lantern cast a golden glow on the slope down to the cove. As the fog moved, I caught sight of Sculder wiping his boots on some seaweed near the bottom of the path, and two other dark lumps clambering over the rocks on each side of him. They didn't have Perkins. He'd managed to spill the oil and hide, but he wouldn't be able to get back up to the throw the bottles in time. I'd have to do it all.

As fast as they'd appeared, the fog drifted and concealed them from me. But thanks to the lantern, those lumpy oafs could see where they were, scale the rocks, and reach the bluff in minutes. Mrs. Dalworth and I wouldn't stand a chance.

"Last chance, Will. You can't have the girl," Mrs. Dalworth's voice came from the opposite side of the bluff somewhere.

"Oh, but see? I've got her precious mutt. Hear that, girlie? If you want to save your dog, you'd better come out."

I shot to my feet. Where was Mr. Jones? He wasn't on the bluff anymore and his warning barks had come from below. They could have got him, knowing it would flush me out of hiding. Or it could be a trick. I started for the path, unwilling to gamble. Mrs. Dalworth couldn't see me, but she spoke as if she knew what I intended to do.

"You never were a good liar, Will." She was near the light-house now. "If you have the dog, then who's up here with me?"

Right on cue, a low and vicious snarl cut through the air.

I crouched back down behind a rock. I'd heard that sound before, behind me in the clearing, the sound that spooked the pirates and made them run.

Sculder recognized it, too. His head and torso emerged from the fog, floating as if he didn't have legs. His face was a sea of turbulent shadows, hollowed out by sudden fear.

"We ain't falling for that dog trick again," he said. "That don't scare me."

"You're the one who thinks this island is haunted," Mrs. Dalworth said with a peculiar, evil-sounding laugh.

Another growl, this time louder and nearby. It felt like a call to arms, like a wolf signaling its pack to circle and prepare for attack.

The men below exchanged anxious words. I heard one of them say "witch" and the other say "voodoo". Sculder shouted orders for his crew to stand their ground, as if expecting another cowardly retreat was about to unfold.

Then Mr. Jones barked three times from below me on the bluff, proof that Sculder had lied about having captured him. Moments later, he barked four more times from a spot opposite the first. Three? Now four? Nearby? Far away? What was going on? The fog had confused everything, including Mr. Jones. At least I knew Sculder didn't have him and Mrs. Dalworth was right, that he was a poor liar. But if Mr. Jones was not confused and all that barking was correct, then Sculder may have organized a small invasion. He must have had more men on board the sloop and had recruited them all to assist. They outnumbered us. We were doomed.

Something moved next to the path. Loose pebbles shifted off to my left on the bluff. My senses were on high alert.

"Perkins?" I whispered. No reply. My skin prickled. I couldn't wait another second if we were to have a chance at all. I spun sideways and aimed at the glowing lantern.

One shot, Charlee. I could hear Papa whispering to me on the homestead when he taught me to shoot. One is all you'll need. I took a breath, let it out, felt the natural pause and squeezed the trigger. I aimed for the glass globe, but my shot pulled low and hit the base of the lantern instead. It teetered back and forth. "C'mon, fall!" I said, pleading with it, and then, as if the force of my voice was enough of a nudge, it toppled. It rolled on its side three times, picking up speed before crashing against a rock, knocking the glass cover off. The exposed wick landed on the spilled oil, which caught fire and sent flames tearing down the path.

"Fire!" someone yelled from below as the oil ignited and made the cliff look like an erupting volcano with orange lava pouring down. That would stop them from using the path. Now I had to keep them from climbing the rocks next to it.

I carefully groped the rocks for the first hidden bottle. Despite my cold, nervous hands, I struck a match and set the rag ablaze. I flung it out over the rocky bluff and hoped for the best. It hit the rocks mid-way down with a crash, followed by a loud "phump" as the contents exploded into a fireball.

The gravel crunched behind me. Someone had made it to the

top. A gloved hand clapped over my mouth and the powerful grasp of an assailant clamped my arms at my sides!

285

CHAPTER FORTY-THREE

"Shshsh! We're here to help," my captor whispered, with a British accent even stronger than his grip.

I didn't fight to escape. There was no way I could get free of his grasp even if I wanted to, but he was telling me he wasn't part of Sculder's motley crew. But who was he and where had he come from? He whispered again, this time to someone nearby, someone still concealed in darkness.

"This one's just a lad, sir. Does the lightkeeper have a son?"

Arms pinned to my sides, I thumped his leg with a fist.

The man nearby whispered back, his voice low and raspy. "No lads. We're looking for three. The woman keeper, her assistant, who's a navy man, and a girl."

I murmured, "That's me!" It came out like "Ah-ee!" and they ignored it because they didn't understand.

"Maybe the boyfriend snuck ashore?" my captor suggested.

"Possibly," the boss man replied.

I thought I'd lose my mind listening to them figure it out. I grunted and banged my captor's leg again, hoping he'd realize I had something important to say and would let me speak.

"Truth now. You with that sloop?" the boss man asked. He'd

moved out of the cover of darkness until I could see the vague outline of his head and shoulders.

I shook my head vigorously.

"You friends with the girl, then?"

I widened my eyes and shook my head again. This captive game of interrogation wasn't getting us anywhere.

"C'mon."

The first man kept his gloved handed clamped over my mouth and lifted me into the air. Following close behind the barely visible leader, we passed more crouched figures creeping across the bluff in the dark. Mr. Jones barked six more times. Six! Preoccupied with my capture, I'd lost count of his barks, but it didn't matter because I knew the place was crawling with unknown intruders. Tucked in behind Mrs. Dalworth's garden shed, the boss man moved close to me and spoke in a low voice. A beam of light from the lantern hanging on Mrs. Dalworth's porch caught his eyes, and they sparkled like two tiny stars.

"Quiet now, lad." I nodded to show I understood the situation. "Now then. Who are you?"

My captor eased his hand from my mouth, ready to clap it back over if I tried to scream or holler. I coughed once and croaked out a weak answer.

"I'm the girl!"

"What?!" The man holding me loosened his grip.

"You're the girl? My sincere apologies, Miss," said the boss man. "We did not mean to manhandle you. We saw you heave that fire bottle and assumed…"

I brushed my sleeves off as if they had rolled me in the dirt and mustered as much outrage as a loud whisper would allow.

"Who are you?"

"Navy," the boss man replied as I realized these men in black were our rescuers. The two men spoke to each other about what to do next while I huddled in the fog beside them.

"How many men did you see on that sloop?" the boss man asked.

"Three. But I think there's a few more. They kept me locked in a cabin all the way from Victoria, so I can't say for sure."

"Any up at the keeper's house?"

"Maybe. We drove 'em away once, but when they returned, we set fire to the path and they had to spread out. I couldn't see in the dark. Their leader was half way up when you grabbed me. He might have made it."

The boss man dispatched a couple of men to check the house. They returned in minutes with a report that Mrs. Dalworth was inside with one man who had a pistol. There was quick planning about surrounding the house and talk of how to create a surprise attack.

"Excuse me. I have a suggestion." They stopped talking and gaped at me, not without a little impatience, because I'd interrupted them.

"The one inside. That's Sculder, and it's me he wants. Let me go in there. I know I can draw him out."

"No. He's armed."

"He won't kill me, at least not right away. See, he needs me alive to take him to some buried loot. I'll get him to follow me outside for it, then you can bushwhack him and nobody gets hurt."

"Buried loot? Where?" Of course, they'd get hung up on the detail that least mattered.

I ignored their questions and kept up with my persuasion. Finally, they agreed to include me, but not before listing several annoying conditions.

On the porch of the lighthouse cottage, I rapped on the door and called out.

"You want me and I'm here. I'll take you to the gold if you let her go."

I turned the knob and swung the door open, shielding myself behind the doorjamb.

"Well, well, Ellie. Didn't I say she'd ride in to save you like some white knight?" Sculder guffawed at his own stupid joke.

"You win. Leave her out of it. I'll take you to the gold right now."

"Move into the light where I can see you, girlie. And put your hands up. I've had enough of your funny business."

I'd promised the navy boss man, with fingers crossed behind my back, that I'd stay on the porch and out of a line of fire. The man closest to me, pressed against the wall on the other side of the door, lurched as I raised my hands and stepped into the light of the open doorway. Bushes next to the porch rustled and came alive. They had the house surrounded, but I didn't flinch, didn't look their way, didn't let on that I wasn't alone.

Sculder stood beside Mrs. Dalworth. He aimed his loaded pistol at my chest.

"The gold's here, you know. Buried in this yard the whole time. But I suppose Mrs. Dalworth's already let you in on that secret."

He shot an annoyed look at Mrs. Dalworth, whose jaw had fallen open. Of course, she hadn't told him that. I shifted from one foot to the other and moved one small step towards them. The man in black on the other side of the doorway, only inches away from me, coiled like a rattlesnake ready to strike.

"And what's this?" I said. "You've been enjoying a lovely cup of British tea? Only British tea can beat this fog. Has to be British tea. Isn't that right, Mrs. Dalworth?"

Her eyes locked with mine, and her puzzled expression shifted to sudden clarity.

Sculder snorted and waved his gun at both of us. "Tea? You think I've been sitting here sipping tea? Women! Here's what we're going to do, ladies. We're going to go nice and careful-like —all three of us—and Miss Smarty Pants here is going to dig up the gold she claims is in the yard. Lead the way, Ellie. Girlie stays in front of me where I can keep a muzzle on her."

As Mrs. Dalworth started for the door, there was a muffled boom from out on the water. It was big enough to rattle the window glass and Mrs. Dalworth's teacups.

Sculder yanked her back. "What's with the cannon?"

"Oh, that must be a big ship sounding out in the strait. They do that sometimes when the fog is thick and they're stuck on the water." Mrs. Dalworth was so convincing, even I wanted to believe her.

"I've never heard of that."

"You've never been fogged in here," she replied. "They only do it if they think they see another vessel approaching."

Sculder accepted her story and waved her on with his pistol. Mrs. Dalworth shuffled to the door and I follow behind, my hands gripping her shoulders. Sculder shoved his pistol into my shoulder blades and reminded me not to try anything. I realized he would shoot me dead when he realized I'd walked him into a trap.

Suddenly, a pane of glass in the side window shattered. Sculder spun sideways, pointing his gun at the source. In that split second, I dove for the porch, taking Mrs. Dalworth down with me, breaking her fall. I rolled her away from the door as navy men swarmed past us. We ended up in a tangled heap.

"Goodness!" Mrs. Dalworth said, clutching her chest as three men piled on Sculder and ground him into the floorboards. His pistol flew from his hand, clattered onto the porch and came to rest beside me. I snatched it up and aimed at him.

"Don't do it, Charlee!" Mrs. Dalworth said, clutching my wrist. "Killing him won't bring any of them back."

"I know," I said, but I wouldn't drop the gun.

"Don't let her shoot! She's a witch, that one." Sculder exclaimed, shielding himself from my following aim as the men dragged him from the house. My hands shook violently as I tracked him down the steps into the yard. Then I dropped the pistol onto the porch like I'd been holding a hot poker with bare hands. One of the navy men picked it up and took it away.

"Are you hurt?" I asked Mrs. Dalworth as she rubbed a knee and straightened herself out.

"Still in one piece. I'll be black and blue tomorrow, though." I helped her up, and she pushed the hair back from her eyes. "Did I just get wrangled like some tough old steer?"

"Nah, if I'd wrangled you, I would have grabbed you by the horns first."

"Good to know."

She steadied herself on the porch railing. She could have broken bones when I threw her down so hard. I checked her from tip to stern for injuries, just in case, even as she insisted she was still in working order.

"Stop fussing now. Our company is returning."

Mr. Jones burst from the darkness ahead of the group and bounded onto the porch. Black oil and soot covered his white coat. He was filthy and quite delighted with his condition.

"Don't you dare set foot in my house like that, mister," Mrs. Dalworth wagged her finger at him and he skulked to a corner of the porch. Had he rolled in dirt and oil so the pirates couldn't spot him on the bluff, just like the men who'd come ashore to rescue us? Could he be that smart? Or was he just a mess from running all over the oily bluff, barking his head off for the past hour?

"There, there, Mr. Jones. Come back here right now. I'm not cross with you. You're a genuine hero."

Mr. Jones wagged his tail and sat his greasy hind quarters down by her feet. The pungent, fishy smell of whale oil wafted up from his coat.

The boss man with the raspy whisper approached with a small group of men. Black grease smeared on their faces caused the whites of their eyes to float, reflected by the lantern light on the porch. Like wolves' eyes, just past the light of a campfire, I thought, but then their bodies took shape as they came close. Three men formed a neat line behind their leader, arms pressed to their sides.

"Mrs. Dalworth, I presume."

She limped down the stairs. "I am, sir. Might I say, I'm delighted to see you chaps, although I would have preferred friendlier circumstances for us to make an acquaintance."

He smiled and his teeth gleamed. "Lieutenant Arthur Hayes, British Royal Navy, at your service, ma'am." He politely took the hand she'd extended to him in greeting.

CHAPTER FORTY-FOUR

In the hours that followed, the patchy fog lifted, revealing a sky full of starry diamonds and a waxing gibbous moon.

The navy arrested Sculder and the other pirates, hauling them away to the huge warship anchored off the north point of Hidden Cove. They'd captured Hample and Quinn in the cove, attempting to paddle their skiff with bare, icy hands. At the bottom of the path, Perkins had cheered the stealth invasion of his navy pals. Unable to get back up to the bluff, he had done his part by stealing the pirates' oars and sabotaging a retreat.

Lenny, the sailor who'd survived the *Salish Wind* shipwreck, had also been aboard the sloop. Mr. Jones had not been mistaken when he barked four times, as Lenny had come ashore the second time with the others. He was only a few feet away from grabbing me when the navy men beat him to it, silently picking me off as well as him. Mr. Jones' string of barks was for the navy men. He'd spotted their arrival and had reported their numbers as they came ashore, just as I had instructed him to do.

After their successful raid, the Navy lit up Anguish Point with dozens of torches, combing the bluff for spoils of the raid and stray pirates. I retrieved the last bottle bomb from the rock slope and gave instructions to the puzzled sailor assigned to get rid of it. Out on the porch, I bathed Mr. Jones in a tub of warm, soapy water while Mrs. Dalworth limped about, restoring order to her kitchen. I could tell she'd hurt her hip in our tumble, but she insisted it was no worse than before and refused to hear another word about it.

I had just plunked a wet and weary Mr. Jones in front of the roaring fire when Perkins burst through the door.

"Mrs. D! Charlee! We did it!"

A bunch of dirt fell from his boots onto the floor that Mrs. Dalworth had just swept, but he didn't care. He bear-hugged her, lifted and spun her around before she could protest. He was about to do the same to me, but pausing to wipe his grimy hands on his trousers, his usual reserved nature caught up to him. Mrs. Dalworth eased the awkward moment by shooing him back to the washbasin by the door, where he recounted the blazing fire on the path, the sneaky navy raid, the impact of our shots and bombs, and Mr. Jones everywhere and nowhere all at once causing confusion and terror among the pirates.

Perkins had noticed as well. Mr. Jones was in one place, then moments later in another; barking at the bottom of the bluff, a split-second later growling from the top. It wasn't possible for him to change places that fast. Things that didn't have a logical explanation bothered me, but this time I knew my mind wasn't playing tricks on me.

"It's the fog," Mrs. Dalworth said, all matter-of-fact but not sounding at all convinced herself. "A person can't tell where sound comes from." We all looked over at the oblivious Mr. Jones, who had settled into a peaceful nap on the woven rug by the blazing fire.

After so much excitement, none of us could sit still. Perkins and I were up and down, out of our chairs, looking out the window, reporting on activity in the yard. Mrs. Dalworth puttered around her kitchen, picking things up and putting them down with no real purpose. She put the kettle on, but then changed her mind and dug a bottle of fine whiskey out of the top cupboard. Perkins didn't drink, but on this occasion, he made an exception and took the small glass she handed him for a toast.

The whiskey took the edge off all of us. We sat down at the table and Mrs. Dalworth refilled our glasses with a very modest ration as we shared our stories of the raid.

Perkins said he had almost finished soaking the path with oil when Mr. Jones barked a warning. Hearing the clunk of oars out on the water, he hid behind a boulder as the pirate skiff came into view. Thanks to the fog, they hadn't seen him on the beach. They landed, started up the path, and he contemplated getting back to the top by climbing the steep rock face next to them. That's when he noticed two navy rowboats landing on the far end of the cove and a dozen of his comrades slipping ashore.

"Mr. Jones barked his head off. He saw them coming and warned us," I said.

"But Mrs. Dalworth had distracted the pirates. They were too busy negotiating and navigating the slippery stones."

"I knew you were trapped at the bottom," Mrs. Dalworth said, "so I set the lantern down, hoping it'd help you see another way back up. But, as always, Charlee had a bigger idea."

"That was a spectacular shot, by the way." Perkins mimed the explosion and the hissing of burning oil as flames raced down the path. He threw back the rest of his whiskey, reached for the bottle to refill his glass, but Mrs. Dalworth pulled it out of his reach.

"Easy, sailor," she said, and he returned a sheepish grin. I'd never seen Perkins let loose. It suited him. He could be quite likable.

It was Perkin's unfortunate burn accident in the fall that gave me the idea to shoot out the lantern. It drove the pirates back, slowed them down, and forced them to pick their way up the rocky cliff. Perkins said the business with Mr. Jones howling had caused two of the pirates to panic and retreat, only to find their oars missing and no way to row back to the sloop.

"But William persisted and caught me in the house. He figured you'd come for me," Mrs. Dalworth said, "and sure enough, you showed yourself. It took me a minute to figure out what in blazes you were talking about, what with saying the gold was in the yard and all. And then all that nonsense about having tea. But when you said British tea…I caught on."

"I don't get it," Perkins said.

"First thing I learned at the lighthouse. All of Mrs. Dalworth's teas have names. Darjeeling, Oolong, Earl Grey," I explained.

"So when Charlee said 'British tea', she was telling me they'd come."

"Brilliant!" Perkins said, his smiling hazel eyes resting on me a little longer than felt comfortable or necessary.

"It's all of us. We're a clever team," I said, and Perkins clinked his empty glass with both of us.

The shots of whiskey mellowed our moods. Stories told, Perkins swept up the dirt he'd dragged in on his boots while Mrs. Dalworth put a cottage pie in the oven. I stoked the fire and sprawled beside Mr. Jones, warming my sock feet on the hearth. A delicious aroma soon filled the room, and I realized I hadn't eaten all day. My stomach growled so loud that Mr. Jones popped his head up, looking for another intruder.

Just then, steps rumbled on the porch. Mr. Jones ran to the door, barked three times, and a knock followed on the door.

"The navy, back for something," Mrs. Dalworth said, signaling to Perkins to open the door.

"Good evening, ma'am," a clean, uniformed naval man said,

removing his cap. "I hope you don't mind two visitors. They insisted."

Behind him, Cook and Jake pulled off their boots and beanies! I threw myself on Cook's neck, then pulled Jake in for a hug.

"You came! I knew you'd figure it out."

Jake, shocked by my affection, reached down and picked up Mr. Jones.

"He told us, didn't you, Mr. Jones? He took us to the sloop and jumped aboard, so we knew you were on there. But we were outnumbered, so we ran for Mr. Brody."

Cook shook hands with Perkins and introduced himself to Mrs. Dalworth.

"Sorry to bust in on y'all like this. We're Charlee's friends. We begged Mr. Brody to let us come ashore, so you'd know we were here."

"Had to wait for clearance though, till they were sure nobody had gotten away," Jake added.

"You must be Amos Jefferson," Mrs. Dalworth said.

"Everyone calls me Cook, ma'am."

"And Jake Miller. I've heard so much about you. What a delightful surprise to meet both of you!"

This was so much more than another joyous reunion. Jake and Cook had come for me. Mr. Brody, too. They had taken the risk to come, knowing it was too late in the day to return to Victoria harbor, with no idea what they might encounter. Everyone in the room had risked their lives to help me.

Mrs. Dalworth saw me wipe the corner of my eye. Bustling us both into her kitchen, she ordered me to put the kettle on and extended a cheery invitation for Jake and Cook to join us for supper. Cook helped in the kitchen, while Jake and Perkins set the table. I stood in the middle of it all, overcome by waves of love and friendship. Mrs. Dalworth and her simple pleasures. I was certain she could conquer the world armed with nothing but a wooden spoon.

Over steaming cottage pie, Cook told us how they'd come after me in Mr. Brody's supply boat. Before they could reach Deception Island, the sun had dropped low in the sky and marine cloud had gathered in dangerous patches along the coastal shore. They had no choice but to stay clear and wait for the fog to lift.

Jake said they lit up their boat like a Christmas tree. That was smart thinking by Mr. Brody. The navy ship, responding to strange distress signals at the lighthouse, might have run them over in the fog and dark. Barreling toward the island, they'd spotted the glowing supply boat bobbing offshore, and dispatched a boarding party.

"At first, they thought we were the problem," Jake said, "but Mr. Brody explained everything. And then they towed us along, because they couldn't leave us stranded out there like sitting ducks.

"Perkins met the sailors when they came ashore," I said. "He told them what was going on. Wait'll you hear what we threw at them."

Jake and Perkins eyed each other without expression. Jake didn't jump on my invitation to find out.

"The best part of all of this? The Captain turned himself in to Mr. Brody," Jake said. "He admitted to surviving the shipwreck and trading Father's gold to save himself. Like you, he saw the dead bodies. He knew he was next."

Cook said, "He also admitted it was his mistake that the *Salish Wind* ran aground, that he'd tried to evade robbery and lost his bearings."

"And then he lied about it," I added.

"He wasn't in on it after all," Jake said, "but his actions are inexcusable."

"Not befitting of an officer," Perkins said, returning to his scowling self, and Jake acknowledged his remark with grim agreement.

CHAPTER FORTY-FIVE

Dishes were still on the table and teacups half full when a navy man returned for Jake and Cook. The supply boat was a day boat, so all who had been aboard were spending the night aboard the naval ship. At first light, assuming the weather didn't sock us in overnight, the supply boat would return for me and we'd make our way to Clamity Cove for Mr. Miller's gold. The navy ship would wait at anchor for us, with the seized sloop in tow, and then escort all of us back to Victoria harbor.

"I'll see you both in the morning," I said, not wanting them to leave.

Jake and Cook joked about letting me out of their sight and whether it was wise to take another chance at separation.

"Keep an eye on her, Mr. Jones," Cook said. "Do not let her leave this house, and all of us might sleep tonight."

Mr. Jones sat down on my toes. He always took his assignments to heart.

"I haven't slept since she left in April," Mrs. Dalworth added. "She won't be sneaking out on my watch."

I poked her shoulder. "You haven't slept a full night since I've known you, up at all hours, nursing that lighthouse like a newborn."

Teasing aside, there was truth in all we said.

Perkins lingered after they were gone and, in yet another uncharacteristic fashion, offered to help clean up the dishes. Mrs. Dalworth thanked him for his thoughtfulness, but dispatched him to check the lighthouse instead and then to his quarters to sleep.

"Well, here we are again," she said, limping across the room and easing herself into her rocking chair. She had disguised her bad hip in front of the others. I tucked one last log on the dying fire and flopped into the rocking chair across from her. Mr. Jones retired to the hearth but kept his eyes on me, monitoring my position as instructed, even though I assured him I wasn't going anywhere.

"Have you really not slept since I've been gone?"

"It's a bit of an exaggeration, but it's one you'd appreciate since you are so inclined to them yourself."

I grinned. "A fairly large exaggeration, then."

"I'm afraid not. I've had much on my mind, what with leaving Edgar, and no idea where I should go next. And this blasted hip aching all the while. Imagine my surprise when you turned up. I didn't think you'd ever set foot here again, since you'd given up on the missing gold."

"I had given up. But in San Francisco, I worked for a doctor who helps people with head problems. A real smart man. Kinda funny, too. He showed me how to get my memory back and I guess it worked because one day I woke up and remembered everything. When I saw myself moving the gold a second time, I knew where to look. A second time! It was too close to the water, see, and I thought a high tide might wash it away. Then I was certain the Captain was after it because he was so eager to get me back here. And now we find out his intention was to come clean, correct the record, and he needed me to return to bear witness. Of course, once I knew Mr. Miller's gold was still here, I had to come and get it."

"And so you'll get it tomorrow morning?"

"Yeah. At last."

"The island will thank you for getting it out of here. I'm sure the Lekwungen people won't be sorry to see the lot of us and all our company gone."

The room was quiet but for the crackling fire and the clock on the mantle. All the knick-knacks and decorations in the room were gone, already packed away for Mrs. Dalworth's upcoming departure.

"What's gonna happen to your privateer friend and his murdering pals?" I said.

My question seemed to upset her, but she pinched her lips together into a tight line.

"He's not my friend, Charlee."

"He calls you Ellie. You call him Will. He used to come by to trade with you. Seems like you're pretty well acquainted."

She took a few quiet breaths. I'd pushed her into an explanation.

"I've known him his whole life. We have...history."

This time, I stayed quiet and gave her room to choose her words. I waited, the way Papa had always done when someone was telling a painful story. Sure enough, Mrs. Dalworth kept talking.

"I had a best friend back home named Anna. Anne, she liked to be called. We grew up together, were inseparable. She was a lovely lass who married a hard man. Wasn't long before he took his anger out on her. Anyway, she didn't have to endure it for long. She passed at twenty, after giving birth to their son. On her deathbed, she asked me to look out for her boy. I'm his godmother."

"Oh."

"William wasn't bad at first, but he fell in with a rowdy crowd. Couldn't keep a job, got into drinking, carrying on. He was throwing his life away in pub fights and scrappy deals. I'd talk to him—Edgar, too—and he'd always say he wanted to get out of Leeds, and make a fresh start somewhere. When Edgar and I emigrated, we offered to bring him along. He jumped at it, seemed ready to change for the good. But when he got here, he wanted no part of homesteads and tough colony life. He got in with a no-good bunch and ran off to sea."

"He killed a man on the *Salish Wind*. I was there, in the cupboard."

"I know. He told me everything, sitting right there at my kitchen table. Said he never meant to do it, but the man in the galley lunged at him with a butcher knife."

I flashed back to the cramped hiding place, where I'd heard it all and seen the horrific aftermath. Drak had tried to defend the *Salish Wind* and died.

"Broke my heart to hear him say it. Edgar and I tried with him, but he wouldn't listen once he came of age. It's so sad. Anne was the kindest soul. How a son of hers could turn out so different is beyond me. I was always looking for Anne in him, hoping her goodness would win. He had it in him, but he let the other side take hold."

"You did your best." I said. "He's a grown man."

"You know, he confessed what he'd done, like he knew it was all over for him. The wreck of the *Salish Wind* happened as you always said. The raid, the murders—all of it. And now, justice will be done."

There was one thing bothering me and I knew I had to talk to her about it while we were alone and still on the island.

"Mrs. Dalworth…"

"Yes, lass."

"Did you have Edgar's body exhumed?"

I hoped the answer was "yes," since his body had vanished from the grave I'd made for him. If his grave had been raided, I didn't know if I could tell her.

"Yes. Oh dear. That empty grave must have shocked you when you saw it."

"Only for a moment. Then I used it to scare those fools."

Mrs. Dalworth laughed. "San Francisco did you good. All this quick thinking."

She was right. I hadn't given my once-broken head a second thought.

Mrs. Dalworth told me that after I'd left, she'd decided she didn't want to leave Edgar on the island. At her request, Brody arranged a sea burial for him at the reef where the *Salish Wind* had gone down. "He's among friends there," Mrs. Dalworth said, and I told her it was the best decision ever.

We stayed up late that night, talking about other things, both exhausted but not wanting to put an end to our conversation. Just after midnight, Mrs. Dalworth pushed herself to her feet. We made up my old bed in the alcove behind the stove and said goodnight. Mr. Jones and I curled up in the warm heart of the lighthouse kitchen one last time.

The next morning, the skies were clear, the breeze cool and light. Mr. Brody guided the supply boat into Clamity Cove, where Jake and another sailor rowed us ashore. Mr. Jones and I marched up the beach to where our raft had landed after the shipwreck. I looked over my shoulder at the cove. Not the view I remembered, but I was very close. Mr. Jones started up the trail and turned. A voice in the wind whispered, "The gold sleeps." And then I knew.

"Of course!" I exclaimed.

"Wait up!" Jake said, as I scrambled up the small bluff to the grove of trees where I'd sheltered that first night. Buried under the tangled roots of a cedar, in the soft, mossy soil, were three canvas sacks I'd made from the torn sails of the *Salish Wind*. Three sacks full of Mr. Miller's gold. The final memory had snapped into place.

"This gold has caused so much misery and death," I said to Jake as we carried the canvas sacks to the rowboat. "Maybe I should have pretended I couldn't remember and left it here forever."

"You couldn't do that."

"Because it's not mine, and I promised to deliver it. But I'm mighty happy to hand it over to you and Cook, and have you sail it home to your father."

"I still don't like leaving without you. Something bad always happens. I wish you were coming back with us on the *Sonoma Wind*."

"Nobody's after me anymore. As soon as we get affairs wrapped up here, we'll catch a nice, richy-rich ride to San Francisco on one of those fancy steamers. Besides, I'll be with Mrs. Dalworth and she won't let me out of her sight."

I rolled my eyes to make him think I didn't like or need supervision, but secretly, I was thrilled she had decided to accompany me to California.

And that's how it unfolded. Mr. Brody took Jake, Cook, and Mr. Miller's gold back to Victoria, back to the *Sonoma Wind*, where the First Mate assumed command of the ship to sail for home. The navy confiscated the black sloop and delivered Sculder and his pals to the authorities. I stayed on the island to help Mrs. Dalworth with the last of her packing. Mr. Brody returned a few days later to get us and to bring in the lightkeeper replacements—two retired naval fellows that looked so much alike I mistook them for twin brothers.

"What happened to the family that was supposed to come?" I asked Brody as his crew loaded the last of Mrs. Dalworth's belongings into the rowboat.

"Got all the way to Victoria and backed out," Brody said. "Probably heard stories. There was a wild story in the paper the other day about a pirate raid at Deception Island," he said with a sly grin. "If you ask me, this is no place to raise kids. But two retired navy men jumped at it, so it'll be a bachelor house like all the rest of the light stations. It's a tough, lonely assignment out here. Takes a solitary sort to stand it, and a strong kind to survive it."

He looked at Mrs. Dalworth, who was giving Perkins last orders about minding the vegetable garden. He didn't need instructions anymore, but it was how she coped with saying goodbye. She took Perkin's face in her hands, and after speaking to him at length, he nodded and wiped his eyes with the back of his hand. I swallowed and looked away. Even places that have been hard and painful, even people who are hard to warm up to and downright difficult, can take the heart hostage.

Perkins had to stay on for two more weeks, to help the new keepers get familiar with running the lighthouse before returning to service aboard a naval ship. Mrs. Dalworth had penned a glowing report regarding his brave actions, with me taking dictation and suggesting a few colorful phrases. With a commendation forthcoming, Perkins was certain to receive a promotion. It was all he'd wanted when he'd arrived at the lighthouse. Now that he was likely getting one, it didn't seem to matter to him anymore. I felt the same way about gold I'd chased all the way from California.

As we rowed away from the island for the last time, the lighthouse winked and the rhythmic clunk of the oarlocks thumped like an ancient drum. Water lapping against the hull was a soothing salve on the pain of leaving. Later, when the supply boat chugged away, Clamity Cove and the rest of the island faded into the vague horizon.

"Fair winds and following seas, Edgar," Mrs. Dalworth said, and tears streamed down her cheeks.

Mr. Jones leaned his head on her shoulder. I wrapped my arms around them and held them tight, silently pledging to Edgar, and to Kuno, that I'd take care of both of them.

CHAPTER FORTY-SIX

In Victoria, Mr. Brody re-opened the investigation and took charge of the statements and revised records. The Captain would be handed over to the Americans across the strait where he would answer for his disgraceful conduct under maritime law. They threw William Sculder and his nasty crew in jail, to await trial with a tough judge who was away upholding the law in the goldfields. When I asked what would become of them, Mr. Brody changed the subject. I kept after him until he said, "They'll not bother anyone again." I didn't press him anymore, because I was afraid of what I might hear.

Mrs. Dalworth and Mr. Brody gave me permission to see Jake and Cook before they set sail for San Francisco. As I boarded the schooner with Mr. Jones tucked under my arm, the Captain emerged from his quarters. A black waistcoat had replaced the blue tunic of his position. He struggled under the weight of the heavy duffel bag slung over his back as he wasn't used to carrying things around himself. He approached in measured steps, violin case in one hand, his collection of books bundled by leather straps in the other.

Nobody came to his aid. Two sailors on deck disappeared

where once they would have dropped what they were doing and rushed to his aid.

I stepped aside to let him pass.

"Miss LeBeau," he said, but I fixed my eyes on a coil of rope near my feet. Mr. Jones' body tensed and he growled.

"That dog has always been a superb judge of character," the Captain said.

His humor caught me by surprise. I looked up and met his gaze. His once piercing blue eyes were watery, red-rimmed and dull grey.

"I hope you know I never meant you any harm. Truly. You must despise me, and I can't blame you for it. I succumbed to the worst impulses and I am deeply sorry."

I didn't know what to say, and he didn't seem to expect a reply. He pinched his lips into a stiff expression of resolve and continued on his way.

Worst impulses. That was an understatement. He had discredited me and Kuno to save his reputation, and had caused so much confusion and suffering. I thought of the first time I'd seen him aboard the *Salish Wind*, when he'd struck me as generous and confident. He was neither of those things. He was a cowardly leader who used his books to escape the misery of an unwanted seagoing career. When faced with life-threatening danger, he'd thought only of himself.

"I understand what Mr. Whitman meant about rough prizes," I said to his back. I don't know why the book of poetry he'd loaned me that first trip on the *Salish Wind* popped to mind just then.

His violin case clunked against the gunwale as he swung himself around. Joyful recognition lit up his face. I tried to smile, but only half of my mouth turned up, which made me feel more smug than sympathetic. My recollection of a favorite poem was nothing more than a few logs laid across a rushing stream. A temporary, unstable bridge.

"Rough prizes. Indeed." He returned my half-smile and sighed. Then, pulling himself together, he swung his violin case around at the horizon. "'*Allons*. The road is before us.' Before us both. Believe it."

"Aye, sir." I'd called him "sir" out of habit.

"Should we ever cross paths again—and I doubt we shall—my name is Sebastian Hart. Good luck to you, Miss LeBeau."

"*Bonn shaans* to you, Captain Hart."

As soon as he was gone, I took the steps from the main deck down to the galley. Cook was strumming his guitar, and Jake was hunched over the table, squinting at a page in a book.

"You're gonna need glasses," I said. "You've already ruined your eyes, reading in poor light."

I dumped Mr. Jones on the bench beside him, and Jake threw an arm around him.

"Nah. Not enough sleep is all. You know, found myself caught up in yet another Charlee LeBeau adventure. Cook says I look like I'm twice my age today. I'll be grey by the time I'm thirty. Or bald. Want coffee?"

He untangled his legs from under the table and stood up, careful not to bump his head on the overhead nets packed with cooking supplies. The galley's low ceiling made him seem taller than the day before. Cook winked at me behind his back and I mouthed the word, 'What?'

Jake plucked a swinging mug from an overhead hook and filled it as I slid behind the table. I peered into the half-empty cup he set down in front of me.

"What's with the rations?"

"Ha. I like to leave room for sloshing, sailor," he said with a grin as he refilled his own cup the same way.

Mr. Jones curled up beside me like we were staying a while. We weren't. We couldn't. Mr. Brody insisted on walking me back to the rooming house where Mrs. Dalworth was waiting. Jake and Cook had to turn in early as they'd be gone at first light and they were both exhausted from the events of recent days.

"I ran into the Captain up top as he was leaving."

"Lucky you," said Cook, tucking his guitar between a couple of bags of vegetables that had yet to be stowed in the pantry.

"It was mighty awkward. Nobody on deck to see him off, crew ignoring him, just a couple of British sailors escorting him ashore." I looked from one to the other, waiting for them to explain.

"I hope the boom hit him on the way out," Cook said, catching Jake swallowing his coffee. He coughed and banged his chest with a fist.

"Oh, so you're holding a grudge, then?" I said.

"And you're not? After what he did to you?"

"It's strange. I'm not mad at him anymore. I kinda feel sorry for him."

"Too soon," Jake sputtered, his voice a choked-off whisper.

"He'll be turned over to the Americans, right?"

"Big deal," Cook said. "They won't do anything. The British never should have let him go. I tell you, if he was a Black man…"

I knew what he meant. There was justice, but its scale tipped in favor of some over others. The Captain's status, as an educated white man and a ship's commander, had spared me jail and punishment only two days earlier.

"He isn't a murderer or a thief. I was wrong about that."

"Still, the British could have charged him as an accessory," Jake said. "I think they'd prefer to wash their hands of it. Could cause quite a stir, prosecuting the son of a high-ranking American military man. But maritime law will get him, and our fellas don't mess around with the rules. He's finished."

"I don't think he cares. I think he'll be relieved to be out. Finally free."

Cook looked puzzled, and Jake tipped his head, pondering what I'd said. I wasn't sure I understood it myself, but sometimes fate steps in when we don't have the courage to fix things ourselves.

~

The *Sonoma Wind* left Victoria the next morning while Mrs. Dalworth and I remained to wrap up final business regarding the shipwreck. Two weeks later, Mr. Brody took us by buggy to nearby Esquimalt, a deep and protected harbor only a few miles through the woods. Where Victoria harbor bustled with merchant sailing ships, old whalers and lumber barges, Esquimalt was where the British Navy anchored its vessels, and where larger and more modern ships on the Pacific routes docked.

We boarded the *SS Commodore*, a big steamer heading for San Francisco. Unlike Mr. Miller's merchant schooners, this ship could carry tons of cargo, scores of passengers, and reach San Francisco in half the time. Mrs. Dalworth had purchased our tickets, spending extra for a cabin. Most of the passengers were below deck in steerage, where they got a bunk and mess hall grub. Most of those passengers were men, and judging from their sickly, haunted expressions, returning home from the goldfields.

Mrs. Dalworth said she only intended to visit California to escort me home and stay on for a little rest. I said she was going to fall in love with the place and her hip wouldn't even ache once she was out of the damp and on a sunny porch having her afternoon tea. She promised to keep an open mind, but I noticed she had brought most of her belongings, leaving only one cumbersome trunk behind that Mr. Brody offered to store.

One pleasant afternoon aboard ship, only a day or so out of San Francisco, we strolled arm-in-arm around the passenger deck like a couple of *high muckamucks*, taking in the fresh sea air and sunshine. Mr. Jones had never seen a parasol, so when he spotted one in the hand of an approaching lady, he barked his head off. He told me he preferred schooners any day over this floating barge with people milling about, poking and prodding things with canes and umbrellas, and stepping on him at every turn.

"I've been thinking a lot," I said to Mrs. Dalworth somewhere during our second lap around the spacious deck.

"Now there's a switch."

"I'm serious. Except for my no-good Uncle Jack, who probably got himself killed last year, I have zero family. So I'm making myself a new one. I've picked Mizzy and Cook, Jake and Mr. Miller, Mrs. Plea, and Mr. Jones and Magic. And you."

Mrs. Dalworth stopped mid-stroll. "I come after your dog and your horse?"

I brushed off her concern and pulled her along. "My list isn't in order."

"Well then. Do I get to accept or decline the offer? And is there a contract you've drafted?"

"Oh. I never thought of that. I mean, I could get Jake to help me..."

"You're quite a handful. A person has to know what they're signing up for. Say I agree, you won't call me Auntie or Nana or some such nonsense, will you?"

"No! But I can't call you Ellie either, even though it is one of the prettiest names ever. You'll always be Mrs. Dalworth to me."

She grabbed my hand and gave it a squeeze. Mr. Jones trotted out ahead of us, turning heads as he pranced by. One didn't see loose dogs on the passenger deck, but Mr. Jones considered himself a naval officer and therefore didn't think of himself as out of place.

A sour-faced gentleman lifted his cane, ready to whack him out of the way as he passed.

"Stay close, Mr. Jones," Mrs. Dalworth said, loud enough for the man to hear. Mr. Jones sniffed the air and waited for us to catch up. I caught the steely eyes of the gentleman and glared. Don't you dare, my eyes said, and his arrogant leer melted into an obsequious smile. I'd seen what Mrs. Plea could accomplish with a perfectly executed gaze. My first use of it was effective.

"So I was thinking..." I continued. "You don't have any family left here either. You can start fresh with me and Mr. Jones. We've got the best people around us."

"I like the ones I've met so far."

"Wait'll you meet Mr. Miller. He's a lovely man. He's also handsome like Jake, except old like you, but not broken down one bit."

"Goodness. He's also married!"

"Oh, that's finished."

"I wouldn't have taken you for a matchmaker," she said, removing her bonnet and letting the breeze blow her hair around. The late afternoon light softened her face, and she looked lovelier than I'd ever seen her.

"Ew! You'll get along, is all I meant. And you'll love Sonoma. The soil is amazing. You can grow so many things. In fact, Mr. Miller planted special grapes from Europe a few years back and Jake says they were rolling in them out on the ranch last fall."

"You don't say..."

She braced herself against the rail and looked out at the horizon as if she'd just seen vines reaching up over the waves, taking her by the wrists and gently pulling her to them.

CHAPTER FORTY-SEVEN

We arrived in San Francisco on the last Friday in June, and Mrs. Plea arranged for us to stay at her house for as long as we wished. Mizzy thanked Mrs. Dalworth for taking such good care of me, and as they caught up on stories, it was as if they already knew each other. Jake and Cook had already come and gone, and would have passed our steamship somewhere out on the open seas as they headed north on their final merchant run aboard the *Sonoma Wind*.

While I returned to my job at the hospice, Mrs. Dalworth took in sights around the city with Mrs. Plea and helped Mizzy in her kitchen and garden. But the joy of a new place wore off fast. By the end of the week, I found her staring into the distance, tapping her fingers on the armrest of a garden chair.

"I'm not much of a reader," she said to me, when I handed her a book from Mrs. Plea's library.

"You'll enjoy this one."

Mrs. Dalworth's face brightened as she read the title. "'The Culture of the Grape and Winemaking?' People are making books about everything these days."

"Mrs. Plea is interested. And Mr. Miller thinks Sonoma is perfect for winemaking."

Mrs. Dalworth didn't hear me. She was already thumbing the pages, her forefinger tilling the lines for fertile ideas.

Although I'd only been gone a month, life at the hospice had gone on without me. Nurse Killjoy welcomed me back, but she seemed busy and distracted. She had turned her attention to an earnest young nurse who followed her around like a shadow, and who had picked up most of the tasks I'd been doing. She didn't need me anymore, which was a relief, because that made leaving the job easier. But I still needed to work, and felt anxious about what I could do next. The hospice work wasn't perfect, but I could have done so much worse.

Seeing I needed something to do, Dr. Benjamin asked me to escort him on his rounds. He didn't bring my file along, and the notes he wrote were on the patients we visited. The woman who mistook me for a doctor had passed away while I was gone. I said to Dr. Benjamin that it was a blessing, which is something Mrs. Dalworth might have said on hearing the sad news. As I saw it, death was her only way out of a fog that would never lift.

I told Dr. Benjamin I wouldn't be staying in the job for long, which surprised me more than it did him, because I hadn't given it any thought until then. He told me he knew that right from the start, which made me think maybe the whole setup had been to help me get my head sorted out and not about the job at all. But he also said he'd find different work for me, if I wanted to stay on.

On the way back to the staff room, he knocked on a door that said, "Laboratory." A tall, grey-haired man answered. The arms of his white coat were too short, exposing his boney wrists as he mixed a solution in a glass tube. He waved us in as we were introduced, and then returned to a flask of liquid boiling over a blue flame on his work bench. Dr. Wallace was a real-life scientist, one like Edgar Dalworth. I gaped at his scattered papers, a sea of numbers and diagrams, and asked questions about what they meant. As he explained, one set of figures and a corresponding graph caught my attention. I pored over the numbers and put my finger on something that didn't make sense. Dr. Wallace checked the numbers and then looked at me in dismay. Although I didn't know what the figures meant, I'd discovered a calculation error.

Dr. Benjamin mentioned I had a gift for mathematics and suggested I stay to observe. From that day on, I spent my mornings in the hospice lab. Nurse Killey would come to get me for lunch every day, and we ate together in the staffroom while her new assistant was dispatched on mundane domestic chores. In the afternoon, I worked with the patients in the courtyard. Mr. Jones was still allowed to visit the old gentleman he'd befriended.

Things seemed to be working out, at least in small ways. But whenever I thought about the big questions—like what I wanted to do with my life—I could hear Papa saying how he couldn't see my future. After everything that had happened, I still couldn't see it, either. When I mentioned this to Dr. Benjamin, he said, "You are destined for something remarkable, young lady. Be patient. It will find you in due time," and then he told me Dr. Wallace had asked if he could teach me chemistry.

Back at the house, Mrs. Dalworth grew restless. She'd endured endless days of dull repetition at the lighthouse because she'd had a purpose. As Mrs. Plea's guest, the only routine she could latch on to had to do with meals. Hanging around the kitchen, she soon discovered Mizzy took no time off and she saw an opportunity to make herself useful. After getting instructions for Sunday breakfast, she'd assumed the work and sent Mizzy off to church. On her return, she was ordered into the courtyard, with a promise she could have her kitchen back in time for dinner.

That afternoon, while sitting in the courtyard enjoying Mrs. Dalworth's tea and scones, Mrs. Plea swept into the yard and threw down her carpet bag.

"What a lovely afternoon! Am I too late for the refreshments?" She closed her eyes, put her hands on her hips, and inhaled the lilac-scented air.

"You're back early!" Mizzy said.

"I am, but for good reason."

"Tea's still warm," Mrs. Dalworth added. "Darjeeling. Would you like some?"

"I would love a cup."

Mizzy put her mending down and rose to pour, but Mrs. Dalworth beat her out of her chair. When they first met, Mizzy had tried to serve Mrs. Dalworth, and she'd said, "Just because you're employed here doesn't mean you have to wait on me. I got a set o' legs, good ones if I do say so myself, and I like to use 'em." Mrs. Dalworth liked to keep busy. The warm weather had given her fresh energy, and the ache in her troublesome hip had almost vanished.

Mrs. Plea took her cup, stirred in a bit of milk and honey, and joined Mr. Jones and I on the flowered settee. He didn't want to make room for her, but she gently shoved him over. After catching up on the day's events, she set her cup down and reached into her bag. She pulled out two envelopes and flapped them in the air.

"I have mail from Mr. Miller. By Pony Express, if you please! Quite a remarkable service."

"You mean someone rode those letters across the country on horseback?" I said.

"Yes. It's incredibly fast. Also very dangerous, I hear."

"I could do that job, couldn't I?"

'No!' they answered in loud unison, and I flopped back on the settee.

Mrs. Plea had already read the letter addressed to her. "Mr. Miller is coming back, and he's opening up the ranch. He wants me to persuade you to return and run the place, Mizzy."

Mizzy turned to me, her forehead pinched with worry.

"Say 'yes' and I'll go with you," I said.

With The Missus permanently gone, I knew I could.

Mrs. Dalworth chimed in. "I hear he wants to start a winery. That happens to be my area, besides lightkeeper. I could lend a hand out there."

Mrs. Plea eyed the three of us. "Mr. Miller will be delighted to see the place brought back to life. Perhaps we'll all end up in Sonoma. I'm looking at a property there myself." She handed the unopened envelope to me. "This one's for you, Charlee."

I tore the envelope open and let my eyes fly across the page.

"What's it say?" Mrs. Dalworth said.

"Everything that Mrs. Plea just told us. He's coming back on his own. Has to get back to his business. Misses the way things were."

"That ranch is going to be in quite a state, cowboys runnin' the place for the past year," Mizzy said.

"He says he'll be back in August. For good, it sounds. And I..."

My mouth dropped open.

"What's the matter, Charolat?" Mizzy put a hand on my knee.

"Nothing, I guess. Apparently, I have shares in one of his companies."

"That's right, you do." Mrs. Plea said. "He explained it in my letter, too. It seems your father invested all his savings with Mr. Miller, so you'd be taken care of when he was gone. Mr. Miller gave your uncle a promissory note on the ownership, explained it all to him, but I gather he never told you. Your ownership is in trust, you see. Your uncle couldn't touch a penny."

"That company certificate? Uncle Jack told me he'd won it playing cards! He used it to cut loans and make deals, told me we'd be rich one day, and then got himself run out of town because of it."

"I knew that man was trouble, first I laid eyes on him," Mizzy said.

"That paper was your record. So you'd know you had something he couldn't take."

"Wait'll Jake hears. This is unbelievable."

"But wait," Mrs. Dalworth said, her expression pained. "I traded that paper away. That's the one you're talking about, isn't it? Oh dear! I thought it was a fake mining claim. It looked so much like the ones I'd seen floating around."

"The paper is worthless and Charlee doesn't need it. The company has registered her ownership as her father's beneficiary."

"So it's mining company shares. I guess I'll have to wait until I'm eighteen, right? Then what'll I own? Some gold pans and picks and what not?"

Mrs. Plea shook her head and laughed.

"You do not know, do you? That little company your father invested in has been running supplies to the British colony on Mr. Miller's merchant schooners. Sound familiar yet? It's made a small fortune these past two years, not in actual mining for gold, but in gold paid by miners buying equipment. It's one of John's biggest successes, so much so that he has to move to shipping by steam to keep up with the demand."

"Wait! That gold I recovered for him was from that company in the gold fields."

"That's right. And almost half of it is yours!"

CHAPTER FORTY-EIGHT

When our buggy stopped in front of the Sonoma ranch house, I leaped out and ran down the hill to the stables. Mr. Jones sprinted along beside me. At the open door, the sweet smell of hay and leather filled my nostrils as I let my eyes adjust to the dim interior.

"Magic?"

I heard a shuffle in the first stall and a long black neck stretched over the half door. Jake's bay mare also recognized my voice and popped her head out of the next stall, and all the other horses in the stables followed suit. I fell to my knees on the dirt floor and burst into tears. My old friends hadn't forgotten me. Joy and pain swept through me—elated to be back with them, and devastated I'd had to leave. I wiped my runny nose on a sleeve, feeling foolish for letting my emotions run wild, even if nobody was there to see. But crying released something bottled up inside and an immense wave of relief followed. The ranch was my home and my horse friends hadn't given up on me.

Mr. Jones pressed himself against my side, as he often did when I was going through some human thing, waiting for whatever came next. Without hesitation, he followed me into

Magic's stall. I introduced them, even though it wasn't necessary. Magic lowered his head and the two of them touched noses, like they were old pals saying hello again. I swear something passed between them—some kind of understanding—and I squeezed them with the longest hugs ever. Mr. Jones said later that he and Magic exchanged news because so much had happened to me. Papa always said animals know way more than folks give them credit for, and I've always believed that. I longed to grab a saddle and ride, but I told Magic I wasn't leaving anytime soon and it would have to wait. Mr. Jones perked his ears, as if I'd revealed a secret even he didn't know.

"Charlee LeBeau?" I almost collided with the ranch foreman as I rounded the corner of the building.

"Paulo!"

"That's me." He politely took his hat off, revealing a pale forehead next to his tanned face. "Mighty glad to have ya back. What's this though? You taller than me now?"

"I must be. And here I thought you'd shortened the cookhouse stools."

His weathered face stretched into a huge grin. He knocked the dust off his hat and put it back on.

Paulo was a friendly cowboy and not the type to carry a grudge. I'd snubbed him cold before I left the ranch because he'd bought Charger, Papa's horse. I was mad at everything and everyone back then, and just plain furious that Papa had died. Paulo understood that. Once I got through my grief, I knew he'd been looking out for me and the horse.

Paulo would have been Papa's pick for foreman, if he'd had the chance to say so. Maybe he'd even told that to Mr. Miller since he'd confided in him about his failing heart and other things I didn't know. Coming back to the ranch, I was glad Paulo had ended up in the foreman job. Although it seemed like a lifetime ago, Paulo's familiar face made me feel welcome, like I belonged again, and I felt myself straighten up and stand tall.

By the time Paulo and I climbed the hill to the house, Mrs. Dalworth, Mizzy and Mrs. Plea's carriage driver had everything unloaded and stacked on the veranda. Mizzy was inspecting the peeled paint on the old porch swing and said she'd add that to her long list of things to fix.

Cowhands had occupied our former cabins near the cookhouse, but Paulo told them that the womenfolk were returning and they had to move out, which amounted to carrying their sleeping rolls and saddle bags to empty shacks farther down the hired row. Mrs. Dalworth didn't want to put anybody out, but Paulo said cowboys didn't much care where they laid their heads, and we shouldn't feel bad for a minute.

While hauling our bags over to the cabins, a new dilemma came over me. I didn't know if I should claim Papa's bigger cabin and share it with Mrs. Dalworth, or stay next door with Mizzy in her old cabin, or invite Mizzy to stay in Papa's with me. Adult thinking can be so complicated. It can snag a person up when you least expect it.

Mrs. Dalworth caught me with my jaw hanging open, stalled on the path, and guessed what I was stewing over.

"Tell you what, Mizzy. I'm used to living alone at the lighthouse," she said. "Since you're in charge now, why don't you take the first cabin with Charlee?"

Mizzy would have preferred her own cabin, if it had been like she left it. But it was barren and had nothing left of her earlier presence. With The Missus gone, she'd be running the house, too, and the first cabin was befitting of a boss. As she mulled over the suggestion, Mrs. Dalworth pulled me aside.

"You two need more time together."

"But Nana!" I whispered, and poked her in the ribs.

"Don't you dare," she said, but then gave me a wink and a warm hug.

Since the ranch house had been closed up all winter, it needed work to make it livable again. Fortunately, the last housekeepers had covered the furniture before leaving, but the air in the closed house was stale and musty. Dust covered every surface and clung to the curtains and sashes. We flung open all the doors and windows, started on the second floor, and cleaned room by room. Wielding brooms, dusters, buckets, and mops, we worked as hard as any ship's crew to make the place spotless.

It took us a week to get the house and cabins in order so the place would be livable by the time Mr. Miller returned with Jake. With the insides done, we tackled the yard. Little could be done about the garden in the middle of summer, Mrs. Dalworth said, but we planted a few rows of fall vegetables anyway and pulled more weeds than I'd seen in my entire life. Mrs. Dalworth pointed out that she didn't miss the rocks of Deception Island, which had bent many a hoe and shovel.

The outdoor cookhouse had suffered neglect in Mizzy's absence. Used only during roundups and harvests, the cowboys hadn't taken care of it. Mrs. Dalworth and I knocked down cobwebs, wiped a thick layer of sticky pollen off everything, and weeded around the outdoor counters and benches. Mrs. Dalworth found some wild flowers and planted them in the empty pots, bringing splashes of color back to the plain structure. Mizzy scrubbed her cook stove from top to bottom, all the while complaining about the baked-on spills and greasy messes left behind by chow wagon cooks. She hunted for utensils up at the main house and assembled her basic supplies, all the while going on about the state of things in her absence, but looking the happiest I'd seen her since before Papa died.

Mr. Jones found a spot in the grass by the cookhouse where he could supervise our progress and keep an eye on the barnyard down the hill. Except for one bossy rooster down by the chicken coop, he liked ranch life, and thought it was a station befitting a distinguished former naval officer. He took a fancy to a pretty border collie that belonged to the ranch shepherd, but not appreciating herding as a canine occupation, admired her work from a respectable distance. And since he'd made quick friends with the horses, he took it upon himself to patrol their stables for critters seeking free accommodations in the hay.

Mrs. Dalworth said the entire courtyard would look better with less pretense, starting by getting rid of the statue of a little boy peeing into a fountain. Once Mizzy knew what pretense meant, she whole-heartedly agreed. That night, I woke up to muffled laughter out behind the cabin. Mizzy's bed was empty. Under the light of the moon, I caught her and Mrs. Dalworth lugging that white statue down to the pond in the lower field. I watched them pick it up, drop it because it was too heavy and awkward, and then collapse on the ground, giggling and snorting and carrying on like a couple of school-age pranksters.

"You two!" I said, interrupting their mischief, and they burst into another round of laughter, pointing at me standing with hands on my hips and wearing a serious teacher's face. I felt ridiculous, so there was nothing to be done but join them. We tumbled that statue across the grass, Mizzy on a dedicated mission to get rid of it, Mrs. Dalworth complaining that she had to pee, and all of us gasping for air between fits of laughter. It was the most fun any of us could recall in a long time. Finally, standing barefoot in the mud, nightshirts damp and dirty, the three of us watched it splash into the black water of the pond and sink out of sight.

We leaned forward and peered after it.

Mizzy said, "Let's send our old hurts down there with that cement baby."

"That's a great idea," Mrs. Dalworth replied.

We put our arms around each other's shoulders. I closed my eyes and let my worst hurts slip away, in the good company of those who went before me and stood beside me now.

CHAPTER FORTY-NINE

On my first day out with Magic, Mr. Jones wanted to come along, so I'd made a seat for him in front of me out of an old piece of rug. He'd perched on it like Prince Ahmed, surveying his domain, ready for that rug to take flight at any moment. It was funny, but too much trouble to explain to anyone who hadn't read the story from Arabian Nights.

The cowboys laughed every time we passed by, no doubt enjoying the spectacle of a dog and pony show. By the time Jake arrived at the ranch, our morning rides were the buzz of the barns. He got my joke right away, because he'd read the story. In fact, he was the one who'd brought me the storybook from his father's library.

Mrs. Dalworth didn't find Mr. Jones' carpet rides amusing. She worried he would go flying off, crash to the ground, and get hurt. I promised to be careful, but she continued to fret. As Jake and I saddled our horses one morning, she showed up at the barn with a burlap feed bag she'd fashioned into a sturdy shoulder sack.

"Mr. Jones is too old to run after you out there on horseback. And if he falls off, well, it won't be good. Sling this over your back for him to sit in."

It was a brilliant invention. He didn't have to dig his nails into the rug to keep his balance, and I didn't have to look past his curly head to see where I was going. The new system was much more relaxing for all concerned, and Mrs. Dalworth was relieved.

Jake watched as I swapped out the rug for the shoulder sack, and Mr. Jones settled into his new lookout.

"Honestly, that dog," he said, shaking his head.

Mr. Miller hadn't been home for more than half a day when I cornered him with my saved wages and begged him to let me buy Magic. He listened as I presented my case, hands clasped behind his back, and then told me it wasn't possible. His refusal crushed me. But then he explained it wasn't possible because Bernadette had already arranged for me to have Magic.

It was supposed to be a surprise—a gift walked out of the stables on the afternoon of the Miller homecoming party on the weekend. Bernadette knew I was returning to Sonoma, so she asked for Magic to be given to me, in honor of my heroic deeds fighting off pirates on the Pacific and recovering the stolen gold, she'd said.

Her gesture left me speechless. I pushed my money into Mr. Miller's hands, insisting on paying fair and square, but he stuffed it right back at me and said Bernadette had given him strict orders and he would not go against her wishes. "You've met her. Her health may not be good, but her spirit is as fierce as ever. Magic is her gift to you."

I left Mr. Miller in his study and found Jake out on the veranda, painting the peeling porch swing. Mr. Jones sat on the top step, looking out for barnyard escapees seeking greener pastures. I plunked myself down beside Jake and told him the news.

"I already knew, but I was sworn to secrecy," he said.

"I'm kind of shocked by it, given how she despised me."

"What? She looked up to you. You didn't know that?"

"All I ever saw was a mean girl who told hurtful lies about me."

"You weren't wrong about that. She was jealous back then, and a real pain for both of us. But she changed after you left. She felt responsible for how it ended."

"I could have been kinder to her. We got off to a terrible start, thanks to her mother, because I wouldn't give you up."

"Good choice. Not giving in, I mean."

The consequences of that choice still echoed inside me. It had been hard.

"I'm going to write and thank her, but I don't know what else to say. I don't think I ever got to know her. Does she still paint?"

"Oh, yes. When she's feeling well enough. You could tell her stories of your adventures. I wrote her about some of them, but I don't do them any justice."

"Maybe she'd like to correspond. I have room for more than one friend my age."

"Who's the other one?"

I stuck a finger in his ear, and he retaliated by trying to dab paint on my nose. I ducked, caught his wrist and as we fell over sideways, I flung out my other hand and caught the paint bucket before it toppled.

"As quick as ever," he said as we sat up. "If you write to her, she'll answer. It would mean the world to her."

The son had his father's compassion, but there was an added warmth in his caring that could melt the ice off a frozen, uncertain heart.

~

The Sonoma Valley shimmered in the bright morning sunshine as Jake and I rode up to the top of the hill.

"So, how do you feel about school starting?" I asked.

"I'm ready. Looking forward to it again. Cook says nothing like a backbreaking job in a risky setting to knock sense into a man. I'm not cut out to be a sailor, that much I've learned."

"That makes two of us. And I'm happy to be here. I bought writing supplies. Reams of paper. Whole pencils and ink."

I remembered how he used to save bits of paper and pencils for me when I couldn't afford any.

"Will you be corresponding with your gentlemen suitors?"

His odd question hung in the air while I tried to make sense of it.

"Suitors. What suitors?"

"Well, you've attracted a few of them. I'm not the only one who's noticed. Cook saw, too."

"Cook is a big brother. He protects me, like Mr. Jones here."

The even rocking of Magic's steps had lulled Mr. Jones to sleep. Hearing his name, he lifted his head out of his new riding satchel, which I'd swung around to my lap as we moseyed along. He smacked his lips and yawned. Seeing nothing important happening, he dropped his head down and I tucked his ears out of sight. Magic snorted.

"Who do you think is interested in me?"

"Well, there's that island fellow."

"Perkins? You can't be serious. I'll never see him again. Even if I did, he's hardly my type."

"Do you even have a type?"

"Do you?"

I glared at him and he glared back. Jake and I never used to fight, but we weren't two peas in a pod anymore. We couldn't finish each other's sentences. We'd grown up and apart.

"I get it. You're jealous. That's what this is about."

"No, it's not that at all."

"Then what is it?"

"I'm…like you. I'm… I don't know what I am or what I want."

His shoulders slumped as he stared at his saddle horn and fiddled with his reins.

What was he trying to tell me? Did he mean he felt lost like me? Did he mean he still didn't have his future figured out, either? Even though we'd gone in separate directions, we were still on unknown parallel paths.

We stopped at the top of a hill, dismounted and sprawled in the grass while the horses grazed in the shade. And then, with Mr. Jones rolling around in the grass between us, it was as if an old logjam broke free in our river. We talked about everything—from our lost mothers and broken families, to our vanishing childhoods and broken dreams.

"You know what? We don't have to know where we're headed to get somewhere," I said, chewing on a long piece of sweet hay.

Jake leaned on his elbows and pushed his hair out of his eyes. "That's downright philosophical."

"I stole it from Mrs. Dalworth, the lighthouse philosopher, queen of platitudes."

He laughed. "Do you think she'll stay in California? She adores the ranch and Father says she won't stop talking about the winery. And I've never seen Mizzy laugh so much."

"She's definitely gonna stay 'cause now she's got a purpose. Plus, I told her I want her in my family. I think everyone is sorted out, except for us.

"Yeah. Except for us."

"But one thing I think of all the time lately? This is where I belong." I stopped short of saying I felt like I'd come home. "All we have to know is the next step to take, not all the steps, right?"

"Go on…"

"I mean, you're going back to school and you're ready. I'm

here. Your father knows a college tutor who'll see me in San Francisco, and while I'm in town, I'll apprentice in the hospice lab for a week. As for where it all leads, well, who knows?"

"I like that outlook."

"Me, too. But I hope you're open to some projects on the side, because I got money. I think we should go into business, kind of like Mrs. Plea and your father. You'd have to do all the talking, but then you're real good at that. It comes natural to you, like when you did your school reports back in the day. In fact, you should run for government office someday."

"Government!" It was his dream not so long ago. Expressing confidence in him seemed to bring back some pleasant memory. He leaned back and smiled at the sky.

"Only if you want to, that is. I'll write for the papers under a pseudonym so they'll think I'm a man. Then they'll publish me. If you represent me, nobody will ever know."

"Are you asking me to be your agent?"

"'No, I'm inviting you to be my partner. I promise I won't lead you on any more outrageous adventures…"

"…she says, having just returned from a wild expedition, where pirates sunk a sailing ship, stole the gold cargo and buried it on a remote lighthouse island, where only she could find the stash."

"I'm inclined to be impulsive. I'll admit it. But I always get out of my scrapes, don't I?"

"Barely. But business. I don't have a clue in that area."

"You study your law and leave that part to me. Mrs. Plea's gonna mentor me."

"She is?"

"Well, she hasn't agreed, exactly. She's tried to discourage me, because it's brutal for a woman. I think she wanted to make sure I understood that. Which I do. She'll take me on if I ask. Did you know they call her the Black City Hall in San Fran? I read it in the paper the other day."

"She's got no shortage of names, or enemies, for that matter. Entrepreneur, slave smuggler, voodoo queen—they love her and hate her in that city. No denying her influence and determination, though. She is formidable."

"They'll love me and hate me one day, too, if I do it right. If that's what it takes to make people pay attention to what's wrong with the world, then let them."

"I'd be the face of your operations, is that right? You want me to back you up, like Father does with Mrs. Plea?"

"Yes. We'll be mysterious and unstoppable."

Jake reached his arms out to embrace the horizons. "Now that's my kind of adventure."

Mr. Jones grunted in protest as we loaded him back into his riding sack. Jake held Magic steady while I hauled myself into the saddle with the extra weight on my back. As I took the reins from Jake, I held his hand for a moment.

"I've never properly thanked you. For coming after me. For believing me."

His eyes were a verdant green, bright and hopeful like the planted fields in spring.

"Sure, you did. What? You don't remember?"

"Very funny," I said.

Grinning, he pulled the brim of his hat down, sprung onto Sitka, and we headed down the hill for home.

CHAPTER FIFTY

By the time everyone had heard the story of the pirate raid at Deception Island, I was weary of repeating it. Ordinarily, I would have spiced it up and dragged it out to make it more interesting. But the events were so thrilling, it didn't need embellishments to keep people hanging on my words.

Of course, Mr. Miller wanted to hear the whole thing. So the day he arrived home, I had to tell it to everyone gathered one more time. I noticed that with every telling, some new question would pop up from someone who'd already heard it, like they'd been stewing on matters, and something curious or unanswered had sprung to mind.

The next afternoon, Jake and I were perched on cookhouse stools, sipping tea and waiting for Mizzy's baking to cool down on our plates. Mrs. Dalworth was kneading dough for the next day's bread. We were all a little talked out from the night before, so we had little to say beyond how nice the weather was and how pretty the ranch looked in the golden shades of late summer.

"Something keeps nagging on me 'bout that island," Mizzy said. My fork slipped from my fingers and clattered onto my plate. "What caused them sailors to go berserk in that clearing? It's like they ran into the devil himself up there."

"Yeah," said Mrs. Dalworth. "When Charlee took me there, I found it peaceful and comforting. Will and his boys were tough as nails, yet they ran off like superstitious fools. You've never explained how you made them unravel, come to think of it. Hiking them up to the clearing could have been your death sentence, knowing the gold wasn't there. Yet somehow you pulled off a daring escape."

It was more than daring. It was impossible, if not for Mr. Jones.

"Well, see, because they were lazy and mean, they made me carry everything. All the tools and water and such. The first time we stopped for a rest, I packed delirium root into their canteen when they weren't looking. The Lekwungen people have another name for the plant, but that's what I call it, because it has a powerful effect on the mind. It grows wild all over the island. I got the idea when we stopped because it was all around my feet."

Mrs. Dalworth's brow furrowed as she reviewed her extensive knowledge of island plants. I could tell she wasn't finding a match, so I pressed on with my story before she could form yet another question.

"Sculder's two side-kicks got mighty thirsty, puffing their way up the steep trail. Swatting flies off their sweaty heads and getting chewed alive by mosquitoes made them even nastier, so when we stopped to rest again, they snatched the canteen away from me and guzzled down the works of it between them."

"Couldn't they tell the water was off?" Mrs. Dalworth muttered.

"Delirium root is tasteless. Anyhow, it worked right away. They started getting all itchy and paranoid, and their little minds started playing all kinds of tricks on them, like imagining hungry animals lurking in the bush, or unscrupulous gold diggers stalking us to beat them to the loot."

"Ha! They were hallucinating!" Jake said.

"Not exactly. They weren't seeing things, just thinking about them. I'd worked them into a frightful lather with made-up legends and folklore. Even Sculder was bothered and told me to shut up. By the time I was done, their nerves jangled like a pocket full of coins. Just as we reached the clearing, I told them about a wild ghost dog who guards the island, hundreds of years old and fierce as can be, known as the Dog of Deception. That one got them good."

Everyone looked over to Mr. Jones, who stood on a rock fence next to the cookhouse, watching the cowboys at work down by the stables.

"Sculder didn't have any of the water, so he couldn't hear anything, but it rattled him all the same because he'd imagined a dog attacking him at Clamity Cove the last time they'd been on the island. That was when they had cornered me on the beach and the Lekwungen chief came to my rescue. Anyway, I can't explain that time, other than he'd drank a lot of bad liquor."

I looked over at Mr. Jones. On more than one occasion, he had mysteriously disappeared and appeared while we were on the island.

"All of them had good reason to think the island was haunted, that the wild dog was real and it had come for them. When the wind in the trees became a mournful howl, they lit off down the path like their pants were on fire. Sculder hollered after them to halt or he'd shoot 'em dead and bury them where they fell, which only made their legs pump faster. He fired two shots over their heads to make them stop, and I got my chance to run. He couldn't cock that pistol fast enough to hit me with his last shot, and I knew he'd never come after me on the unmarked lighthouse trail, with his men running the other way.

That's how I escaped the clearing. They thought the Dog of Deception was coming for them."

"Delirium root in the canteen. Fresh root or powder?" Jake asked, gazing at the horizon.

"Fresh," I said, probably too fast, and Mr. Jones saved me by barking for a long minute at something moving in the yard that none of us could see.

I knew a little chemistry. It would take fistfuls of plants crammed into that canteen and steeped in the hot sun for days to make a powerful infusion like the one I described. But thankfully, nobody found my explanation lacking, and nobody asked another pesky question.

"That was real smart thinking," said Jake, blowing on his fork and sampling his peach cobbler. "You'll have to use that in a book one day. It's such a clever twist."

Everyone agreed, and the conversation turned to Mizzy's delicious dessert.

I would use it in a book one day.

Sometimes facts are stranger than fiction. Sometimes fiction comes alive with strange facts. As for what happened on that island, I'd told the whole truth. I didn't make any of it up or change anything to make the story better. Well, except for one tiny detail.

There is no such thing as delirium root.

ACKNOWLEDGMENTS

The drafting of this book was fast, leading to the golden deception that editing and completing it would be equally quick and smooth. But like Charlee's journey in this novel, I ran a parallel course of struggle and disorientation. Looking back, I can say this is exactly how it had to be for me as the author, for I was able to fully embrace what my character experienced in her world.

I am often asked if Charlee is based on me, or if any of the characters in the book are real people. None of the characters are real, but all of them are a complex mixture of those who live and have lived. In historical fiction, the echoes of those who have gone before are summoned. In writing the Charlee LeBeau series, I've listened to the whispers of my own Métis lineage.

This book would not be possible without the understanding and support of my dear friends and family. There are too many of you to list in the space of a few pages. Suffice it to say, all of you believed this book would one day appear, even when it took much longer than expected to finish.

To the devoted readers of the previous Charlee LeBeau books, thank you for your enthusiasm and grace as you waited for the release of this third novel.

To my fleet of diligent beta readers and copy proofers: Brenda McGuire, Celine Kaufman, Norm Root, Jan Carley, Marty Dolan, Jim McCaul, Gayle McCaul, Josie Steeves, Richard Scott, and Adua Porteous. Every little point raised, question asked, typo found, has raised the story, and the published book, to a new level. I am so grateful for your time and attention.

Special thanks to my long-time friend, Marty Dolan, for her creativity and inspiration; to Raman Dhoot, for rendering our endless ideas into the beautiful cover; to Cita Airth, for crafting Charlee's bookmarks from off-cuts of magnificent *qathet* cedar.

To Heather Larson and her dear mom, Anne. Stories endure even though we must leave them behind on the page.

To my amazing editor, Glenda MacFarlane, who held the lantern for me on a foggy bluff and guided my way.

To my editorial assistant and canine consultant, Cory, who helped me bring a wonderful, now extinct, Salish Wool Dog back to life.

ABOUT THE AUTHOR

C.V. (Cindy) Gauthier is a Canadian author, living and working on the traditional, ancestral, and unceded territories of the Coast Salish people.

Before turning to fiction writing, Cindy spent over three decades as a secondary school educator in Vancouver, primarily working with students who found themselves in the margins, or who simply didn't fit within the traditional model of education.

With Métis ancestral ties to the Red River on her father's side—lineage almost lost through relocation, disconnection and erasure—Cindy's historical fiction writing brings forth the echoes of those who have gone before, through engaging stories of struggle, resilience and hope.

~

To order books directly from the author, join the author's email list, or get further information, please visit the author's website at www.cvgauthier.com.

Books can also be ordered online and through local bookstores. Libraries will add the books to their collection when requested by readers. And finally, reviews help indie authors reach new readers and audiences. If you are willing and able, a short review or mention online would be greatly appreciated!